TUNNELING

by
SHELLEY MUNIZ

Word Project Press of Sonora, CA

Tunneling

Published in the United States
by the Word Project Press of Sonora, CA

Requests for permission to make copies of any part of this work should be submitted online at
info@wordprojectpress.com

Credits:
Cover and Interior Design:
Melody W. Baker, Graphic Design by Melody
Author Photograph: Katy Lind

Word Project Press, Long Barn, CA

ISBN-13: 978-0-9970349-4-3

Also by Shelley Muniz:
Eagle Feathers and Angel Wings: Micah's Story
One Great Tribe

This book is dedicated to:

Suzan Still and Ann St. James

"It depends on how you look at things…"

—The Churkendoose,
Ben Ross Berenberg

-CHAPTER 1-

*L*oretta circled her mother's room, searching for some clue that might explain the chaos of their lives. Road trip memorabilia, glossy photographs and vintage promo posters covered the walls, alongside a flyer announcing the Lone Pine Film Festival, five years prior. More souvenirs from her mother's work as a movie stylist crowded closets and shelves, including a dried rose from a long-ago boyfriend, a guitar with no strings purchased from a hitchhiking roadie, an antique silver hairclip with several missing teeth, and a framed card that read: *Good things come to those who wait...greater things come to those who get off their asses and do anything to make life happen.* That was *so* Greer.

Tucked away on the dresser like an afterthought sat a few personal photos: one of Loretta as a toddler, and a couple of school pictures. There was one of her in that hideous green dress she wore when graduating from eighth grade. But there were no pictures of her teen years. Quite a testimony to the time she'd spent practically orphaned. Loretta flipped the graduation photo face down on the dresser and rolled her eyes. "Stylist to the stars, whatever," she muttered. She snagged a gold-sequined camisole from a pile of clothes on her mother's bed and slipped it on over her t-shirt and shorts, breathing in the hint of hibiscus perfume that clung to the fabric. Then crinkled her nose and sneezed.

Scattered on the dressing table were half-used bottles of moisturizer, tubes of mascara, a rainbow of eyeshadows and blush. Lipsticks, foundations to color-correct and powders to prime. Why her mom would leave these products behind and stash others in the pockets of her professional makeup kit was a mystery. How far away was Las Vegas, anyway? Not that it mattered. Soon her mother would be fussing over Rachel Maxim's hair and makeup, with some big-shot director *oohing* and *aahing* over both women while bragging about his fabulous movie set in some fancy casino. The film's production designer would be onsite too—an edgy science-fiction geek, known for making last-minute changes to the script and set design while leaving actors and crews on standby. His over-the-top ideas could mean extra days to wrap up the shoot. Add those to the six weeks already committed, and *bam*. School break was over.

Loretta inspected the many containers before opening a jar of blush, applying the rosy powder in a circular motion. The choice of lipstick was easy, Dragon Girl Red—her mother's favorite. Creating Emma-Watson-worthy brows was tricky, so she saved those for last, leaning toward the mirror, grinning as she applied the brow pencil the way her mother had taught her.

Even now, all done up, it was hard to believe she and her mom were related. Her mother was never shy. Or quiet. Her mother's skin was pink-toned. Hers was olive. Her mother's hair was red, and Loretta's mousy brown. Her mother loved white chocolate. She loved dark. Her mother loved Johnny Cash. She loved Johnny Depp.

As if on cue, her mother's voice bounced up the stairs, brash as always: "Hey, Lo-retta! I can't leave without my good-luck necklace. Have you found it? Are you looking?" A string of muffled curse words, the banging of cupboard doors, followed the questions.

"No to the first question, yes to the second," Loretta barked back.

"Loretta Lynn Duvall, don't snap at me like that."

"Loretta Lynn. Right. Once again, my name gets dragged into the argument."

"A name needs to be sturdy enough to hold the baggage of a lifetime. I gave you a good one, so don't complain."

"Like naming me after a country singer has lessened the crap in my life. Don't think so, Mom. But thanks for the effort." As Loretta walked down the stairs, the mini-lecture stopped, and she could see her mother boot-scooting in the kitchen, wearing a peasant blouse, knee-length skirt, and cowboy boots, looking like a B-grade version of the star she would pamper for the next six weeks. Loretta grinned, despite feeling annoyed. "Hippie Cowgirl," she swore, feeling proud of her witty double descriptor. Mostly, her words caught in her throat, bubbling up like empty comic-strip speech balloons—so this perfect character-smack felt like vindication.

"Ha! Found them!" Her mother was standing in front of the refrigerator, waving the beads.

"In the frig?"

"No, silly. In the flower pot beside the fake daisies."

"You're so weird," Loretta said.

"Says the apple to the tree. *Biscuits and gravy*," her mother then sang, sashaying across the room, spinning to a Willie Nelson tune as it carried through the radio. "You ready?" she crooned. "It's now or never."

"Why do you always say biscuits and gravy? You never cook biscuits and gravy."

"Snarky, this morning, are we? That's not like you, Loretta," her mother said, smiling.

Breakfast was toast cut in a heart shape, topped with peanut butter, topped with Loretta's initials spelled out with raisins, all served up on a pink paper plate. Loretta grabbed the plate off the kitchen counter, walked into the living room and plopped on the couch. On the TV, the newscaster reported about car bombs in Syria and then turned his broadcast over to a reporter in Louisiana, who showed a burst oil pipeline dumping crude into the Gulf of Mexico. "Why is the news always so depressing?" Loretta asked, injecting a subject meant to distract her mother's rush out the door.

"Don't talk with your mouth full," her mother responded from the kitchen.

Loretta tossed her last bite of toast onto her plate, irked at her mother for using the news as background noise, but never taking it, or her, seriously.

"Hustle up, Lo-retta, I've got to go," her mother hollered. She swooped in and picked up Loretta's paper plate. "Are you ready for tomorrow?" she asked.

"How could I not be? You've reminded me enough times." It's not as if someone had handed Loretta a death sentence, really. She wanted a job, just not one working for the craziest woman in Lone Pine.

"Don't get huffy. This isn't my fault."

"Then whose is it? I didn't *ask* for this jo—"

"Noleen Deerborne *offered up* this gig. It's a win-win-win. The old lady gets her chores done, I have someone to watch over you for the summer, and you'll end up with some jingle in your pocket at the end of it all."

"I'm seventeen. I don't need someone to watch over me." Noleen Deerborne. Alias Granny Noleen. She wasn't like some sweet granny pictured in a children's book. No. Granny Noleen acted more like the Wicked Witch of the West. She was not soft and cuddly, nor was she the kind of person to read bedtime stories or bake chocolate-chip cookies.

"Lo-retta, this will be good for you. Trust me."

"Trust you? How can I trust you?" Loretta said. "You lie. You *said* you wouldn't leave town for a while. And you never listen—"

"I listen," her mother said, turning away.

"Really, Greer?"

"Oh, you're calling me Greer now?"

"Well yeah, lately, or haven't you noticed?"

Greer raised an eyebrow, calling attention to her overdone lashes. "Tell me one time, name one time I've missed my cue."

"Just one? Okay, how about last week, when I asked you if I could have friends over while you're in Vegas? You never gave me an answer, you—"

"I love you, Lo-retta, but I'm no fool. I don't want a bunch of kids showing up while I'm gone."

"I would never—"

"Cora can come over. She's got some sense. You, on the other hand, are morphing into a lemming, darlin' girl. You'd follow Jemma Griffin and her wannabees over a cliff if they asked you to come."

"Good one, Mom. Thanks."

"You're welcome."

"You're the only mother I know who—"

"Cry me a river, Lo-retta. That line was around when I was a kid, and I used it plenty. 'You're the only mother who won't let me wear makeup. You're the only mother who won't let me date at fourteen. You're the only mother blah, blah, blah.'"

"Yeah, but—" Just once, she wished she could finish a sentence. But that would be like wishing that unicorns were real, or that Batman existed, or that the guy she was crushing on liked her back. *If wishes were kisses*, her mother would say.

"Be good. Stay home tonight and rest up for tomorrow."

"But I, Jemma and Brady, we—"

Loretta heard Rachel Maxim's big black tour bus drive up in front of the house, and from the window in her living room, could see its trailing cloud of diesel.

"Gotta go, curtain call. Kisses, right here," Greer said, as she opened the front door and walked out, suitcases in hand. "The truck keys are on the counter. Don't forget to feed Toby. Collect the mail. Water the geraniums. You know the routine."

"Water the geraniums. Right." Loretta yawned. She touched that spot on her cheek where the kiss would have landed. The muscles in the back of her neck bunched up as the sunlight dimmed and the room grew shadows. "I was *about* to say, I'm going to the knoll," she whispered. "I'm not officially employed until tomorrow morning. Tonight is mine. As if anyone cares." For just a second, she reconsidered her plans. Her mother *had* told her to stay home, after all.

Greer waved one more time as she stepped into the bus, and then she was gone. The massive Star Coach farted a series of exhaust bombs as it backed up and crept past the house and down the road, disappearing in sections as it slogged onto Main Street. "That clunker's as inefficient as a wood-burning VW," Loretta snapped. She took a deep breath and walked into the kitchen, stewing about the dirty paper plates her mother had left on the kitchen counter.

As with everything her mom organized, the kitchen "office" conveyed minimal effort covered with maximum crap: a card table set up in the corner loaded with stacks of receipts and invoices, unpaid bills, and the reservation confirmation for her mom's Las Vegas hotel. Of course, she forgot to take that, and the MapQuest route planner she'd printed before she left. The bus had a driver, yes, but having her own navigational info was mandatory for a backseat copilot such as Greer. Lying on top of the paperwork were the good-luck beads Loretta had searched for most of the morning. Good *God*. What else was new?

Between the modem and the laptop sat a glitter-framed picture of her father. Every year the photograph faded a little more, but her memory didn't. That playful smile, the way he tilted his head a bit to the left as if he were listening to every word she said. "I can't talk to her," Loretta told him, for the millionth time. "There's no reasoning with her about anything." She wished he could answer. *If wishes were kisses.*

As a child, she had a recurring dream—one where he threw her in the air and caught her with loving arms. So often she prayed that if she wanted it badly enough, the dream would come true, and he would magically appear and stand beside her mother and love them both enough to stick around.

Their family story read like a steamy romance novel. In 1996, Atom Brimley strolled into Lone Pine, California—the lead guitarist for a hopeful country band. Loretta could just see her mother in her Daisy Dukes and tank top, dancing in front of his stage as the band played honky-tonk. Of all the men in Greer's life, he was, or could have been, the *one*. He must have meant something to her because his was the only picture she kept. "My baby-daddy," she called him, always with a smile and a dreamy look of pride.

Since then, there had been a long line of "uncles." Some of them were kind enough, reading her storybooks, tossing the Frisbee and shooting hoops, chomping popcorn through G-rated movies on Saturday nights. Manny Holcomb could blow cigarette smoke through the gap in his front teeth, forming perfect rings one after the other. Joe Sully loved whiskey too much and was the only one ever to hit Greer. She kicked him between the legs before he had time to do it again, though, and then threw him, his clothes, and his boots out the door. "Pay attention, Loretta," Greer told her afterward. "A man treats you roughly, nail him where it hurts. He's outta here. No excuses."

Toby's thick basset-hound tail pounded against the kitchen counter, pulling Loretta free of her funky mood. "Okay, boy," she told him, rubbing his ears. "Let's get you fed. Brady's invited me four-wheeling, do you believe it?"

Loretta frowned as Toby gave her a woeful, cock-eared look. "Yeah, me either," she said, shrugging her shoulders. "Whatever. I'm going to go out for a while, but I won't be gone long, I promise." She rolled her eyes and scratched his back. "Sucks, doesn't it? Mom takes off again, only this time she decides I'm old enough, not only to stay home alone, but to work my friggin' ass to the bone for some wild woman and her goofy cronies."

+++

The clock on the dashboard showed 9:00 p.m. Loretta could see the lights of Lone Pine in the distance, but here, beyond the Alabama Hills, there was no road, only rocks and gullies and dried-up creek beds. Rock crawling the Star's Butt seemed crazy foolish. The enormous granite boulder was smooth and rounded, about six feet of climb, with enough ridges to provide a grip but still challenge the meaty tires of any four-wheeler.

She sat next to Brady in his tricked-out Jeep, cursing the center console and the restriction of her seat belt as she leaned in, trying to close the distance between them. She felt self-conscious about every sweaty part of herself, doubting her choice of clothes and the casual way she'd tied back her hair, worrying that he might notice her peeking at his shirtless chest. As he shifted gears, she tried to think of something to say.

"Ready?" he asked.

"No," she wanted to scream. *"I can't do this…"*

Instead, she nodded, feeling the blush in her cheeks, hoping he wouldn't see.

The tires spun and then gripped. The vertical climb left her breathless. Her head bobbed and her lungs seized as she bucked and banged in the seat of the mud-spattered monster truck.

As she white-knuckled the roll bar, she prayed: *Please, please, God, don't let me scream or pee my pants or fall out of this damn truck.* She felt a tremendous need to jump and run as if she had to expel herself immediately, or she might explode. Like, literally. Like brains on the dashboard and guts on the floor. *Maybe I should have listened to my mother,* she thought. *Maybe I should have stayed home.*

The whoops and hollers of people watching climaxed as Brady reached the top of the boulder. He pumped his arms, hooted and hollered back while inching his Jeep down the far side of the rock. Totally oblivious to Loretta's bulging eyes, to her heart beating in rhythm to the engine's grind, he bellowed on, singing some song about shooting the shit and tempting fate, as he led the lineup of trucks up the next hill, through narrow gorges in the rocky terrain, down dips and over rises, taking corners with angles nearly impossible to maneuver.

Back at the knoll, a tendril of black smoke curled upward, ringed by the red glare of a bonfire. In the light of the full moon, a flock of geese veered to avoid the plume.

Friday night fires on the knoll were Pierce Lukeman's idea. He supplied the paper trash, pitchy wood, and rotting slash—items he got from his cousin Jack, who worked at the Ridge Creek Sawmill. Environmental concerns were not on Pierce's priority list. In fact, issues of responsibility were nowhere on his radar. Loretta sent mental warnings to the geese: *stay away, stay away, stay away.* Knowing Pierce, he had his .22 rifle in his truck—bad news under any circumstance—and when showing off for the girls, anything with wings or four legs would be fair game.

Brady jumped from the Jeep. Other classmates, including Jemma Griffin and Pierce, were already gathered. Loretta fought to release her seat belt and staggered to Brady's side, hoping this was the moment that he would hold her, kiss her like she'd seen him kiss other girls. Instead, she heard Jemma teasing in the distance. "Loretta thinks Brady likes her. What a twit. He brought her out here as a laugh…to scare the crap out of her is all."

The first time she kissed a boy, she was eight. Stevie Monroe was ten, devilishly charming, and had just eaten a worm. He had ruffled blonde hair, an appropriate number of bandages that covered numerous scrapes and contusions, a new BMX bicycle, a Star Wars Ewok figurine, and a shark's tooth given to him by his Grandpa Tim. Stevie cornered her beside her mother's tool shed, but even if he hadn't, his many treasures would have been hard to resist. Too bad he tasted, well, wormy. The possibility that Brady had tricked her left another bad taste in her mouth. She wished she could talk to her mother about it, but there was no way. Not now.

Nearby, voices were cheery, but Loretta stood alone. Anxious to look busy, she grabbed the rear handle on Brady's Jeep, pulling to release the hatch.

"Hey," said Jemma, walking up beside her.

"Hey. Um. Just getting my sweater," Loretta said, reaching into the back of the Jeep. *Damn.* Why, with Jemma, did she always feel the need to explain herself?

Jemma's red hair shone brightly in the moonlight. An alligator clip secured her curls, but her bangs hung loose, spiraling about her face. She pushed them aside with a flick of her wrist, a move she had recently perfected. As much as Loretta hated the purposefulness of that gesture, she couldn't help but stare. How *did* Jemma manage her sexy charm?

Pierce's truck was next to the Jeep. Jemma slid onto the open tailgate and patted a spot beside her. "Sit here by me," she said to Loretta, with her fake smile and big eyes.

"I'm good," Loretta said. "I think I'll head home."

"Aw, come on. Hang out a while," said Brady, taking the spot on the tailgate beside Jemma.

People were still chatting. Pierce stood by the fire pit, talking about some hunting trip, swigging a beer. "Yeah, I keep seeing this six-pointer. Huge buck. I'll get him soon as deer season starts, no problem." He shot multiple rounds with his index finger, blasting holes in the night sky. Loretta shivered, glancing at Brady as he ran a hand through his hair.

Some guy was talking about up-ending his Bronco the weekend before: "Took two trucks with winches to turn me right side up. Dented the passenger door, did some damage to the front axle."

"Hey, you okay?" Jemma asked, faux-concerned by Loretta's scowl.

"Yeah, I'm good," Loretta said, clearing her throat, pretending she hadn't heard what Jemma said earlier. *"Loretta thinks Brady likes her. What a twit. He brought her out here as a laugh…to scare the crap out of her is all."*

"How's Cora? I haven't seen much of you guys lately." It looked like she rolled her eyes, but Loretta couldn't tell for sure in the dark.

"She's great. Busy. We're working this summer, full time."

"I heard."

Silence.

"So, what's up with her? I mean, she seems so put-off."

"Cora? She's not."

"Did you know that her dad refuses to let her drive?"

"Not refuses, exactly."

"So what then?"

Loretta shrugged her shoulders. That was Cora's business, not Jemma's. No way was she going to share that Cora had other priorities, like discovering some new species of insect, or fostering a chimpanzee, or watching and drawing anything Manga (she was a fanatic).

"She's sort of weird," said Jemma. "Her clothes, those boots she wears. They're so, like, retro. I mean, she's super sweet, but really?"

Loretta nodded toward the music blaring from Brady's stereo. "Hozier. He's great. When he sings, there's something in me that always wants more."

Brady glanced at her, bobbing his head to the beat.

"That's kind of random. Is that supposed to be funny?" said Jemma.

"No, I just…"

A twinkle of orange, a rush of flashing lights near Willow Grove caught Loretta's attention.

"Check that out," Brady said. "Kinda late to be welding. That's way out there too, past Noleen Deerborne's place."

Jemma leaned her head on Brady's shoulder. "There's some construction going on out there. My dad knows about it. It's all cool."

Loretta shifted uncomfortably from one foot to the other and said, "Did you know that over nine hundred and fifty man-hours are spent welding and fabricating before a NASCAR race car hits the track?"

"Where'd you hear that?" Brady asked.

Loretta chewed on her fingernail. "Ethan."

"Bor-*ing*. Like, yawn, yawn, can we talk about something else?" said Jemma, as she wrapped her arms around Brady.

+++

Thirty minutes later Loretta was home. She'd barely had time to get out of her truck when her cell phone buzzed, displaying Jemma's name in bright blue letters: 2 BAD UR NOT HERE...I'LL KISS BRADY GOOD NITE FOR U. LOL.

HO, she texted back, too angry to let that one go. Her finger wavered over the send button. She sighed, and punched "delete." Who was she kidding—like she would have a chance with Brady, anyway? He followed Jemma around like a puppy dog. If Jemma told Brady to bite Loretta, he would do it.

It was nearly 11:00 p.m., but the air hadn't cooled. The house was hot and stuffy inside. She grabbed a piece of beef jerky and shared it with Toby, opened the windows and doors, then took him outside. The front lawn was patchy and browning but felt good on her bare legs as she lay down beneath a cottonwood tree. The glittery sandals and new yellow tank-top she wore were from her mom, the typical "My job is taking me out of town, and I'm sorry but deal with it" gifts. She kicked off the sandals and pushed them out of reach. Pacifiers from her mother, nothing more.

She wondered what Brady was doing, and if he and the others were still at the knoll. She probably should have stayed longer. Maybe she should have talked more. "Engaged in the conversation," as Ethan would say.

But it was different with those guys. It's not like she

hung out with them—she rarely saw Jemma's bunch outside of school, but tonight, Brady had invited her to go four-wheeling. Odd, but exciting, and she couldn't say no. Cora, on the other hand, could.

Another fountain of sparks dotted the skyline near Noleen Deerborne's, reminding Loretta that tomorrow she would begin her summer job. She shivered, feeling apprehensive. As a child, she'd heard lots of gossip about Granny Noleen and her friends, tall tales about stolen children kept in hidden cellars and fed rotten vegetables and rattlesnake pie. These days, the stories she heard involved the property more than the people who lived there, and were mysterious rather than scary. The house at Willow Grove was old and isolated, and rumored to have been a safe refuge for runaway slaves during the Civil War. Supposedly there were tunnels and trap doors throughout the property, leading to and from the Alabama Hills. According to her history teacher, the Alabamas themselves were named after the Confederate warship, the *U.S.S. Alabama*. The possibility that a well-known safe house for runaway slaves might have existed under the noses of those Confederate sympathizers who homesteaded the region was obviously, incredibly ironic. Reporters wrote magazine articles about it. Her history teacher was obsessed with it.

In the distance, the weird lights faded, but the pops and sputters droned on long enough that she lost interest in Willow Grove and let her mind float with the voice of

Toby Keith crooning from a neighbor's car stereo.

As if he recognized the voice of his namesake, Toby waddled across the lawn, plopped down next to her, and rolled onto his back, legs dancing in the air. Loretta nestled beside him as he grunted and groaned and drifted with her into uneasy dreams. It was well past midnight when she woke up. Stumbling into her room, followed by the dog, she didn't bother to undress, just settled Toby on his pillow and fell onto her bed. As an afterthought, she pulled her cell phone from her pocket and checked it for messages, feeling foolish for thinking Brady might call. If there *was* a voicemail, it would be from her mother, with some nagging reminder that the summer from hell was about to begin.

-CHAPTER 2-

*E*than knew Loretta was at the knoll with Brady and his friends. If he listened hard enough, he could hear their music blaring, Hozier maybe. He stood on his tiptoes, looking for the dust clouds that always trailed the four-wheelers, and hoped Loretta was taking safety precautions, such as wearing her seatbelt and some earplugs.

A large plume of bonfire smoke carried ash particles into the sky, toxic residue from the chemically treated mill-wood Pierce collected from the Ridge Creek Sawmill. Ethan was surprised local environmentalists didn't protest these weekly summer burns. Whether initiated by teenagers or not, this was a violation of air pollution laws, he was sure.

A flock of geese veered away from the smoke. *Smart birds*, he thought, but still he shivered. He watched them fly until he was certain they weren't doubling back toward him. Just the idea of being near those birds, with their big bodies, short, spindly legs, and angry hissing, left him breathless. If they traveled this direction and chose to land here, he'd have to act quickly in order to avoid them, or abort his plan to visit the bunker altogether. And that upset him. He didn't like changing his plans. He'd driven from town through the hills and to the bunker site tonight on his own. His being there felt important, though he didn't understand why.

The yellow-orange sparks generated by The Group's welders and their oxygen and acetylene torches spiraled upward toward the Big Dipper. The crew, including his father, was occupied and busy, thanks to the Committee's updated deadline for completion of this phase of work.

From behind Pistol Rock, the bunker looked like a man-made gopher mound. Ethan flicked his fingers. He crept forward and climbed into the steel-encased hole surrounding the entrance, down the metal staircase and into the staging area—a circular maze that led to all rooms within the bunker compound. Decorating the main hallway was a forested mural painted by his mother, Raina. She had planned every detail of the landscape, color-matching the local flora and fauna to appease the committee in their quest for authenticity. He admired the cedars, pines, and aspens, the red-tail hawk and bluebirds that flew through the fake sky. Raccoon, deer, porcupine, and fox scampered along the painted forest floor. He wondered how much he would miss seeing those things for real. His fingertips skimmed over tree stumps and mounds of granite, places where the paint was marbled and dense, and the softer bends and dips and swirls in feather and fur. He closed his eyes and smiled, warmed by the colors and textures.

A loud clang startled him, and he jumped. He checked his watch. 8:25 p.m. Seven minutes since he entered the bunker. He blinked his eyes and flicked his fingers. Time to move. Slowly, carefully, he positioned himself.

Inside the conference room, the Committee held its weekly meeting. Through the bulletproof glass insert on the steel door, Ethan could see his father, Sim, and Brock and the others deep in discussion. The people in the room looked distorted, just as he would expect the world would appear through Loretta Duvall's eyeglasses, the ones she had worn until two years ago when her mother, Greer, negotiated payment arrangements for contact lenses. The memory made him smile—until he remembered the mounted surveillance camera that spied 24/7 upon this section of the corridor. He glared at the device and sucked in his stomach, wishing himself thin enough to go unnoticed.

Feigning interest in the mural rather than the conference room, he leaned closer, drawn by the fake green water in the fake stream that meandered across the painting. He imagined himself fishing for trout in the Owens River as he had as a child or hiking the moon-rock vistas of the Alabama Hills with his mother, things his family had done before joining Brock's Group. Now Brock encouraged members of The Group to travel together rather than to take private outings. Safety in numbers, he preached.

Officially, Brock did not allow him to wander the bunker halls during the construction phase; no one but the construction crew and the Committee could enter the facility. Even though he had accompanied his father and worked beside him many times, welding and carpentering both inside and outside the bunker project, Brock called Ethan an "unnecessary risk" and told him to stay away. Ethan had argued the validity of this decision many times over the past months and had climbed down the ladder into the bunker repeatedly. Each time, Brock wrote him up, documenting and filing every violation.

"I'm a nonpaid employee," Ethan said too loudly, "and an official youth member of this organization." In the narrow corridor, every noise amplified, sounding hollow and tinny. His feet twitched, ready to run, but his busy mind protested. "Besides, today is Friday, and Friday means father-and-son night." He paused, considering. When his mother worked nights, it meant guy time. But now things were changing, and as the bunker grew closer to completion, this rule, along with others, was being trumped, and Brock's reasoning was harder to understand.

Each family in The Group had received detailed instructions on how the descent into the bunker would occur and what to expect after. Every family was to study and discuss all phases of the process and to memorize a manifesto Brock had recently penned, detailing The Group's mission, criteria for inclusion, rules and regulations for post-cataclysmic life down to the tiniest detail.

After the descent, there would be strict enforcement of all the rules: where you could go, where and when you could eat or sleep, when you went to work or school. Would he be able to take a dump in private, or would that be monitored for color and content, as were the brown hues used to paint the deer in his mother's mural? A word somersaulted through his mind: *domination: control or power over another or others.*

The steel door of the conference room opened with a whoosh of air, and Brock stepped out. "Ethan. What are you doing here?" he asked. Brock's dark eyes were like murky pools, something an ancient worm might swim in. His brows, set in a grimace, crushed together in unyielding ridges.

All six feet, one inch of Ethan shrank. He felt like a kid again, without whiskers or defined pecs and biceps, with a voice that cracked as it did when he was twelve. "I…I'm just…I was waiting for Sim." He avoided Brock's glare, focusing instead on the man's shoes. Spotless. Not a construction worker's shoes. A business person's maybe, or a banker's: brown, shiny, and smooth.

Brock spoke in his deep voice, the same tone he used when driving a point home in one of his lectures. "The staging area is a good place to wait," he said. His look was dismissive, as if he were thinking, *"Leave now, and don't question why."*

It took a minute for Ethan to focus on the words rather

than the shoes. "The staging area is a good place to wait," he repeated. "Yeah, I'll wait up above in the staging area."

"Good boy," said Brock, resting his hand on Ethan's shoulder, nudging him toward the exit.

Ethan drew back. "Don't touch me," he said. "*Good boy* is an affirmation you give your dog, and I am not your pet." He then bolted toward the stairs, thinking only of getting away, of escaping the lecture he knew would come: "I can't control what you think or say, nor do I want to," Sim would tell him. "But I can set consequences for your rude behavior." He had heard this spiel so often he knew it by heart—and this time, Sim would expect him to say "I'm sorry," which he most definitely was NOT.

He climbed the metal steps two at a time, crested the mound of dirt surrounding the entrance to the bunker, and launched himself toward Pistol Rock. A nearby welder dropped his torch, startled by Ethan's sudden appearance and the Vulcan greeting he offered as he passed. The moon shone with an eerie light. Ethan took a deep breath and tried to relax, but couldn't. The air was too hot, too dry. His feet moved faster, faster, until he was sprinting through the loose breccia, up the hill to the rocky outcrop where he had left his Enduro. Without thinking, he mounted and kick-started the bike, revved the engine, spun a dusty brodie, and drove up the bunker's access road. He moved slowly at first, acutely aware of the flashes of light from the welder's torches, and the acrid odor of mixed gases coming from the construction site.

He wondered how far the stench drifted and if Brady and his posse could smell it over the fumes from their burning wood fire. Most likely not. The Committee counted on the weekend parties at the knoll, the bonfires, and the kids' lackadaisical attitudes. They planned the construction on Friday and Saturday nights to protect the confidentiality and integrity of the project, and the noise from the four-wheelers, the loud music, and the bonfires all helped.

Once on the access road Ethan accelerated, enjoying the warm air as it sailed past his face. He turned off onto a BLM trail leading back to town, soothed by the placement of his hands on the rubber handlebar grips and the pressure of his knees on both sides of his bike. His breathing slowed. His muscles relaxed. This was his favorite time of day in the Alabama Hills. The mood was always surreal, the scenery otherworldly. The grays, the browns, the blacks and faded greens were calming; they matched that corner of his brain where he sometimes went when the world became too intense and he needed to disconnect.

Summer vacation, he reminded himself. No more classes or hallway detentions, no Brady and his boys. He nibbled at his lip, bothered by his frequent banishments from the classroom. Talking in class—that was something he couldn't help, like the blinking and the finger-flicking. His doctor and teachers called those behaviors *stimming*, and he had always done those things, at least for as long as he could remember. He wasn't ashamed of his Asperger's. The word circled and landed softly in his brain. *Asperger's.* A while back, his doctors declared that this disorder that contributes to his social awkwardness and all-absorbing interest in specific topics had a new name: *autism spectrum disorder.* But Ethan would have none of it. He had Asperger's, and he adamantly refused the change.

Ethan shifted his focus and felt proud of his ability to do so. "Ten-a-cious," he mouthed, enunciating each syllable. He loved the way words slid off his tongue and was fascinated with the definitions and feelings associated with those words. With lightning speed he formed connections between other words and other feelings in his mind: *afflicted, tormented, frustrated, determined, encouraged.* He remembered how hard it had been as a child to understand what *hot* and *cold* meant—what *happy* and *sad* and *love* and *rejection* meant. He glanced down at his steel-toed work boots and his army green Dickie cargo pants, both constant sources of amusement for Brady and Pierce. He blinked, flicked, rubbed a bit of dirt off his pants. He liked his clothes. He chose them. The sameness brought him comfort and no one could tell him otherwise, not even Brady or Brock.

Ethan whizzed past the rock formation he called Tonto's Fingers. The aura around the granite felt magical, as if the rock had eyes and ears and a mouth open to gossip, spreading stories about the movie heroes who had filmed there: Gene Autry, Roy Rogers and Dale Evans, and the Duke, John Wayne. He'd watched TV reruns a hundred times of Roy's golden horse Trigger, his hooves pounding stone as he loped along the trail with Roy riding snug in the saddle.

On the road into town he slowed, pulled into reality by the smell of burning pitch-wood. The rolling roil of smoke on the knoll had withered to a thin trail of gray. To the west, the welding flashes at the bunker were barely visible. Just ahead was the turnoff toward Willow Grove, where tomorrow morning Loretta would begin her tenure of servitude for Granny Noleen. It was funny to imagine Loretta doing chores for anyone, especially the woman she referred to as the Wicked Witch of the West.

In Lone Pine Ethan drove along Main Street and turned on to Alpine. He parked the bike under a cottonwood at the end of Loretta's block and hoofed it the rest of the way. As always, Loretta's house looked bright and colorful and felt comfortable and safe. The light from the windows was fuzzy yellow, the ruddy front door slightly ajar. Ethan knew the open-door policy was a matter of convenience for Loretta and a source of annoyance to Greer. He and Loretta had been study buddies since the 4th grade. Even back then she was patient. She gave him space when he needed to expound about the treatment of Native Americans by Spanish missionaries or when he rambled on incessantly about the miner 49er's or when he repeatedly enunciated words like *dry digging* and *river damming* and *rocker box*—his favorite descriptors for how to find gold. Nothing disrupted his thoughts when he was on a backward roll, and he was on one now, remembering how anxious he used to get and how he had struggled when he was younger to learn that *anxious* was a word associated with a feeling. He flicked his fingers, but only three times, recalling a meltdown he'd had in Loretta's living room when he was ten years old. He had screamed until Greer called Raina to come and get him. As Greer panicked, Loretta sat calmly beside him. She did not touch him or try to talk to him. She just sat and rocked slowly back and forth while his meltdown ran its course.

Ethan calculated the length of their friendship, though math was not his thing. They had just ended their junior year in high school. That meant they had known each other for eight years; eight times three hundred and sixty-five equals two thousand nine hundred and twenty days.

When he spotted Loretta on the grass, he stopped. Her chest rose and settled into a pattern of sleep, her brown hair, high cheekbones, and lips illuminated in the moonlight. He sat cross-legged a few feet from her, protective, watchful. The word *friend* nestled in the pit of his stomach.

An hour into his vigil, his stomach rumbled. He peered past the window light into the kitchen, thinking about Greer. There was nothing predictable about her, but he liked her, and he loved the after-school snacks she made: peanut butter-and-jelly sandwiches cut into stars, or pizza with faces made out of olives and raisins, or backward root-beer floats (lots of ice cream with a tiny bit of root beer). "Crazy food for a c-r-a-z-y guy," she would say, mimicking Ethan's love of vocabulary as he blinked and flicked in gratitude.

He checked his watch. Two minutes after midnight. If his parents were home, they would be worried and calling his cell or Loretta's. Thankfully, he didn't have to stress over Sim; he would be in the bunker until dawn. Raina, however, would be off work in an hour. The Iron Gate closed at 1:00 a.m. and as soon as her last customer hit the door, she would be two steps behind. She enjoyed her job waiting tables, and she made good tips, but done was done, and she was always out of there in a hurry when her shift ended.

And he liked that. She worked close by and was home every night—she was always available if he needed her. For Loretta, it was different. Greer usually worked out of town, sometimes far away. When Loretta was younger, she would stay with her best friend Cora while Greer was gone, but now she stayed by herself. *"Independence,"* Ethan mouthed. *"Exemption from reliance on, or control by others."* The definition was precise, but the meaning was not clear to him.

He looked at his watch again and timed his trip home, calculating how long it would take to get into his pajamas, brush his teeth, and get into bed. He would have to leave in fifteen minutes to beat Raina and avoid adding a second strike to his evening's list of *rebellious activities*. He tensed and flexed his jaw. He blinked his eyes. "Rebellious activities." That's the way Brock would put it when he tattled to Sim and claimed the right to name Ethan's punishment for breaking bunker rules.

Across the street at Mr. Gorman's house, an oversize flag snapped in the wind from the holder beside his door, the red and white stripes gleaming fluorescent in the moonlight. Ethan wondered if the Committee would still salute Old Glory, or if they would design their own banner of allegiance once the time came for separation.

There was a sudden screech and a loud bang, and several porch lights came on. A cat scurried across the lawn, chased by the neighbor woman. "Damn people, abandon their animals, just leave them to wander. What the hell's the matter with this crazy world?" she said.

The pitch of her voice raised the hair on Ethan's arms. He leaned back into the shadows of the elm tree. Loretta moaned, stood and stretched, then stumbled toward the house. Ethan opened his mouth to speak but decided against it.

-CHAPTER 3-

The alarm buzzed at 8:00 a.m. *A few more minutes, just a few more*, Loretta thought, as she punched "snooze" and slithered deeper under the covers. The alarm resounded just as her cell phone pinged with a text from her mother: CURTAIN CALL. RISE AND SHINE.

"Crap!" Loretta said, scratching a fresh mosquito bite as she typed out a response: REALLY, MOM? HAVE A GREAT DAY.

The longer she stalled, the more her stomach knotted. She was no handywoman or gardener, or whatever else might be expected of her at Willow Grove. The day had barely started and was already a downer. She groaned and climbed out of bed, a sleepy tangle of arms and legs. The cut-off jeans she still wore were giving her a wedgie, so she unzipped and stepped out of them, then pulled the sequined shirt and yellow tank top over her head and tossed them on the floor.

Once in the shower, she let the water do its magic,

massaging her face and shoulders, soothing her swollen eyes, until her brain interfered and she remembered the *big D*. Word about California's drought had resounded at school and on the local radio and television stations. Signs posted in neighborhoods and in town stated the concern very clearly—*Conserve water. Brown is the new green. Every drop counts*—so after only a few minutes, she shut off the spigot.

Half an hour later, she was stressing over socks. Her choices were limited: white tube socks, white ankle socks, or a pair of her mother's that had found its way into her drawer: black knee-highs decorated with cheeseburgers. She wore a clean pair of cut-offs, no contest there. A green t-shirt, okay fine. But the socks were, like, cool versus uncool, and hey, they mattered. "One two, sky blue, all out except you," she said to the white anklets.

Still stalling, she arranged the covers on her bed, fluffed her favorite teddy bear and propped him against the headboard. Though it was disturbing to her seventeen-year-old ego, she still loved snuggling her nose into Teddy's well-worn fur, holding him tight when she was upset. The bear, along with her *Divergent* throw pillow, had survived her most recent redecorating. Loretta sat for a moment, admiring the new bedspread she had picked out of a J.C. Penney catalog, green with sapphire stars. Posters of One Republic, Imagine Dragons, and Green Day decorated her walls, along with pictures she had cut out of *Seventeen* and *People*. Her bookcase bulged with well-read books and CDs. She had a great

CD player (antiquated but appreciated) and an iPad—gifts from Uncle Manny Holcomb.

Cora's face smiled at her from a snapshot on her bulletin board, tacked up alongside her fall class schedule and her junior class picture. She kissed her finger, found Brady in the back row, and transferred the kiss with vigor.

Downstairs in the kitchen, she picked up her daypack, brooding over the contents: her swimsuit, an extra shirt and shorts, the new book Cora's dad had given her for her birthday. The *Classic Movie Anthology* was a surprising choice, though it did have a historical theme. As an anthropologist, Dr. Gomez was majorly analytical, thriving on scientific theories and data. On past birthdays, he had given Loretta subscriptions to *National Geographic* and *The New Yorker*, offering culture into a home where her mother thought Louis Leakey was a plumber and Margaret Mead a folk singer. It was nice to know *somebody* made an effort.

Loretta fed Toby, then trudged out the kitchen door with her movie face on, all droopy and sulky, wishing someone would notice. The sun seemed as angry with her mother as she was, bearing down heavy for a mid-morning in June. Every breath she took left her feeling flat, constricted. "'It's hot enough to cook the geraniums,'" her mother always said, and on that point she had to agree.

Old Blue, their Chevy truck, was parked in the driveway. Loretta slid into the front seat, turned the key, and gunned the engine, goosing a full *ba, ba, ba* from the exhaust pipe. She eased up on the gas pedal and sat for a minute, upset about the heat, her too-tight shoes, the broken knob on the CD player in the truck, and the fact that she would be spending her summer working hard labor rather than pursuing *the Brady bunch*, as Cora called Brady and his friends. "Why can't you get a *regular* job?" she hollered at her mother's hummingbird charm, draped around the rear view mirror. She sighed in frustration, then checked the time on her cell phone. It was one thing to be late for school and quite another to be late on her first day of work at Noleen Deerborne's. She could always finagle Mrs. Brown in the attendance office into a tardy slip, but convincing Noleen that her alarm clock was on the fritz would be another matter entirely. "Bummer," she said, another of her mother's favorite expressions. She revved the engine once more and settled into the seat. First gear had died long ago, so after easing out of the driveway in reverse, she wiggled the gearshift into second and bumped along with Old Blue into town.

+++

As usual, even on a Saturday morning, most of the people wandering Main Street were truckers, strolling out of the coffee shop and Motel 6 to head back to their big rigs and finish their runs to and from Los Angeles. The line was growing at Carmen's Tamale Stand, truckers waiting to buy her homemade tamales, fresh-made every morning. Loretta breathed in the aroma of corn masa and spice, the cinnamon-and-apple sweet tamales Carmen was famous for up and down Route 395.

A flicker of movement caught her eye. She slammed on her brakes, swerving to the right and barely missing a pedestrian in the crosswalk. "Ethan! Oh, dang!" she screamed, though it was clearly her fault. Ethan stood and stared, blinking his eyes and flicking his fingers. His longish dark-brown hair appeared neatly combed. His clothes were boho grunge: baggy Dickies, a red t-shirt, and a green plaid flannel, left unbuttoned, tied at the waist. His usual steel-toed work boots. Loretta pulled Old Blue to the curb and parked, looking over her shoulder at the unaware truckers and also at Carmen, busy at her tamale stand. Ethan smiled his lopsided smile, still frozen mid-stride, a stack of papers tucked under his left arm. He saluted with his right hand, looped around a passing car, and hopped onto the sidewalk.

Loretta dug her cell phone from her purse and texted Cora: I NEARLY RAN OVER ETHAN. BE THERE IN 10.

Cora's response was immediate: HAVE U NOTICED??? ETHAN = JOHNNY DEPP. CU IN A FEW.

Loretta edged away from the curb and onto Main Street. She had noticed—Ethan was growing into his own and then some. If Cora had picked up on this, other girls had as well. She pictured Jemma putting a move on Ethan. *Over my dead body*, she thought, her protective mode kicking in.

From her rearview mirror, she could see Ethan, and he

waved again. Behind him, the Iron Gate pool hall remained dark, the neons that typically lit the bar's windows noticeably absent, as was the country music that pulsed through the doorway every day and every night, twelve months a year. In yesterday's paper, in the News of Record, she'd read: *A theft was reported at the corner of Main and Pine. Mustard was involved.* Mustard was involved? Where were the newspaper reporters when a real crime happened? She had nearly run over Ethan, Jemma could potentially cop a move on him, and the music had died at the Iron Gate. Something was off-kilter. She returned Ethan's wave and put her fist to her ear, signaling that she would call him later.

To her left, a herd of white clouds surrounded Whitney's peak, and the sun beat down over Lone Pine. She pulled Old Blue back on the road, her mind spinning with memories of mornings spent playing beside Lone Pine Creek with Ethan and his parents, Cora and her dad, and her mother's movie crew friends—and afternoons watching actors dressed as cowboys and Indians, starship captains, even gladiators, declaring war on each other in the Alabama Hills.

As she neared the Deerborne place, the reason for Hollywood's fascination with the Hills became evident. A sea of metamorphosed volcanic rock and hippopotamus-shaped granite rose out of the desert floor. Shadows snuck among the massive boulders, rugged arches, twisted rock formations, and rounded hills, disappearing into caves and playing tricks before her eyes. She blinked, and blinked again. Some of the old-timers, people who had lived in Lone Pine all their lives, swore that the ghosts of movie stars haunted the Hills and the ghosts of miners walked among the craggy cliffs at night.

Loretta drove into the yard at Willow Grove and parked near the garden shed. It had been several years since she and Cora had come snooping and really, very little had changed. The house looked the same: two stories with a wrap-around porch and shutters, flanked by an out-of-control wisteria vine that seemed determined to devour the whole thing. As badly as the house needed a new roof and fresh coat of paint, it would have been difficult to accomplish either one. Thinking back, it was easy to see why local kids had been fixated on the rumors that surrounded the place. She and Cora had done their fair share of trick-or-treating-type stunts at Willow Grove over the years, leaving bubble gum on fence posts and ritualistic bones and dead worms on the doorstep.

In the side yard, Noleen quit hoeing and peered squinty-eyed at Old Blue. *Uh-oh*, Loretta thought. *Busted.* She slid out of the truck and kicked a rock, launching it unexpectedly at the shed. The rock ricocheted off the old wood-sided structure and into the brush. Her aim was never *that* good, so why today, of all days, should it be any different? Noleen one-eyed her, muttering some crazy gobbledygook.

"Weirdo," Loretta mouthed, as Noleen walked over to the rock she had kicked, picked it up, and tucked it into her shirt pocket. An entire conversation between Noleen and her mother played out in her mind with the rock as evidence: a reason to extend her sentence on Noleen's work crew. Accident or no, she was screwed. At this rate, she could be working at Willow Grove for the rest of her life.

Cora Gomez sat slumped in the rocking chair on Noleen's front porch. "Nice," she said, between bites of peach. Her stringy black hair framed her face like an Easter bonnet tied within the rolls of her chin. She wore hard-gripping hiking boots, bush-beating cotton khaki shorts, and a button-up top with a vest to match. With one hand she swatted a fly and with the other lifted the peach to her mouth for another bite.

Loretta tried to take a deep breath. The air, smelling of sage, was hot going down. It was not easy to fill her lungs with the full weight of summer. Whatever possibility there had been for a decent breeze that morning seemed trapped in the snow atop Mt. Whitney. Perpetually icy, Whitney was as promising as a mirage along Highway 395, and she imagined herself crawling to it, parched and near death.

She plopped on the porch beside Cora and for the first half hour listened to Noleen complain to some invisible friend about how undependable teenagers were; the wasteful nature of Lone Pine's citizens as evidenced by the treasures her son, Paiute Bill, found after dumpster diving behind the new superstore being built near the highway; the high price of ham; and Ralph the Butcher's habit of skimming her pocketbook by refusing to trim the fat. While listening to this tirade, Loretta wondered

if Noleen wanted her and Cora at Willow Grove even less
than they wanted to be there.

It was a standoff, pure and simple.

-CHAPTER 4-

*E*than stood in the middle of the road. It took con-centrated effort to register the closeness of Loretta's vehicle and verify that she was the driver. She had nearly run him over, but he was still happy to see her. He smiled and waved and she waved back, then gestured him on. He started toward the curb, then hesitated, shading his eyes to see her more clearly. Loretta waved him forward more insistently this time and held her fist to her ear, a sign that she would phone him later. Knowing that if she said it, she meant it, and would call, he smiled. Then he saluted and continued his trek from the middle of the street to the sidewalk in front of the Iron Gate.

Various ads and for sale notices filled the bulletin board on the wall outside the entrance to the bar:

For sale: Rain barrels, $50.00.

For sale: Coonhound puppy, dog bed, dog toys, puppy pads. Best offer.

Oak Firewood: $350.00 per cord—$325.00 per cord— price negotiable.

Farmer's Market: Saturday afternoons in the park. Local farms, organic produce.

Barely visible beneath the flyer advertising the Farmer's Market was a small, yellowed piece of paper, an ad written in faded blue ink:

Carmen's Tamales, fresh made daily. Open seven days a week.

Ethan unpinned Carmen's sign and rubbed it against his thigh, trying to smooth out the creases in the weathered paper. He picked at the edges of the posters tucked under his armpit and curled his upper lip at the crinkling sound they made. There were only a couple of people on the sidewalk nearby, but it suddenly seemed crowded. He thought of his Enduro and wished he was on it, riding in the open hills as he had planned to do that day. But the trip didn't happen because he was here instead, walking the streets, hanging posters—the consequence Brock had set for his *rebelliousness* with the price of a box of thumbtacks and fifty copies of the poster. No Enduro. No friends. His Saturday morning ruined.

"Need help?" MaryAnne Archer had been sweeping a neighboring storefront, a touristy souvenir shop called the Bait and Buckle. Now she stood beside him, creating space for his poster. She unpinned the outdated and faded flyers and index cards and threw them in a nearby trash can.

"There now. That's better," she said, brushing her hands together, wiping away the dust.

"Thank you," said Ethan. He waited until she walked away, then placed his poster just so, following the straight edges of the bulletin board—one inch from the left side, one inch from the top—and secured all four corners with thumbtacks. Satisfied, he stood back and studied the poster. The blue-gray background was a watermark, a vague picture of a classic A-bomb mushroom cloud. The header above the picture announced the event, place, and time: "Group meeting, Grange Hall. Tonight, 8:00 p.m." He noted the late hour. Was that to weed out attendees or protestors, he wondered? Only the resolute need apply?

Near the left margin, off-center from the watermark, was a photograph of a Group party. People were smiling, playing Frisbee, enjoying a picnic beside the river. Ethan's eyes shifted from the mushroom cloud to the photo of the happy people enjoying each other's company. Seeing the two images made his skin prickle. Bouncing from one foot to the other, he read the fine print near the bottom of the poster: "Interested candidates may now apply for our catastrophic episode shelter project. We are looking for individuals who will contribute best to our shelter community as a whole, those who can provide the financial and emotional stability necessary to secure the greatest chance for long-term survival of the entire Group." Underneath that, in bold red print: **THE COMMITTEE WELCOMES YOU.**

"*I'm* not welcome," Ethan blurted, "So this is a lie." This recent news from his father was not a huge surprise, but its delivery was startling. "Behave yourself. Stay home," Sim had told him. The sentences were clear but the meaning was double-edged. Mind the rules *or* stay home. Stay home *and* mind the rules. With no clarification, Ethan was confused. All he knew for certain was that Sim was majorly ticked off—that he had ranted and paced the floor as he spoke, not his usual M.O. "Your behavior is an embarrassment to our family," he'd said. "These ridiculous outbursts have got to stop." Ethan knew these last words were Brock's, not Sim's, but still they hurt. He thought about and carefully measured the wording of another lecture from Sim's oft-repeated repertoire: "Rudeness and disrespect can have a high price. How you talk to people influences the way they see you." It wasn't like his father to disregard one of his own declarations.

Ethan had tried to explain his reason for coming to the bunker, but Sim wouldn't listen. He'd stated his argument calmly at first: "I needed to talk to you. Yes, it was important, and no, it couldn't wait." His brain retraced the detailed plans he'd wanted to share, ideas for the bunker he'd come up with on his own: an area to house family pets (people won't want to leave them behind) with hospitable cages, runs, food bins and proper sanitation units, all drawn out following the bunker's circular design. "It was Group-related business!" he'd shouted before he shut down, before he withdrew from the conversation.

If he'd spoken his mind, his punishment would be much worse that the minor annoyance of hanging posters and purchasing thumbtacks. He'd wanted to discuss the Committee's edict that children call their parents by their first name. He'd memorized the ruling, word for word: "Using given names rather than terms of endearment is a protective measure meant to promote bonding among all members of The Group rather than segregation of family units."

"Dad, it sucks" he wanted to say. "It sucks big time. And I don't trust Brock. And I don't like it when you and Mom ignore me." Ethan didn't like the feeling he had in the pit of his stomach. It felt raw and uncertain, like his perception of The Group and the Committee and the bunker. He thought of something his father had once told him: "Look at the *original* painting, not someone's interpretation of it—otherwise you may miss the artist's real intent."

He flicked his fingers, and Carmen's tamale note fluttered in his hand. His mouth watered as he gazed at the faded blue ink; he could almost taste the fresh masa, the seasoned chicken, green olives, and little potato chunks hidden in the middle of the tamale. "The potato is a gift, Carmen often told him, "from me to you." He held the yellowed paper to the bulletin board, centering it appropriately: "giving it prime advertising space," as Raina would say. He pulled open the lid to the box of tacks and looked inside, but dared not use them to hang anything other than

Brock's posters. Instead, he plucked four micro-nails from the well-used cork and secured Carmen's sign, then stepped back, nodding in approval.

"A one-hundred-count box," he said as he shook it. "One hundred minus four equals ninety-six thumbtacks. Ninety-six thumbtacks, four per poster, fifty posters…not enough!"

He chided Brock in absentia: "You demanded that I purchase these thumbtacks at the Penny Saver, and the only container available there was this one. Your estimate of materials needed to finish the job is incorrect, so I'll do the right thing and equalize." Ethan looked over his shoulder, to his right and left, rounded the corner to the alleyway, found the dumpster behind Quill's Pet Emporium, and slid twenty-five posters in between old cat-food boxes and discarded fish food. The smell of the sour tubifex worms brought to mind his aquarium at home and the fish food he kept on the shelf below the tank. The angelfish, neon tetra, African cichlids, silver hatchetfish, rubber lip pleco and his favorite kuhli loach—were all gifts his parents had given him for birthdays or Christmas. Sometimes they bought him a fish for accomplishing a task or managing a behavior: washing up after dinner without breaking a single dish; controlling his wiggles through an entire movie at the theater; going to sleep without flicking, blinking, or pounding his head against the pillow.

Ethan remembered the affection he used to see in his

parents' eyes when they looked at him, particularly after such a milestone. He thought of the confidence they used to inspire, how they had always listened to what he had to say and encouraged his individuality. Something had changed, though. There was a darkness to Sim now, and it felt too Brock-like. Even the inflections in his speech—the rolling pauses and inhales, slow rises in tone and pace—mimicked Brock's.

With a rush of heat, Ethan felt himself slipping into his own world, that peaceful place in one corner of his brain that he owned absolutely. This time, though, he pulled back, teasing himself slightly to offset the threatening images of Brock. "I *will* not disrespect. I *will* not be insubordinate. But I'm not sorry. I'll never be sorry for barking in your ear." Just as he said it, his smile disappeared. He sucked his lips behind his teeth, where he wished his words had stayed. He looked up and down the sidewalk. If anyone heard him, he could be punished. Worse than now. Something gross even, like latrine duty.

Or cage clean-up at The Group's organic farm.

Ethan felt a tingle in his chest, knowing that in truth, this scenario was no joke. There were many things he didn't understand and many things he'd learned to deal with in his life, but there were some things his Asperger's still controlled. One was his aversion to bird legs. He didn't mind little birds like sparrows or robins or towhees. It was big birds like ducks, geese, and chickens, with long spindly legs comprised of concentric scaly orange rings and probably crawling with minuscule parasites, that set his skin afire. Just thinking about the possibility of shoveling bird crap in the hen house at the organic farm led Ethan to plop down on the curb, blink his eyes, flick his fingers, and go to his peaceful place. This time, he stayed.

Some time later, loud voices and swearing from inside the Iron Gate caused a ripple of conscious thought, then a wave that pulled him back to reality. Glass shattered, and chairs scraped across the wooden floor inside the bar. Pierce's cousin Jack and Paiute Bill stumbled out the door, assisted by the Iron Gate's bouncer, Frey. "Beat it, you two!" The pointy toe of Frey's cowboy boot caught Bill behind the knees. Bill stumbled forward and lost his footing, landing chin first on Ethan's back. Ethan dropped his stack of posters. The wind created by a passing big rig sent them flying.

"This bar has turned to shit," Jack slurred. "You can't turn people away. That's discrimination."

"Ya, well, tell it to the cops," said Frey. "Management has the right to refuse service."

"Drop dead."

"Now that was uncalled for." Frey peered through the door into the Iron Gate, nodded his head and grinned. "The boss says, "Ante up." His fist struck Jack in the jaw, knocking him sideways, a spray of bloody saliva raining on the sidewalk. Frey chuckled, turned, and walked back into the bar, rubbing his hands on his jeans.

Paiute Bill scrambled on his hands and knees, over Ethan and into the street, picking up the flyers within his reach. He stank of yesterday's beer and stale cigarettes, and the spidery veins in his cheeks were cherry-red. His Wranglers had holes in the knees, and the soles of his tennis shoes had no tread. The sleeves had been cut off his green flannel shirt, his brown arms bare from the shoulders down. His biceps slouched south of where they should have been, and his left forearm suffered a patch of fresh road rash.

Paiute Bill struggled to his feet, wiped the grime from one of the posters and pushed the batch of them into Ethan's hands. He cocked his head to the side and smiled a nearly toothless grin. Hyper-aware of the warmth that radiated from the dark centers of Bill's eyes, Ethan found a word and let it circle his brain: *Compassion: a deep awareness of the suffering of others coupled with the wish to relieve it.*

Jack grabbed Bill by the elbow and pulled him along. With their heads tucked to their shoulders, both men slunk away. Ethan checked his watch. Even with the delay, if he didn't dawdle, he could finish hanging posters by noon. Then he was free to do summertime stuff: maybe a little trout fishing in Tuttle Creek, or even riding out to Willow Grove to check on Loretta and Cora. He flicked his fingers, thinking of Granny Noleen's long skirts and big funny hats, her scowl and sour attitude. Other kids were afraid of her, but he wasn't. She was different and he was curious about her—plus, he liked her funky style of dress.

He walked along Main Street, tacking posters on the bulletin boards near the tourist shops, in front of the gas stations and motels and near the entry to Eastside Deli. His stomach growled at the smell of freshly baked ciabatta bread. He went inside and stood by the cash register, waiting for Ruby.

Ruby came in from the storeroom, wiping her hands with a dishtowel. Her rosy cheeks matched the color of her shirt, which read: "The West Wasn't Won With Tofu." Her smile was as broad as her belly. "Ethan, my man, what's happening?" she asked in her raspy Midwestern drawl.

"Hi, Ruby. I need to hang this in your deli." He held up the poster.

Ruby nodded her approval and pointed to a bulletin board near the door. "Go for it."

Ethan hung the poster, recalculating his count of thumbtacks. "I smelled your bread baking clear down the block," he said. "What's the special today?"

"Anything that tickles your fancy, darlin'. I've got some excellent roast beef. Provolone from Maggie Grayson's cheese factory up near Bishop."

"Provolone cheese, lettuce, tomato, pickles, olives, a tablespoon of mayo, and a teaspoon of mustard."

"You got it. Make yourself at home. It'll be right out."

Ethan slid into a booth, and watched the traffic outside. The long-haul truckers' rigs were mostly gone now, replaced by locals and tourists with their pickups, minivans, and

SUVs. A man and woman stopped to read the poster he had tacked up near the Shell station across from the deli. Ethan's gut reaction was to jump up, run out the door waving his arms and tell them, "No, no, don't go to The Group meeting." He slid down in the booth and shot a quick look at Ruby, then turned his shoulders so he couldn't see her.

Ruby was not on the Committee, but she was a regular at meetings and never hesitated to add her two cents. She was part of the bunker design team and had instigated the addition of television monitors in each sleeping compartment rather than just in the main conference hall. She had been the first to fork out her savings to get the project started. Ruby, Sim and Raina, Pierce's parents, and Jemma's had all contributed funds to hire the architect and the construction crew. The bunker was not a project propelled by the community's poor and indigent. Big money had come in from wealthy contributors. Ethan knew this from his parents' conversations.

"Here ya go, big guy. Enjoy." Ruby set a plate in front of Ethan laden with his sandwich, potato chips, and two homemade peanut butter cookies. "On the house," she told him. "My treat today."

Ethan looked up and away, staring his appreciation into the corner of the diner. "Thank you," he said.

"My privilege," she said, smiling broadly.

He relaxed a little, and as he ate his mind wandered, formulating possibilities for how the descent could happen.

He had eavesdropped on enough adult conversations over the past months to understand that if a threat, catastrophe, or cataclysmic event occurred, bunker co-owners would only have one hour to get into the shelter before a Committee member sealed shut the doors. The bunker would be ready, stocked with food and beverages, furnishings, fixtures, and all the equipment needed for long-term survival. Every person would receive clothing, bedding, toiletries, and medical supplies. A deep underground well serviced the complex, a continuous water supply guaranteed to last the duration of the *incident*. A hospital and dental facility were part of the structure. Hydroponic gardening supplies, computers, generators, fuel, security devices, books, tools, radios, gym equipment—all provided. Off-road vehicles parked in the garage component and maintained by the best mechanics were an additional perc. Brock assured his investors that their comfort and safety were the Committee's top priority.

Would it be a terrorist attack, Ethan wondered? A nuclear event? Anarchy? Maybe a natural disaster like an earthquake. He recalled from tenth-grade geology that the Owens Valley was home to basaltic cones and flows created over the past 1.2 million years. North of Lone Pine, in Mammoth Lakes, earthquakes were a regular occurrence. Even though eruptions in that area ended 57,000 years ago, Mammoth still produced volcanic gases that killed trees and had even caused ski patrol fatalities. The skiers had been digging out an old fence line near a volcanic vent when the ground gave way. They landed in a deep hollow and were overcome with carbon dioxide fumes.

This same type of event was something that could happen today. Ethan shivered and then swallowed whole the bite he had just taken from his sandwich. He choked, coughed, and took a sip of water from the glass Ruby had set beside his plate. He made a mental note regarding the location of his parents and the time it would take him to reach them. Loretta and Cora popped in his head, and he worried, knowing that neither Greer nor Cora's father, Doc Gomez, had bought into the bunker idea, and that both families had nixed the philosophies of The Group. If a disaster happened, Loretta and Cora would be on their own. If the ground shook and the earth sucked the town of Lone Pine down to its core, there would be nothing he could do to protect them.

Ethan flicked his fingers and groaned. The facts as he saw them looked bleak, so he listed them for easier evaluation:

One. Pierce's father and Jemma's parents are Committee members.

Two. Pierce and Jemma are both assured a place in the bunker.

Three. A lockdown with those two and no friends to provide comfort and offset their teasing will be a nightmare.

Surely Brock and his Committee would set rules regarding bullying in their precious bunker. Surely his parents would intervene on his behalf if things got out of control. "I'm still a kid," he said, loudly enough for Ruby to hear. "I shouldn't have to think about this crap." He kicked the table leg, stood up, and marched out of the deli without saying goodbye.

The Enduro was parked near Mail and Such, where he had run off copies of Brock's flyer that morning. He hopped on the seat, turned the key, and revved the engine. The high-pitched whir was a welcome relief from the busyness of his mind. He pulled out onto Main Street, drove to Whitney Portal Road, and let the wind and the speed and the power of the motorcycle carry him away.

-CHAPTER 5-

Noleen's brown skin was weather-beaten, her face deeply furrowed. Her white braids hung below her hat, were chest length and tied with leather cording. She wore a three-tiered skirt, faded red, and a blue flowered shirt with rolled-up sleeves. Draped around her neck was a wet bandana, and her boots were hardcore Neanderthal. Hunched over her work, she tossed flower seeds around tree stumps and into shallow pockets of earth, her body swaying to the rhythm of her prehistoric stride. "Pretty clear what needs doin'," she said, pointing with her nose to a wheelbarrow and a patch of weeds invading her tomato vines.

"What? I mean..." Loretta hesitated, unsure which way to go.

Noleen left her hands where they sat on her hips, daring Loretta to question her further.

Loretta's mind spun with images of dungeons and missing children, the notion that her life would change now that she and Cora worked every day at Willow Grove.

"Alright-y then. Guess this is it." Cora grunted as she stood up. Shuffling toward the garden, she picked up a stick, broke it in half, stopped to study a dragonfly on a nearby lilac bush, and then again to pull a copy of the National Geographic *Field Guide to the Insects and Spiders of North America* out of her pack.

"Ah," she said, "a twelve-spot skimmer. Cool. *Very* cool."

Loretta muddled along behind her, glancing at Cora, glancing at the dragonfly, glancing at Old Blue, but keeping her eyes mostly on Noleen. When she finally reached the garden, she stood surprised. The orderly rows of vegetables were in various stages of growth. The plot was big and needed a good weeding but was obviously well-tended.

"Lord a-mighty, you girls have a hitch in your gitty-up? Come on now, day's a-wastin'," Noleen said, her naturally growly voice sounding more so.

Loretta felt her face flush and bent to remove her shoes and socks. Mud squished between her toes as she stepped into the wet soil—at least an eight on the *yuck* scale. She gagged, but her mouth stretched into a smile as she watched Cora do the same.

"*Ew, ew…ew, ew, she's a dreamer, and a dancer, the ultimate romancer,*" Cora sang, off-key, as she wiggled her toes in an oozing pocket of muck.

"Don't even go there," Loretta told her, giving *there* a nasal drawl, as her mother might do.

"What? This doesn't remind you a bit of home? I mean…a vegetable garden. A super talented karaoke-type singer? What more can you ask for?"

Loretta gave Cora *the look*, the one that said, "Stop, or I'll dance my way right out of here and leave you to fend for yourself."

The fact was, this garden was not at all like her mother's: a tomato here, a cucumber there. Most of the seeds her mother planted lived long enough to poke their heads through the soil, but as her watering routine followed the same pattern as her life, the vegetables soon shriveled down to nothing or grew long and leggy and turned an unhealthy yellow-green. If she grew a tomato, it dried on the vine. If the cucumber plant produced a cucumber, the gophers ate it before Loretta did. Here in the garden at Willow Grove, each row of vegetables was precise and well managed—there were several varieties of tomatoes marked by stakes bearing the names Beefsteak, Early Girl, Roma, and Cherry. There were rows of corn stalks nearly up to her waist, zucchini plants growing on round knobs, green and red peppers, jalapeño and Anaheims, pole beans climbing teepee-like contraptions made of wood and tied together with string. Cucumbers, strawberries, and kale.

The sky was alive with the whirr of wings—flies and bees and dragonflies—and bird song—robins, bluebirds, mourning doves. Loretta picked a weed, disturbing a red-ant colony. Instantly, the ants were swarming her feet and legs, their pungent smell filling her nostrils. She swatted them, then hopped and ran through the zucchini beds, demolishing the plant identification tags, plowing down wooden stakes and wire vine holders.

"Good Lord, girl. Glad it wasn't a hornet's nest you unsettled."

Loretta stood stiff-legged, breathing hard. She wanted to tell Noleen to take her nasty ants and her garden and stick them where the sun don't shine. Instead, she cursed her mother between closed lips, hexing her for life for forcing her into this job and sticking her in this hell-hole for the summer.

Noleen turned her back and sowed her seeds, ignoring Loretta's attitude. "Fix them vine holders," she said. "We'll not worry about the name stakes."

Hours went by without a break. Loretta and Cora threw weeds, hurling them into a pile to the side of the garden. Loretta launched a few in the wrong direction, decorating the tool shed with muddy brown graffiti. Her back hurt. Her knees were dirty and her hands were scratched and sore. From behind her, a shadow grew over the beets: long, lanky, and crowned with a cowboy hat. She turned and saw the scrunched-up face of Paiute Bill, peering at her as if trying to remember who she was and why she would be in his mother's garden.

Cora jumped up, her legs like two thick stumps, her khaki shorts glued to her thighs with a thick coat of muck.

Bill nodded his head, tipped his hat, and retreated with his shadow. "He gives me the creeps," Cora scowled, her lips in ventriloquist mode.

"Get used to it," Loretta said. "He lives here, you know. With the others." She frowned, thinking of all the old folks in Willow Grove, their wrinkled skin, liver spots, and boxes and boxes of Depends.

Noleen pulled a handkerchief out of her pocket and dropped it. "Hrumph," she said, as she leaned over to pick it up.

"That's Paiute," Cora whispered, "for shit." Both she and Loretta giggled.

Noleen wiped her face with the handkerchief. "Come on, then," she said. "Pick a couple of them tomatoes, Cora, and let's break for lunch." As she breezed past Loretta, the leaves along the brick walkway whirled and eddied at her feet, clearing a path to the house and the door.

"Did you see that?" Loretta asked Cora. "I swear this property creates its own weather. It's like some vortex exists in the blackberry patches down there." She nodded toward the creek.

Cora rolled her eyes and then turned to the tomato vines, picking two red Early Girls. "I'll get you my pretty and your little dog Toto too," she said, with her back hunched and her arms swaying back and forth.

As Loretta chuckled, her stomach growled, reminding her that it had been hours since she'd eaten breakfast. Still, the thought of entering Willow Grove and having lunch with the old folks soured her appetite.

Noleen turned on a water spigot near the porch, washed her hands, and then dried them on a towel flung over the porch railing. She untied her boots, slipped them off, and stood them beside the door before entering the house.

"Don't dawdle," she hollered, as the screen door banged shut behind her.

"This is too weird," Cora said, following Noleen's path to the porch. She set the tomatoes on the railing, turned on the water, and stuck her hands and feet under the spigot. "We're going inside? Nightmare city."

"We could run for it," Loretta said.

"She'd jump on her broom. We'd never make it."

While Cora dried her hands and feet, Loretta thought of excuses she might make, some reason for leaving early: her dog was sick, she had to check on him; the house payment was due, she had to mail it; she had a dentist appointment, a doctor visit; she'd started her period and had cramps. She needed to go home.

Paiute Bill bounced past them into the house and re-turned with two fresh towels, gesturing that they should wipe the mud off their shorts as well as their arms and legs. Loretta knew that Bill was deaf, but had never observed his sign language up close. Although rough and callused, his hands moved with ease, suggesting they should hurry.

The story, as her mother told it, was that Noleen had

birthed Bill on the Paiute Reservation near Bishop. Two women had tied her legs together when she was in labor to keep her from having the baby before the doctor arrived. The delay had caused permanent damage, resulting in Bill's deafness. "That's the way it was back then. Paiute were lower-class citizens." Loretta thought her mother's explanation was nothing more than an original argument for birth control, but now, up close, she could see Bill's misshapen ear lobes and the scars and discoloration near the outside of his left ear canal. Cora raised her eyebrows, indicating that she had seen the same.

As Bill opened the door, Loretta held her breath, prepared for an onslaught of smells: dust, old socks, mildew, mothballs. Vicks Vapo-Rub. Geriatric armpits. Urine. What greeted her instead was the smell of roses. The windows were open, and with the breeze, antique lace curtains saluted them as they entered the house. The living room was large and roomy, with a floral couch facing a massive river-rock fireplace and a coffee table on which the vase of roses sat. Near the windows rested two rocking chairs, a recliner, and a small table piled with books. Laughter distorted the image she had spun all these years of dark, dusky rooms and ghoul-filled halls. The laughter came from the kitchen, she assumed, by the rustle of silverware, cafeteria-style murmurs, and the aroma of homemade bread. "Got those tomatoes?" Noleen shouted.

"Set seven plates," someone ordered.

"Bill will take two plates." Three sharp claps followed the speaker's gristly chuckle.

"That's right, Billy, it was a joke. Apologize, Earl. We've got company," Noleen scolded.

"You go in first," Cora told Loretta.

"No, you." Loretta pushed Cora's shoulder with her own toward the kitchen door.

"Come now, dears. Lunch will get rusty if you dilly-dally much longer." The woman speaking was elf-sized and came upon them from behind. "Excuse my war paint," she said. "I barely had time to do my eyes." She smiled like a little girl, fluttering her lashes, one eye slathered with mascara, the other butt-naked. Her hair was clipped into a mass on the top of her head and was as red as her rouge-covered cheeks and the swath of lipstick on her pencil-thin lips. With her oxford shoes and white folded-down socks, a yellow knee-length full skirt, and a white ruffled blouse, she looked ready for a square dance. She sashayed past them, twirling and scurrying them along.

Loretta gave Cora an "are you kidding" look, the one she had perfected for her mother: a slight roll of her eyes, a quick lift of her eyebrow, pursed lips.

+++

In the kitchen, the countertops held baskets filled with green beans and peaches, stoneware bowls and canning supplies: Mason jars, lids, funnels, tongs, and spoons. A large pressure cooker hummed on the kitchen stove, erupting short bursts of steam. On a shelf above the cabinets sat two huge oval baskets and several smaller round ones, some with conical lids, others without. "Winnowing and storage baskets," Cora exclaimed. "Nice!"

A pinewood table was set with seven white plates, silverware, and blue cloth napkins. Two platters filled the center of the table, one stacked with butter-browned biscuits, the other with sliced apples and cheese. There were also a gravy boat, salt and pepper shakers, and a small bowl of olives.

"Biscuits and gravy." Loretta bit her lip, remembering her mother's tendency to announce breakfast by hollering "biscuits and gravy" even though what she fixed was nothing close. Suddenly Loretta missed the smell of "designer" pancakes, even though the ingredients came from a box.

Long benches were on both sides of the table, and a captain's chair occupied each end. Noleen sat in one chair; a lanky man with tousled white hair and a white mustache, wearing Wranglers, a flannel shirt, and cowboy boots, sat on the other. Another man sat beside Paiute Bill on one bench.

"My name is Parnethia, but my friends call me Pansy," offered the woman who had come to fetch them. She walked around the table as if she were playing duck, duck, goose, tapping each person on the head as she introduced them. "You know Noleen, Granny Noleen, to most. This is Yoshi Koyama, next here is Bill, and filling the captain's chair, Big Earl."

Loretta knew their faces; she'd seen them in the grocery store, the pharmacy, the park, and the bus station. Pansy waved her and Cora over. "Have a seat, dears. Here by me," she said as she sat, patting the bench beside her.

Earl grabbed two biscuits and reached for the gravy boat.

Noleen cleared her throat. "Good Lord, thank you for this food and for Pansy, who cooked it. I suppose you know Yoshi's last biopsy came back clean. Thanks for that. And forgive Big Earl for forgetting his manners. It appears he likes biscuits more than prayer. Hallelujah, amen."

"Don't be shy, dear," Pansy told Loretta, pointing at the platter of nectarines and cheese.

Loretta took a nectarine slice and a piece of cheese and set them on her plate.

"Good Lord girl, you're gonna waste away, you eat like that." Big Earl forked up two more nectarines and another slice of cheese and dumped them on her plate. "Way I see it, Noleen's got herself a couple of new pack horses. Best feed up. You're gonna need your strength." He laughed so hard the table jiggled against the weight of his belly.

Yoshi's hands spun words into sign language, interpreting the conversation. Paiute Bill nodded and grinned. He galloped his fingers along the edge of the table.

"Yep. Well, then." Earl patted his belly. "Noleen's serving her specialty for dessert today. Homegrown rattlesnake pie." His teasing spurred another round of laughter.

Noleen's face was as pointed as her rebuttal. "Stop now, no more pestering," she said.

Cora added items mindlessly to the pile of biscuits and gravy on her plate. As Loretta waited for the biscuit platter to reach her, she thought of other traumatic events in Cora's life and how each triggered food binges. It started with the death of her mother in third grade. That was the biggest heartbreak of all, resulting in Cora's gaining twenty pounds in less than a year. Loretta recognized the manic look in Cora's eye and the uneasy way she scooped her food. She expected a reaction from the people around the table, but none came. No one threw criticism here like in the cafeteria at school, as Jemma or any of her clones did. Jemma was ruthless. There wasn't a day went by that she didn't fill her cheeks with air and pop them in Cora's face, or make fun of her clothes, or imitate her slow gait during gym-class workouts.

"Cora, your father has been quite helpful to me," Yoshi said, breaking Cora's trance.

"Oh? Oh yes, he told me about you. You're writing a book?" Cora's eyes grew wide and attentive.

Loretta smiled. Anything scientific or archaeological, or something regarding Cora's father, hooked her attention like the creamy center of an Oreo cookie.

"Yes. About this house. And its historical significance to this community."

"My father says you've uncovered some interesting stuff, like finding tunnels where runaway slaves used to hide. Or maybe freed slaves running from bounty hunters?"

"Quite right. The story of California's participation in the Underground Railroad is significant and little known. A piece of that story lies here, on this property," Yoshi confirmed, bowing his head and closing his eyes.

Cora echoed his movements, respectfully. Loretta grinned, knowing Cora couldn't maintain such a pose with the smell of biscuits so close to her nose. A second later, Cora's eyes were open and she was nibbling contentedly.

Loretta tasted Pansy's gravy with the tip of her tongue. It was thick and creamy with just the right amount of salt, pepper, and sausage. The biscuits were buttery and moist, melt-in-your-mouth delicious. Even still, there was a sense of trickery, as if something wicked and sinister was cooking in the kitchen, maybe an evil plot meant to destroy humankind. Just as she was ready to swallow, a bit of biscuit stuck in her throat. She glanced up at Noleen, forgetting the pleasure she'd felt for Cora a moment earlier, wondering suddenly if her soul had been breached, her thoughts snared in a rusty old trap. Too many who-done-it movies, she chided herself. Too many online conspiracy theories.

Noleen glared at her suspiciously and leaned back in her chair.

A rumble, a revved-up dirt bike engine somewhere outside brought Loretta's gaze to the window.

"I love historical tidbits," Pansy said, still lost in the early part of the conversation. She smiled and batted her eyes at Yoshi.

Earl grinned at Yoshi. "You still got it, partner," he teased. Noleen shushed him and turned toward the kitchen window, cocking her head and concentrating on the disturbance outside.

Just west of the driveway along the creek bank, a dirt bike and its rider bumped along the uneven ground. Moments later, it returned going the opposite direction, back and forth, back and forth. Then all was quiet.

Until outside the kitchen window stood wide-eyed Ethan.

Loretta opened her mouth to speak, but nothing came out. She nudged Cora and pointed at the window, at the empty air that now filled the hole Ethan had just occupied. She tried again, in a whisper this time. "I'm losing my mind. One day out here and my brain cells are fried."

Noleen held her nose in the air. "You're not losing your mind. And your brain cells aren't fried," she said.

Loretta stared at Noleen. Nobody ever heard her when she mumbled. Most people didn't acknowledge ever hearing her at all.

"Ask the boy to lunch," Noleen commanded. "If you don't, he'll keep riding that contraption all over creation and back, disturbing our peace." She flicked her napkin up and onto her lap. "And if you know he's gonna show up anyways, do us a favor and give him a lift in your pickup truck. An extra pair of hands around here won't hurt."

-CHAPTER 6-

*T*he sky was a soft gray, the trees webbed with evening shadows. The first stars shone bright, yet the day's heat held and sweat ran down the faces of the people gathered in front of the old Grange Hall. Some of the men talked in hushed tones while others had their hands thrust deep into their jean pockets, just nodding and listening to the conversation. The women were animated, debating ballot measures and supervisorial candidates in the upcoming election.

"I wouldn't vote for O'Malley no matter what he promises. The man's a scumbag. He won't deliver." Ruby's raspy drawl stood out in the jumble of voices. Ethan observed them all as they waited for Brock: Sim and Raina; Ralph the butcher; Crystal the county library clerk; Esmina; William; Samuel; Frey, the bouncer from the Iron Gate; and Mr. and Mrs. Griffin (Jemma's parents). The Committee. The folks who made the rules.

There was nothing that set these few apart or gave them importance above the others in The Group. Yet somehow that had happened, and what he also noticed was that sub-Groups were forming within The Group. The pattern was clear. Where in high school the jocks and cowboys, nerds and stoners stood out, here the alignment fell into a classification like that of the animal kingdom. From Ethan's perch on a limb in a nearby pepper tree, it was easy to spot how the Group members ranked themselves. The pages of his biology textbook flipped definitively in his mind. His internal dictionary went to work:

Alpha leaders: muscular, strong, and cunning.

Subordinate or beta members: the food gatherers, laborers, warriors—the army.

Predator: One that victimizes, plunders, or destroys.

The double doors swung open and there stood Brock, arms spread wide in greeting.

"Brothers and sisters!" he proclaimed with a wave of his hand. "Come on in, please. Let's get comfortable." He smiled, his teeth white and gleaming. He wore casual dark-blue trousers, and a white short-sleeved dress shirt unbuttoned at the neck. His shoes were loafers, Ethan noticed—preppy style, no socks.

"Family, my family, bless you for coming," he said as people filtered past.

"This is bogus!" Ethan blurted. He flinched and shushed himself, nearly falling off his seat in the pepper tree. His eyes scanned the parking lot and the nearby bushes, finally locking on the entryway to the Grange building itself. There, Brock was welcoming The Group: he patted Frey on the back, kissed Esmina on the cheek, and helped Crystal with her crutches as she navigated the stairs up to the landing in front of the hall. Sim clasped Brock's hands and shook them heartily. Raina hugged him, and Ruby gave him a high-five. Mr. and Mrs. Griffin stopped and talked for a minute before passing through the doorway.

Feeling alone and out-of-sorts, Ethan tried, as Cora would say, "to make an attitude adjustment." He *wanted* to picture Brock the way his parents and the others did. The man was well-respected and thought to be an innovator within the community, a sharp business person, and a self-motivator. Ethan watched as Brock hugged and loved and praised all these people, and he hoped that they were right—that this person they admired was legit—but his gut told him otherwise.

At first, he'd liked Brock. The early meetings were simply conversations in the park, no more than thoughtful discussions among a group of friends—just as how he and Loretta and Cora would discuss an assignment in their political science class: like that, friendly talk and nothing more. In the beginning, Brock was thoughtful. He laughed a lot, and if the discussion got off-color or too wild he would bring it back, bring *them* back, his parents and the others: "Enough," he would say. "I don't know about you, but my stomach is rumbling. Too much politics makes me hungry." Chances are, he would wink at Ethan and throw him a sack of chips or a peanut-butter-and-jelly sandwich, and then pat the lawn beside him, inviting Ethan in. His treatment of Ethan, the way he welcomed and included him, was one of the things his parents had come to love about Brock.

Today, Ethan didn't feel welcome. He knew he should smile and wave, or climb down out of the tree and approach the hall, but something held him back. His brain was full of questions and thoughts about all the priority shifting, the adjusting of schedules and routine lately, and how much he disliked change. Still bothered by the day's events, he puzzled over them.

That morning before he left home, he'd checked the wall calendar: Saturday: Raina, Iron Gate -- 4-7. When Raina worked, Sim stayed home. If Sim worked, Raina stayed home. The routine was important; it was everything, yet when he got back from Granny Noleen's that afternoon, the doors were locked and no one was there.

Ethan didn't like walking into an empty house. He had wandered from room to room before settling in the kitchen and deciding to play games on the computer. The screensaver was activated, so his father couldn't have been gone long. This realization and the fact that he would surely be home soon was comforting, at least. He had repositioned the mouse, preparing to click on the *Minecraft* icon, when the draft of an unsaved letter populated the desktop. "Holidays this year will be a little different," the letter announced. "We're breaking tradition. Spend Thanksgiving and Christmas with your Group family," it read. "Good food. Games. Conversation that matters."

When Sim walked in the door, Ethan asked him to explain.

"Ethan, believe me, this wasn't an easy decision," said Sim. "But times have changed. We need to take precautions, and Brock has promised that he'll watch out for you in the event…if something should happen, if your mother and I are no longer able to care for you…" Sim took a breath, and then blew it back out. "The bunker, The Group is like an insurance policy for your future. Don't you see? We've grown to know and love these people. They're family now."

"Family means you, and Mom, and Papa, and Nona, and Aunt Sue and…"

"Brock's request regarding the holidays is for the best, Ethan. It's his way of weaning Group members from our blood relatives," Sim said, "and redirecting our lives toward a total commitment to the project."

"Brock's request?"

Sim let loose an exasperated sigh. "When the time comes," he continued, "it'll be hard enough to explain to parents, brothers, sisters, or cousins why no one can come into the bunker with us—leaving loved ones behind in the face of a catastrophe or imminent threat will be painful. We've got to prepare for that now by limiting contact. You understand, right, Ethan?"

Ethan shook his head. No, he didn't understand.

The people in The Group were not his family. His *real* family lived far away, in Connecticut, but still. No more turkey and dressing dinner with Papa and Nona Williams, and no more sharing of presents at Christmas time with Auntie and Uncle and cousins Jack and Minnie. Would there still be stockings lined on the hearth? Would Raina still make her special egg, cheese, and vegetable strata for breakfast? Would they drink eggnog? Spiced cider? What about their tradition of reading Dickens's "A Christmas Carol" aloud each year?

Ethan shifted his position in the nub of the pepper tree. He rubbed his temples and scowled, thinking. Other families will continue their traditions. Some people might even establish *new* ones with *new* friends they *chose* to hang out with, not those they are *forced* to hang out with, like those in The Group. He pondered this idea, considering the people—friends and otherwise—around the lunch table at Granny Noleen's earlier today.

Loretta had looked good, a bit scruffy, maybe hesitant, but not surly. Cora was good-humored and contributed to the conversation on numerous occasions. Not a surprise. Granny Noleen's offer of lunch was unexpected but well-received. The food looked delicious. She was apparently treating the girls well and would keep them safe. He trusted her and he trusted Paiute Bill, though he wasn't entirely sure why. He didn't know the cowboy or the red-haired lady but had seen them around town, and they always appeared jovial and considerate of others—a big thumbs-up, as far as he was concerned.

He *did* know the Asian gentleman, the docent who had spoken to his history class during a recent tour of Manzanar Internment Camp, just outside of Lone Pine. He liked this docent. The man spoke softly and articulately, in a tone that was pleasing to the ear. The memories he shared, though, the facts provided, had bothered Ethan's dreams for many nights after. It still made him uncomfortable to think about walking through the dusty, desolate camp that day, hearing true stories of hardship and suffering. "During World War II, the Japanese Americans were forced to give up their homes and all their possessions, and were taken to makeshift detention centers, made to live in horse stables filled with old manure and urine and places infested with fleas," the docent told them. "Eventually, they were driven by bus or train to internment camps like this one, where they were assigned a tent to live in, and provided the most meager of food rations."

"Why?" Ethan had asked.

"After Japan declared war on America, the American government became suspicious of all Japanese, even those born here in the United States."

"Why?"

"People thought that Japanese-Americans might be

connected in some way to the bombing of Pearl Harbor or were spies for Japan. The majority felt that no Japanese could be trusted."

"Ethan!" Brock's directive came through the fog of Ethan's thoughts, distant, inconsequential.

"Ethan!"

Ethan glanced at the Grange Hall, regaining his focus. Sim was standing beside Brock with his hands on his hips. Not a good sign.

Ethan flicked his fingers, looked up and away.

"Now!"

Ethan jumped from the tree, but lost his footing when he hit, landing butt-first in the dirt. He sat while his heart settled, peeking through the crook in his arm at Sim and Brock. From this distance their faces looked painted on, abstract. Brock's lips morphed into something reptilian, slithery, as he whispered to Sim. Sim nodded, stepped off the porch, and strode toward Ethan.

Ethan stood and dusted off his pants and shoes.

"What was it this time, Ethan? A buffalo in the clouds? Ant trails up the tree?"

"Dad, I mean, Sim, I…"

"You embarrassed me again, Ethan. In front of someone I respect." Sim pointed his finger, motioning Ethan forward. "Move," he ordered flatly.

Ethan stared at Sim's eyes, and he frowned. Who was this man? It was as if some stranger had swallowed his father—as if an alien body-snatcher had plucked away his life. Ethan looked up and away. He blinked fast and then faster, creating silent-picture footage in his mind of the old and familiar father that he loved.

From the corner of his eye, Ethan saw Raina walking toward him from the Grange Hall. In the midst of his chaos, her quiet serenity, her graceful stride worked like a pacifier, and he relaxed and then smiled, knowing it had always been this way. It was as if he and his mother shared a special secret, as if a little piece of her was with him when he disappeared inside his head, and even in the blackness he knew unequivocally that the whole of her would always be waiting for him when he returned. Her blonde hair had appeared like the halo of an angel many times as his eyes refocused and his brain kicked into gear.

Raina touched Sim's arm with her fingertips, and his shoulders relaxed. The corners of his mouth softened into a half-smile. "Come on, Ethan. Let's go," he said, letting Raina lead the way. "Sorry, buddy, I just get so..."

"Irritated," Ethan guessed. "Shook up. Perturbed. Grouchy!" He followed behind Sim and Raina, spouting words, despising this new version of his father.

+++

The lights inside the building were bright and hurt Ethan's eyes. Most people were already seated; a few, like Sim and Raina, stood with Brock on the stage, near the podium in the front of the room. Ethan glanced at his watch as the minute hand clicked over: 7:57 p.m. He slid into a metal chair near the back of the meeting hall, sat up straight, and hung his heels on the chair's support bar. In spite of the swamp cooler, the room was hot and stuffy. With the doors closed, it was hard to breathe.

Sim banged a wooden gavel on the podium. "This meeting is called to order. Glad you all made it. Man! It's hot enough to blister a snake's skin!"

The crowd laughed.

Out of the window, Ethan saw Pierce and his parents pulling into the parking lot, driving their not-so-new Ford pickup. Late, as usual. Odds were when they barged through the entry doors they'd do it with flair, tromping into the Hall as if they owned it outright and, by God, people should be honored that they had arrived. A second later, as predicted, the Grange doors burst open and the clocking of cowboy boots on linoleum echoed through the hall.

"Hey. Hey there. Happy to see ya." Handshaking. A couple of hugs. A flow of commotion comparable with paparazzi-tailed A-listers.

"First order of business, construction progress," Sim continued, once the Lukemans were seated. "I'm happy to report that Phases 1 and 2 are complete. All meeting rooms, the hospital, dental offices, supply and service bays are operational. As we enter Phase 3, individual requests for personal living space will be considered." Sim pointed at Ruby. "No Ruby, that does not mean you get your gourmet ovens and Le Creuset cookware."

Whoops of laughter and clapping erupted throughout the room.

"Any questions before we continue?"

"If I'm living months or more in the dang ground with only freeze-dried and canned crap to cook up, you better give me a decent pot and spoon," said Ruby.

"Ruby darlin', you can cook it up and dish it out with the best of them, with or without your Le Creuset!" Brock teased.

The room exploded with laughter. All eyes were on Brock now, but he waved the attention back to Sim.

"Charlie, what's up, man?" Sim asked.

"Just wondering about the munitions bay. We supposed to supply our own rifles, or—?"

"The answer to this question is in the manifesto, Charlie. No guns from home. We can't take a chance on used weaponry. Everything deemed necessary by the Committee will be provided. I'm talking rifles *and* ammunition."

Several people thumbed through their copies of the manifesto.

Ethan's mouth formed an O big enough for a bullet to pass through. Rifles? Ammunition? Until eight months ago Sim and Raina were anti-weapons of any sort. They never even let him play with toy guns growing up. *What the hell?*

The World Trade Center attack had effected them greatly, as had all the school shootings, particularly Sandy Hook (his cousin was among the injured), and the Boston Marathon Bombing, and the bombing of Charlie Hebdo in Paris, on and on, but really?

"I heard the newspaper wants to do a story," said Esmina. "Are we granting permission?"

"Yes. Someone from the Committee will meet with a reporter. People are curious about the construction site. We'll answer what we're legally bound to put forward, nothing more."

Sim looked around the room. "Anybody else? Nada? No? Okay, then, Brock?"

"Crystal, Raina, do your thing, sweethearts," Brock said.

The county librarian and Raina stepped toward the podium. Crystal cleared her throat. "We're making a list. Checking it twice," she joked. "We're looking for donations, any household goods with enough value to trade in the fair market, to increase our monetary assets. Mike Smith, thanks for the car, by the way. Got it sold. A penny in the coffer. Yahoo! And Frey, that silver of your mother's. Awesome. Thank you."

Brock stepped between the two women, draped his arms around their shoulders and gave them a squeeze. "I know it's hard sometimes to give up the things you love." He sucked in his lips, blew out a puff of air, and dropped his arms. "Remember, though, possessions mean nothing in the face of a terrorist attack. Better to be prepared, and every silver spoon, every collectible we can put together adds to our store of provisions." He strode forward and stared at Rachel Smith, seated in the front row. "What better way for a mom to provide for her children, her grandchildren, than to pass her treasures into the hands of those who will protect them from harm." He lifted his eyes and searched the crowd. "Frey, where are you? There. Stand up, man. Stand up!" He raised his arms. "Frey, bless your soul, and bless your mother's for the generous donation she gave posthumously.

"Look here," said Brock. "Check this out." He tugged a pocket watch out of his pants pocket and held it up. "This belonged to my OmPa," he said, then paused. Inhaled. Held the watch to his heart. "He raised me. Me and my sister. Best years of my life." He hesitated. Took a deep breath. Wiped tears from his eyes.

Ethan craned his neck and narrowed his eyes to focus in on Brock. The man was like one of those child actors who could cry on cue.

"I gotta do it. Gotta do it," Brock said, making a show of his wet fingertips, the tears he flicked at the crowd. He turned slowly and stood before Crystal, staring at her, nodding. He held up the watch, waited, then dropped it in her hand and clasped her hands in his.

There was a palpable sigh, a wave of appreciation throughout the audience.

"Brock, I've got a set of china…"

"And I've got a pretty decent collection of baseball cards."

"A boat I never use."

"A motorhome!"

Brock raised his hands in praise. "Oh, it's good to be here and see my family, my brothers and sisters, make witness to your love for one another and your faith in me. Say yes!"

"Yes!" The Group exploded.

"Pierce, my man. Come pass the hat, will you? Let's keep the momentum going." Brock handed Pierce an old straw hat that he kept beside the podium. "If we were in church, the clergy would *suggest* you pay ten percent. We're not in church, but we're the closest you'll come once Doomsday happens, folks. The closest you'll come is this right here. This family. This…right…here!" He stomped his foot and pointed to the crowd. He bowed his head, and his leg twitched like Elvis Presley's in the old movies Ethan had seen with Loretta.

"A while back, while at Santa Monica Pier, I'm talking Big Bucks City, folks. Hollywood-land. Porsches and Jags. Designer clothes. Two hundred dollar bikinis…*what*? For two teensy strips of material that covered…well…that's *another* story." Whoops and laughter echoed throughout the hall. "Anyway, here we go; I'll get to the point, and it's short and sweet, I promise." Brock lowered his head and raised his arms, fingers spread wide. "That day in Santa Monica, I learned a lesson." Brock paused, making eye contact with as many people as he could in those few long seconds. "As I walked along the beach, no one paid any attention to me. Not the bikini girls, or the jocks playing volleyball, or the lifeguard in his little beach box. After surveying the situation, it became so apparent. All around me were plastic people living in their plastic worlds of credit cards and Styrofoam cups, tummy tucks, and genetically modified lifestyles. I could have been anybody. I might have been carrying an assault rifle or wearing a backpack with a bomb inside. Nobody looked at me. Nobody cared!" Brock's voice resonated with a gritty, deep-throated tension when he yelled this, and all the room was quiet, including Ethan, who couldn't help but stare into the eyes of this man who held his audience captive.

Brock shook his head and continued, very slowly: "All. I. Could. Do, was…cry. Because I *knew*, folks, I *knew* that these people were dead men walking. No one could help them unless they were willing to change…*sacrifice*! Open their eyes to the truth!

"Indulge me for a minute, if you will. Sherlock Holmes and Dr. Watson were going camping. They pitched their tent under the stars and went to sleep. Sometime in the middle of the night Holmes woke Watson and said: "Watson, look up at the stars and tell me what you see." Watson replied: "I see millions and millions of stars." Holmes said: "And what do you deduce from that?" Watson replied: "Well, if there are millions of stars, and if even a few of those have planets, it's quite likely there are some planets like Earth out there.

And if there are a few planets like Earth out there, there might also be life." And Holmes said: "Watson, you idiot, it means that somebody stole our tent!"

The audience laughed. As Ethan searched his brain for a definable explanation, the word *master* came to mind— *Master: a skilled practitioner; one who gains control of, who overcomes; a man who enslaves...*

"I'm telling you, folks, I saw a video the other day. Scary. The way of things to come, I guarantee it. The way of things to come!" Brock shook his head and clasped his hands in front of his chest. "The hospitals, the grocery stores, Social Security, the DMV, all telling people to get a Federal ID Number implanted under the skin of their left hands if they wanted to shop there, qualify for, or get a license from their facilities...that all things purchased, all transactions with the government, such as taxes, and veterans' medical care, would require this implanted documentation of personal identity." His face twisted. "I say, *'What?!'*"

"What!" The Group yelled back.

"I say, 'No way!'"

"No way!"

Brock paced back and forth. Crystal and Raina crept to their seats. "The other day, a *hater* called my lecture a sermon, and I said, 'You don't know me, and I've never seen you at a meeting, so don't you crit-i-cize!'"

Brock's voice was loud and higher-pitched; his words coming so fast, Ethan covered his ears.

"I'm not a preacher, and I'm not a prophet, but I can call the bluff of any nonbelievers out there who say there is no change coming!" He paused again, wiped the sweat from his brow, and circled the stage behind the podium. "There is a foul wind blowing our direction. Maybe it's created by our government or someone else, or maybe it's a storm of biblical proportions swept out of nowhere by some nowhere man, leaving his trail of destruction for those who choose to ignore the signs! It's coming, brothers and sisters, it's coming!"

"I believe you, brother!" yelled Frey.

"We believe you!" others repeated.

The whites of Ethan's eyes grew dry and chilled. He couldn't blink. For the first time in as long as he could remember, he couldn't blink. Panic rose inside him like basalt from the earth's core.

"Open your wallets and pull out the biggest bill. Drop it in the hat here and secure the futures of yourselves and your children. The future of our family!"

As others dug in their wallets and moved toward the podium, Ethan launched from his chair and sprinted for the door. Raina followed him with her eyes but let him go. "Be safe," she hollered after him. "Wear your helmet!"

The engine growled and vibrated beneath Ethan as he sped onto Main Street, and the velocity-induced wind whipped past, turning his cheeks and lips to Jell-O. The storefronts blurred as he accelerated, and he only vaguely worried about policemen and speeding tickets and being safe as Raina had asked of him. Instead, he focused on racing through the hills to the Mountain, the safety of Mt. Whitney.

On Whitney Portal Road, near the Red Dog Bridge, the dry air, the heat, and the pressure of the helmet against his ears provoked a coughing spell. He pulled to the side of the road and reached for the shoulder strap of his pack, realizing suddenly that it was not on his back—he must have left it, and his water bottle, beside the pepper tree at the Grange Hall. He gazed toward the night-capped silhouette of the Mountain in the distance but thought of the BPA-free water bottle Loretta had given him. He gritted his teeth, adjusted his helmet, edged off the berm, and made a U-turn.

The asphalt road felt spongy beneath the Enduro, the one-hundred-plus-degree temperature still holding. Road ripples wavered in the headlight beams. Oddly shaped shadows slogged along the roadside, affecting his peripheral vision. The minutes it took him to drive to the bridge felt like hours on the return trip to town. By the time he got to Main Street, there was little traffic, just a few cars parked here and there. The owners of a Jeep 4x4 and a Ford pickup were pumping gas at the Lone Pine 76; a few people were strolling, window shopping: some locals and a sprinkling of out-of-towners. Most businesses had closed down for the night, all but the Penny Saver and the Iron Gate.

At the Grange Hall, there were only two trucks in the parking lot: Brock's and the Lukemans'. Ethan stepped away from the bike and stood quietly for a minute, feeling nervous about being on the Grange property without his parents. Finally, hesitantly, he walked toward the tree, and could see his backpack still leaning against the trunk. As he looped the strap over his arm, he noticed that the window on the north side of the hall was open. He could hear voices.

"I didn't see anything unusual. Families milling around. People talking, laughing. Ethan exploring the corners, as usual," Brock said, chuckling

"The kid's weird. There's no doubt he could be our thief. He knows the Grange Hall backward and forwards. He knows the collection plate, or hat, was full," said Mr. Lukeman.

"Right. Right. Good point, Lukeman."

Ethan wished his father was there. He flicked his fingers, listening.

"He's always been weird," Pierce piped in. "It wasn't until sixth grade that they stopped pulling him out of class to go to the Special Ed room."

"Why was he put in Special Ed, Pierce?" Brock asked.

"He interrupted the teacher. Did his wacko flicking crap. He watches people, in his freaky, off-the-wall way. It gives me the creeps."

"You're right," Mr. Lukeman said. "He does watch people. He watches everything."

"Now, now. The kid's odd, but he's not a thief. He could never, he would never...I mean, you're savvy, Lukeman, street-smart. If you think there's cause for alarm, maybe we *should* question Ethan…"

Ethan ran. Righted his motorcycle and pushed it until he reached Main Street. His mind flew as fast as his Enduro and he drove. Hard. To Tuttle Creek.

At the creek, he chose a spot he was familiar with, one where he had fished, swum, and sunbathed alongside Loretta and Cora. A large cottonwood stood nearby, its limbs and roots reaching through the heat to the cooling water. He swerved to a stop, unzipped his backpack, and grabbed a notebook, pencil, and flashlight.

As he sat down, the nearby cottonwood doubled as his backrest. The roughness of the bark was soothing in a way, something tangible and substantial. He turned on his flashlight and propped it against the tree trunk, then opened his notebook to a blank page. Tapping his pencil to Macklemore's rap song, *Inhale Deep,* he began to compartmentalize his afternoon, grouping experiences in numerical sequence:

Group meeting.

Drove toward the Alabamas, but backtracked. Forgot my water bottle and the Red Vines I bought for L & C.

Grange Hall.

"Grange Hall" was all he wrote, but what happened there had imprinted in his memory.

Ethan tapped his pencil on his notebook quickly, repeatedly. This was like a nightmare, and he wanted to wake up: wake up or slip away, the latter being the easiest but also the most dangerous. After what he'd just experienced, he had to think.

He fought. Stiffened. Wrote.

Tuttle Creek.

As he was preparing to add to his notes, he noticed an approaching car. The bright headlights became blinding as it grew close. Ethan covered his eyes with his forearm, and the vehicle stopped near his bike. When the driver's door opened, he heard the *click, click,* the static of a CB, like a police radio.

"Ethan, my man," the officer called out.

Clive. Clive something. He had dated Loretta's mother once. "Ol' Clive...he thinks he's too good for penny candy" –that's what Greer said of him. Even she had been smart enough to dump him after their first date.

"Yes, sir. My bike's registered if that's what you're checking."

"That's not what I want to discuss. Follow me, son. This should only take a few."

Ethan followed the officer up the embankment, wondering what a *few* meant in police-speak. A few minutes? Hours? Days?

At the police cruiser, Clive retrieved a small clipboard. "You better hope this amounts to a hill of beans, *boy.* Inside, you'd be no more than a meal for the lifers, you know. A pretty guy like you...no chance at all."

Ethan frowned at Clive's basketball-shaped head, his wire-rimmed John Lennon glasses. *Hypocritical. Yes. You're no John Lennon*, he thought. "I want to call my parents," he said.

"Do you get who you're talking to? You're in trouble, or I wouldn't waste my time, you little shit. Yes, sir. No, sir. Yes. Yes. Yes. That's all I want to hear from you, understand?"

"I want to call my parents."

"I hear you know Paiute Bill?" Clive cocked his head, shined his flashlight into the back seat of the squad car.

Inside sat Bill, rubbing his temples with his thumbs.

It was hard to see through the glass, but it looked to Ethan as if Bill had a black eye and a bloody nose. "No sir," Ethan said. "I've met him. I mean. I guess I know him a little." His fingers moved though he tried to still them. Flicking. Flicking. He couldn't stop. "I want to call my parents," he reiterated loudly.

"Calm down, kid. No need to get testy. Answer me this and I'll let you go. Where were you this morning?"

"This morning?" The question threw him, as he expected Clive would ask him about the missing money at the Grange Hall.

"That's what I said. No need to repeat."

"Hanging posters for Brock?"

"Downtown? You see Bill?"

"Yes. But I don't like you asking me questions. You're not following protocol. This isn't a proper interrogation technique." Ethan was sweating, and he hated to sweat. He turned to leave.

"Don't walk away from me, Bucko." Clive yanked him by his arm, hard.

Ethan jerked away. "Okay! Don't touch me!"

Clive held his hands up, palms facing out. "Just answer my questions, Bucko, and we'll have no problems. Hear?"

Ethan nodded.

"And this afternoon? Where were you?"

"Riding my bike. Then there was a meeting. My parents were there."

Clive yawned and rolled his eyes. "You're boring me, kid. It's like this. Pay attention. Eye contact, right?" He passed his index finger from his eyes to Ethan's and back to his. "Word is you've been doing some vandalism. Graffiti. There's been a lot of spray-painting around the Penny Saver and the Iron Gate. You know anything about that?"

"No."

"Bullshit."

"Stop. You can't ask me these things. I know my rights!" Ethan could no longer see Clive standing there, only a yammering mouth and angry eyes—a monster truck with a big-ass motor and wheels that could crush him with one single shift of gears.

"What the hell? What's wrong with you, kid? Stop that shit! You're as crazy as they say you are."

The CB in the squad car chirped to life: "33. We've got

a 415 at 123 Main. What's your 10-20?"

Clive sauntered to the squad car and spoke into the microphone: "Tuttle Creek. I'm on it. Over."

Clive pointed his long, spiny finger again. "Watch yourself, Bucko," he said. "I'm on you like slick oil."

He laughed, climbed in his police cruiser, and sped away, leaving Ethan sitting in a heap on the ground.

CHAPTER 7

*I*n Loretta's dreams, Brady held her tight. Their lips were nearly touching when the ringtone on her cell went off. Still half asleep, disoriented and disappointed, Loretta jumped out of bed and grabbed the phone. "Hello, hello?"

"Hey, Lo-retta, sugar, you awake?"

"I am now. Why are you calling so early?"

"Las Vegas never sleeps, darlin'. You know that. Lo-retta, you'll never guess who I met last night. I was playing blackjack and this guy sits down next to me..."

Loretta held the phone away from her ear. *Blah, blah, blah,* she mouthed to Cora.

Cora put her pillow over her head and waved Loretta off.

"...and he had on a Gucci suit, string tie, real alligator boots. To die for, Lo-retta. To. Die. For."

Loretta could hear someone talking in the background. Her mother giggled, smothering the receiver with one hand while speaking to her new friend.

"Mama, Cora and I are going hang gliding today. Tandem. We're being dropped off Whitney with no parachute."

"Okay, darlin'. Be safe. Love you. Kisses!"

"I love you too, Mama. So much. I…"

"We're gonna hang up on three. Ready? Kisses, Lo-retta, right here."

Once again, Loretta rubbed the spot on her cheek where she knew her mother would be pointing. From two hundred and fifty miles away, that fish kiss found its way through the phone line to the soft spot in the center of her face.

"One, two…three!"

The hang-up click startled Loretta even though she knew it was coming. "Dang," she said, nudging Cora's sleeping bag with her foot until she got a response.

"Huh? What?"

"She so ticks me off."

Cora wrestled with her pillow. "Is Mommy Dearest okay?" she asked.

"As predictable as a B-grade western." Loretta shrugged her shoulders. "Everything is fine until it isn't. You know how it goes, and goes, and goes with Momma."

Cora sat up. She took a slow deep breath, stood and stretched into a downward dog position.

"Yoga. Are you serious?"

"Completely."

"Since when?"

"Since a week ago. You should try it."

"I will. Tomorrow."

Loretta slumped out of the bedroom and down the stairs. Toby did his watchdog dance, tail at attention, a lopsided military jog-in-place. He woofed, and then howled—loud enough to attract her attention, but soft enough so as not to earn a scolding. She opened the back door and waited while he wandered outside, sniffing the perimeter of the yard and marking his territory in the usual places. "Come on boy, bacon, bacon, bacon," she finally said, filling his food pan with kibble, scratching him behind the ears after he tromped inside. "Arthritis bugging you this morning, fella? Come on then. Easy does it."

Toby grabbed and shook his favorite cuddle toy. It was something she had bought him when he was a pup with the birthday money she'd received from one of the Uncles—Fred or Beau or Willard—she couldn't remember which one. The stuffed basset hound was as worn around the edges as Toby and smelled as bad too. She waved her hand in front of her nose. "Whew! Toby, you need a bath. This afternoon, I promise. If the old lady lets me off before dark, that is."

It had been ten days since their first visit to Willow Grove and each work day had been the same: mucking through the mud in her bare feet, pulling weeds, hauling leaves, burning dead branches in an old fire pit between the house and the creek. Choking on smoke. Getting chased and pecked bloody by the rogue rooster that Pansy called Spike. Leaving dog-tired at nightfall, falling asleep before the movie credits rolled on whatever film she'd been watching, rising at some absurd hour so the whole show would play again.

A door slammed, and Cora walked downstairs carrying last night's pizza garbage. "There's a cop cruiser out front," she said.

"What? Where?" Loretta came to stand beside Cora at the window. The police car drove slowly to the end of the block, then turned around and drove back past the house and toward town. "Wonder what that's all about?" Cora said, rubbing her hands together.

"You're such a dork," Loretta said, laughing.

"No, you're a dork."

"You're the one who's rubbing her hands together as if you were conjuring up a clue. You can't stand it when there's a mystery going down without you knowing the details, Cora."

"Yeah, well. Point taken, I guess."

"Remember the Gomez and Duvall Detective Agency?"

"And the detective kit Dad gave me for my eighth birthday. OMG, we were so into that magnifying glass and that crazy fast drying plaster."

"We tracked wild turkeys...and Toby." Loretta gave Toby a pat. "Poor old dog." She held up Toby's tail and wagged it. "Remember the tail caper?"

"Of course," Cora said, laughing. "We tried to convince your mom that he'd been the victim of a hit-and-run. Seriously, pouring catsup on his tail—what were we thinking?"

"You never complained, did you, boy? Not ever," Loretta said, ruffling Toby's ears.

"You see a crime, we'll do the time. Call 1-800-IF-YOU'RE-IN-A-MESS-WE'RE-THE-BEST." Cora grinned and then shivered. "Did we really believe someone would call us, let alone dial a phone number *that* ridiculously long?"

A car horn honked outside. Loretta could hear the crunch of gravel in the driveway.

Cora peered out the window. "It's my dad," she said. "He's early." She grabbed her shoes and socks and a bottle of sunscreen. "Oh crap, no breakfast?" Her shoulders slumped, and the hangdog expression on her face was an example of what her mood would be like for the rest of the day if her stomach remained empty.

"Got it covered." Loretta jogged into the kitchen and grabbed a box of doughnuts. On the counter beside the telephone, she spotted the pink leopard-print sunglasses her mother had given her after a recent trip to L.A. She'd never worn them; she wouldn't have been caught dead in them, especially in front of Brady or Jemma. The glasses were as out-there as her mother. But still.

"Oh, hell," she said, grabbing the glasses. She slipped them on and sashayed out the door behind Cora.

"Nice glasses!" Doc Gomez gave Loretta a thumbs-up. Loretta imitated her mother's walk: swaying hips, left-hand palm down and horizontal, chin up, confident.

Doc's rumbly deep-throated laughter was contagious. Cora's chuckle was so similar it was like listening to "Dueling Banjos," a tune so joyous it was impossible not to strum along. He slid out of the car and opened the front and back doors. "Your laughter feeds my soul, Mija. Yours too, my darling Loretta Lynn," he said.

"Enough, already, you always say that, or you say: 'Music to my ears, girls, music to my ears.'" Cora puffed up like a cockatoo preening its feathers.

"Aristotle said that a baby does not have a soul until the moment it laughs for the first time. Do you believe that?"

Loretta glanced at Cora and snickered. "Not for a minute, Doc. Sorry."

"Self-expression embedded in humor. I like it," Doc said grinning.

Loretta adjusted her legs to as comfortable a position as she could manage in the back seat of Doc's Mini Cooper. If a car could conform to its owner, this one, with its stumpy body, enviro-conscious fuel system, and techno-savvy dashboard gadgets, was a mechanized second child for Doc and an only slightly mismatched sibling to Cora. Loretta grinned, recalling her mother's favorite song. That old Janis Joplin tune about a Mercedes Benz and Porsches and making amends...

Janis's cackle at the end of the song was her mother's specialty. She had it down pat. Many a nighttime kiss was preceded with that cackle, and it tickled Loretta to think of the raw and raspy *yeow*.

Doc and Cora synchronized watches, chatting about the day's schedule and making dinner plans for later. "Chilis rellenos," Cora said. "We've got all the stuff, and it's easy to throw together."

"Yes, but Loretta doesn't love the *heat* of the Ortegas as much as we do, Mija."

The consideration of her feelings was comforting, and Loretta liked that she felt invisible in the back seat.

"Right," Cora said. "Well, then. Tacos. Yeah?" She turned her head to confirm with Loretta.

Loretta nodded and the conversation shifted to garbage pickup, chore schedules, and finally to the reason Doc was going with them to Willow Grove. "According to Yoshi, the tunnels are well-built. There's only been one substantial cave-in over the years, and as far as he knows, the remaining passages are intact."

"Can we come?"

"Mija, you have a job to do. It wouldn't be right to abandon your responsibility, even for an adventure such as this."

"No fair."

Doc laughed. "Life's like that, eh?"

"What do you expect to find?" Loretta asked.

"Good question, my dear. I'm hoping to find the truth behind the gossip that surrounds Willow Grove. Perhaps view a history that few have been privy to."

Loretta smiled. There was no way Cora would let this opportunity pass by—no way would she stand aside and watch her father enter the tunnels without her.

Cora turned to Loretta and rolled her eyes. "Dad, come on," she said. "You drive like an old lady."

"I drive like a contemplative anthropologist," Doc corrected, winking at Loretta in the rear view mirror.

"Sorry, Dr. G. Cora's right. Old lady, for sure." Loretta smiled at him.

They had just turned onto Main Street and there was not much traffic—no big rigs, only a few four-wheelers. Loretta recognized some local cars: Sam's from the Rock Shop, Garrett and Colleen's, owners of the Whitney Bookstore, and Mr. Waldman's, the bank manager.

Down the block, she saw Ethan's parent's Subaru parked in front of Milne Hardware. Sim and several other men stood near the store, watching as one of them rattled the locked door. Sim motioned the man aside and tried the door again, then pressed his nose against the glass and peered inside. He shook the handle and banged on the glass, then backed away.

"What's up with that? Nug Milne should have opened up by now. Are the lights on in the store?" Loretta goosenecked, straining to get a better view.

Cora did the same. "No. No lights. Aren't those the guys from that Group, Brock's group? What do they call themselves, the Committee?" she asked.

"Whatever it is, it's their business, girls. And we have an appointment. Mine will be more pleasurable than yours, but nonetheless." Doc laughed. He turned onto Whitney Portal Road, then passed Tuttle Creek Road and Tuttle Creek.

Loretta touched the freckles on her forearm, connecting the dots. She and Cora had spent a lot of time during summer vacations riding their bikes and playing in Tuttle Creek. During the Leonids meteor shower, they had camped there with Doc. It was cold—mid-November. Greer had thought them nuts, but Doc insisted that braving the weather would be worth it, and he had been right. He had even managed to talk Greer into coming along. The four of them watched fireballs in the sky that night, one after the other, shooting stars lighting up the heavens. Cora had drawn the path of the largest meteor across Loretta's arm, ending in a star-shaped patch of freckles near her wrist. They both were convinced that it was a sign that the meteor had not been a meteor but a space ship coming to check on Loretta because she was not the daughter of Greer Duvall after all, but the spawn of alien invaders.

The idea may have been farfetched, but it certainly explained a few things as far as Loretta was concerned.

Through the tinted glass of the Mini Cooper and through her sunglasses, the Alabamas looked overcast. Even

Bertha, the giant boulder that locals had named and given a spray-painted face, appeared sullen and gloomy. The blue star surrounding her left eye, her floppy red tongue, and her chubby cheeks looked in need of a make-over. "Rock Biter," Loretta murmured, imitating one of her favorite characters from *The Neverending Story*.

"Yessss," Cora confirmed. "Loretta, show us what you got, movie trivia queen. In *The Neverending Story*, what and who was the character, the Rock Biter."

"A hunky piece of granite, big boy riding a scooter... solumn, but adorable. He fed on rocks and had a particular fetish for limestone."

"You haven't lost your swagger, Loretta."

"I've got one, an old classic," Doc said. *"All About Eve*, with actress Bette Davis. Can you give me a line that became famous from that movie?"

Loretta paused, but had the answer in less than a minute: "Quote: *Fasten your seatbelts; it's going to be a bumpy night.*"

"Contact, Jodie Foster," Cora said. "Movie plot, please."

"Creationism. Scientist Ellie Arroway, Jodie Foster's character, finds evidence of extraterrestrial life. She's chosen to make first contact and her quest for the truth tests everything she knows about the barriers between science and religion."

"Stunning, Loretta. Quite remarkable." Doc reached over the backseat and offered Loretta a high-five.

Loretta sat quietly, trying to reinvent the image of her father, wishing that there could have been a mistake seventeen years ago and that it was not aliens or Atom Brimley but Mannie Gomez who had bedded Greer Duvall and created the life that was hers. She spent so much time with Dr. Gomez, so much time with Cora, that they were family. Doc even liked Greer, and that was a miracle given their differences intellectually. Loretta assigned absurd personality quirks to each of them: if Doc was an eagle, Greer was a cuckoo bird. If Doc was a dolphin, Greer was a clown fish. If Doc was a chimpanzee, Greer was a capuchin. Yet something bonded them as friends. And there it was again—that magic magnetism her mother possessed. It was impossible to hate her or even stay mad at her. Already Loretta had softened and was worrying how her mother would manage the Las Vegas world without her nearby to handle the men, and women, and circumstances that seemed to swarm around her like bees to a field of poppies.

She had the urge to snuggle up to her mother as she had done as a small child. To hear another one of the silly songs her mother sang to her rather than the typical lullabies most children grew to love. *"I took my gal to a dance one night, it was a social hop. She danced upon my toes so much I thought that I would drop..."* Or to listen to a bedtime story, happy or sad, short or long, but always starting the same way: "It was a glorious night in the Alabama Hills." Most of the time she and Cora were the main characters in those tales, hiking through the rocky crags, climbing jagged peaks, discovering diamonds, swordfighting ogres—or meeting a handsome prince.

"Aw, geez," Cora said, pulling Loretta from her reverie. "The whole clan's out front. Check it out. Looks like a meeting of the Lone Pine Hysterical Society."

"Mija, really!" Doc pulled the car to a stop in a side yard near the house, nearest to Pansy's flower garden.

The scent of roses fused with sage and lavender; the tangled mass of perennials was as colorful as Pansy herself. Loretta breathed them in, then coughed, mildly amused by the disarray.

Yoshi sat cross-legged on a big wooden bench in the middle of the garden.

Doc got out of the car and shook Earl's hand. "Everything okay?" he asked.

"No," Earl told him. "Something's happened."

Yoshi stood up, bowed to the east with his hands in prayer position, and then approached. The ground was rocky, but his stride was smooth and light. He was barefoot, but dressed in his usual casual slacks and a collared t-shirt.

"I hope it's not serious," Doc asked, concerned.

"Yep, well. It's pretty bad. There was a robbery at the Iron Gate. The glass mirror in the bar back was broken, and some rude-ass racial crap was scratched into the wood."

"How do you know this?" Doc asked.

"The cashier at the grocery store was eager to share the

news this morning," said Yoshi. "Frey apparently told the police that Bill was loitering around the bar when he locked up last night. Frey says Bill has a vendetta against him. He says they often argue, but that the other day it got physical. And that the fight was three against one."

"*Frey* being the *one*, against Bill, his friend Jack, and some young boy," said Earl.

"Frey thinks the young boy is Bill's accomplice in the vandalism," Yoshi added. "He said he often sees them talking… "conspiring" was the word he used, according to the clerk at the store. Frey says the boy is trouble. He says the kid is mentally ill."

"Wait," Loretta said. "It's not possible! That kid is Ethan! He told me about the thing between Bill, Jack, and Frey. He said Frey was out of line. And Ethan's not mentally ill. You've met him. He's coming over again this morning. You'll see…" It was the most she had said since she had been at Willow Grove, and she caught herself, startled. Everyone was looking at her, including Noleen.

"This Ethan," Noleen said. "I've heard he has autism."

"Autism Spectrum Disorder…Asperger's," Cora said. "But he's high-functioning. Most times you can hardly tell. He's a genius, in my opinion. It's hard for him to make friends, is all. He hangs with Loretta and me. Especially Loretta."

"Ethan has difficulty interpreting social cues," said Doc, "but I agree with Cora. He's very smart and has learned a lot about how to manage himself over the years. He would never vandalize, nor would he assist anyone in doing so. He's a good kid. He always has been."

"There's something else," Yoshi said. "This morning there was a break-in at Milne's Hardware." He closed his eyes and rubbed his balding head. "Bill is a good man too. He would never do this vandalism, or break into a business. Something is wrong here. Very wrong. I know this thing, this categorizing of people, jumping to conclusions. It's not good. Not good at all."

Noleen sat on the porch with her head slumped. It was hard to tell where her neck stopped and her torso began. "This is ridiculous!" she grunted angrily. "There's more to this story. I'd bet my hat."

"There's obviously been some misunderstanding," Doc said. "Once the facts become clear, I'm sure this will all settle down."

"*Whose* facts?" Noleen said, stiffly. "When it comes to Bill and others around here, the truth doesn't seem to matter."

Earl leaned on the porch rail beside Noleen, his face in the shadow of his cowboy hat. He grunted and then spat. A large golden horse stood like a guard dog by his side, leaning in protectively, snorting and nodding his head.

"Okay, this is me, returning from the dark side," said Cora. "I've got the heebie-jeebies, so can we change the subject? And by the way, who's this?" she asked, frowning.

"He's beautiful. May I?"

"His name's Dakota. Yes, gal, go ahead. He loves to have his forehead scratched, and here between his ears," Earl told her.

Loretta tried to concentrate on the horse and not what she'd just heard. She recognized him as a palomino—the same kind ridden by so many of the Western movie actors who had worked in the Alabama Hills. However, this horse was old. Gray hair shone through the gold and he was slightly swayback, though it was evident that he was healthy and sound. Dakota's hooves were in good condition, his blonde mane combed. His tail swished from side-to-side at flies, and the way he moved his feet and his body it seemed like he was trying to keep them off Earl as well. And there was something about his eyes—their long lashes and oval shape—and the soft creases of his brow that immediately inspired trust and warmth.

"How come we're just now meeting you, boy?" Cora asked.

"He's been grazing in the meadow up by Cow Camp. I trailered him down this morning. Nice to have him home, right, ol' fella? Missed you some. Yep," said Earl.

Dakota pressed his muzzle into Earl's chest. Cora scratched where Earl had shown her and Dakota's lips relaxed; his withers quivered. Loretta moved closer, and the horse nickered. She offered her hand, palm up, and he laid his muzzle there, nibbling softly without biting. As a small child, she had wanted to be a cowgirl. She wanted a horse of her own to ride like the wind through the boulders and over the landscape of the Alabama Hills, to dance to fiddle music and sing old ballads and confide her deepest desires to her cowboy buddies in the light of a full moon. The feel of Dakota's muzzle in her hand and the tickle of his whiskers made her smile.

"Lord Almighty, I've never seen him take to young'uns like this," Earl said. "Dakota's a good judge a character, Noleen. Yep, well. These two are keepers, I'd say."

With a sudden start, Dakota's ears flattened and his eyes rolled wide. He shook his head, stomping his right front foot. Loretta heard a familiar whine like a mosquito buzzing in her ear. The Enduro's clacky buzz grew louder, closer. Ethan must have been on Horseshoe Bend Road. Judging the distance from the sound, he hadn't yet turned onto the driveway heading into Willow Grove.

Pansy came out of the screen door carrying a basket full of muffins. "Hello, my dears," she said, smiling. "Nothing says lovin' like something from the oven." She walked from person to person offering her baked goods, oblivious to the strain in their faces.

"Pansy dear, you're a notion," said Noleen. She smiled at Pansy and took a bite of the muffin. "Banana nut, my favorite."

Yoshi motioned Loretta and Cora toward the barn. "We didn't tell Pansy about Bill," he said, when he was sure she couldn't hear him. "This news would upset her. She's kind of…delicate, you know? Change, turmoil, trigger episodes of her Alzheimer's."

"Alzheimer's. That explains a few things," said Cora.

-CHAPTER 8-

*I*t was a sit-down conversation, the worst kind, the kind where *he* had to sit. But his parents were in motion, so much so that it was hard for his brain to keep up with his eyes and stay focused. His father paced the living room floor, and his mother shifted her seat from the couch to her recliner chair and back to the couch.

Questions were fired from every direction: first Sim, then Raina, then both of them together. "You *can* account for your whereabouts, right?" Sim asked.

"Was anyone with you, Loretta, maybe?" Raina's voice was softer than Sim's.

"Ethan! Answer our questions. Please."

Ethan couldn't think straight, let alone respond. His father just said there was a robbery at the hardware store, and that there was money missing from Iron Gate as well. The whens and wheres were as confusing as the accusation itself. "Late evening or early morning at the Iron Gate," Sim said. "Before opening, or just after, at Milne's Hardware," he stated, in a wobbly, concerned tone.

"Ruby!" Ethan volunteered. This morning, he had stopped by the Eastside Deli and bought six fresh-baked peanut butter cookies. Surely Ruby would have noticed how calm he was—in no way would he have displayed a behavior indicative of a would-be robber. After Ruby's, he'd sat on the cement planter box in front of the hardware store, eating cookies until Mr. Milne unlocked the door at 8:00 a.m. Right now in his lap lay the new work gloves he'd purchased, the tags still attached. Somehow, between the times he walked in the store and when Mr. Milne rang up his sale, a robbery occurred. Cash was taken from the register. "Maybe the money was stolen last night?" Ethan offered. "Mr. Milne was with me when I picked out the gloves. He helped me choose."

"Not last night. At least, the police don't think so. And Mr. Milne did tell them that he was with you the entire time you were in the store, Ethan. But Officer Belcher isn't so sure. He says Mr. Milne is old and gets easily confused. He would have only had to turn his back for a minute…"

"Officer Belcher. You mean Clive?"

"What does it matter? Think! This is serious, son." Sim was in no mood for a cross-examination.

"The hardware store is one of a series of recent break-ins. And Clive saw *you*, sitting in front of Milne's this morning. He thought at the time you acted, in his words, 'preoccupied, and suspicious…that you displayed malicious intent by your attention to the storefront and door's entry keypad.'"

Was Clive serious? "Preoccupied" maybe, but "suspicious?" "Displaying malicious intent?" He would never steal or vandalize or deface public property. Most people knew this about him. His parents knew this about him. At least they used to. Before Brock. Before the Committee.

"I was eating cookies. And waiting." There was a valid reason for his being at the hardware store that early in the morning, and if that question had been asked, he was ready to reply. Granny Noleen had invited him to come over. He had planned to spend the afternoon working with the girls and needed proper gloves to protect his hands from splinters and crawling insects such as ants—proof being the gloves in his lap.

"I don't want to talk about this. I want to discuss the bunker. Why can't I go to work with you, Dad? I mean, Sim."

"We've had this conversation before," Sim told him.

"I want to have it again."

"Another time. Right now we need you to…"

Raina shot Sim a look, then turned to Ethan and said, "Ethan, darling, you can't go down the stairs into the bunker right now."

"I can always go to Dad's work. That's just the way it is."

"Yes, you can always go where I go," Sim said, "but for now, just for now, for safety's sake, no using the main entrance into the bunker. Understand?"

"Why?"

"Construction. There's too much going on, too much equipment being moved, too many men working in that area. You can explore the bunker when the time is right. Until then, no." Sim waved his hand in a catawampus circle. "Enough," he said. "We've gotten off topic."

After fifty-seven minutes and twenty seconds, according to his watch, of more yelling and talk, talk, talking, Raina finally said: "We believe you, Ethan." When she hugged him, it was like snuggling his old teddy bear. Though intimate touch had always been hard for him, he accepted this hug gratefully, breathing in the scent of her vanilla essence oil, relaxing in her warmth.

Sim exhaled the way he always did at the end of an argument, or when Ethan came out of a trance-like episode. "Give us some time to clear this up. It will be okay. Honestly. It can't turn out otherwise," he promised. "Just think before you act. Stay away from town for a while and drive the speed limit, please. It'll probably be a good thing if you hang out with Loretta this afternoon," he added. "If memory serves, you had planned to do so anyway, right?"

+++

Ethan spotted Noleen and the others beside the porch, stopped, and waited near the archway and path to the house. "Come on ahead, Mister," she called out, waving him along.

Ethan bounced from one foot to the other, his eyes on Loretta.

"It's okay," Loretta told him. "You're invited. It's okay."

The pounding in Ethan's chest felt like his insides were about to blow. He glanced at Cora and his eyes exploded tears, but still he strode forward. All morning, this is where he had wanted to be. At Willow Grove, with Loretta and Cora. Where better to verbally vomit the crap he held inside than with people he knew he could trust? "He didn't follow procedure. I know my rights, and he didn't abide by proper police protocol. Not before, at the creek, and definitely not today."

Ethan paced the ground and flicked his fingers. "The first time, he tried to pin me for vandalism...*without* my parents being present *or* suggesting that I obtain legal counsel. Strike one. Today he accused me of stealing money from Mr. Milne. *And* he spoke with my parents about this without my being there to defend myself...an issue that's as much illegal as immoral, but still. Strike two. Twice, he's jumped to conclusions without having evidence to substantiate his claims. That makes no sense."

"Who? Ethan, what happened?"

"Officer Belcher. That guy with a crew cut who dated your mom."

"You mean Clive?"

"I asked my dad that same question! Yes, Officer Belcher, *Clive.*" Ethan blinked, looking up and away before wiping his eyes with the back of his hand. He flicked his fingers. "Clive didn't follow procedure. He accused me of painting graffiti on the wall outside the Penny Saver Market and at the Iron Gate. He said there had been all kinds of vandalism around town lately, and that I was a suspect. Me and…"

Ethan turned to Granny Noleen and Earl. "He didn't follow procedure. He arrested Bill without probable cause. Strike three."

"Today?" Granny Noleen asked, jumping to her feet.

"No." Ethan shared his observation and its definition aloud. "Clive's arrogant…full of himself. Ar-ro-gant!"

"Definitions are Ethan's thing," Loretta said.

"It's the way his brain works," added Cora. "Weird, but very cool, I think." She shrugged her shoulders.

"Lovely: the things I treasure." Pansy's attempt at mimicking Ethan's fetish for definitions tickled him. Her eyes were sweetly innocent and her smile so big. He liked her. But he still felt the tremors and the heat as he retreated back to his experience with Clive.

"Where's Bill? Is he home? I bet they didn't read him his rights," Ethan shouted.

"Slow down, cowboy. We know about the vandalism charge, but did something else happen?" Earl stepped away from Noleen and toward Ethan. Ethan backpedaled, sideswiping Loretta and nearly knocking her down.

Loretta steadied herself and without touching Ethan sat

down on the ground, arms to her sides. Ethan stared into the distance, and when he felt ready he sat beside her. She smiled—not at him, but at the heart he had formed with his hands as he laid them in his lap.

Soon Ethan's breathing grew steady; his shoulders settled and his muscles relaxed. For the first time since he got there he was able to focus on the people around him. Granny Noleen stood rigid, eyes sharp, lips pressed so tightly together it looked as if it would take a crowbar to pry them apart. Earl's eyes were pointed at his boots, the knuckles of his right hand stretched tight over a pocket knife as he fed Dakota apple slices. Yoshi sat on a stump beside the porch, looking contemplative and concerned, his hands clasped and flexing one against the other. Pansy was in the chicken coop, giggling and cooing over the Rhode Island Reds while feeding them her leftover muffins. Cora and Doc stood side-by-side, their faces grim, serious. Loretta still sat beside him, enforcing the behavior she had invented so long ago: calmly befriending without words and supporting regardless of the issue.

The crunch of gravel drew Ethan's attention to the driveway.

Paiute Bill shuffled along it and up the path to the house. The horse saw him, and Ethan saw him, but both let him come without announcing his presence. Bill walked hunched over, his long gray braids more disheveled than usual. His hat was missing. He had a bright red abrasion on his cheek and also a black eye.

When Noleen noticed him, she ran. "Billy!" She hugged him, then held him at arm's length, surveying his eye and his damaged cheek. Using sign language, she spoke with him privately for a moment. Bill nodded, and she led him to a rocking chair on the porch, helped him set down, and then bustled into the house. Moments later she came out with a wet rag, a bowl of soapy water, and a glass of cold tea. Bill took the glass in his shaking hands and gulped greedily until the glass was empty.

Yoshi stood up, came and sat beside Bill's rocker on the porch. He asked Bill questions with his hands and translated as they spoke. "Yes, Office Belcher did arrest Bill today."

Bill shook his head.

Yoshi started again. "Wait, no." He gestured with his hands as if he was wiping the slate clean. "Bill says the officer did not arrest him, but *detained* him, as he did before when you saw them at the creek, Ethan."

Granny Noleen gently patted Bill's cheek. "This?" she asked.

Bill nodded yes. "And this?" she asked, turning his head to show the other cheek, an older bruise, yellowed and fading.

"That one's from last time," Ethan said. "I saw that Bill was bleeding, there, on his face," he pointed, "when he was in the squad car at the creek."

"Why didn't you tell me?" Noleen asked.

Bill shrugged his shoulders.

"Bill says not to worry; they can't charge him," Yoshi explained. "There is no evidence to prove his guilt. He *is* a suspect in the robberies, however, and so is the boy." Bill pointed to Ethan.

Ethan shrank beside Loretta.

"Officer Belcher claims there was money taken. Bar money. Money from The Group meeting and now from the hardware store. Bill was walking down Main Street this morning, and Officer Belcher picked him up and asked him questions. Then took him behind the restroom at the park and got...more serious with his interrogation."

"Harassment!" Noleen hollered.

Bill's hands were signing rapidly, his eyes on Yoshi.

"Later, at the station, Bill saw Group members speaking with Sheriff Atkins. Bill was in a holding room at that point, but could see clearly into the area where the members sat. It wasn't difficult for him to lip-read their conversations. Bill says the rowdy blonde-haired boy and his father were there."

"Pierce," Ethan said.

"And Brock was in the room too. He didn't speak but listened to the others, gesturing as if he were thinking things over." Yoshi lowered his head and paused as if praying. He rubbed his eyes.

"No way," Ethan interrupted. "Brock would *not* be thinking this over. He's made up his mind."

"Bill says you're right, Ethan. He saw this in Brock's eyes. Not that you're guilty. That you're a threat. Every time your name came up, he tensed up. His eyes narrowed."

Ethan internalized the word. *Threat: regarded as a probable danger; a menace.*

As the heat in his stomach started to erupt again, Bill's sign language became a necessary distraction, creating words different from those Ethan loved, but still powerful and distinctive. The creation of each handshape was a fluid thing of beauty, his forearms, fingers and thumbs fully involved. "Bill says that Frey was waiting for him outside the police station when he was released," Yoshi said. "Frey told him to watch his back. By interpreting Bill's sign, Frey's threat, as close as I can get it was this: 'Regardless of what the department decides…you're guilty, you son-of-a-bitch. From now on, every move you make, I'll be watching.'"

Yoshi's head dropped forward again. He hesitated as if considering his next words carefully. Finally, he raised his head and said: "Frey *will* be watching Bill. And Ethan. To think otherwise would be pure folly.

"And here is something else. Bill heard this later, from a friend of a woman who works a dispatch desk in the police department. Apparently Clive is in big trouble. Repeatedly, he has acted without departmental approval. How he handled Bill and then Ethan was the final straw. He is suspended from duty until further notice."

·CHAPTER 9·

*L*oretta knew Ethan wasn't involved. And despite Frey's insistence that Bill was guilty, there lingered in her mind a nagging doubt. She had seen movies about cases where mistakes were made: screwed-up DNA or blood samples, evidence lost or tampered with inadvertently—or purposely. She thought of Bill's inability to talk, his gentle eyes and the tender care he gave Cora when he came to her rescue so long ago. It was one of those goofy moments of adolescent miscalculation (Doc called it poor judgment). They had stopped at the creek to catch pollywogs on their way to school one morning, and Cora fell in the icy water. In a matter of seconds, Bill appeared out of nowhere and pulled her out, took off his flannel shirt and wrapped it around her shoulders to ward off the chill. Cora was more humiliated than hurt and ran away before she thanked him, but Loretta remembered the shock of it all, seeing the concern on his face as his fingers talked a language she didn't understand. She couldn't remember saying "thank you" either, just standing there with her mouth agape, then following Cora's trail of dripping water down the street and to the Gomez house. It was hard to imagine that the person she encountered that day, and the man she saw now, wilting into an old rocking chair on the porch at Willow Grove, could be involved in a crime of any sort.

The granite-like lines of Noleen's face, the opaqueness of her eyes projected the persona Loretta was familiar with—the face of the woman she had shied away from and avoided all her life, the Witch of Willow Grove. Yet there was something else as well, and Loretta marveled as she witnessed this transformation: the long stretch of Noleen's arms as she reached for Bill, her hands as rough as old leather forming words, gentle in the way they caressed and soothed the bruises on his face, lips that plumped and softened when she *tsk, tsk'd* to calm him. In some weird way, this reminded her of her mother—as strange as that seemed, in the middle of Bill's drama, her mother had popped into her head again, and she couldn't get her out. Images of Greer fussing over her sheets at night, crooning country-western songs, wiping away tears, and punching *Uncle* Jason in the gut one time, after he had patted Loretta on the backside, warmed her stomach like sweet farm-fresh butter.

"Bi-Polar weather," Cora said, rubbing the goose bumps on her arms as a phantom breeze rolled off Whitney's peak.

Noleen clicked her tongue and wiped her hands on her

skirt. "Enough," she said. "I've had it with those bloodsuckers Frey and Clive. They're light-stealers. They've stolen my time and, it seems, our summer sun. Criminy! The weather won't even cooperate today." Raising a fist, cursing the clouds that straddled the yard, she strode to the coop where Pansy was feeding the chickens, put her arm around her, and gave her a squeeze.

"Doing okay?" she asked.

Pansy smiled and danced a little jig, sang, *"Lovin' me some good times, so much more to go. Though it takes a while to get there, I'm baskin' in the glow…"*

Noleen tugged at the pockets of her skirt, pulling free a tangled mass of parsley and some carrot tops. She shoved the semi-fresh vegetables through the fence to the hens, and the two women clucked and cooed, watching as the chickens attacked the green glob and began a feeding frenzy. When Big Mama, a goliath Rhode Island Red, ran off with the last of the leafless stems, and the smaller hens lost interest and resumed pecking the dirt for worms or grubs, Noleen took hold of Pansy's hand and led her toward the house. Before the steps, she groaned and arched her back, reaching for the handrail. "This wonky hip a mine's actin' up," she said. "To heck with this. I'm declaring a play day. For the whole lot of us. Doc, you and Yoshi here had plans to explore the tunnels, right?"

"Yes, ma'am. That was the plan."

"Well, we're crashing your party. What say, y'all? You

ready to see those dungeons you heard about? Can you handle the truth?"

There was a poster on Ethan's bedroom wall. Before you assume, *learn the facts*. Before you judge, *understand why*. Before you hurt someone, *feel*. Before you speak, *think*. Loretta's mind whirled with half-formed ideas. Long dresses and a big funny hat, so what? A bike with a basket, big deal. An old woman, protective of her home and family, certainly wasn't so out of line.

+++

Earl and Yoshi took their time lifting and moving the couch, rolling aside the braided rug that covered a portion of the living room floor to reveal a small, rectangular trap door. The simultaneous intake of breath was notable, and Loretta felt the rush. She, like the others, leaned forward to get a closer look at the old hatch. Built solidly into the wood-plank flooring, its edges were curled and swelled with age, the hinges rusted but solid.

Cora sniffed the air. "Smells mysterious," she said. "Myst*er*ious."

"Gomez and Duvall Detective Agency, active once again," Loretta said.

Earl straddled the door and tugged on the iron handle, tugged again and again. On the fourth try, with a *whoosh* and a shudder the hatch door released and popped open. Beneath it was a rustic set of stairs, like basement stairs, only steeper: nearly a vertical drop to a floor hidden in shadow.

The stairs were narrow and creaky, and leaned slightly to the left. Loretta's toes hung over the tread nosing of each step as she descended, and with no banister to steady herself, she felt dizzy, off-center. She groped the rocky wall, feeling her way down, concentrating on the position of Cora's feet in front of her to keep from losing her balance.

Getting everyone down the stairs, with the issues of hip pain and sciatica, dressed in skirts and wearing loafers or cowboy boots, seemed monumental. Although it was midday, there was no light, except for the lanterns carried by Noleen and Earl and the flashlights held by Doc and Yoshi. The air was cool, unnaturally still, and filled with a myriad of odors: mysterious, invasive, not entirely unpleasant but strange, reminiscent of numerous bodies pressed into tiny spaces, stale tobacco, old saddle blankets, and some sweet woody herb.

"Wow," said Doc.

Loretta had never heard such a simple expletive slip from the lips of Cora's father.

They stood in a boxy room, no more than six armspans wide. Water-worn river rock, varying in size from two to eight inches and entombed in a sandy matrix, formed the walls of the room, and those of what appeared to be three connecting tunnels. Hand-hewn cedar beams, varnished by age, reinforced the ceiling in the center of the room and wrapped around each tunnel entrance like dwarfish limbs.

Loretta scanned the area, imagining that she might see cellar windows half buried in the dirt: this could be the dungeon of childhood fantasies, where children disappeared and were kept and tortured, prompting many a Halloween fear-fest.

"These marks were made by a tool called an adze," Doc explained, running his fingers over a chipped depression in one of the beams. "An adze was used for smoothing or carving wood and is similar to an ax, but with the head mounted perpendicular to the handle. The carpenter would actually straddle the wood and swing the adze front to back as if it were a pendulum. The broad, curved blade removed a chip at a time; the smaller and closer the chips, the smoother the finished beam."

"Extraordinary, really," Yoshi said. "Quite beautiful. Art in another genre."

"Yes, and unusual, considering the timeframe that would have been involved and the proposed use of the materials," Doc added.

"Someone cared," Cora said.

Doc put his arm around Cora's shoulders. "Yes, Mija," he said, smiling.

Loretta peered into the tunnel to her right. It was shallow enough that she could see its rocky end. "Sweet," she said, just above a whisper.

"Plenty fine. We'll start here, then," Noleen said, her grimace smoldering in the diffused light as she held her lantern aloft.

"Right," Yoshi agreed. "This tunnel is the easiest to access, and the ceiling is higher than in the others. Most of us can stand comfortably…"

"All but Ethan and ol' Stretch here," Noleen teased, pointing to Earl. "And maybe you, Doc? How tall are you anyways?"

"Five-ten."

"Luck of the draw. The entrance might give you grief, but other than that, I expect you'll manage. It's six feet, give or take, floor to ceiling in the tunnel proper."

Doc nodded, smiling and barely able to stand still.

Loretta had never seen him this excited. His eyes scoured the rock walls, stopping now and then as if he were snapping mental pictures.

Following Ethan, she entered the tunnel. She could stand without hitting her head, but the minuscule space between her scalp and the granite bedrock was unsettling and a bit claustrophobic. The air seemed thicker than in the anteroom and sweat began to form on her forehead and upper lip. The now-familiar smells swelled in the dead space. Every sound magnified: a cough, the chatter of voices, the crunch of pebbles beneath her feet. Just inside the entryway, a smaller cavern had been chiseled into the rock. Four flat hollows were dug into the walls, two on the east side, two on the west.

"Sleeping quarters, we figure," Granny Noleen said. "Look here." She held up her lantern. Scratched in the beam above the hollow, in a scrawled and barely readable script, a message read: *"Who made it here is nearly free. I wonder where is my wife and 2 chilren."*

"And there," she pointed. *"Brackish water hole 50 paces down tunnel next. Best not to drink of it."*

A foot above each hollow was a much smaller depression, and Granny Noleen set her lantern in one of them—a perfect fit. The light danced about the room, projecting shadows and raising goose bumps on Loretta's arms. She ran her fingertips over the wall. It was rough with a chalky feel, a mix of stones, rounded and of various shapes and sizes, just as in the anterior room. The wall felt sturdy and secure. More stable than a tunnel wall that old should feel, in her opinion. She wanted to hoot and to hear an acknowledging echo, but couldn't open her mouth; she felt her face flush, and that familiar restriction of her vocal cords.

Cora did it for her. "Woot! Woot! I love this place!" she hollered.

Woot, woot, woot…I love, love, love…

"Hella cool!" Ethan circled the room, sniffing the walls. *Hella cool, hella cool, hella cool…*"It smells *real* in here. Like hard work." He lay down on one of the hollows, his legs longer than the rocky bed by a foot. "Five feet. The people who stayed here were very short."

"Curl up on your side, Ethan. Back toward the wall. The people who occupied these rooms may not have been as short as you suspect. More likely, they lay in defensive position, ready to bolt," Doc surmised.

"Eyes on the entrance. Yes. I see," Ethan said. "Of course. That makes sense."

Beyond them, the tunnel ended in a crumbled alluvial fan of rocky debris, but there was something else atop the rubble. Loretta, Ethan, and Cora approached slowly and knelt down. Cora turned to Noleen. "May I touch?"

"Go on ahead. But be careful."

The grouping of four flat granite slabs sat one on top of the other and was distinctly different from the surrounding rubble. "The object on the stones is an incense burner," Yoshi explained. "The technique used to make the pattern you see here is called cloisonné. Creating a work of art such as this is time consuming, but the results are quite beautiful. In this case, the incense burner is made of bronze with gold inlay and the tiny lotus flowers are lapis lazuli, jade, and red jasper. This piece is very old."

"Fascinating," Doc said, kneeling beside Cora. "It's still an assumption, but likely these tunnels did provide some sort of refuge for interned Japanese."

"It is more than an assumption," Yoshi said. "Here." He pointed to pictographs on the walls. "The Japanese who occupied these tunnels chose not to leave their names. The evidentiary truth could implicate not only their family but the people who owned this house during wartime." Yoshi lifted his lantern, pointing to childlike drawings of clouds and rain over what appeared to be a vegetable garden.

Children playing. A dog. Perhaps a cat. Happy images of a former life. "No one knew at that point what would happen. In our minds, the United States had already betrayed us and forced us to leave our homes and come to Manzanar. If anyone chose to steal away, to find respite here, it would have been prearranged."

"When you say *us*…" Doc said. "You mean…"

Noleen raised her finger and her lantern. "Yoshi, I believe it's time to spill the rest if you're willing." She plopped down on a sleeping shelf, scooching deeper until her back met comfortably with the rock wall.

Yoshi closed his eyes and cleared his throat. "It's easy to discover the first part of the story," he said. "That piece is public record. My family's name is listed in the Inyo County Archives as internees at Manzanar."

Cora gasped and clasped her father's hand.

Yoshi opened his eyes and ran his index finger across the drawings on the wall, lingering on the cat, the dog. "The rest of the story, my story, until now is *not* a part of that record." He smiled. "When my family was interred at Manzanar, my father became gravely ill. It wasn't a sickness of the body, but of the mind. He lost faith. He lost heart. At that time, my mother was part of the camp's furlough program and each day she worked the fields around this house, here at Willow Grove. She grew close to the property owners, Abel and Sybil Barlow. One day, while helping Sybil with house chores, she broke down and cried. She told

Sybil that she feared her husband would die if he remained at Manzanar. That afternoon, she and the Barlows concocted an elaborate plan. They faked an influenza outbreak. For several days, my mother applied hot compresses to our heads…my father, my sister, and I. We refused to eat. Soon after, Abel requested that the officials at Manzanar allow my mother's family to come and help finish the picking. He hired a doctor to pronounce the diagnosis of influenza and quarantine us to Willow Grove. After a week, he faked our deaths. Because of the high possibility of spreading the disease throughout the camp, the guards did not question his word and did not ask that our bodies be returned. Abel swore that he would bury us on his property, and as far as I know, there was no further inquisition. After that, we came into these tunnels and stayed until Abel secured safe passage for us to Canada.

"I met Noleen and the others when I traveled back here from Quebec, to see if the things I remembered, and the stories my mother told me, were true."

"And were they true?" Cora asked.

"The entry from the living room floor was the first thing that struck me. I remembered the weight of the wooden lid and the steep stairs that led into the tunnels. Long ago, I was frightened to go to that dark place, as any child would be. And then there were the artifacts. This incense burner belonged to my grandfather and was passed down to my mother. If I close my eyes, I can still smell the frankincense and sweet cloves and sandalwood she burned. I also have vague memories of sleeping on shelves, as my sister called them. And of the taste of rock dust and the writings of the Civil War-era slaves who cleared and built the tunnels. When I first revisited the tunnels, I remembered my small hands tracing the letters of those etchings and my mother saying the words. *'Who made it here is nearly free. I wonder where is my wife and two children.'*"

"Fascinating," Doc said.

"I'm sorry," Cora said, "for your family's losses."

Yoshi shrugged his shoulders. "What's done is done." He turned away from the pictures and the incense burner as if he were through talking for now and ready to move on.

"There are tools in the next tunnel over. Couldn't have been left by the runaway slaves that hid here because they're too modern. Shovels. Picks. A hammer. Could be the property of the last owners. But maybe not," Earl offered.

They each took the time to study the pictographs, but Ethan was struck more by the inscriptions. Loretta got a kick out of watching him study the text, his fingers probing the chipped-out lines and spaces, forming the words with his lips. The support beams into which they were inscribed were old, but there remained a sense of the trees from which they came, and Ethan stroked and sniffed the wood, smiling and nodding as he recognized that lingering essence of cedar.

Sometimes Loretta wished she had a fraction of Ethan's brilliance, his knack for memorization and skill with building words and managing definitions. His grades were better than hers by a long shot. Even with his tics and repetition, he managed better than some and understood the important stuff more than most kids at school. She took a deep breath, wishing she could suck in half of what he was observing right now and had the confidence to repeat that information later, to her mother, or in an essay for school, or in a conversation with Brady.

Cora and Doc had inspected the tunnel and were now at its mouth, ready to move on. Loretta laid her fingers on Ethan's shoulder and tapped lightly.

"Ready, big fella?" Earl asked him. "We can stay on for a bit if you'd like."

"I'm good," Ethan told him. "Thank you, though."

After everyone had left, Loretta looked back into the tunnel, watching as the lantern light flickered and bounced and dimmed; as the cavern browned and then blackened, much like a ride at an amusement park when the attraction fades and the rider's attention is diverted elsewhere. She wondered if the ghosts of the runaway slaves had settled and if the spirits of the Japanese, of Yoshi's family, had forgiven their intrusion.

"Are we ready for a break? I brought granola bars and juice boxes," Doc said.

The rock walls of the anteroom amplified the sounds of their munching, swallowing, and satisfied lip smacking. Doc slapped his knees in rhythm with the crunch, crunch,

crunch, and Pansy began to hum. Earl tapped his foot against the rocky ground, following the cadence of Pansy's song. Catching on, Cora mashed another granola bar still in its wrapper and shook it like a rattle, slapping it against her hand to the makeshift beat. Loretta giggled as Doc rapped harder on his knees. Bill smiled and rocked back and forth while Noleen sang: *"Ahey, ahey, ahey."* Ethan's eyes darted from one person to another, and then he danced, a methodic stomp and sway, stomp and sway, glide, glide, stomp, and sway.

"I hate to break up the party, but we better move on. There's more to see," said Yoshi.

+++

The next tunnel they entered was to the left of the first one and ran deeper. The ground was smooth, and, as in the first tunnel, there were four sleeping hollows, two on each side of a man-made cavern. Inside the passageway itself, darkness thickened. Even with the lanterns, it was hard to see. Loretta lagged behind the others this time. Her eyes were dry and watery from the strain of holding them open. The air smelled musky, dusty, yet a faint breeze managed to find its way there, teasing the short hairs around her forehead and neck. She was alert, but her mind wandered, envisioning the people who passed through these tunnels, imagining their whispers and cries. She tried to tread softly, but her feet found every chink of wood and loose rock on the tunnel floor. She tripped and her arms flailed, reaching for the crumbling wall that was knobby and cool to the touch. Her breathing quickened; she noticed a shift in the airflow and smashed into Cora, who had stopped just in front of her.

"I wonder if this is what it feels like to be buried alive," Cora said, her voice scratchy and subdued.

"Creepy," Loretta said, standing motionless, feeling as if her muscles were made of tin and that her arms and legs were rusty and in need of oil.

Just ahead, the others ogled another message written on the wall. In the distance, Ethan stood alone near what appeared to be a side tunnel, staring into the dark. His fingers flicked in the dancing light of Noleen's lantern.

Doc read aloud the message: *What do freedom meen?*

"Check this one out." Earl shone his lantern on a nearby support beam. "*We darnt be catchd with pencil an paper so let this wall tel our histry.*"

"Let's see if we can recreate an atmosphere like the one these folks must have experienced," Doc suggested.

"Like an experiment? Cora asked.

"Yes. Very simple. I'll give a signal. Lights out. No talking. Everybody okay with this? Yes? Here we go, now. Lights out."

As the lanterns were extinguished and the flashlights switched off, Loretta shuddered. Noleen hesitated—one, two, five seconds longer than the others—until her quivering lantern-light melted away along with her shadowy self. Loretta opened her eyes as wide as she could, straining to see some beginning or end to the blackness that grew around her. The absence of light left her queasy and off-balance. She fought to stay upright. She tried to find an edge, a corner, something tangible to grab hold of, something her mind could track and manipulate into a memory of some place warm and pleasurable. The air or lack of it was suffocating. She could hear people breathing but couldn't identify where the noises were coming from, or from whom, other than Ethan. She knew he was behind her, but couldn't gauge how far. The sounds coming from his throat were similar to ones she'd heard him utter as a child, ancient noises, as if he were communicating with himself in a pre-language of his own making. After some minutes, he said: "Experiments. Some are good, and some are bad. Adolf Hitler's experiments were bad. He felt his people were superior, and that other races, especially the Jews, should be eliminated."

"Every life, no matter our differences, is important and has a purpose," Noleen offered.

Someone stumbled, said "Sorry, *oops*." Pansy. She must have bumped into one of the others in the dark.

There were noises. Some close. Some far away. Pings. Groans. Creaks. And something else—a hiss, subtle, snake-like, that moved Loretta's imagination to things nasty and slimy.

"That's enough. Good golly, that's enough!" said Noleen.

One by one the lights came on—first the flashlights,

then the slower, propane-driven lanterns.

"The Milgram experiment." Ethan was stuck on his earlier thought pattern. "In 1963, Stanley Milgram decided to test a theory that there was something special about the German people that had allowed them to participate in genocide during the Holocaust. Pretending that he was doing an experiment about human learning, Milgram asked randomly chosen people to question his test subject, a man who was supposedly attached to an electric shock generator. They were told to shock 'the subject' in stronger and stronger increments each time he answered incorrectly. The man was an actor, and the shocks were fake, but the participants didn't know this. They each obeyed the commands of the man conducting the experiment, even when the person being 'shocked' screamed in agony and begged for mercy."

"Dang," Cora said. "If I didn't have the creeps before, I do now. Can we get out of here? Please?"

"Sorry, Mija." Doc stroked Cora's hair and kissed her cheek.

As always, Loretta marveled at this show of affection. Her mother cuddled her, but always in those quirky ways: fish kisses from across the room, neck nuzzles at the most inappropriate times (such as when she had friends over to spend the night or when they were at the movie theatre), long sessions of practicing her make-up skills by using Loretta as a model (hearts and flowers on fingers and toenails, perms, temporary hair color that always lasted longer than she'd intended), during which times she'd babble and rave about how pretty Loretta was and how thick her hair was and how she'd inherited her mother's bedroom eyes. And the dance lessons in the kitchen, the living room, before bed at night if the music was good and when there were no *uncles* visiting.

"The Stanford Prison Experiment. Male students were assigned roles as guards or prisoners in a fake prison set up in the basement of the Stanford psychology building. The 'guards' got carried away and did ugly things, psychological torture, far worse than was intended. The experiment was aborted after six days."

"Let us be done," said Yoshi.

This was one of those times as in school when Ethan would alienate classmates and teachers alike. It was just something Ethan did when he was uncomfortable, or when a topic of discussion caught his attention. He'd get stuck. His brain would assemble knowledge that he had learned from books, movies, and articles, words falling from his mouth like an endless cascade of water.

"The Monster Study: In 1939, twenty-two orphaned children were separated into two groups, one with a speech therapist who praised the kids' progress, and the other with a speech therapist who chewed out the kids for every little mistake. In the end, the kids who had been treated badly were a mess. Their speech problems got worse instead of better."

No one stopped him. In the tunnels, these outbursts seemed mildly appropriate. Everyone appeared to understand Ethan's need to talk and bury his emotions in facts just now, though all Loretta wanted to do was to get home, crank up the stereo and climb into a hot bath where she could massage her feelings with a soft cloud of bubbles.

Earl hurried them along, gently pushing the pace. "Best move on outta here," he said. "Dakota will raid the hay barn if I'm late with his dinner."

+++

As Loretta climbed the stairs, it felt as if she were entering a time-warp, re-entering the present to the soft sweet smells of roses and the warm breeze coming through the open windows of the living room at Willow Grove. She breathed in the comfort, familiarity, and openness of the place.

"Lemonade?" Pansy said, as much a request as an invitation.

"You sit. I'll get it," Yoshi offered.

Suddenly, there was a knocking at the door, then a pounding, followed by loud baritone voices.

Noleen peered out the window, then opened the door a crack. Miraculously, the old wooden doorframe cooperated; it rattled, but at least it didn't stick. The men outside had walked to the edge of the porch, mumbling and pointing toward the toolshed and the creek beyond. Noleen stood silently, waiting for them to speak to her.

Officer Clive swiveled toward the door, ready to knock again. He jumped back when he saw her standing there. "Ah, shit, Noleen. You look like a damn ghost."

"And?" Noleen's shoulders rose a few inches.

"We the people..." Clive handed Noleen a piece of paper. " ...the County of Inyo... have concerns. There have been numerous complaints. Some of your neighbors insist that you're running an illegal boarding house, Noleen."

"What neighbors? I don't have any, not for two miles down the road, and those folks are friends of ours. They wouldn't complain. Besides, I don't run a boarding house, Clive, and you know it."

"Willow Grove is a rundown, ramshackle piece of crap," Clive said. "The best thing that could happen involves a bulldozer and wrecking ball."

"You and your friend here got nothing better to do than harass an old woman?" Noleen nodded toward Ethan and Bill, both helping Pansy to her easy chair. "What, no major crime ring that needs busting up?"

Yoshi cleared his throat. He placed his hand on Pansy's shoulder.

Earl chuckled.

"It appears that you're receiving rent money from these folks, Noleen. That makes this a boarding house. Period."

"Period nothing. We're friends, helping each other out. End of story." She tried to shut the door, but Clive blocked it with his boot.

"Hey, man," Earl said, rushing to Noleen's side. "Let it lie."

"I don't see the problem," Yoshi added.

"We've obtained bank statements that verify our concerns. Noleen, you've been depositing checks from these folks for years."

"It's a joint account. We pool our money, buy groceries, tend to our needs from that fund," said Yoshi.

Doc flashed a smile, walked to the door and offered his hand to Clive. "Look. I don't see what the problem is here. Noleen and her friends have found a creative alternative to the housing and financial dilemma that plagues many older adults. They deserve accolades."

Clive kept his hands to his sides, rubbed the right one on his pants as if ridding it of dirt. "Not according to the law. She's never been granted a permit. She's not established herself as a business, therefore never paid taxes as one, county, state, or federal. The paper I gave Noleen is a cease and desist order, handed down by the Town Court of Lone Pine. The way I figure it, with back taxes, permit fees, et cetera, she might as well shut 'er down, 'cause she'll never be able to meet her obligations. We'd like to have her out of Willow Grove by summer's end."

"Impossible! We won't leave." Earl's face was splotchy red and deeply furrowed.

"Calm down, calm down. I've got good news with the bad. My friend here knows of an investor who will buy

Noleen out, pay her back fines and fees. Clear her name, no questions asked. It's a win-win."

"Who's your friend?" Noleen asked, standing firm. "I've never seen him before."

"Simon Brown." Simon tipped his Stetson fedora. His black hair was short and curly, tidy behind his ears. His sunglasses were not something you would pick off the rack at K-Mart, nor were his suit or shiny brown shoes. "I'm an attorney out of L.A. My client is anxious, Ms. Noleen. Anxious."

"A-N-X-I-O-U-S. Which do you mean? Uneasy and apprehensive, or intensely desirous?" Ethan paced. Loretta sat near him on the floor. Ethan slowed, then stopped, then sat beside her.

"It doesn't matter who he is, Noleen. I'm not arguing with you about this. I'm here to give information. To let you know that you are served and that with that service, I've given you an option. Rather kind of me under the circumstances, don't you think? As they say in the movies...don't shoot the messenger." Clive turned to walk away.

"We're not moving!" Noleen yelled after Clive. "So take your offer and stick it up your..."

"Suit yourself." Clive and Simon stepped off the porch and sauntered slowly to the car. They seemed in no hurry, as if they were waiting for Noleen to change her mind and make a deal. Clive held in his belly and adjusted his belt, pulled the keys from his pocket, and unlocked the car with his remote. Simon opened the door on the passenger side and slid into his seat. Clive hesitated and cocked his head, glancing toward the creek before doing the same. He started the engine of the big black Hummer.

"No police cruiser. Maybe what Bill heard is true, and Clive's been canned," Earl said. "Anyway, I'm wondering how, on the County payroll, he could afford a brand-new car like that."

"Someone's padding his pockets, I'd say. Just a knee-jerk reaction, but hey..." Noleen pursed her lips.

"If he's not delivering the cease and desist order on behalf of the police department, then whose payroll is he on? Being the braggart that he is, he'll be yapping up a storm before long. Somehow we'll hear who's behind this mess. Don't worry, darlin'," Earl said to Noleen.

As the Hummer circled the driveway, Clive slowed to a near stop, grinning satirically at Noleen. The windows of the vehicle were all open, and in the back lay picks, shovels, and what looked like oxygen and acetylene torches.

-CHAPTER 10-

The longer Ethan sat, the more difficult it was to keep his body quiet. He fidgeted and flicked, wondering if Granny Noleen and the others had noticed the big trucks and other vehicles coming and going and if they ever heard the construction noise. Depending on where Willow Grove's escape tunnels lay in comparison to the bunker, the work might sound like rumbling or perhaps a series of vibrations or minor explosions, maybe. Who knew? Sim's expertise at muffling sound was legendary, but still, blasting was a noisy business. Ethan slid the back of his hand over his forehead, wiping away the sweat. He pinched his lips to dull their tingling. The fact that the day was waning didn't help his anxiety. Group workers would begin their shifts at nightfall—hammering, drilling, sawing—and he wasn't sure he could keep from talking about the project if questions were asked. No doubt, Noleen knew something about the building site—most people did—but she didn't know everything he knew about the secret deliveries, and the extent of the plan, and the rules and the bylaws and the manifesto.

Another thing kept picking away at him, pulling his thoughts back underground. In the second tunnel, a slight but persistent airflow was present that logistically shouldn't exist. He tried to reason it out, but there were too many unknowns. Then it struck him. The workers at the bunker had made intrusions into *some* tunnels. He had overheard Sim and Brock boast about this "unexpected but thrilling discovery." They had blasted through on one occasion at least and had used picks and shovels to gain access on another. The fresh air in the tunnel could be coming from some new shaft leading outside or into the bunker itself; the facility was well ventilated, the ducting and circulation system state-of-the-art.

Should he tell what he knew? That somewhere near these historic tunnels was a bunker with enough stored ammunition to blow up the Alabama Hills, Willow Grove included? He tried to weigh his options, but there was no baseline from which to draw a conclusion. His father called this type of decision-making a crap shoot, and instead of reasoning things out, all he could think about presently was what an awful picture that phrase painted. *Crap shoot*—who in the world would have thought to use that expression in the first place?

He mulled this over for a while but got nowhere. His

mind was so full he couldn't separate his feelings from the facts, or the facts from the silliness. The faces of all the people he knew began to appear in rapid-fire images, similar to those in the flip-books he had played with as a child. He wished for an epiphany. *Epiphany: a moment in which you suddenly see or understand something in a new or very clear way.*

Ethan tried to focus on the problem at hand; he had no loyalty to Brock at all, but his parents were another matter. If he opened his mouth, he could get confused and say something he shouldn't; then Brock would accuse him again of being a rebellious, disrespectful kid. His mind bounced from light to dark, those flip-book pictures of the people he cared about warping into photos of Brock smiling, Brock frowning, Brock yelling, Brock pointing a big long finger in his face. He shook his head and tried to shoo away the evil thoughts. He glanced at Loretta, but she was distracted by the cease and desist order that Doc now held and was reading.

"I need to go!" The words came out of his mouth like stiff little jabs. He stood up. Then again: "I need to go!"

"Ethan, man, it's cool," Cora said, trying to reassure him.

Staring at him now, brows furrowed, Loretta said, "Clive and his clone, they're idiots. Let's eat, like Pansy suggested, huh? Drink some lemonade maybe? You love lemonade."

Ethan gazed at Loretta. Looked up and away. Should he

tell her it was not only Clive but other things that troubled him? He turned and padded across the braided rug and out the front door, dismissing that idea before it even jelled.

"Ethan, you come back now, hear? In this house, you got equal footing," Granny Noleen yelled after him.

+++

Walking outside was like heading into a blast furnace; the cool breeze that had kept the heat at bay earlier in the day was gone. Ethan ran his hands through his hair, pushing it back off his face. All he knew was that he had to ride. He had to see his father. Speak to his mother.

There was a Committee meeting—something about money and priorities. In Brock's office. That's what Sim had told Raina in the kitchen over hot tea and biscuits that morning, before their ill-advised interrogation regarding his whereabouts during the hardware store robbery.

On his Enduro, Ethan forced the throttle to a place it had never been, teasing the bike faster, faster, until its tires hissed and wobbled. Past Movie Road, through the mutated shapes and ogre faces of the worn and rusty granite, over the creek to the private access road that led to the bunker.

Ethan turned the key and silenced the engine, but let the bike roll as far as it would go before coming to rest. It was another mile to the site, but he didn't care. He pushed the bike along the shoulder of the dirt road and prepared to duck for cover if someone approached by car. When nearly there, he pulled the Enduro into the scrub willow where he could hide it from view. His legs felt like spaghetti, but he walked at a fast clip until he reached the familiar cottonwood stand, the breccia outcrop and piles of gravel at its base. There were multiple cars in the makeshift parking lot: his father's Jeep Cherokee, Brock's Land Cruiser, Pierce's dad's Ford pickup, Frey's '56 Ford. Clive's new Hummer.

Ethan stopped short, wondering what the Hummer was doing there, what Clive was doing there. And Frey. Always Frey, who had been promoted from a bouncer at the Iron Gate to a bodyguard for Brock in recent days. "Curious," Ethan said, then nearly at a whisper: "Curiosity killed the cat."

There was no guard at the bunker entrance. A soft beam of light shone through the steel trapdoor, turning the trees into blackened trunks with ghoulish arms. Ethan could see Pistol Rock, but on this visit, he didn't stop to hide behind it. His thumbs flicked wildly against his middle fingers as he tiptoed toward the bunker. He tried to still them by concentrating on the hole, the railing, the metal staircase as he climbed down and into the circular hallway that led to all rooms within the compound. As before, his left hand followed a zigzag trail along the forested wall mural painted by his mother. He could hear voices this time. The door to the conference room was open.

"We need to enforce the ten-percent rule. Pass the hat. These folks have money. We can't preach social justice if this practice isn't followed within our own congregation."

"We're not a congregation, Brock." It was Sim speaking now.

"We *are* a congregation, Sim. As close to one as any group of people can get. And we need to *believe*, man. It's a war zone out there, and our members have to be protected. To do that we need money. The time is near. We *must* move. Gather the flocks."

"Time for what?" Sim asked, louder. "The whole idea of this bunker was to provide protection in case some future catastrophe happened, something we couldn't escape from, such as volcanic activity or a terrorist attack, or, heaven forbid, nuclear war."

"Aside from any of those, you think the government will sit by and let us activate without interfering? *Someone* will always be after us. If it's not North Korea or Iran, it'll be the IRS or the FBI, or some home-grown SOF unit."

"Special Operations Forces. Wait a minute. You're talking about issues we've never discussed."

"The future is now. Get a grip. Read the papers. Watch the news." Brock cleared his throat. "We're there, man. Please, for God's sake, let's get on with it."

"Are you saying that it's time to activate? If so, I seriously disagree."

"Really? One day you walk into a meeting with your silver stash, Sim, and everyone thinks, oh, look at the big man. Oh, he's the greatest. The next day, you're ready to stab me in the back? That the way it is, buddy?"

"I didn't say..."

"I know, I know what you didn't say. But here and now, in front of God and all you people, let me make one thing perfectly clear. Do *not* underestimate me. I made plans for treason long ago. Believe me. My mind is never idle."

Someone shouted and cheered. Someone else applauded.

"Shut up, Sim." It was Frey. Ethan could tell by his scratchy drawl.

The sound of metal chair casters sliding across linoleum hurt Ethan's ears. There was scuffling. A thudding sound. Shouting.

"Let him up, Frey. This does no good," someone said.

Ethan peered around the door jam and saw Clive pulling Frey to his feet, saw his dad on the ground, saw Brock leaning back in his desk chair, hands clasped as he watched the men tussle. The smirk on his face was sickening.

"No!" Ethan screamed.

"Ethan?"

Ethan saw Sim scramble to his feet.

"Again. Really? You've got to do something about that boy of yours, Sim. The kid's issues, his quirks, could disrupt our plans in a major way. We've had this discussion before and it still isn't settled. Make arrangements. Be done with this. Prove your allegiance. Now."

The voices faded. The buzz of electronic equipment rose up in their place, droning, alien, and Ethan ran. He heard

Sim calling him but couldn't turn back. If he did, he'd fall away into his quiet place, where no one was yelling at his father, where he could call his father *father* instead of Sim. "Father!" he hollered over his shoulder. "Dad!"

Think. Stay focused. Picture a place where the river runs and the fish swim and a time when Mom made picnic lunches with peanut butter sandwiches and deviled eggs, and delicious chocolate brownies for dessert.

Willow branches clung to the foot pegs and the front tire as Ethan pushed his Enduro out of the brush. He took a moment to pull a twig out of his shoe and swish the leaves off his pants. One kick, two kicks, and the engine turned over. The bike sputtered. Roared. Home, he needed to be home, with Raina. His mother. Right now, at this moment, he needed her more than ever.

The Alabamas stretched and distorted as his speed increased and the dirt road veered to the right. Then there was loose gravel, and pavement, and a screeching of tires and the clash of metal on asphalt, severe pain, sky, darkness.

+++

It was Earl who found him, woke him. Dakota's soft nose nuzzled Ethan's cheek. "Lay still, cowboy. You're okay. Nothing looks broken." Dakota stomped and snorted as Sim's Jeep rounded the corner and pulled to a stop.

Sim nearly fell from the cab as he opened the car door. "Son!" he yelled. "Are you okay?" He ran to Ethan's side and squatted beside him.

"What are you all doing out here?" Earl asked. "Long way from town, Sim."

"Yeah. Some buddies and I…we're out here. Hunting."

"Hunting."

"Yes."

"Don't see no gun in your truck."

Sim ignored Earl's remark. "Ethan, let's get you home. You think you can stand?"

"Yes." Ethan let Earl and Sim help him to his feet. "I crashed," he said.

"Earl, I can't thank you enough, man."

"Just get the kid home. The bike is toast. I'll get Billy to help me haul it to the house."

+++

At the kitchen table, Ethan broke. "I don't! I can't! I feel like… Who *are* you? I don't want to call you Sim and Raina! It's worse now than ever before, and I don't trust Brock." He flicked his fingers. Blinked his eyes. The room was growing distant, as were the voices of his parents. He fought to stay in the present.

"Ethan, we've been committed to The Group for a while now. Brock is a little out there, but he's a good man. He wants the best for all of us." Sim put his hand on Ethan's shoulder, but Ethan pushed it away.

"How do you know? Are you listening, really listening?"

Ethan screamed.

"Sim." Raina pursed her lips. "I don't know anymore. I think we need to discuss this and listen to what Ethan's saying. This thing has taken a different turn. Besides, I don't like seeing him so upset just now. He's had a major crash on his bike. He's hurt."

"I'm fine. Just a couple bruises on my arm," Ethan said.

"Ethan, you passed out," said Raina.

"Just for a minute," Ethan told her.

"I want to talk about this thing with Brock. Now," Ethan said, pushing his chair back, standing.

"Look. Let's just slow down here. I'm not ready to…all I'm willing to say right now is that we need to be vigilant. *If* the time comes, we'll make a decision together as a family, and if we choose to back out of this deal, I'll talk with Brock personally and try to come up with a solution that works for everyone.

"We've invested a lot," Sim continued.

"Yes, we have. All of us have. But there have been… instances…lately, Sim, that make me uncomfortable. Suggestions regarding our own family that I can't abide, and you know that."

Sim nodded. "The new addendums to the manifesto. Yes, I know. " He slid his arm around Raina and winked at Ethan with a bloodshot eye. "I'll handle this. Let me talk to the others. Please, try not to worry."

+++

Later that night, when Sim, Raina, and Ethan arrived at the mandatory meeting, Brock was in full preaching mode. As often as he said he didn't sermonize, Ethan could think of nothing else to call it.

"I've tried so hard to add meaning to your lives. But in spite of all my trying, there are a handful of people here who are spreading lies and deceptions. We're sitting on a powder keg, folks."

"No!" Frey hollered.

The crowd moaned.

"Oh, yes, my friends. I didn't want to rush. Trust me when I say this. Say you believe!"

"We believe!"

"There's no way to detach from the outside world other than to take ourselves out of it. Some people have betrayed us. Some mistrust us. Some take the law into their own hands and do the unthinkable. Thieves. Vandals. Crooked politicians. Vulgar television and movie producers who create filth to poison our children's minds. Terrorists. It could be a checker at the grocery store, or the clerk at the post office, your friend, your neighbor. Others who will soon try to prevent our efforts, perhaps even stop our mission at the bunker."

Brock paced the floor at the front of the room. His voice softened, and then rose. "Sitting here and waiting for a catastrophe to happen...that's a fool's game, people."

Some men stood and hooted and raised their arms to the sky. Ruby was on her feet, clapping, hollering: "Right on!"

"Think of me as if I were a ship's captain. There are those of you who want to blow up the ship and the captain along with it. I know that. I didn't plan it, but I know it to be true."

"We won't let that happen, Brock! You're the man!"

Raina glanced at Sim. "What the...?" she mouthed.

"Billy, who came to help you when you had a broken hip and couldn't mow your lawn and take out the garbage? Hell, even take a shower. And Neil, who paid your electric bill last month? Jenny, who babysat your kids so you could go to work last week?"

All were shouting, pointing at Brock.

"No, no, not me folks. It was your friends here in The Group...not your neighbors, not your community, or your government. The Group!"

The crowd clapped wildly.

"I've never lied to you. I'm not going to start now." Brock rubbed his temples and moaned. "So much pressure. Pressure on the brain. It hurts, folks. Treason makes me sick." He stood tall, seemed to grow by several inches. His voice magnified, reaching a crescendo: "I've got plans. Big plans, and you're either with me or against me. Make your choice. Draw a line in the sand. We've got weeks, maybe a month, but no more. Questions are being asked. Curiosity seekers and bloodsuckers are on our heels."

Brock looked The Group over, then said softly: "Go

home now, people, and give this some thought. Dig deep, both in your pockets and your hearts. Committee and their spouses, please stick around." He waved his arm, dismissing the crowd, and row by row they exited the building.

"Ethan, wait outside," Sim said. "We won't be long."

When it was all but the chosen, Brock spoke again. The one thing he had forgotten to do was close the window, and Ethan knew it, hiding beneath it now, listening. He had promised to sit still during the meeting, but he hadn't promised not to eavesdrop.

"I heard one of you today say we're on the wrong track." Brock shoved something heavy, the podium perhaps, and it groaned as it hit the concrete floor. "If you think love is the answer, you're on a fool's mission. If you think negotiations will do the trick and cookies around the kitchen table will solve the world's problems, you're an idiot. Love won't do when you need a weapon! We need to stay focused and protect our dreams and ideas regarding the future of society and the world. We got claws and teeth, guns and grenades. Stockpiles of them." The noise that emanated from his throat sounded animalistic, only sicker, fiercer.

"Follow me! Soon! Let me hear your commitment to the cause!"

Ethan peeked in the window.

All were standing now except for Sim and Raina and a few others in the back of the Grange Hall.

Ethan watched wide-eyed and counted the people who

left the building. One, two, three. Four. Five, six.

"That's it. We're done." The man speaking was Jemma's father. "I'll sue to get my money back, count on that."

"Won't happen."

"You're crazy!"

"The money was a donation. Nonrefundable."

The discussion went on but in muffled voices, and the six disappeared into the night. Inside the Grange building, Ethan could hear Sim, but his words were not audible.

Soon Raina came to find him. "You feel okay? Can you walk home?" she asked.

"Yes. And yes."

Raina nodded her head. "Okay then. Visit Loretta, then straight home. No other side trips. We'll be there as soon as we finish up. I promise it won't be long."

She kissed her hand and blew the kiss to Ethan.

- CHAPTER 11 -

"Loretta? Pick up. Loretta, Lo-retta! This isn't funny any more. This is your mother speaking. I'm getting a bad vibe here, girlfriend. Call me."

Loretta replayed the recording. "Loretta? Pick up. Loretta, Lo-retta!"

"What, now she's trying for the mother of the year?" Loretta rolled her eyes and stared at the answering machine like she was expecting it to spit out something more substantial. Maybe a "yeow" or a "yee-haw" or a "just kidding" in cowboy drawl, or perhaps some tale spun by a new member of the club, the Greer-keteers—a new boy toy.

Cora shook her head.

"What! It's been a month, and she's barely checked in. Her weekly calls amount to diddly-squat, no more than five minutes each, and that's with me pushing for more time by babbling on about something or other. So now she's worried? Are you kidding me? What the heck," Loretta growled. She filled Toby's dog bowl with kibble and topped off his water bowl. "Come on, boy. Come and get it." Toby had followed them in the door, his growly hound-speak reaching a crescendo while he waited for his supper. "At least you stick around, don't you, boy. No commitment issues here."

"Hashtag, salty."

"Me? Salty? Don't even go there."

"At least you've got a mom. I'd give anything to have a five-minute phone call or a female-type lecture, or breakfast pop-up waffles slathered with peanut butter and jam and served on a paper plate."

Loretta cocked her head to one side. Crinkled her nose. "I'm sorry," she said.

"She loves you, Loretta. No way she doesn't. She's just peculiar in the way she shows it, that's all."

"Okay, I concede. Maybe. A little. Can we move on now, talk about something else?"

Loretta fumbled with the hot-pink envelope she'd found in the mailbox when they got home from Willow Grove. There was no return address. Her name was on it, and Cora's. First names only. She tore open the envelope and pulled out the card within. It was hot pink as well, sprinkled with glitter on a field of multi-colored daisies.

Cora looked over Loretta's shoulder, then moved on to Toby, ruffling the fur around his neck. "Hey, boy, did you miss us?"

"So. This card is an invitation. To a party at Jemma's tonight."

"No way." Cora opened the refrigerator and pulled out two colas. She popped one open and passed the other to Loretta.

"Yes, way. Eight o'clock. Pool party. The invite's a little late, but still. It could be fun."

"Don't think so," Cora said, slurping her soda.

"Come on. Ple-e-e-ase." Loretta drew the word out as long as she had breath to hold it.

"I'm not going, Loretta. There's no way I'm spending a minute, let alone a couple of hours, kissing up to Jemma. Sorry. Not happening."

"Brady will be there. Come on. I need this."

"You need what, Loretta? To be humiliated again? Those people are not your friends. You get around them and you change. You can't say no. It's like…like you mutate into some kind of wannabe. You ignore me. It's like I'm not even there when you're with those guys."

"Not true. You're my best friend. And I could care less about Jemma. It's Brady I want to see. They're not that bad, really. A little snooty. Jemma's got an attitude, but she's not horrible. This should prove it. Look." She shoved the invitation under Cora's nose. Her voice trailed from a high-pitched whine to a cat-like purr. "Ple-e-e-s-e?"

"Oh, man…really?" Cora gave her a death stare.

"What?"

"She's not the same girl we knew in elementary school, Loretta. She's worse."

"Yes, but..."

"It's more than an attitude problem, and you know it."

"We used to be friends, the three of us. Can't you just go with that and give it a chance?"

"Jemma lives in a fantasy world..."

"She baffles me. The boys like her...all of them do, including Brady. I don't believe it's her money, or her big boobs, or the parties. There's something else. What is it? I don't get it," Loretta said, throwing her hands up.

"I don't know. Whatever *it* is, your mom's got the same *gift*. If you want to know about that kind of stuff, ask her. Seriously, Loretta. Ask your mom."

"You're going to go there? *Really*? I can't believe you just said that."

+++

Loretta changed clothes several times, settling on a short jean skirt that belonged to her mother and a pink cami tank top. The heels on her cowboy boots looked worn and the toe boxes a little done in, but who cared. It was going to be dark. No one would notice.

"How do I look?"

"Like you're about to commit a sin."

"Just what I was trying to achieve."

"This is against my better judgment," Cora said, as she

helped her comb her hair and twirl it into an upsweep, using a bejeweled barrette that belonged to Greer.

Loretta collapsed her hands to her sides and scrunched her lips. "Seriously, though. I look like a fashion misfit with a country fetish."

Cora hugged her around the waist with her chin on Loretta's shoulder, staring into the floor-length mirror in Greer's bedroom. "You look beautiful. If Brady doesn't notice, he's more of an fool than I think he is."

"You're not still mad, are you? I mean, you wanna go? Right?"

"I'm not mad. Just. It bugs me that you put yourself in these positions."

Loretta sighed. "Come on. What about you? You want me to fix your hair?"

Cora held a slinky silver blouse under her chin, glanced in the mirror, then threw it on the bed alongside other rejects Loretta had tried on. "No way. I am what I am, and that's all that I am. They can deal with it or not. Peace, sister."

Loretta had at least talked her into putting on a clean set of khakis and a cute green t-shirt shouting 'SUPPORT FREE TRADE' to the world. This was Cora's new favorite cause, and she had purchased the shirt from an online store selling purses, blankets, and jewelry made by women in Guatemala and the Congo. Luckily she had brought extra clothes in her overnight backpack—something she usually didn't do.

"Let's get this over with," Cora said. "It's now or never."

Loretta texted her mother: "I'M FINE. CORA'S SPENDING THE NIGHT. NO STRESS. GET BACK TO RACHEL. HOPE THE MOVIE SHOOT IS ALL YOU HOPED IT WOULD BE. I'M OUT-Y." Out-y. Her usual sign-off seemed a bit shallow, but "I love you" was not what Loretta wanted to project at that moment.

"Let's go, buddy," Loretta said, settling Toby on his pillow in the kitchen. As an afterthought, she scanned the cupboard, choosing her mother's favorite porcelain tea plate as a snack dish for his dog biscuits. "Hmm. Works for me," she giggled.

Outside Loretta turned on the drip system to the flower pots on the porch and the vegetable garden out back. The mist settled on her face like dew off a willow tree and smelled like an old rubber boot. A brittle drip emitter broke into pieces in her hand. She reached for a pocket knife on a nearby stump, whittled one end of the connecting tube to a point and shoved it into the main line, hoping another repair might keep the old irrigation system alive a few days longer. So many things around their house were jerry-rigged. Do-it-yourself-videos on the Internet had pretty much kept their home livable. Glue and spackle, caulk and duct tape—she and her mother had done it all. When the toilet got clogged last winter, they used a borrowed shop vac to suck the water until a pencil popped out, clearing the trap. Who knew how the pencil got there. Loretta hadn't done it, but Greer wasn't admitting guilt either. Aliens, most likely. That was the Duvall standard for unresolved issues regarding anything they wanted to mask over and leave to chance. The oven door hung catawampus, low and to the right. The window in her mother's bedroom would finally open, thanks to a long string of cuss words and a can of WD-40. A brick held the pantry door closed. It came from a planter box started last spring, but now it was summer. The bricks were there, and two sacks of mortar that had been watered so often by the sprinkler they had turned to hardened cement. There also sat the wisteria bush Greer had intended to grow, leafless and as dead as the idea to plant it in the first place. She was in the habit of putting grave markers on her unfinished projects, kind of a reminder of dreams that had fizzled or plans that had failed. Her reasons were simple and Loretta knew them by heart. "The idea may have died, but the intention didn't. All that creativity deserves a proper burial, to my way of thinking."

Loretta had been missing her mother all day, and this didn't help. "Hold on," she told Cora. "Be right back." In the house, she dumped Toby's dog biscuits into his food dish, washed and dried the porcelain tea plate, and placed it with the others back in the cupboard.

+++

The light was dimming over the homes on her street but it was not dark yet, so they decided to walk to Jemma's.

It wasn't that far and even when the party was over, they knew they would feel safe about walking home. A family of quail scurried across the pavement and then launched into a mini-flight toward the field at the end of the road. Turning to the left at the end of the block was like entering a new zip code. Large homes on huge lots glittered with bright light from bay windows and outdoor pathway lanterns, recessed deck lighting, and backlit beveled door glass.

Cora walked behind Loretta as they followed the curving slate driveway to Jemma's house, the last on the cul-de-sac of Raven Hills. The main house, a beautiful combination of richly textured fieldstones was built villa-style, high and wide, with perfectly manicured gardens bordering a lawn the size of a football field. The porch in front of the house was like a grand hall, with a vaulted ceiling and bronze pendant lighting. Like stone-faced palace guards, two marble pillars flanked each side of the doorway. No matter how many times Loretta had seen Jemma's home, she felt in awe of its regal appeal.

"Cora, you afraid?"

"No, just a little nervous."

Loretta wondered how long Cora could keep up her stoic image while facing Jemma and friends.

Cora's pace had slowed to a shuffle; she was obviously in no hurry to arrive at the party. "S.O.O.F.," she said warily.

"Swear on our friendship...about what?"

"That if I give you this signal," Cora said, clearing her

throat, "Brady or no Brady, we'll scoot."

"S.O.O.F. Don't worry, okay?" Loretta took a deep breath and rang the bell.

Jemma answered. "Well, well, nice to see you, even if you *are* a little late." She turned and, with her arm, ushered them into the house.

The inside was a continuation of the outside: an entrance hall, wood-vaulted ceilings, and tile floor that extended into the living room and open kitchen. Beyond, on the other side of a double set of French doors, were a courtyard, patio, and swimming pool, an outdoor barbecue, and a movie theater, set up tonight to play video games.

Loretta's first instinct was to turn and run, but she didn't. And neither did Cora. Something came to mind her mother once said, after Loretta had been teased for having only one parent. "Jemma's veins run on the same fuel as yours do, Loretta. She steps on a nail, she's going to bleed, same as you." Good advice, but then it got ruined because Greer followed up with: "You got the best example of someone who can yawn away a bully right in front of you, Lo-retta. Ta-da, look at me!" And the dancing commenced, and Loretta had laughed until her insides hurt, forgetting completely what Greer had just told her. Until now, when that old conversation popped like a bubble in front of her nose.

Steeling herself, she followed Jemma into the backyard. Kids were milling about everywhere. A large group gathered near an outdoor kitchen with a countertop filled with chips, dips, cookies, and a bucket containing soft drinks. A beer keg. People were laughing and eating, and only a few glanced up when Loretta walked onto the patio.

"Hey, Loretta, Cora, how you doing?" Joan Bashley called out.

Sweet girl, Loretta thought. *Always has been.*

"Well, look who's here. Nice that you both could make it." The gleam in Pierce's eyes made Loretta uncomfortable.

Brady stood on the other side of the pool with a group of guys on his basketball team. He smiled at her and waved. This was more than Loretta had hoped for, and her heart lightened a bit. He motioned for one of his friends to come with him, then walked around the diving board and to the outdoor kitchen.

"Something to eat?" Loretta asked Cora.

"Nah, I think I'll hang here on the patio."

"Come on, we haven't eaten dinner. Maybe just a little."

"Okay, sure. I guess I could eat something."

"I'm sure you could," Jemma teased, as she walked past them.

"Why did she invite us, if all we're going to get from her is sarcasm?" Cora asked.

"Let's give it a bit. Maybe it'll get better."

"Seriously, help yourselves," Jemma said, waving from within the circle of girls that now surrounded her.

Loretta smiled at Cora. "See?" she mouthed. She took

a step, concentrating on her feet, her boots, afraid she might trip and cause a scene. The farther she walked, the more her shoulders slumped in an attempt to make herself smaller.

Jemma broke free of her friends and walked toward them.

"I'm going to check out the sound system," Cora said, nodding toward the stereo components housed near the bar. "I'll meet you at the food tables when you're done kissing ass."

Loretta raised a finger, intending to ask Cora to stay, but Jemma interrupted before she could get a word out.

"So, you brought Cora," Jemma said.

"Yeah, I did. Cora's name was on the invitation, re-member?" Loretta told her. "Anyway, she's cool. You should come hang out with us some time. Like you did when we were kids."

"No can do. My parents are on a rampage. It sucks." She took a sip from the paper cup she held in her hand, shivering as if drinking something bitter. "I can have friends over here, but that's it. No more sleepovers away from home. No study sessions at friend's houses. Nothing like that at all."

"Seriously? Why?"

"It's all a bunch of *shit*," Jemma slurred. "Don't take it personally, *Lo*-retta. I'm not supposed to talk about it, but it's a Group thing, a *Committee* thing, kind of *hush-hush*, or so say, my parents." She giggled and motioned toward the house. "Didn't you notice my "bodyguards" when you came in? Such a joke, right? Like two old biddies can keep me clean and sober." She took another sip from her paper cup.

It was true. Loretta hadn't noticed the women before, but now, looking through the picture windows into the living room, she could see Esmina, the librarian, and Ruby, from the deli, sitting in recliner chairs and watching television.

"Kind of crappy, right? My parents are *so* controlling."

"No way. I don't know much about The Group or the Committee, as you call them, but your parents are great. Your mom is always there for you. She takes you with her wherever she goes, and your dad, well, he's at every school function. I've never known him to miss a play or a volleyball game or a band practice, even."

"Yeah, well. My parents hover. Every minute of every day. And like I said, it kind of sucks." Jemma shrugged her shoulders and smiled her perfect smile. "Well, better go mingle," she said, flipping her bangs off her face a little less delicately than usual. "See to Cora, will you?" she added, stiffly. "Make sure there are cookies left for the rest of my guests."

Cora looked up as if she'd heard her name. She fidgeted with her coke can, then turned and walked away from the bar and toward the pool.

The pool was kidney-shaped, and on the far side, a waterfall rippled from cascading granite, resembling the toppled stones in creeks and rivers surrounding Lone Pine. Three round tables covered with lavender tablecloths were to the right of the pool. On each table was a rose-colored candle in a clear glass jar. The candles were lit and glowing. The air smelled like vanilla and cinnamon, and when Loretta ate one of the cookies she'd chosen she tasted the same fragrances that she smelled. She sat in a chair at one of the tables and motioned Cora over.

A few of the kids were playing with a karaoke machine, singing old tunes they knew by heart. Pierce walked out of the garage, carrying a pitcher, drinking from it freely. At the karaoke machine, he handed the pitcher to Brady and took the mic. The girls were egging him on. Pierce slicked back his hair and chose his song.

"Kill it, Pierce! Do it, brother!"

The soundtrack to Aerosmith's, "Walk this Way" blared from the stereo system.

"Check it out! He's a legend in his own mind!"

Pierce was going for it; jumping, strutting, and gyrating like Stephen Tyler.

"Dude looks like a lady," someone yelled.

Pierce dropped the mic and flew at the kid. He slapped him in the face and punched him in the stomach, sending him face-first to the ground. Pierce jumped on him again, hitting, pinching, and gouging. The table where Loretta and Cora were sitting tumbled sideways, Cora jumping one way, Loretta the other. Brady grabbed Pierce by the neck of his shirt, jerking backward until he had Pierce restrained.

"Cool it, man. That's enough!"

Already, Ruby was banging on the window. Pointing her finger at Pierce.

Pierce jerked his arm free, but Brady grabbed him again.

Brady scanned the crowd. "We need a diversion. Now. Hey, Loretta! What you got, girl? Show us your stuff!"

Loretta's gut flipped, and her mind grew foggy. "Oh no, I don't sing. Only in the shower. And maybe in my truck, you know."

"Come on." Jemma had the mic now and shoved it in Loretta's face.

"No, really, please." Loretta pushed it away.

"Okay. So how about movie trivia. I know you got that in you. How about…give us something from *Twilight* or *New Moon*. Who was the actor that played Jasper Cullen? How about Emmett Cullen? Who were you rooting for, Team Edward, or Team Jacob?"

Jemma's breath stung Loretta's eyes. It was not vanilla and cinnamon. More like homemade margaritas.

"No. Please. Don't," Loretta begged.

"Oh, come on. I've heard about this big talent of yours for years."

Loretta could see Cora poolside, but the circle of people between them was growing.

"Don't you guys have anything better to do? You're jerks, really!" Cora hollered. "No means no. Listen to her words. Leave her alone."

Pierce twisted free of Brady's grip, ran towards Cora,

and elbowed her into the pool. "God. You're such a freak," he yelled. "Loser. Give it a break."

Cora splashed and sputtered and made her way to the side. Brady ran to help her, shouting at Pierce. "What are you thinking, man? That was low, even for you." He offered Cora his hand and pulled her out of the water.

"What? Look at her! She doesn't know whether to save herself or swallow her pretzels," Pierce said, laughing. "You're swinging for the wrong team, Brady. You should have let her flounder."

Loretta pushed past Jemma and toward Cora. Jemma tried to stop her. "I didn't know it would go this far. I'm sorry, I really am."

Loretta turned back, and this time she was in Jemma's face. She opened her mouth, but nothing came out.

A few kids were laughing, but the majority looked stunned. Loretta pulled Cora free of Brady and walked with her to the pathway, the street, and home.

+++

Ethan was sitting on the lawn, waiting for them. Loretta barely looked at him, and he was on his feet, arms at his sides, fists clenched. "What happened? Where have you been?"

"Not now, Ethan, really."

"Jemma. Party. Pierce. Need I say more?" Cora said.

Ethan flicked his fingers and scowled.

Just then, Toby raced out the doggie door and across the yard, pawing at the bushes by the fence, barking frantically.

The nearby houses were dark and the curtains were drawn.

"Toby, come!" Loretta called. A shadowy figure walked across the neighbor's yard, turning back to look at her as he reached the street.

"Someone you know?" asked Cora.

"I can't tell. Could be Mr. Gorman's son."

"Creepy," said Cora. "Let's go inside."

- CHAPTER 12 -

*O*nce again, Ethan couldn't sleep. Nightmares, night terrors—whatever his parents wanted to call them—had been a regular occurrence lately. In the weeks since Sim and Brock had argued at the bunker, he had had many, always climaxing with a replay of Brock's threat: "You've got to do something about that boy of yours, Sim. The kid's issues, his quirks, could disrupt our plans in a major way. We've had this discussion before. Make arrangements. Be done with this."

Sim's apology and his excuses for Brock's tirade were shallow and rambling, and left Ethan more fearful than ever. "This is nothing for you to worry about, Ethan. Your mother and I are handling everything as best we can. Please understand, Brock wants an optimal outcome for The Group as a whole. His red flags are a bit...much...they have to do with long-term survival...it's not you personally...trust me. Besides, there are options we can take to address his concerns in a manner that's fitting and appropriate for everyone.

"We love you. That's the bottom line."

Since the incident, Ethan had tried his best to stay busy by doing chores, helping around the house and in the yard. He even spent time at Granny Noleen's, raking leaves, brushing Dakota, cleaning stalls—almost everything but messing with the chickens. He got up early, went to bed late, and made sure his parents knew where he was and with whom, but even so, there were questions.

"How long were you at Noleen's, Ethan? What did you do when you left there? Did you come straight home or stop in town? Are you sure there's nothing else we should know?"

Ethan felt as if his insides were being scraped raw, a slow and steady ache that grew worse day by day. Every morning before he left his room, he took a clean sheet of paper and a pencil from his desk drawer and wrote his daily list of buzz words and phrases: One. Stay focused. Two. Pay attention. Three. Smile. Four. Trust your instincts. Five. Remember everything. When he was finished, he placed the pencil back in the drawer, folded the paper and tucked it into his shirt pocket, easy access should he need a reminder later on.

He bought a composition book at the drugstore and stashed it in his backpack alongside his older, well-used note-book. His habit of journaling had started in third grade, and he remembered well the very savvy special-education teacher who recognized his love of language and who encouraged his keeping a diary of vocabulary words, thoughts, and feelings toward his parents and classmates. The composition book attracted Ethan straight away; its thick black-and-white cardboard cover was both durable and practical, providing a sturdy enough writing surface to satisfy his needs anytime and anywhere.

This morning Ethan copied one of his mother's favorite affirmations: *Earth, help me to remember kindness as the days grow dark, and the mountains weep.* After he had written it, he read it several times, as he loved the essence of the wording and the musical feel of the phrasing as it slid past his lips. The next few pages were left blank, to be used later for daily schedules and lists. On page ten, he recorded what had happened at the bunker, and after that, documented Cora's experience at Jemma's party. He concluded by noting:

Pierce is a bully. He is most obnoxious when he is with his squad of friends, his cousin Jack, or his new buddy, Frey. He shoots animals and harasses birds. He's particularly rude to Cora. BAD NEWS.

Something positive: He owns a truck. Old. But it runs well, better than his father's beater Silverado.

Ethan tried to think of more good things to write, but his mind kept stalling on an image of Pierce, sitting in the corner in the conference room at the bunker, watching Frey attack Sim.

Instead, he wrote:

Note: Pierce has been invited to at least one Committee meeting. Why?

Confession: I have not been invited to any meetings. But I have eavesdropped numerous times on conversations I was not supposed to hear.

Ethan slipped his journal into his backpack. He checked the time on his watch and glanced at the wall calendar above his desk, verifying his plans for the day: *Monday. Meet up with Loretta and Cora. Go to Granny Noleen's.*

He had been up since dawn, showered, and tidied his room. He was dressed for farm work: faded blue jeans, an old red t-shirt with the sleeves cut off, thick socks and work boots. He viewed himself in the mirror, shaved the stubble on his cheeks, finger-combed his hair, put on extra deodorant as a preventative measure, and flapped his arms to dry it.

In the hallway, he stood with his finger on the light switch but decided not to flip it. His parents' bedroom door was ajar, and if they were still sleeping, he preferred not to wake them. He tiptoed into the kitchen and turned on the fluorescents, waiting while the overheads hummed and buzzed and came alive. Thanks to his mom, there was no need to rummage through cupboards, as his favorite breakfast foods were easily accessible. He chose what he wanted and arranged his meal mindfully on the table: an eight-ounce glass of milk to the left of his plate; muffin in the center of the plate beside but not touching the dollop of peanut butter; fork to the right; the banana on a napkin to the side. He took a sip of his milk, peeled his banana, slathered it with peanut butter, and ate it. He took a bite of the muffin but spit it out, shivering. Too dry. And there were raisins. He stood and carried the muffin into the half-bath off the kitchen, tossed it in the toilet, and flushed. "Down you go," he said, as it swirled and sailed into the trap. He smiled as he watched it go, knowing this way he wouldn't break the leftover rule, and Raina couldn't lecture him about ignoring the merits of bran fiber.

+++

The sun was creeping over the horizon as he left the house. Tree branches resembled long gray fingers, coyotes howled and the neighbor's dog growled in response. He could hear his own footfall, his rubber-bottomed boots crunching gravel, riding asphalt and plodding along the cement sidewalks in turn. He checked his watch and was half an hour early when he reached Main Street. The plan was that he would meet up with Loretta and Cora in the parking lot at the Penny Saver Market. Since his bike was trash, he would ride with them to Willow Grove. Today there was a rock pile to move, and a new fence and shelter to build that would house a baby goat Earl had purchased for Pansy.

The driver of a Kenworth Semi flipped his Jake brake and pulled the eighteen-wheeler into the vacant lot near Carmen's Tamale Truck. He opened the door of the cab, hopped to the ground, and signaled – "One, please." Ethan's mouth watered, and he wished he'd thought ahead of time to skip breakfast at home and bring money to buy one of

Carmen's chicken tamales with green sauce on the side.

The air was warm even at this early hour. Ethan raised his t-shirt and rolled it high onto his chest, enjoying the sensation of a slight breeze on his bare skin. His leg muscles were tightly strung, and he loved the feeling of control that gave him. If a dog were to give chase, or a speeding car were to drive too closely, or a random bird should attack from above, the odds were in his favor that he could run, jump, or backpedal out of the way.

The log bench in front of the Penny Saver was chain-saw-fitted back to shoulders, butt to back, and knees to pavement. Ethan wondered how one learned to use a chain-saw so skillfully and decided that one day he would inquire about taking lessons. He sat down, noting that by doing so, he was in a perfect position for people-watching, one of his favorite activities. The light in the Eastside Deli blinked on; a liquored-up man poured around the street corner and tugged on the locked door of the Iron Gate; a woman in much the same condition soon followed him, staring at the neon light fixture in the bar window as it flickered and blinked the message CLOSED. The two kissed outside the entryway for a long while, then stumbled arm-in-arm down the street.

As his eyes followed the progress of the stumbling couple, Ethan noticed Paiute Bill near the north end of the Penny Saver. Bill sat cross-legged and slouched against the building, mouth open, and hat askew, his long braids shadowed in the new dawn light. As he slept, his arm jerked, he hooted once, and exhaled a half snore. There was an open quart of alcohol on the ground beside him. Ethan thought of waking him but chose to let him snooze. Instead, he picked up the bottle of gin, nestling it among the wilted produce and discarded packing debris in the garbage bin behind the store.

Soon Bill's snoring hit a smooth pace, a low pitched *zzz zzz* of wheezy snuffles. Before long, though, there was a shift in his rhythm, a series of hoots and puffs and snorts. With that, Brock's voice crept into Ethan's head, flat and calm and controlled at first, then staccato and tense and raucous. "You gotta do something about that boy of yours, Sim. The kid's *issues,* his *quirks,* could disrupt our plans in a major way." This hurt Ethan's ears, and the intensity of the noise throbbed inside his head. His arm muscles twitched, and he flicked his fingers and shifted uneasily on the bench.

"Ethan, you ready?" Cora hollered, climbing out of Loretta's truck. "Sorry, we're so late, man. Gotta go."

Cora's call woke Bill, and he struggled to stand and gain his footing.

"It's gone," Ethan told him, shrugging his shoulders, as Bill scoured the ground for his bottle.

Bill stumbled forward. Ethan ran ahead and lowered Old Blue's tailgate.

"Got him okay?" Loretta asked from inside the cab.

"Yeah," Cora said. She grabbed Bill by the seat of the pants and pushed as he scrambled into the truck bed. Ethan hopped from foot to foot, then grabbed Bill's hand, pulled him forward, and slammed the tailgate. He lunged for the passenger door and opened it for Cora, and they both climbed inside.

"Let's hit it," Loretta said. "We're late."

Almost immediately, Cora began talking about the party again. Ethan listened on the first go-through and was mildly distracted during the second, but by the third time, he was thinking only of the Telephone Game—whispering a word in someone's ear, hearing it morph and change. *Pool. Rule. Cruel. Ghoul.*

"Ethan, you seem distracted," Loretta said.

"A little."

"What's up?"

"I have to get back in the tunnels."

"No. Are you crazy? Why?" Loretta asked, in a tone both plea and protest.

Ethan flicked his fingers, mumbling: "I've got to tell you something." His voice rose an octave and sped up accordingly. "The Group...The Committee...They, we, it's..."

Loretta turned her attention from the road to Ethan. "Deep breath, man. Spit it out, slowly this time."

"Something bad is going to happen. They said...I mean, I heard some things..."

"Wait." Cora turned down the radio. "If you're

talking about those meetings at the Grange Hall, I already think they're creepy. I mean, posters with atomic bomb watermarks?"

"Yes, the Grange Hall meetings, The Group...one and the same. My parents are a part of The Group, and Ruby, and a lot of other people."

Once Ethan started he couldn't stop. The story gushed from his lips. "In the beginning, our meetings were held in the park or at the river. People brought food, organic stuff, a lot of fruit and veggies, homemade bread, and cakes, and pies. My dad always called the outing a 'get-together of like-minded folks.' People laughed and played games, but there were serious discussions too, about sustainability and environmental issues. About family. Kids. 'The challenges of growing up in modern times,' Dad would say."

"My mom and I came a few times, but when Brock moved to town and joined The Group, she lost interest," Loretta said. "For some reason, Mom didn't like him. She never talked much about her reasons for quitting...but she did say the guy gave her the creeps."

"It's funny that my dad never showed interest in those meetings," Cora said. "He's usually so supportive of anything proactive, environmentally speaking."

"I think my mom turned him off to the idea. At least, I remember a conversation between the two of them about your parents, Ethan, and the others...about Brock."

"Where was I?" Cora asked.

"We were on a picnic. You had your nose buried in a book."

"Seriously?"

"Big surprise." Loretta chuckled, and Cora fluttered her eyes, smiling.

"So Ethan, what's Brock's story? Cora asked. "What the heck's going on?"

"At first, Brock was listening more than talking, participating just like everybody else. Then one day, he started telling stories about snipers and bombings and talked about immigration and homegrown terrorists. He said that we are 'one group among a chosen few' and warned that we should protect ourselves against outside influences and prepare for violent attacks and events that are beyond our ability to control."

Ethan rubbed his temples, thinking of instances when Brock soap-boxed people to a boiling point by sermonizing about issues that were meaningful to them, like climate change, global warming, GMOs, food additives, and poisons being imported in food, clothing, and toys from China and other parts of the world. "They are conquering our country without using a gun," he would say, almost tearfully. "It's a planned takeover from the outside in. They're a major holder of our national debt, lending freely but keeping score, snatching up homes, acreage, and public lands as if they were properties on a Monopoly board. And they're laughing all the way to the bank."

Ethan concentrated on all he had seen and heard as he described what happened next: "Conspiracy theories were downloaded from the Internet and read aloud at meetings. The more Brock talked, the bigger he grew. His lectures punched holes in the philosophy of The Group. The whole thing felt...greasy." Ethan quivered. "He talked about stockpiles of caskets in secret locations within the United States, government spying, drones, eventually tattooing citizens with information-driven barcodes. Terrorists.

"He goes on and on, and my head gets so full!" Ethan hit the dashboard with his fist. "Stop the truck! I have to get out!"

Loretta swerved to the side of the road and jammed the gear to park. Ethan stumbled from the truck as he opened the door. He paced the berm of the road, still talking. Cora crawled out and braced herself against the truck bed. Loretta did the same, leaning in, watching Bill resettle himself into sleep.

"A while back, the Committee was formed," said Ethan. "Talk changed from homegrown potatoes and heirloom vegetable and flower seeds to stockpiling 'doomsday supplies' like water filters, cooking systems, first-aid kits, emergency food, and water. Rad stickers. Nuke alert kits. Knives. Guns. Ammo."

Then Ethan told Loretta and Cora about the bunker. As he said the words and called it what it was, he broke out in sweat. The word *betrayal* stuck in his throat.

"Eerie. There's got to be some good movie trivia for this one, Loretta." Cora's eyes resembled cat's-eye marbles, glazed over and alien in shape and size.

"*Conspiracy Theory*," Loretta nearly whispered.

"You're talking about the movie, right?" Cora asked as if she knew what movie trivia was coming. "Perfect...what you got?"

Loretta took a deep breath and let it out slowly. She recited: "There's this New York City Cab Driver, right? He's all into conspiracy theories and believes NASA is trying to kill the president and that militia groups...the survivalist-type guys on the right-wing side, are really U.N. troops, ready to take things over when the time is right. The thing is, some of the stuff he believes is true. The bad guys in the CIA find him, hold him captive, and feed him drugs. The poor guy is ruined, no matter how you look at it."

"Good Lord. You had to come up with that one?"

Ethan flicked his fingers. "I've got to go back into those tunnels," he said.

"I need to tell my dad about this," Cora countered.

"No! I need to get inside the bunker, Cora. Please. If you tell your dad, if anyone else finds out, Brock will deny everything, blame me for...whatever, and have time to hide any evidence that could prove him guilty of deceiving The Group."

"And there lies another question," Loretta said. "Why is Brock after Ethan so hard? I mean, theft, vandalism, really?"

Cora shook her head. "Okay," she said to Ethan. "But only if you let Loretta and me come with you. Only if we work as a team, and if we find anything illegal or potentially harmful, we tell my dad. Deal?"

"I can't agree…"

"Deal?" Cora's cheeks were puffed beyond their usual chunkiness.

"All right," Ethan stammered.

"Say it."

"Okay, deal!" Ethan counted to calm his nerves. "One, two, three, four…"

"It's going to take some convincing. What excuse can we give Noleen?" Loretta asked.

"We may not need to tell her," Ethan said.

"No way, she knows all, sees all," Cora said.

"Down in the tunnels…there is a side tunnel…"

"I remember," Loretta said.

"Between Willow Grove and the bunker, in the same direction that tunnel would run, is a venting system of some sort, at least that's what I believe, now that I've seen the tunnel itself," Ethan said. "I found metal pipes sticking out of the ground, nearly buried by dirt and leaves. Close by is a small cave, another entrance to the tunnels, I think."

Ethan remembered the day he had discovered the pipes. He had had a confrontation with Brock at the bunker and had simply slunk away, his feet gliding over the ground until he stumbled over a metal stub, the rusty lip of it catching his boot and cutting his hand as he fell. He'd had to get a tetanus shot—at his mother's insistence—though he didn't tell her where and on what he'd gotten cut.

"I think those pipes may drop into that section of the side tunnel. I could feel, like, cool air on my face when I was standing in front of it, and there were weird odors too… things you shouldn't smell underground."

"Tobacco," Cora offered.

"Yeah," Loretta agreed. "I smelled that too."

Ethan loved Loretta for so many things, and Cora too, but the fact that they listened to him, agreed with him even, felt good. Their voices were thoughtful and responsive. Not like others that held a choppy-trill or sharp-edged wallop and made him want to cover his ears and run away. "This isn't going to be easy," he said. "They're watching the bunker all the time. But…"

"But what?" Loretta asked.

"But next Sunday, there's a big barbecue. Attendance is mandatory. There'll only be one guard at the bunker. Old Man Bale. And he shouldn't be a problem. Sim says he sleeps on duty. He stations himself in the television room and comes out when it's time to go home."

"Just one guard? You're sure?" Cora asked.

"Yes. Brock wants everyone at the barbecue. I don't know why, but he's pushing big time."

"Pushing what?" Loretta asked.

"I'm not sure. I don't know. I'm just not sure." Ethan

shook his head and started to pace again. His mind whirled with half-formed thoughts.

"Okay then," Cora quickly agreed. "Sunday. We'll go on Sunday. That gives us six days to make a plan."

- CHAPTER 13 -

At Willow Grove, Pansy cuddled her new baby goat, its floppy Nubian ears bouncing side to side; Earl groomed Dakota at the tie rail beside the tool shed; Yoshi read a book in the shade of a cottonwood tree. As Loretta pulled Old Blue into the driveway they all looked up, but no one waved. Noleen never broke her stride with even a sideways glance. Eyes to the ground, she swung a long machete with quick flicks of her wrist, clearing a wide swath of weeds and brush. Instead of her flowered skirt and apron, she wore faded blue bib overalls, with her usual mud-crusted work boots. An old white t-shirt exposed her arms, more sinewy and muscled than seemed natural for someone her age.

"Uh, where's the fanfare?" Loretta asked, overwhelmed by a sudden melancholy. She looked around the now-familiar yard, wondering how she'd come to expect a gleeful welcome. She had fallen so naturally into a routine that felt so comfortable, with people who only weeks ago she barely knew.

Ethan jumped out of the truck and ran toward Earl, grabbing a curry comb off a bench beside the tie rail. Dakota snorted and shook his head and nudged Ethan hello as he began brushing his neck and withers. Even strokes, firm, purposeful. Therapeutic, Loretta knew.

She closed her eyes, giving herself a moment to relax and transition from Ethan's bizarre stories to her upcoming tasks at Willow Grove. Beneath her eyelids, detailed images of her *uncles* intensified her gloominess, faces she'd known and cared about, real people who had become faded memories like the grayed-out image of her father in the worn-out frame. She shivered, wondering how many others might come and go from her life, including losses that would be harder to take, like maybe Noleen, or Earl, or Pansy. Yoshi. Ethan. Cora?

"There's humor in this somewhere," said Cora, interrupting Loretta's thoughts. "Us. Here. Becoming chummy with Noleen and clan." Her neck extended turtle-like out of her shirt as if she wanted to inhale the day in one big gulp. "I love it. Imagine what the haters would say." She giggled, breaking the tension as if she had snapped a barbed wire fence with a pair of wire cutters.

Loretta didn't speak, because what she was thinking might pour out of her mouth, and she would say that she wanted to go home and back to bed. That she wanted to spend the day playing Frisbee with Toby and watering her *own* garden, heading to the creek to take her shoes off and wade in the water, sunbathe and do summer things, kid things, instead of worrying herself over grown-up decisions and choices. She hadn't intended to *care* about Noleen and the others, and it terrified her now because she did. Silently she stewed over Ethan's mysterious spy mission and wondered how his plan to investigate the bunker would affect them all.

Cora crossed her arms and tapped her foot on the floorboard. "So what are you planning on doing? Sitting in this truck all day?"

"If I need somebody to criticize me, I'll call my mom," Loretta fired back.

"Oh. Wow. *So* pissy." Cora glared at her as she climbed out of the truck and slammed the door. "And by the way, thanks heaps. You're comparing me to your mom? Really? Besides, we're halfway through summer. Why hold on to something until it rusts, Loretta? What the heck good does that do?" She turned and huffed away, beelining for Ethan. Loretta looked down at her chest and rubbed the place between her breasts where her heart sat. A familiar tightness gripped her there and she tried to massage it away. Her history with heartburn was a lengthy one. The first time she used fruit-flavored Tums was at her doctor's recommendation when she was in the fourth grade. Her mother was away at work, and she'd been staying with Cora. During

Greer's absence were a school play and STAR testing, and Loretta had broken her left arm after a fall off a neighbor's trampoline. She'd gone through bottles of the antacid since and should buy stock in the company, her mother often teased. "Lo-retta, darlin', you're sensitive to every shift in the wind. Make lemonade out of lemons, that's my motto." Tickling fingers, dancing eyes, and a stupid song about crazy love or blue-tick hounds, beat-up trucks and dead-end roads characteristically followed this type of banter.

"Mama. Come. Home." Loretta blinked back tears and searched the sky as if she would find a reason there for her angst. She sunk her head against the steering wheel, feeling lonelier than ever and far removed from everything, even herself. The rumble of the engine, the vibration of the steering wheel against her forehead, and heat from the floorboard reminded her that the truck was still running. She reached over and killed the ignition, and Old Blue disputed her command with a buck and a series of groans.

A glint of light crossed Loretta's face, and she raised her hand to shade her eyes. From somewhere nearby, a humming pierced the gloom, and then the humming became a song. *"Gotta live it like you love it, gotta give it a chance..."*

Pansy stood beside the truck's window, grinning so wide it looked as if her face might split. *"Gotta live it like you love it, gotta give it a chance, sing yourself forward, give it up to the dance,"* she sang. Her cheeks were as pink as strawberry ice cream. Her skin was talcum-dusted, and she smelled of yeast, like bread dough, rising. "Come, dear, come to Pansy. *Da-den –do-wha…*"

Loretta opened the door and slumped out of the truck.

"There, there, Loretta Lynn. What you need, dear girl, is a cookie and some milk." Pansy kissed her baby goat on the nose and set her down, then helped Loretta to the porch and to Granny Noleen's rocker.

"Pansy, darlin', the cure for all ills, to your way of thinking, is always sugar." Noleen teetered up the steps, rubbing her right hip.

She felt Loretta's forehead and Loretta drew back, as childish visions came to mind of bony witch's fingers, dungeons, and stolen kids.

"You're as clammy as a snail in a sauna, girl. When's the last time you ate something worth talkin' about, eh?"

"We had donuts this morning."

Noleen wagged her finger in the air.

Loretta forgot about the food question and backpedaled some. "Pansy, you called me Loretta Lynn. How'd you know my middle name?"

"It's a small town, no more, no less," Noleen spouted.

"We've known your mama a long time," Earl added. "Since before you were born."

"Wait. What?"

"Like Noleen said, it's a small town," said Pansy.

Loretta reached for the glass of cold milk and the plate of sliced apples Pansy brought her. Each apple slice was decorated with raisin eyes tooth-picked into place and a broad peanut-butter smile. "Oddly familiar," she said, looking squint-eyed at Noleen.

Bill poured over the tailgate of the truck, wobbled toward the tool shed, and fell to a squat beside Yoshi.

"I'm sorry," Loretta said, directing her gaze at Cora. "I didn't mean. I'm so...I'm not usually so..."

"Grumpy?" Cora said, smiling.

"What's done is done. Let's hear no more of it." Noleen's words came out as a growl but had no menace to them.

"It's just. My mom..." Loretta frowned, transforming her face with an uncooperative pucker. "She's kind of gone a lot. And I guess sometimes I get a little upset about it."

Yoshi nodded. "You were always an introspective child. Even as a baby, you had this look on your face, as if you were trying to make sense of the world around you." He grinned, raising his left arm and grabbing his forearm with his right hand, stretching his shoulder muscles.

"You knew me when I was a baby?"

"We did." Yoshi finished his yoga pose, right arm up, left hand grabbing his right forearm and stretching. "Noleen babysat for your mother quite often back then," he said.

"Why didn't I know this? I don't understand."

Noleen stiffened, set her mouth in a pucker. "It don't matter much, really," she said. "Your mama had her reasons for not telling you, I suppose."

"But why did she stop coming? I mean, she's never

mentioned this at all."

"We agreed to disagree and part ways, is all," Noleen said, her voice graveling up as she gained momentum.

"A long time ago, Noleen ran a daycare. Your mother had her own ideas about coming and going," said Earl. "Noleen called her on it, and that didn't set well. Neither of them was at fault. It just ended when it ended, and no one was worse for wear."

Noleen cleared her throat and threw him a look. "Your mama called last night," she said.

"She called here? Why? Was she checking up on me?"

"Checking *up* on you and checking *in* on you are two different things," said Yoshi.

Noleen cleared her throat, and said, "I'll spit this out once, then we're done with it. She tries hard, that one. Works her tail to the bone. She helped out around here when you were little, doing every odd job she could think of to keep food on your table."

Loretta fixed her eyes on the old woman sitting next to her on the porch and felt a quiver in her chest to match the buzz in her brain. So when she was little, Noleen was a major presence in her world? Another omission to her life story, a missing puzzle piece? This was hard to believe, but somehow it rang true.

Noleen continued: "After Atom took off and left her, your mama never looked back. She thought he was, or could have been, *something special*—but she also knew his future was in Nashville. Besides, she had a new kind of love growing inside her, and that seemed to be enough. She got a job at the Penny Saver and put herself through beauty school. Worked for Darla at the Clip and Curl Salon for eight years before that movie crew filming some cowboy flick, I've forgotten the name...anyways, their starlet needed a hairdresser on account of hers had quit...Rachel Maxim...a pain in the butt even then, if I recall. Your mama had done side work for film crews before so her name came up, and getting the job was the luck of the draw, or not, depending on how you look on it." Noleen pulled a handkerchief from the pocket of her overalls and wiped the corners of her mouth. She ran her gnarled fingers over the sagging flesh of her cheeks as if contemplating what she wanted to say next. "I don't often go on so much," she said. "Tires a person. Anyways, might as well spit out the rest, 'fore I give in to the heat.

"Greer never took no help from no one, did it all herself. Never asked for nothing, no welfare, no charity, and that's a big deal in my book. Only thing that turned her head now and again was being in love with love, hoping for, wanting more, seeing them films being made, all with handsome princes and fairy-tale endings." She wiped her forehead this time.

"Bling," Loretta said. "Mom calls any fanciful thing bling. Love or what comes from it. Doesn't matter. She always tells me, 'Reach for the brass ring, Loretta, reach for the bling.'" She rolled her eyes as she said this.

"Bling," Noleen said, repeating the word as she thought about it for a while. "That's a good one, yep. It fits right fine. Greer goes breathless over shiny baubles and assumes them into promises not one of her men has meant to keep. Only person did her any good was crazy Tom Perkins, a Southern California real estate agent whose commission included fringe benefits not mentioned in the contract. Sold your mom a house super-cheap, signed it over lock, stock, and barrel. She thought he was *a keeper.* Bought a dress. Came out here asking about flowers and such for decorating at her wedding. Had you dolled up cute as I've ever seen. This was before Tom admitted to having a wife in Anaheim and two kids he wasn't about to leave fatherless." Noleen swatted at a fly with enough force to knock it off the planet.

"She mentioned him once. There's a grave marker in our yard. An old broken pot, lava rocks in a pile, a short wooden plank with the words 'Slick Tom' carved into it."

"That'd be him."

"She said he was a rat."

"That'd be him."

"I thought he was a pet rat."

"He was a rat all right. Just not the kind you're thinking."

In Loretta's mind, Tom was faceless. To have had a big old trap back then, to snare *the uncles* one at a time before they hurt her mother and left them both, would have been good. Lemonade out of lemons. You bet. That and enough local granite to plant a grave marker in the front yard for each one who came and went. Good riddance. For her mother and herself.

"Granny Noleen?"

Noleen stole a glance at Loretta, swept the moisture from her eyes.

"Yes, deary?"

"Was there ever one who loved her?"

Noleen rubbed her cheek, picked at a chin hair. "I believe there was. More than one, likely. It's just that your mama don't tend to choose the kind that sticks around." She stood slowly, mechanically, as if her bones had turned to metal. "Life is full of boulders, Loretta, like the Alabama Hills…some are smooth and easy to climb, others require a bit of stamina, a leap of faith, requiring fingers and toes and every muscle you got, to struggle your way to the top. But the view…the sweat, and blood and heart it takes to get there, those are the challenges that remind us how great life is and how important it is to keep living it."

Loretta thought of her mother, all the ups and downs, and how she kept climbing those boulders, day in and day out. "I know Mom's worked hard for me," she said warily. "I know she loves me. But she's so checked-out most of the time. So…not there. I don't feel like I'm *part* of her. Maybe it's because I don't look like her. I don't act like her. Mostly, I feel like I'm somebody else's kid…like I'm half, not whole, like my body's here, but parts of me are missing." She felt herself blush, embarrassed that she was sharing so much.

"You may not see it, Loretta, but your mama's inside you. Your papa too. The best part of you, though, is what you've come to be on your own. You're a good girl, darlin'. It's not what you're given by birth, but what you do with it that matters."

She moved her arm in a broad sweep. "Look around here. Round faces, long faces, old and young. Some people see only the brown color of my skin, and they miss the green in my eyes, the piece of my great-grandmother that I see every time I look in the mirror. She was Irish, and her eyes was all I got from her, other than maybe her temper, some say." She paused. "You're not half of anybody, Loretta; you're a whole bountiful person. You got sturdy DNA from folks that worked hard and played hard too. Stick-to-your-ribs spunk and vigor that you earned on your own. What a combination, if you ask me. A whole, grand person named Loretta Lynn Duvall. And there—what a gift your mama gave you. A name that sticks. A name that has grit and meaning."

Noleen finished her talk as she would a good meal, by wiping her mouth and smacking her lips. "Welp, Loretta-girl, best get at it," she said. "Pansy's goat pen won't build itself, and it's gettin' hotter than Billy-Be-Damned out here." She waddled past Earl and jabbed him in the side, depositing a kiss on Dakota's muzzle.

"Damn, woman," said Earl. "As disinclined as you are

to give up words worth noting, we should be celebrating, because a miracle just occurred. Anyone track the speaking minutes on that spiel she just gave?"

+++

There was a new pile of fence posts beside the garden shed and two rolls of hog wire. Loretta had never built a fence before, and she wondered where they would start. Cora ignored her pre-assigned duty of measuring corners and setting stakes, and waylaid Noleen. "I've been wondering—any more word on the cease and desist order? What happened with that? Have you heard any more from Sheriff Atkins or from Clive? Do you have a plan?"

"One question at a time, girl, one at a time." Noleen looked amused.

"Your exuberance overpowers your tongue," Yoshi said, chuckling. "Charming. And smart."

"Well, I'll be…" Earl talked out the side of his mouth as he tethered Dakota to a tie rail beside the barn. When he laughed, his whole body shook. "Both you girls are a caution today. Good for us old folks, to my way of thinking." His knees popped as he walked. "Let's get this fence built. Then it'll be time for more talk and storytelling. We got a good pot of chili cooking and Pansy's delicious honeyed-up biscuits to go alongside. Kindling's laid out in the fire pit, and there's plenty of hollowed-out sitting stumps. What say?"

"It's a yes from me," Cora said. Loretta smiled and nodded.

"I'm using the Internet on my phone, and found information stating that a three-sided corral is appropriate as long as the shelter itself provides protection from the sun, the wind, and rain," said Ethan. "The shed looks secure, but I think we need to extend the perimeter of the corral to measure ten by ten, so she's got more room to run and play."

"Smart man. All right then. Ten by ten it is." Noleen jammed a shovel in the ground near a stake Cora had pounded. "Cora, hop to the rest of these markers and extend them all two feet. Loretta, haul those posts, one to each hole as we dig them. The rest of you lazy sons-a- beaches, you know where the shovels are. Let's get 'er done."

- CHAPTER 14 -

The honey was local; Ethan could tell by the hint of blackberry and sage, maybe lavender. Lavender Farms on the south side of Lone Pine was a honey farm as well as a lavender farm and their bee colonies were well known to locals. The honey was a golden brown, mildly floral, and it melted in his mouth along with the biscuits Pansy had baked. His stomach was thankful for the food, but his mind was busy calculating the distance from the fire pit to the tunnels, the vent holes and small cave he assumed led to them. By walking the path beside the creek, rather than following the road to the bunker, they would gain minutes—ten, twenty, at least.

Granny Noleen bent over her plate and went at her beans again. Though she was thoroughly engaged in eating, Ethan suspected she was aware of each person's whereabouts around the fire and the amount of food left on their dishes. When Earl's plate was nearly empty, she brought him more chili. As Bill stood with an empty glass, she offered him her water. She fed the fire before it had time to die. Tossed grapes to the chickens. Snuffed out an ember that flew free of the pit and landed on the nearby grass.

Pansy's goat frolicked in her new pen, jumping from boulder to soft ground and up onto the boulder again. Pansy waved and cooed at her, giggling through dinner. Loretta laughed as well, which was good to see, considering her mood earlier in the day. Her eyes had brightened and her gait seemed light, bouncy even. Maybe it was the food, as Pansy had suggested. Whatever the reason, Ethan was happy to see it.

The dinnertime tea had an earthy taste and lemony aroma. Ethan drank one glass and poured another. Drank that, but hesitated to pour a third. He finished his bowl of beans and biscuit and honey, his eyes darting from the creek to the fire, his mind racing. He tried hard to relax, but his leg was bouncing and he couldn't seem to still it. Names turned to faces in his mind as he made a mental list of men who might be on duty over the next weeks, those who could be stationed at the bunker after dark. There was probably a work schedule written up on The Group's web page, but that information would be difficult to access since the site was monitored and passwords were often changed.

Loretta snapped her fingers in front of Ethan's face. "Lighten up!" she said, laughing as she chucked a marsh-mallow that hit him on the cheek.

"Oh, you didn't!" Ethan grabbed for it but missed.

"Run, Loretta, run!" Cora laughed.

"Gimme!" Ethan growled, coming at her with his arms extended, hands clawing the air, zombie-like. He loved marshmallows. There was something about their soft and gooey texture, the way they melted on his tongue, that made him happy.

Yoshi passed around long whittled sticks. Earl handed out chocolate squares and graham crackers.

"Oh, yessss." Cora was lit up with stars in her eyes. She stuck a marshmallow on the sharp end of her stick and held the stick near the coals in the fire pit.

"I've thought of a name for my goat!" Pansy proclaimed. She jumped up and pirouetted around her log seat. "S'more. Her name is S'more!"

"Sweet," said Cora. "Perfect."

"So it is spoken, so it is done." Yoshi raised his marshmallow stick in the air and waved it as if it were a magic wand, pointing it then at the baby goat. He did a little jig alongside Pansy.

Willow Grove was just a mile out of town, but it felt like another world. Things were light and comfortable here, even with the issues pressing heavy on his mind. Ethan sprang from his own stump and plunked down next to Loretta, pushing and shimmying sideways until she landed on the ground. "Not fair!" she whined. "You've grown guns over the past year. Look at those arms. You're bigger than me and stronger."

"I can't believe you admitted that, Lolo Ninny," Ethan teased. They laughed. "Lolo Ninny" was a nickname he had given her when they were kids. Not out of disrespect, or playfulness, but because it was the best he could do when he was angry or frustrated. Loretta: Lolo, like Lo, lo, (stutter, stutter) and eventually, Loretta, if he was lucky. The Ninny part came later after their friendship cemented.

It felt good to laugh, like a million tiny rainbows were growing inside him. In the distance he could hear the creek bubbling along its bed, and felt as secure as he always did when near running water, the water itself as much a part of him as his own blood.

Loretta climbed back on the stump, hip-checking Ethan until there was enough room for both of them. They jostled for position, still laughing. The fire burned low, red embers crusting to black near the edges of the flames. Smoke circled upward, a curlicue of gray. The singing started on this side of him and then on that side, moving around so swiftly that it seemed to be everywhere at once. The sound was sad and wistful: a cowboy ballad, started by Earl, added to by Noleen, Pansy, and Yoshi. *"As I walked out in the streets of Laredo…as I walked out in Laredo one day…I spied a young cowboy all wrapped in white linen…wrapped in white linen as cold as the clay."*

Ethan listened with every inch of his body, feeling, smelling, tasting the old days as Earl described them with a story: "Cowboy Eddie wore his blue jeans 'til they was glazed and shiny, ripe enough to stand on their own. Him and me, ol' Jim DeMill, Lou Brandsom, we played up in those mountains in the horse camps. We worked for the pack station, but we was mostly on our own." He pointed to Mt. Whitney, toward meadows Ethan knew to be up there—old corrals for keeping packhorses, barns nearly useless now but still managing to stand.

"We'd pack folks in, put up the horses, get the chili pot out, and throw in whatever we had, a little bit of this, a little bit of that. Sometimes we'd get ahold of a cowboy who was a pretty good singer. Guitar player, maybe. Harmonica man. Nighttime was special, magical even. Stars so bright their light flooded the sky." He shook his head and tipped his hat. "Old-timers pullin' on them whiskey jugs. Sleeping a little. Bragging a lot. Settling in with a smile on their faces and a tale to tell."

Noleen leaned over and poked the fire with her marsh-mallow stick. "You go to a person's camp back then, you'd bring something to share, and leave with something better…a good feeling…peace of mind. It was a matter of trust and respect. Of course, there have always been scoundrels, like the one who came waltzing in here with his fancy friend and crazy accusations." She didn't say his name, but Ethan knew she spoke of Clive. This recollection could have soured the story, but it didn't, and Earl moved on. His face was shadowed, but light bounced off it as the flames in the fire pit flickered, highlighting his words now and again with a pop or sputter.

"One year, a fella came up…a little scrawny kid with a mop of red hair and a freckled-y face. Said he wanted to be a cowboy. Said he knew about clicking his teeth and saying whoa, making a good cup of coffee and baking biscuits. So we made him our camp cook. His name was Walter, but the boys called him Cookie."

Ethan leaned in to hear more.

"We had a little buckskin up there that year, two-year-old, green-broke. The horse trailered okay, but you couldn't trust him on the mountain. Cookie took a liking to that horse, though, and decided to take him on. Named him Ransom. Welp, first trail ride out, Ransom argued a bit, ears laid back, but he let Cookie ride, no trouble. We headed up from Horseshoe Meadows toward Tyndal Creek, Crabtree Meadows, Rock Creek, like that."

Earl's word choices, the way he enunciated and truncated language fascinated Ethan. Each phrase became a picture or smell, as of lathered-up horses and aging saddle leather, campfires and chili seasoning and sweat; he could taste the air, feel the breeze on his face as the cowboys ascended Whitney.

"Anyways, Cookie's snaky horse did fine on the trail, but when we got to the first creek, he wouldn't cross. Finally, out of frustration, Cookie spurred him a little, and that buckskin took to the sky. Jumped straight up and into the middle of the water, then stood there refusing to come out," Earl said, laughing. "Cookie, well, he pushed and pulled, and reined him up, but that stiff-legged mule wouldn't budge. 'Til the moon come up, and a cougar screamed, and set that horse to running, past the boys, down the hill, all the way to the basecamp."

The quiet at story's end was palpable. Ethan swayed to some unsung song while the fire popped and sizzled and a puckish light danced in the trees. An ember burned at the tip of his marshmallow stick, and he swirled it slowly in the air like a sparkler.

"So, is this a good time? Can we talk about Clive's cease and desist order?" asked Cora.

"The truth is, I don't know," said Noleen. "I made some calls today, but didn't get any answers I felt kindly toward."

"My dad's on it. I know that. He went to the courthouse to look into the legality of the document, right?"

Noleen nodded. Her shoulders slumped, and even in the dark, the circles under her eyes seemed more pronounced than ever. "Tomorrow's another day," she said. "Not to worry now, you hear?"

"It's just that, tonight, with the barbecue and all, I figured it was okay to bring it up."

"You've a right to ask. Like I said, though, not to worry."

Not to worry. There was big meaning in those three little words. In the silence that followed, Ethan gathered and then grouped and prioritized his growing list of concerns:

One: His parents' commitment to Brock and The Group.

Two: Brock's threats, both real and implied.

Three: The cease and desist order against Granny Noleen.

Four: What's Clive's deal? How come he's involved in this, anyway?

He moved them around in their chronological order, put more emphasis on one and then another, but no matter what their sequence, he was uncomfortable with the results. However he chose to pattern his worries, the days ahead would most definitely suck.

A sudden scuffling noise in the blackberry thicket drew his attention. The scuffling grew closer, a subtle disturbance that could have been the result of a passing animal—or something else.

"What was that?" Loretta whispered.

Earl stood and walked toward the thicket, motioning for the rest of them to stay put.

"The berries are gone along this part of the creek, so it can't be a raccoon foraging for those," Noleen whispered.

"I've eaten them all up," said Pansy, cheerfully. "Four and twenty blackberries baked in a pie…"

Noleen spoke then, but her eyes were on Earl and the thicket. "Yes, dear one, you certainly have. Next time you're hunting berries, you'll need to go further." As if thinking twice about what she had said, she added, "But you can't go by yourself…we'll need to make a plan."

Ethan paced back and forth. Outside the ring of light cast by the fire, it was jet black, but he could see Earl in his white shirt, moving steadily away and to the north. He wished Earl would come back, and worried about what could be out there: some animal or worse, maybe a person, maybe his father, or Frey, or Brock. Ethan tried to think about the distance to the cave logistically this time—as the crow flies—one-half mile maybe, or a little more. In his mind, it was like a wormhole had been punched through the night sky, a glowing passage leading to the bunker.

- CHAPTER 15 -

5:45. Loretta stared at the numbers, willing them to move backward. Another hour. Just one more hour. She blinked her eyes, checking the time again and wondering if Pansy was up making breakfast, if the kitchen in the old farmhouse smelled like coffee and cinnamon rolls, and if there would be hot cocoa waiting for them, even though they were stopping for breakfast in town.

She got up and went about her routine in a bit of a daze: showering, dressing, feeding Toby, watering a garden that now grew more weeds than flowers and vegetables. Her mother would not be happy with her for letting it go, but hey, priorities, right? She was spending most of her days working for Granny Noleen. There was no time for anything else.

She glanced in the mirror before heading downstairs. No makeup either. She hadn't bothered with it for a while now. If Greer were home, she would receive the four-S's lecture: shower, shave, slather, and sizzle: body lotion, lip gloss, mascara were a must.

In her mother's room, the same stack of clothing was strewn across the bed. The vanity was still cluttered with half-used blush, outdated foundation, lipsticks Greer had chosen to leave behind. In a tray on the table were various bottles of fingernail polish: Glitter Frenzy, Nail Junky Blue, Elusive Black, and Red Divine. Loretta picked up the Glitter Frenzy and shook the bottle, tapping it against her wrist as her mother had taught her to do. "Mixes the pigments so you get good coverage," she told Loretta often. Even when Loretta was little, Greer had painted her fingers and toes, decorating them with accents like pink hearts on Valentine's Day, green four-leaf clovers on St. Patrick's Day, tiny flowers and polka dots for no reason at all. "Twinkle, twinkle, little star," she would say as she painted, and again when she put Loretta to sleep at night; when she dropped her off at school her first day of kindergarten; before she went on stage the first time in a school play in third grade. Loretta had a minor part and only a few lines, but they were important ones, and she remembered them still: "*Churkendoose! What kind of animal is that? Chicken, turkey, duck, and goose.*" *Churkendoose.* She bonded with this little storybook creature, a character whose mixture of DNA set him aside from others and left him on the outside looking in, teased and tormented until he proved his worth. A sweet, aching sorrow ran through her, and one at a time, meticulously, she rehung blouses and slacks, shut drawers, dusted bottles and tabletop curios, straightened the bedding—cleaned up her mother's messes, as she had done a hundred times before.

+++

Though Loretta willed her mother to call, it didn't happen. Even this morning, she checked and rechecked her cell phone, making sure it was charged. As she drove to the diner where she was meeting Ethan and Cora, all kinds of reasons for the ringer's silence ran through her mind, but she knew the most likely one, and he was undoubtedly wearing a wide-brimmed hat and boots. She kept at the speed limit for once, pulled into the dirt lot beside the Black Bear and parked. Texted: MOM. WHERE ARE YOU? CALL ME.

When she got out of the truck, she leaned down to check her shoelace.

"Hey, Loretta!" someone hollered.

As she looked up, she saw Brady drive by in his Jeep with a couple of buddies. He honked and waved, and she tried to wave back, but got her finger caught in her shoelace. "Perfect, just perfect," she said, blushing.

He stopped and backed up, then pulled into the parking lot. "Yeah, what's up?"

"Uh, nothing, I just, I'm meeting Cora and Ethan."

"Okay, well. Just thought I'd say hi." The other guys in the Jeep were punching each other, teasing about some silly joke. Neither of them looked at her or said hello.

"We're going to the hot springs," said Brady.

"Sounds hot," Loretta countered, and again, she felt herself blush.

"Yeah, well. Hey, I kind of wanted to say I was sorry too. About the other night. Things shouldn't have gone that far."

"Yeah. That kind of sucked. I mean, it wasn't your fault, but..."

"Right. Anyway, yeah, it *did* suck. Gotta jam, though. See ya, huh?" he said, waving as his Jeep bumped out of the parking lot and onto the street.

+++

When she pushed open the door to the diner, the suction created by the swamp cooler slammed it shut in her face. She pushed again, her hair blowing wildly in the artificial wind, and she huffed it out of her eyes and mouth.

"Whoa, really?" said Cora, staring at Loretta's puffy eyes as she plunked herself down on the bench seat next to Ethan. "You have a fight with your pillow, or what?"

Ethan fidgeted with his place setting, adjusting his fork, knife and spoon, then his water glass into their proper positions.

"Something like that." Loretta leaned down and rubbed her calves. "It felt like I was walking lying down, twitching all night. Crazy legs, Mom calls it."

Cora clucked her tongue, then chugged down half a glass of chocolate milk. "I should have stayed over. I'm sorry.

But Dad wanted me home. He said he missed me."

"Hey, no problem, really," Loretta told her.

"FYI, I didn't sleep much either. Nightmares," said Cora. "Ethan, I've been thinking about this whole bunker thing, and it all seems so bizarre. I have to say, I really wanted to tell my dad last night..."

"You didn't, did you, Cora?" Ethan was standing now, flicking his fingers.

"No, I said I wouldn't, but my gut instinct is to abort this whole mission..."

"Shhh, this is why I didn't want to go to Ruby's place. If she overheard, if she talked to Brock..."

"Okay, I get that, but man. You have to understand. I'm not entirely convinced..."

"I think Brock wants my dad to choose between The Group and me. He's dividing families. We're not supposed to visit relatives on holidays anymore, and he's making crazy rules, like kids can't call their own parents *mom* and *dad*, only their names, like Sim and Raina. He's buying guns. Lots of them. The only details I have are from the documents I've read, papers my dad didn't mean for me to see. I know the money that's being poured into the bunker. I know," Ethan said in a hushed tone, "that Brock is hiding something. I also know that if we tell, just put it out there, and an adult, any adult, confronts Brock, he'll laugh it off. He'll say that it's me, my Asperger's. He'll come up with a million excuses, and people will believe him because he's a master manipulator. He knows what he's doing." Ethan was talking louder, tapping his fork on the table. "And what he's doing is…wrong. It just is. It goes against…the rules."

"Everything okay here?" Carol, the waitress, asked, depositing plates of French toast at their table.

"Right as rain, no problems," Cora told her. "Breakfast looks great. Thanks so much." And she dismissed Carol with a big thumbs-up.

"Okay, so say you're right. What do we do?" Loretta asked once Carol had busied herself with other customers.

"We get into the tunnels, and if I'm right, one will lead to the bunker. From there, I don't know. Brock made a rule, and it's written in the manifesto. No access granted except to members of the Committee. No one gets in the bunker without his permission."

"Manifesto. This gets creepier every second." Cora scrunched her eyebrows together. "The Unabomber wrote a manifesto. Ugly. *Ug*-ly."

"Brock's office is where the records are kept. But there's no way in, not from the main entrance. Not without being detected. There's always someone there, twenty-four/seven."

"So, your hunch about the tunnels is valid. And you said that this Sunday there will be a gathering, and the bunker will be unguarded," Cora said.

"Not unguarded. But the guard will be Bale, remember, I told you…and he'll be sleeping an hour into his shift, no doubt."

"So we're aiming to find a way in, is that correct?" Cora asked. "This first mission is strictly reconnaissance?"

"If I'm wrong about the tunnels, all bets are off. We, I, will start from scratch."

"So Sunday, we meet up," Loretta said. "We'll drive my truck to the access road behind Willow Grove."

"No, not there. It's too close to the bunker. We'll leave the truck near Red Dog Bridge and hike in from there."

"What? No way. That's miles in the heat. No way!" Cora protested.

"You have a better suggestion?" Ethan asked.

"Yes," Loretta said. "We park at Willow Grove. Right in the yard. Granny Noleen won't care and neither will the others. We'll tell them that we'd like to take a hike along the creek. They'll encourage it—you know they will. Anything to get us in the woods rather than sitting in front of TVs or our phones."

"It'll work," Cora agreed. "I'll even pack a lunch. Make it more convincing."

"And, in a way, we're telling the truth. We're just leaving out the details. That will make it easier, I mean, to ask her permission, right?" Loretta said.

Ethan blinked his eyes. Flicked his fingers. "Okay," he finally said. "All right, then."

+++

That morning, pulling into Willow Grove, things felt

off-kilter. The driveway was muddy. The chickens were loose. The shed door was open and tools were strewn about. Loretta turned off the engine and rolled to a stop near a pile of shattered support beams and crushed hog wire lying crumpled, ruined. Tire tracks and traces of spinouts circled the wrecked goat pen. A jagged piece of PVC pipe marked a broken irrigation line near the garden—corn stalks hung broken and wilting in the morning sun and perfect rows of radishes, lettuce, and tomatoes were strewn about and ground together into a green, slimy mush.

Pansy sat on the topmost porch step, rocking and sobbing while Yoshi tried to console her. S'more lay in Pansy's arms, bleating piteously, her right front leg jutting at a strange angle. Noleen pushed through the front door with a basket of bandages at the same moment that Earl appeared from behind the barn carrying several small, flat boards.

"Oh. My. God," Loretta said once she could speak. She keyed off the truck's ignition, pushed the door open, and ran to Pansy.

"How? Who would do such a thing?" Cora asked, her breath coming in short, uneven spurts as she ran behind Loretta.

Loretta stroked the goat's head and Pansy's knee. "She's gonna be okay, Pansy. Don't cry, please. It's going to be all right."

"Whoever did it is beyond wicked," Cora cried. "I'll call my dad. Did you call the sheriff?"

"Be specific!" Ethan hollered. "Wicked can mean evil, sinful, or morally wrong, but it can also mean very, really, or wholly cool, as in, *that truck is wicked!*" He paced the ground in front of the goat pen. "Be accurate with your description! This is bad, really bad. Wicked, as in evil!

"Number one. This is no prank. Number two. They, the truck, was focused on the yard, not the goat, or she would be dead. Number three. We built this fence according to safety specifications for housing goats. It was strong. The tire marks are significant. Off-road big. The ruts are deep." He pulled his composition book out of his backpack and flipped through the pages. He paced, smacked the side of his head, flicked the fingers of his free hand.

Pansy held her baby goat while Earl splinted its damaged leg. The goat screamed, chest heaving, eyes bulging. Chickens flapped their wings and ran from the noise, scattering all over the yard. Ethan flung himself toward the porch, away from the squawking birds.

"Whoever it was had been headed toward Dakota, but Earl got to the horse first with his shotgun. He fired three times at the truck, knocking out a taillight before it sped away," said Yoshi.

Earl was dressed in summer pajamas, long johns with the sleeves cut off at the shoulders and legs cut off at the knees; his feet were bare, and several toes were bloody. He'd not had time to dress. His callused fingers moved as if he had done this before—splinting, applying vet wrap, filling a syringe from a vial and injecting the contents into a vein in S'more's leg. He sang some cowboy song, a gravelly mix of scattered words Loretta could barely make out. *"Oh say, little dogies, when you gonna lay down...Sleep, little one, sleep."*

A trail of dust announced a car approaching the main drive into Willow Grove. A police cruiser. Sheriff Atkins. He poured from his vehicle, eyes gathering evidence before he even spoke. "Good Lord, Noleen. Do you have any idea who might have done this?"

"No, but I'd like to have a word with an ex-deputy of yours."

"Number five," Ethan yelled. "This was purposeful and done with malice. M.A.L.I.C.E. A desire to cause harm."

Sheriff Atkins glanced at Ethan, giving him a moment to finish his rant. "Can you I.D. the vehicle?" he asked Noleen.

"Earl thought it was a 4 x 4 pickup. Older. Big-bodied. Couldn't tell the color. Porch light was out. Sun wasn't up yet."

"Well, Noleen, I'm going to look around the yard a bit. I'll do my best to resolve this, I assure you. This kind of vandalism is incomprehensible. Inexcusable."

"Leastwise you can't blame my Bill for this. Or Ethan over there."

"No ma'am. And believe me, nothing's been settled on that count. No charges have been filed. The theft at the Iron Gate is still an open investigation. The vandalism and theft at the hardware store too." Sheriff Atkins nodded at Bill. "Keep your nose clean, Bill. Avoid town for a while if you can. I'd like to be able to say you were nowhere near the area if another instance occurs, understand?"

Yoshi translated, his hands forming words Bill could follow. Bill nodded.

"Darn shame," the Sheriff said, lips sucked in, eyes surveying the damage.

"Tell me something," Noleen said. "You know anything about the cease and desist order Clive brought out here?"

"No ma'am."

"Can you take a look?" Noleen stepped into the house and back out with the order. She handed it to Sheriff Atkins.

"You mind?" he said, pointing to the porch.

"Help yourself," Noleen told him.

Sheriff Atkins sat on the porch and read the letter. Loretta, Cora, and Ethan stood beside the remnants of the goat pen. Loretta felt violated, angry. Ethan was near a meltdown. He was mumbling, and his eyes looked vacant. He rocked from one foot to the other.

Cora spoke for the three of them. "Whatever you need. Whatever we can do…" And then to Ethan, in a whisper. "I'm still not sure about this plan of yours, the tunnel thing, but the worst detective in the world can see that something is going on here besides vandalism. So I'll do it." She shook her head, scowling. "And I won't tell my dad. I promise. Tomorrow. Tomorrow we ride."

"Noleen," said the Sheriff. "This order was not issued by the Court. It looks to be written by an attorney. The complaint appears to be valid as far as the language goes, but it wouldn't hold much weight legally unless the concerned parties go through the proper channels and get the law involved."

"So anyone can serve this kind of letter?"

"Pretty much any document can be printed off the Internet these days. In this instance, this appears to be the case, except the verbiage is professional, no doubt about it." He scratched his chin. "You say Clive brought this by?"

"Yes, sir."

"How long ago?"

"A bit."

"Mind if I take this?" Sheriff Atkins folded the document in thirds and tapped it against his forehead, as if he were hoping it would summon up names, faces, maybe more.

S'more snored through the sedation Earl had given her, her chest heaving despite her relief from the pain.

"Coincidence?" Earl asked, his gravelly voice deeper than usual.

Sheriff Atkins didn't answer, but he frowned as he stepped off the porch. He tossed the cease and desist order onto the front seat of his cruiser, pulled out a digital camera, and began snapping pictures of the wreckage in the yard.

"Man-quake," Ethan said. "Human-caused damage to our infrastructure."

-CHAPTER 16-

Where Ethan lived there were no sidewalks, and lawns met the asphalt with irregular patches of browning Bermuda grass. Most of the yards had flowerbeds, though this year drought-tolerant plants like lavender and yarrow replaced the usual zinnias and daisies and sunflowers. Back in his own yard, he avoided the dying roses, focusing instead on the tall stems of his mother's hollyhock plants, picking a red flower, a pink, a white one for her table.

Once inside, he removed his boots, placing them on the shoe tree in the hallway, right one on the right side, left on the left. He circled the dining room table and stood for a minute, confused by the missing vase. His mother kept a cobalt-blue vase on that table and she always had flowers there, though he had noticed this morning that the flowers needed to be freshened. The idea had popped into his head several times during the day: pick flowers for mom, pick flowers for Mom, pick flowers for Mom.

He glanced at the clock on the kitchen wall. Five forty-two. Saturday night. Family night. Where were his parents? He found the vase in the sink, removed the old flowers, filled it with fresh water and arranged the hollyhocks he had picked, seating them just so.

In the living room, he counted steps the way he had as a child, though his stride was now longer, the final wall-to-wall count fifteen rather than twenty. He checked the grandfather clock standing near the foyer, his great-grandfather's grandfather clock, a fact that had always intrigued him. Six-twelve. Twelve minutes after six. He stared at the hands as if willing them to tick backward to the prescribed time his parents should have been home.

A car pulled into the driveway. He recognized the thrum and grind of his father's Jeep Cherokee and sprinted for the door. Hearing his mother's laugh gave him gooseflesh, as she called it, the little hair-raising bumps that happened on his arms under a multitude of circumstances: joy, anxiety, cold, fear. He had never fully understood that concept, how those bumps appeared whether he was happy or sad or scared to death. It made no sense to him that his body should react so without his knowledge or permission. His mother climbed from the car and waved to him. His father did the same. Ethan stood gazing out the screen door but didn't open it. There was someone else. The rear car door opened and that someone, a man, stood, stretched, then turned around. Brock. No. Yes, it was Brock.

Ethan bristled. This wasn't right. "Saturday night is *our time!*" he hollered. His parents had set that time aside, a time for his family to reconnect after a week of work and school or whatever. He wheeled around, facing the fireplace, the blackened bricks around the hearth, jagged and out of sync with the comfort he typically drew from it. There was so much he wanted to tell his parents this night: all that had happened at Granny Noleen's, and more pressingly, his concerns about Brock. His mouth tasted bitter, sending a wave of nausea through him.

"Ethan," announced Sim as he entered the room. "Son, we have a guest. Can you welcome him, please?"

Ethan watched his father's face but didn't know what he was thinking. Loneliness crawled up his stomach and into his throat. He turned to face Brock, knowing full well the words that were expected, though nothing but dead air escaped his lips. His eyes followed Brock as he crossed the room and plopped into Sim's favorite chair. Too relaxed, too familiar. Raina went right into the kitchen and to the refrigerator, returning with two Budweiser Talls, handing one to Sim and one to Brock. The third item in her hand was a bottle of lemonade. Natural, not pink: Ethan's favorite.

Ethan's fists clenched too tightly to take the bottle. He blinked his eyes, still staring at Brock.

"Ethan, dear, have a seat on the couch." It was an easy command, given by Raina in her gentle but firm tone. Ethan backpedaled across the room toward the couch. Brock popped the cap off his bottle of beer and took a long, slow swig, his Adam's apple bobbing up and down. From where Ethan sat, he could hear the slop, slop noise of liquid pouring down Brock's throat, and it made him want to scream something foul that would make it stop.

Brock's legs stretched out before him, canvased in pants and boots that hadn't seen much wear. "Thanks so much, folks, for this respite," he said. "Twelve hours at the site have left me a bit stressed. So much to be done. So close but so far, as they say."

Those longs legs stretched across Raina's comfortable old braided rug were out of place. The entire room took on a gray cast, yet certain things stood out. The empty spots on the mantle that once held Raina's silver candlesticks, sold as an offering to help fill the Committee's cash coffer. The vacant space near the front window where Ethan's prized red recliner once sat, the recliner now housed in the reading room in the bunker.

Ethan's mind grew fuzzy. No word fit how he was feeling. He tried to compartmentalize his thoughts, clear back to when he first met Brock—the time Brock taught him to clean a fish. One. Make sure the fish is healthy by checking its eyes. Are they misty? Bloody? Two. Wash the fish. Three. Scrape off the scales. Four. Starting at the gills, cut off the head. Five. Slice open the belly. Six. Using your finger, carefully remove the guts.

During that first summer, Brock would come to Ethan's

house every couple of days, always cautious of Ethan's space and anxious to learn from Sim and Raina about appropriate speech and touch, or lack of, that would keep Ethan comfortable. There were rules. There had always been rules about how to act and what was appropriate to say, when to enter a conversation and when it was okay to leave a room if visitors were present. Now, as when he was a child, those rules rolled together like a squirm of worms, and there was no pulling them apart or recalling a definition that fit the moment.

Ethan thought of the time last summer when he and Loretta had walked to the Penny Saver for an ice cream. They were licking their cones and looking at used books outside the bookstore next door to the market. Brock came out of the bookstore and grabbed Loretta by the elbow, moving her away from the bin. "What the hell's the matter with you kids?" he said gruffly. "Do you suppose I might have liked to buy one of these books? Do you think I would, now that they are smeared with ice cream and your filthy germs?"

So much had happened. It felt to Ethan as if he had lived one life and was now living another; as if he were swimming upstream in the river he loved toward something unsure and less comfortable.

"Ethan. How are you?" The voice was Brock's.

"Ethan. How are you?" Ethan repeated. He flicked his fingers. Blinked his eyes.

"Something the matter...other than the usual?" Brock

asked, chuckling. He blinked five times and then rolled his eyes.

"Brock, Ethan's just…being himself. He often repeats what he hears. It's something he does," Raina said.

Brock scratched his beard stubble.

"Can we move on?" Raina admonished, rather bluntly. She shifted uneasily, moving closer to Ethan on the couch.

Sim pursed his lips and peered at Raina. "Any news regarding the food storage units?" he finally asked Brock.

"They're being delivered the end of the week. Nonperishables will come shortly after. Canned goods, sacks of dry goods: beans, corn, bulk stuff like that. Flour and that kind of thing, items that could become buggy… those things will come later. I'm still doing some research. Research, you know about that, Ethan, right? Gotta get the facts before we act, right?"

Ethan felt Brock's eyes on him again, dark and focused, waiting for an answer.

Raina stood. "You all must be starving. Chicken enchilada casserole and salad. Sound good?" She moved toward the kitchen with hesitant steps, turning back toward Ethan, sidling closer to where he sat, as close as she could get without touching him. "I just have to heat the casserole. It should be ready in twenty minutes." She turned toward the kitchen and back again. "I'll be right back," she said, looking at Sim now. "I'll pop the casserole in and be right back."

"Was it something I said?" Brock said, glaring at Sim.

"Let's talk more about the food stores…"

"You know that there are defectors among us," Brock said, lips turned down in a pout.

"Yes, I know. A few have decided to leave The Group. There's talk…"

"Talk, talk, talk. I wasn't going to complain, but damn, Sim, it's so hard, working day in and day out for you people, pouring sweat and blood into something that's going to save your asses when the time comes. Sim. The bunker is going to save you. You know that right?" Sim nodded.

"We've got to think ahead, man. It'll be a new world when we come out."

Sim offered Brock a peppermint candy from a dish on the coffee table. Brock refused, waving his hand in the air and patting his stomach. He glanced at Ethan.

"You look mad," Ethan told him. "Your eyes look angry. You're a flim-flam man, all shuffle and jive."

"Ethan! Apologize." Sim scolded.

"You know he can't, Sim," Raina said from the kitchen door. "As hard as it is to hear sometimes, Ethan is painfully honest."

Brock turned his dagger eyes on Raina. "Well, well. Like mother, like son." He smiled a lipless smile. "No, no, she's right," he corrected himself. "Let the boy talk. He doesn't understand, could never understand…what we're doing here, the importance of what we're doing here and the stress that can cause." Brock ran his fingers through his hair.

"Now, wait a minute," said Sim, standing now.

"I do understand!" Ethan shouted.

"Yes, yes. I'm sure you do." Again an eye roll. "But back on point. Defectors, cynics, this is why…it's the reason that decisions must be made, regarding *some* people in The Group, and those old folks out there at Willow Grove. Frey caught that old man on his horse poking around near the bunker the other day. Not good, not good at all."

Ethan ran through the list of tools he used to calm himself: slow your breathing, count to ten, focus on the white light, find a word. It popped in his head then, effortlessly and definite: *Duplicity: deceitfulness, speaking one way and acting another.* He picked up a Rubik's Cube from off the end table beside the couch and busied himself with it, thinking of the argument his parents had a few nights back. People *were* leaving The Group. Jemma's parents and others. Raina was worried. Money invested was an issue for Sim, and the time, his commitment; he had given his word and signed a contract. "Good people can turn this around," he told Raina. "This isn't a lost cause."

Brock hesitated, and nodded toward Ethan.

"It's okay," Sim said. "Ethan loves his Rubik's Cube. Right, buddy?"

Ethan worked the cube, matching reds, blues, yellows, and whites.

"You've been my right-hand man for a while now, Sim."

Sim nodded.

"Lately, I've been feeling…like you've got doubts. And if that's true, I need to know."

"I don't have doubts exactly, as much as, well, we're questioning, Raina and I, some of the motives, the new rules. We don't understand where some of this stuff is coming from, who's making it up, the family stuff, for instance, the concern about genetic…tinkering, long term…"

"It's all for the good of The Group. You know that." Brock held up his hand. "Let's don't do details, please."

Ethan worked his Rubik's Cube. His fingers moved more slowly than usual, but Sim didn't seem to notice.

"Why are we using the term *genetics*?" Brock asked. "What we're thinking is, what we're talking about is…going in…clean, if you will. Starting out with a strong gene pool will give us an edge…"

"It's just that, when we joined The Group, we had one school of thought, one philosophy, with all the others, regarding ecology, improving our planet, our ecosystem, our families' lives," Sim said. "Even the bunker idea seemed like a good one at the time, a way to preserve our way of life should something happen…"

"At the time? It *seemed* like a good idea at the time?"

"What I mean is, it still is a good idea, Brock, as long as we keep the focus where we started, and that was to preserve a way of life…"

"That, Sim, is precisely what we're talking about here.

We're moving quickly, and God forbid, should something happen, some threat present itself, we'll be ready." Brock stood up and paced the floor. "Regardless of the scenario, we need to be prepared." He calmed himself, sat again, glanced at Ethan and away. "These defectors...the few who know our plans, and who have been privy to the ins and outs of our operation..." He hesitated again, rubbing his beard stubble. In a quiet voice, he added. "This can be dangerous, you know. I'm not saying these folks need to be punished in any way, but still, there is the issue of...security for all."

Ethan glanced up just long enough to catch the look that passed between his parents.

Sim fidgeted, picking at his thumbnails. "I hear you, I do, but my family comes first."

"So I'm asking you." His eyes were targeting Sim. "Your loyalty is without question. Correct? You're answering *me* now, Sim. The man who's taken care of you when you were sick, brought your family food when you couldn't work... the go-to guy, the guy who writes Raina's paycheck."

Ethan stopped spinning the Rubik's Cube. He knew Mo Chespick had sold the Iron Gate and moved out of state awhile back, but never really thought about who had purchased the business. How could he have missed that? How could it have escaped his radar?

He wondered if Brock thought of him as a trout sometimes, if he would like to see him skinned and belly-cut and gutted by his own hand. Everything he knew that was tidy and right felt lost. He wrapped his arms around himself and started to sway, seeking comfort in his quiet place.

- CHAPTER 17 -

*T*he breeze off the mountain brought with it the scent of something unfamiliar. All morning Loretta had fretted over the smell. A dead animal? Some obscure pollution carried on the wind? Even Toby seemed agitated and refused his morning walk. The neighbor's cat had growled and twitched his tail as she left the house. Birds sat on wires and in the willow stands along the creek, and cows stood under trees in their pastures with their heads down, their tails limp.

In town, Carmen's Tamale Stand was deserted—no truckers, no locals, not even Mr. Milne, who made a habit of having coffee with Carmen each morning and breakfasting on one of her apple tamales. Lights were on in the shops, but no one was out on the street sweeping their storefronts, or watering the flowers in their flower boxes, or rearranging sale items in the rolling display tables they commonly kept outside. Cora commented on this and not much more—even she was stilled by the oddity in the air.

When they arrived at Willow Grove, Ethan leaped for the round corral. Dakota swished his tail, flared his nostrils, but he leaned into Ethan's chest so hard it looked as if they both might topple over. Earl propped his arms on the wooden railing near the gate. His eyes followed Ethan's hands as he stroked the horse's muzzle, steady and predictable—relaxed. Yoshi was there too, braiding a set of split reins out of blue and green Paracord. He worked the nylon rope between his thumbs and fingers, weaving the multicolored strands, tugging the plait gently to tighten, and then weaving some more.

All morning Loretta had practiced what she would say to Noleen, but now she couldn't get the words out. Cora glanced her way occasionally, urging her on. "We feel kind of bad asking," she finally said, "with everything that happened yesterday…but we really need a break." Instantly she regretted the boldness of her comment, restating it: "Or, I mean, after chores, maybe, could we take a hike around Willow Grove?"

The wind blew Loretta's hair across her eyes, obstructing her vision and hiding the expression on Noleen's face in a rippling of shadows.

"Which is it then? Say it straight up, girl."

The sharpness of the statement caught Loretta off guard. "Which is what?"

"Do you want the day off, or do you want to do chores?"

"Well, yeah...I mean, we figured...we've been working so hard..."

Noleen slapped her thigh. "Dang, girl, spit it out!"

Wow, Loretta thought. Everyone is grumpy. She stiffened. Coughed. "We'd like the day off," she muttered outright.

"Say again?"

"We'd like the day off!"

"Well, there it is then. You've got a strong voice when you use it, Loretta." Noleen plopped down in her rocker on the porch and slapped her thigh again, staring out into the yard. "That's all well and good," she said, huskily. "Funny thing, though, today is Sunday, not a work day, or did you forget?" She rubbed her forehead and then stretched her back muscles, leaning over so far that her head was nearly in her lap.

"It's just...we thought...we want to be here to help fix things up."

"Nothing much can be done until tomorrow. Earl says we need new wire, posts, and such from the Building and Supply. Get on with you now. Go with our blessing, but be careful out there. Stay safe."

Ethan eased away from Dakota and sauntered to the paddock gate. He leaned down and fiddled with his shoestrings, his face buried beneath a mass of dark brown curls. Loretta recognized his avoidance tactic. It was impossible for Ethan to lie, and she knew that their reconnaissance mission would be difficult for him on multiple levels, more so if Granny began asking questions about their upcoming "hike."

"Thanks, Granny," Loretta said, "tomorrow we'll make up for this. We'll rebuild S'more's pen and…"

"Hmmm. I like the sound of that."

"Rebuilding S'more's pen?"

"No, not that part, the Granny part. You called me Granny, with nothing attached."

"I did?"

"Yes, girl, you did."

Loretta felt the blush come, her crimson cheeks betraying her attempt to hide her embarrassment. "I'm sorry, I…"

"Sorry you called me Granny?"

"No. Yes."

"It's kind of fitting. Proper, I'd say. Go now, get on with it, before I change my mind." Granny hid her smile with her shirtsleeve. The pace of her rocking set the porch boards to creaking.

Loretta started to walk away, then turned back. "Sorry it took me so long. To call you Granny," she said smiling.

Earl leaned against Dakota's tie rail, rolling a strand of oat hay between his fingers. "Watch out for those bogey-men!" he teased.

"Funny, real funny," Cora said. "Thanks a bunch."

Earl picked a currycomb out of the beer cooler on wheels where he kept Dakota's grooming tools: hoof picks, fly spray, mane and tail detangler. "You're good with him, son," he said to Ethan. "He's fond of you, that's true enough."

Ethan nodded but didn't answer. He beat out a slap-snap rhythm as he met up with Loretta, already heading to the truck. Cora filed alongside, slapping her thighs, snapping her fingers to Ethan's rudimentary beat. Lap, lap, snap, snap, lap, lap, snap, snap…

Dakota whinnied, disrupting their pattern, and they continued their walk in silence.

Loretta grabbed her daypack from the rear of the truck. She checked the contents: water bottle, beef jerky, extra socks, and a long-sleeved overshirt rolled into a ball and shoved beside the rest. She watched Ethan inspect his gear, all neatly packed and arranged by order of need: his overshirt, folded neatly, his water bottle, one sack of twelve cherries (she watched him count them), and three muffins stuffed into separate baggies. Naturally, he'd included Loretta and Cora in his snack planning. So typical, and so Ethan. Since they were kids, he'd taken her into account, not with words, but with his actions. If she said something he didn't understand, he would stare at her or out into space as if her words were important enough to give them maximum consideration. He wouldn't respond verbally, but the fact that he stayed and stood his ground let her know that he cared and that she mattered. When everyone else disappeared, or did their mean-girl thing, or flirty thing, or played judgmental jock games, Ethan was solid. Sturdy. Like the granite on the mountain she loved.

And Cora. Well. There she was, pack set on her back, mind on the trail ahead. Planning, always planning their next move. She scouted the path from the yard to the creek, turned back, and waved them on, giving the okay to proceed.

"Lovely day for a walk," Pansy said. Her rouged cheeks were brighter today than on previous mornings. She held S'more in her arms, dancing her about the yard as she would a newborn baby. The little goat didn't seem to mind and rested her head on Pansy's arm. The splint had held overnight, and the pain appeared to have subsided, as she was relaxed, adding only an occasional bleat to the rhythm of Pansy's humming.

+++

A canopy of branches shaded the trail beside the creek. Last year's fallen leaves littered the ground, crunching beneath their feet as they walked. Ethan led the way around the bend, across a straightaway, and up a low hill. Loretta turned her head for a last view of the yard at Willow Grove, the house ghosted within a forest of limbs and the unruly bramble of blackberry vines that grew in dense thickets. She picked a berry and popped it into her mouth, juicy and sweet, perfect for one of Pansy's pies.

Ethan led them up a second, steeper incline, through a small meadow, and up another incline. Then he turned, glanced back, and flicked his fingers. The brush was thicker now, the path disappearing amidst an outcrop of rock massed with scrub willow and sage. He knelt down, eyes scouring the ground, and Loretta stood still, waiting. Cora sat on a rounded granite boulder, pulled her water bottle from her pack, and took a swig.

Ethan pointed to a mound of dirt and signaled them forward. On the far side of the mound was a metal pipe, eight inches around, its top lip barely exposed. On an average day, out on a casual hike, Loretta never would have noticed it, so overgrown with weeds.

Cora ran her finger along the edge of the pipe and showed Loretta the resulting orange residue. "This pipe is ancient," she said. "Maybe Civil War vintage."

"Ancient implies something belonging to the early history of the world," Ethan corrected. "This is cast iron. During the last two years of the Civil War, the state of Alabama produced seventy percent of Confederate iron. Thirteen iron companies were located there, and they had six rolling mills that traveled from location to location. Some of the iron they produced could have made its way here to California."

"Weird connection," Loretta said.

"What do you mean?" Cora asked.

"Alabama. The Alabama Hills. *The U.S.S. Alabama.* This place is named after a warship that hauled enough iron to forge enough guns and bullets to kill...thousands? And now here we are, near a tunnel fortified by some of said iron, a bunker which predictably houses enough guns and ammo to do what? Kill who and how many? What kind of war is Brock planning?"

"Oh, my God. You totally amaze me. Your brain is a masterpiece, I swear," Cora said.

"Oh, yeah right," Loretta huffed.

"The Civil War was white against black," Cora said. "WWII was us against the Japanese. And then, throughout history, there were a zillion religious wars. Actually, religion tops the list of reasons people go to war. Ironic, if you ask me. What's this guy's agenda, do you suppose?"

"Who knows? So the runaway slaves could have placed the original pipe and used it for air ventilation in the tunnels," Loretta said.

"Could be," Cora answered.

"Or Yoshi's story fits as well…a Japanese family hiding here during the Internment to escape Manzanar," Loretta said. "If there were a family with children down in those tunnels, they would have appreciated fresh air."

"Bingo," Cora said. "Ethan, are there more of these?" she asked.

"I've found three. But there could be more. And there's this." Hunching down, Ethan crawled through a low-slung willow to another mound, this one higher and closer to the creek. On the far side of the mound, facing the water, an earthen overhang formed a small cave, three feet high by four feet wide. When Ethan cleared the entrance of rocks and brush and other debris, they could see that the mouth of the cave dropped down sharply. The air coming from it smelled dank and rotten, like moldy leaves and standing water—a place Loretta normally would have avoided.

"Are you kidding me?" Cora asked. "Brunch first. Please."

They sat quietly, eating the snacks they brought. Ethan glanced nervously and often to the northeast. He stood and paced, then took a pee break on the far side of a boulder, as did Cora and Loretta in turn.

Ethan checked his watch. "Time to go," he said. "Brunch is over." He slid the empty baggies into the appropriate spot inside his backpack, removed his flashlight and a rock hammer, flicked his fingers, and blinked his eyes. Using the hammer, he tapped the beams supporting the entrance to the cave, checking for stability. The wood itself looked to be the same type as in the interior of the tunnels, to shore up the entrances to the small sleeping rooms and to serve as brace beams.

Ethan turned on his flashlight and peered into the cave.

The beam of light searched haphazardly through the dark cavity. In those few long minutes of Ethan's inspection, the only noises were the skittering of a ground bird, quail maybe, and the hoarse screech of a red-tailed hawk.

Ethan pivoted and squatted in the entrance. "It looks okay," he said, "The ground seems solid and so does the cave roof. From here, I can't see much beyond the first few feet, though. Past that point, we'll have to gauge safety as we go."

"Good enough. I'll go first," Loretta told him.

"No."

It was all Ethan said, but his intention was clear. He would lead the way.

+++

The light grew dimmer as they entered the cave, the bedrock itself blocking the sun and the sky. The air felt thinner, the oxygen less pure. It seemed to be a place that held secrets, a chamber people had escaped to, lived in and withdrawn from—and where they had left parts of themselves behind.

Ethan had been right. Behind the main chamber, there was a narrow opening, a downward slope. He crab-walked forward, but Loretta and Cora sat and slid on their butts, down into the belly of the earth. Inside, the tunnels ran to the right and to the left. It didn't take long to see, however, that there were notable differences between these passageways and those under the house at Willow Grove—these were much shorter than their counterparts, barely five feet high from floor to ceiling. The ground was littered with gravel and eroded rock. Water trickled down the walls, and the dirt smelled metallic.

Ethan stepped into the tunnel to the left and Cora followed behind him, their combined flashlight beams forming a disorganized pattern of dots and lines, flickering over muck and granite. "Watch the sharp bend to the right up ahead," Cora warned, just before the light from Loretta's flashlight dimmed.

Loretta was well inside the tunnel by then, and the sudden brown-out startled her. She stared down at the Maglite in her hand, flipped it off and then on again, banged the barrel on her wrist, and checked the reflector and lens. The flashlight emitted a feeble glow, but not nearly enough to guide her way. "Typical," she blurted, blaming her mother, and then herself, for the failed batteries. "I should have known better. I should have checked."

She imagined a plotline for a horror movie with herself as the star, she being the victim of a wizard's spell. She wondered what it would be like to turn into stone, to live as a stalagmite in this rank, damp place forever. Then she heard something—a soft padding, plodding footfalls over rock. A whirl of light bounced off the conglomerate walls in ever-growing concentric circles, and the tunnel appeared to spin. She leaned against the wall and slid to the floor, wrapped her arms around her knees, and waited for the worst to happen.

"Loretta?" Ethan whispered.

She reached out to touch him, her arms flailing in the dark, fingers probing the air. Her eyes widened, trying to see.

"Loretta?" Ethan's voice echoed off the rock walls. Suddenly he was there. She touched him, and then lost him as he pulled away from her—but that movement, that typical wonderfully manic aversion to touch that was Ethan's alone, made her muscles quiver and tighten. She stood up, grounding herself.

"Claustrophobic?"

"A bit. Thanks. I can't remember the last time..."

"Winter, 2012. We took an elevator to the top floor of the courthouse in Independence. The lights went out. You panicked."

"School field trip. Right."

Ethan handed her his flashlight, and as he fiddled with her Maglite, she heard things. Tunnel whisperings. Rocks groaning. But there was something else, coming from behind her in the dark. A series of shuffles. A released breath of air. Loretta shivered, remembering a conversation she'd had with her mother once about the ghosts of the Alabama Hills. It would make sense that one or more spirits could have become lost in these tunnels. A slave running from a bounty hunter. The child of a displaced Japanese-American, separated from his parents in their effort to escape the horror that had become their lives during WWII.

"Dead," Ethan confirmed, regarding her flashlight. He pulled a spare from his backpack and handed it to her, retrieving his original.

As the second flashlight came on, the walls relaxed, and so did Loretta. "Walk slower," she told Ethan. "Don't lose me again."

"Hook your finger in the belt loop on my pants."

"That's okay?"

Ethan didn't reply, but he didn't pull away either. His

breathing was steady, even. As they rounded a corner, she saw it. Another thirty feet or so down, the chamber widened into a grotto-type room with high ceilings braced with metal beams, shiny, new. At the far end of the grotto, Cora was examining a large metal door, also new, its touchscreen deadbolt lock system blinking a hostile red warning.

Cora whispered as they approached, "This thing is intricate. Expensive. There's a keypad. It requires an entrance code."

"This is not surprising. I'm not even sure all the Committee members would know the combination," Ethan said.

"What do we do?" Loretta asked.

On both sides of the door were stand-up canisters, supply cabinets with flashlights, liter boxes of drinking water, waterproof ponchos, first-aid kits, and boxes of bullets. Loretta picked up one of the boxes. "Nine mm Luger," she read. On a second, she read: ".38 Special."

"There's only one option," Cora said. "We make a new plan. We go in through the main entrance. Ethan's right. This is creepy. We need to find out what Brock's up to."

Ethan plopped onto the ground and sat cross-legged, swaying back and forth. He flicked his fingers, blinked his eyes. "We can't," he said. "It's against the rules to go into the bunker's main entrance. I can't go in. That way, anymore. I can't."

Loretta tried to channel her mother, to spout philosophy,

or come up with some grand statement or advice to defuse a situation that could technically destroy their plan, and Ethan along with it. But she had nothing. Just empty thoughts and a mouth full of dusty air.

-CHAPTER 18-

It was dark by the time Loretta drove into her yard. Cora pulled her iPhone from her pocket and texted her father. She translated aloud: *Tired. Long day. OK to spend the night at L's?*

Brrrring. The text alert response was immediate. *"I'll drop dinner by on my way home. Something other than pizza."*

"Thank you," Cora typed, relaying her part of the conversation to Loretta as well.

"Tell him to bring us a movie. No, two," Loretta said.

"Loretta says bring movies. Something spooky."

"Loretta wouldn't ask for something spooky, Mija."

"Busted. Just get us something good."

Looking satisfied, Cora opened the passenger door and slid to the ground, brushing the dirt off her clothes and stomping her boots to clear the accumulated rock dust. "I still can't wrap my mind around this bunker thing. So many questions. The variable appears to be Brock. Is he a nut job, or not? I just don't know."

Loretta fumbled to match the door key with the keyhole in the dark. "That security door, the size of the grotto, the supplies and ammo. Incredible," she said. "That project alone took time and mucho manpower. We're talking money here. And we've only had a sneak peek. Imagine what's inside that frigging place."

The house inside was as dark as the street outside. Loretta flipped on a light.

"It gives me the creeps. The whole thing. The bunker, the Committee. All of it," Cora said.

"Like I said the other day, my mom went to those meetings for a while." Loretta bit her lip. "I didn't want to hurt Ethan's feelings, so didn't say this in front of him, but after quitting, her commentary went something like this: 'Hell no! Give me an In-and-Out burger and a shot of Jack Daniel's. Skip the sprouts. Pile on the pickles. Organic okay, sustainable, I get it. But these folks are taking things a high-step too far.'"

"For chuckles, let's have a conversation," Cora said.

"We are having a conversation."

"No, I mean, hypothetically speaking, a powwow regarding spillage of the beans."

Loretta pursed her lips, unsure of where this was going. "Huh?"

"We need some advice. So what if we told my dad? What's the worst that could happen?"

"Ethan would lose it." Loretta shook her head. "No. We can't, not yet. Like he said, at this point, we have no evidence, only speculation. Your dad will want to investigate, maybe go to his parents, or, worst-case scenario, to Brock, and either way, the finger will get pointed at him. If he's told to stay away from the bunker again, or from us even, he'll have no choice. You know how he gets. If the rules change, he falls apart. Ethan needs to keep order, even in this kind of circumstance."

"Okay. How about this. You talk to Greer."

"My mom?"

The cell phone in Loretta's hands vibrated, then rang.

"How does she *do* that?" Cora asked, stunned.

Loretta rolled her eyes, shrugging.

"Hello?"

"I've called, like, twenty times. Where have you been?"

"We've been...we went on a hike."

"A hike? You? And Cora?"

"Yeah, mom. Me. And Cora. Ethan too."

"We're wrapping up here. Another week, and I'll be home."

"Mom, I need to ask you something."

"Did you hear me? I'm coming home."

"You know that guy, the one who runs the meetings for The Group, those people who..."

"I know who they are."

Over miles of lines and cables, there was a cessation

of sound. "Why?" Greer finally asked, the single syllable hanging there like so much dead air.

The strange silence caused Loretta to fumble her words. "Well, we're kind of thinking. Maybe. He's up to more than he's telling his friends."

"Loretta. Listen to me now. Stay away from Brock. You hear me? Under no circumstances do I want you involving yourself in…"

"Oh. Right. You're supermom now, is that it? Really? I mean, *really?*"

"You asked, and I'm giving it to you straight. I'm serious, Loretta. You stay away from him."

"Whatever. Thanks for the help."

"Loretta? Loretta!"

Loretta muted her phone and threw it on the kitchen table, watching it vibrate its way to the edge and into Toby's food bowl as her mother tried again and again to reach her.

An hour later, Doc arrived with the requested DVDs and two plates filled with enchiladas and beans, a green salad, and sliced oranges. "Eat well, niñas. Sleep tight." He kissed both girls on their foreheads. "I love you. Enjoy movie night. Call me in the morning, Mija."

Loretta brought forks and napkins and glasses of milk from the kitchen, then she and Cora sprawled out on sleeping bags in front of the TV. "Your dad is beyond awesome," she said dreamily.

"Yes, he is. Which is why I'm feeling guilty."

"For what?"

"For not telling him what's going on."

"About that…"

"Mmmm. He does whip up a mean enchilada."

"About the bunker thing…"

Cora's mouth was full, but she tried to answer. "What about it?" She licked her fingers. "You gonna eat those orange slices?" Loretta slid them on to Cora's plate.

"We've got to get inside. According to Ethan, there's another meeting tomorrow night, and this one's a double-header. First, the regular get-together at the Grange, then a late-night hen-and-rooster-fest at the Iron Gate." Loretta snagged a cherry tomato from Cora's salad, wiped the salad dressing off on her napkin, and popped it in her mouth.

Cora guzzled her milk. "Oh, that's good. Cold," she said, wiping her mouth with her napkin. "Tomorrow morning, when we pick Ethan up, we'll try to convince him to take us in."

"His dad forbade him to go into the bunker. To be more accurate, which we know Ethan will be, his dad forbade him to go into the bunker *by way of* the main entrance. This he won't do. But I've been thinking…"

"That's always good news…"

"If we ask the right questions, he'll tell us what we need to know. He'll lead us *to* the bunker, for sure. He can draw a map…he's good with maps…and give us directions about where to go once we're inside."

"Ethan can be our guard. He'll like that." Cora pushed the pause button on the television remote. "Loretta?" she asked. "Are you scared?"

"A little." Loretta's stomach was full, her mind a bit food-foggy. "No, a lot," she said, reconsidering. She rubbed her chest, grimacing. "Acid indigestion, here it comes." She coughed, then drank some milk. "But we have no choice. Whatever is happening is hurting Ethan, and others too. The members of this Group, like his parents, are good people. They genuinely care, which is why they got hooked into this crap in the first place."

"Do we know that it's all crap?"

"Well, I'm assuming…"

"Big assumption. My dad always says don't judge a man until you've walked a mile in his shoes. Or in this case, don't judge people until you've seen *their* truth through your eyes."

"I'm not sure I want to walk in Brock's shoes. Or see the world through his eyes. I'm afraid where that might lead me."

Both girls turned their attention to the still life on the television. Cora pressed PLAY.

Sean Penn's voice trailed away, eerie music setting the scene. Michael Douglas was sitting at a desk, dressed in a suit, his attitude judgmental, suspicious.

"We've seen this. Title, please?" Loretta asked.

"*The Game.* Shhhhh!" Cora's shoulders rounded forward; her forearms were taut, the veins in her neck visibly pulsing.

"Oh. My. God. You're sucked in, and the movie's barely

started!" Loretta teased.

"Yeah, right." It was a barely concealed sneer. Cora hid her face in her pillow and laughed. "The plot of this flick could be, like, serious propaganda for Brock's Group," she said, adding air quotes with her fingers.

+++

When Ethan walked into the house, he did so quietly. It was late. His parents should have been asleep, but they weren't. Coming from their bedroom, their voices were loud and strained. An argument was a rare occurrence in their household, but nonetheless, that's what was happening.

"This kills me," his dad said.

"And what exactly do you mean? What is killing you, Sim, the fact that we've made a mistake in trusting Brock with our entire life savings, *or* that he is asking us to do something so morally reprehensible that neither one of us can stomach the reality of his proposal?"

Ethan considered what his parents were saying, but their words rambled around in his head without landing in a precise order. He covered his ears, not wanting to listen to their private conversation, but this action unnerved him even more. He let his hands drop, struck by the anguish in his mother's voice.

"Both! My God! We…our friends…we've invested up to our eyeballs. Financially. Physically. Ethically. Did you notice the faces of folks in the crowd today? We're not the only ones doubting him, Raina."

"The guy's talking genetic modification, Sim. He's talking about the perfect gene pool to 'repopulate the planet' after end times happen."

"He can't be serious about that, Raina. You know how Brock jokes around. This has to be one of his dumb attempts at humor."

"He rolls his eyes and laughs, yes. But I don't think he's joking. Not one bit."

And then he was in it, the argument behind the wall. "So how would you tell Ethan, exactly, that Brock's plans don't include him?"

"You know I wouldn't let that happen, Raina. And that's the last thing Ethan needs to hear, or feel, on any level."

"Say it, Sim. Say it out loud. Brock wants us to leave him behind. His excuse is and has been of late that Ethan is a troublemaker. That his Asperger's is a threat to the cohesion of The Group. And that's bullshit, Sim! All of it! The truth is, the only truth there is, is that Brock doesn't consider Ethan *worthy*. Ethan doesn't fit into Brock's plan for a perfect society, with perfect people, in his perfect little afterlife!"

Ethan wished the money in his pocket would buy his parents a minute. Maybe that minute would buy them an hour, and that hour would buy them a week in which to consider what they were saying more carefully. He wanted to join the argument. He wanted to retreat into his quiet place.

Instead, his body reacted, and he sprinted out the door,

down the street, across town. At the intersection of Inyo and Lake View, a car swerved to avoid hitting him. Cats scurried out of his way, and dogs barked their chain of alarm as he sprinted even faster. The glow from Loretta's house only made it so far, the unlit street partially hidden in shadow. Ethan tried to will himself forward, to step onto the driveway and up to the front door, but his muscles constricted and refused to move further. He crouched into a ball. Sweat dropped from his forehead off the tip of his nose, but then he smelled—stale beer? Is that what it was? Whatever the odor, it was unpleasant, noxious, and it mixed with the scramble of thoughts in his brain. Ethan screamed. Loudly enough that neighboring lights went on and faces peered through windows.

+++

Toby howled and wouldn't stop. Loretta scrambled to her feet, ran to the front door, opened it, and peered outside. At first, she didn't recognize Ethan, as he was shrouded in shadow, crouched in the dark beneath the cottonwood tree. When he saw her, he stood, though his body was still oddly bent over itself. Loretta opened the screen door and walked slowly toward him, talking softly, urging him into the house. "Hey, Ethan," she said. "Glad you're here…we're watching a movie…come on in."

She stood beside him then, giving him time to consider her offer. Neighbors turned their lights off. Loretta took a few steps toward the house, hoping he would follow. She soon heard the swish of his pants, his boots crunching gravel as he traced her footfall, both of them making a slow procession forward. She sighed her relief and made her way up the steps and back into the living room. Ethan dogged behind.

Still howling, Toby ran out the door, rounding the cottonwood and into the street. Did she hear footsteps? Someone running? Maybe so. Toby was on it, regardless. Cora brought three mugs of hot chocolate and placed them on the coffee table beside Ethan, who was now sprawled on the carpet. They sat in silence waiting until Toby returned and Ethan was ready to talk.

·CHAPTER 19·

*L*oretta wondered if the others felt as disheveled as she. None of them had showered; both she and Cora had changed clothes, ponytailed their hair at least, but Ethan was dressed in the same blue jeans he'd worn the day before, the same long-sleeved blue tee and faded blue sweatshirt. Even with his grunge style of dress, he always looked handsome—as a matter of fact, downright *hot*. That's what Loretta thought when she looked at him, that he was *hot*, and it didn't matter if his hair was unruly; a finger comb was all it took to capture his style anyway. Greer had prompted that look for Ethan. When he was a young teen, she'd ruffle his hair and tell him he was *hip* and as good-looking as any actor she had worked with on movie sets, with his hair all mussed and his layered shirts, the jeans and Timberland boots. Loretta smiled. Her mother—her fly-by-the-seat-of-the-pants, loud-mouthed, country-loving mom. As difficult as it had been to live with her throughout the years, there was that side of her that was loveable.

Ethan trusted Greer. Loretta remembered back when she and Ethan were kids, Ethan deciding one day that he wanted to be invisible. All day he had yelled at anyone who glanced his way, which the teasers at school did maniacally, just to see him react. That afternoon, during homework time at her house, Ethan screamed, "Stop staring at me! Don't look at me!" After a few minutes of bouncing her knee and puckering her lips, Greer held up her index finger. As if she'd sucked an idea out of space, she jumped up and danced a music-free hip-hop, popping and locking, boogalooing to the kitchen cupboard and back with three large paper bags and a pair of scissors. She cut holes in the bags where eyes and noses might be, and cut large smiling mouths with no teeth. She plunked herself down on a kitchen chair and put a bag on the table in front of Ethan and one in front of Loretta. The third bag she opened fully and put over her head, talking then to Ethan as if nothing had happened, as if nothing whatsoever was unusual. Loretta caught on and did the same. Eventually, so did Ethan. They completed that night's homework session with their heads in paper sacks, but it was done with no more tantrums and no tears. Ethan decided when it was time to remove the paper bag from his head. He did so, then Loretta and Greer did also, and afterward, they ate dinner: pigs in a blanket and watermelon cut into daisy shapes, and no one mentioned again about the bags or Ethan's desire to be invisible. After their meal they watched television, and Ethan laughed while Greer shot gummy bears across the living room, trying to hit her target—Loretta's open mouth.

Loretta allowed herself a moment of pride, but even with that pleasure there was the niggling desire for Greer to be a *normal* mom, like Jemma's, who made chocolate-chip cookies for school bake sales and arrived at teacher conferences at the scheduled time. Who squeezed lemons for homemade lemonade, wore respectable clothes, and made her daughter feel like her life was not complete without her in it. Loretta's mother was a jumble of contradictions, fierce but funny, off-color and a bit slutty, but she owned her style with pride. She was permissive but protective, the queen of TV dinners, but a champion of fruit art and cookie-cutter sandwiches—and with no more than a high school diploma, she had managed to help Ethan when others had failed.

And today, regardless of the tunneling they'd done the day before, aside from the emotional crap he'd experienced the night prior, Ethan was present, emotionally and physically. He'd grown so much and had learned how to manage life at his own pace. Last evening had been trying for all of them. Ethan had finally dozed off around two in the morning, and Cora shortly thereafter. But Loretta couldn't sleep. She jumped at every sound, tossing and turning each time Toby grunted or jerked; she watched his little legs run while he slept, wondering what he was chasing or fleeing. She couldn't clear her mind of the things Ethan had shared, the snippets of conversation between his parents. It took forever to coax even that from him, as his words clumped together like cold, sticky oatmeal. He blathered about "viability" and "worthiness" and "a perfect society," but the glue that should have bound these ideas together was no more than mumblings. Whatever was going on with Brock and within the confines of the bunker was affecting life as Ethan knew it. His default assumptions about the world he lived in relied on the credibility and forthrightness of his parents. Whatever he had heard had broken his core of trust, enough so that Ethan didn't want to go home, change clothes, brush his teeth, or even comb his hair—and those were biggies to him.

Add this to what Loretta already knew about Brock and The Group, the bunker—and her imagination flew. Her fear of involving others, Cora's dad, her mother, Granny Noleen, the police even, scrambled with what-if scenarios such as those she and Cora had invented when playing detective games as children, or those she had seen in movies. What might be real blended with improbabilities, but one thing became very clear: their next call to action was the right thing to do. She needed to see the bunker for herself before she alarmed others; she needed facts, as Doc would say, to present a probable cause for alarm. In those final minutes before dawn, this had become more than a game, bigger than her curiosity and movie-centered fantasies. The bunker was real. Whatever was happening there was going on now.

But there was also guilt, particularly regarding Cora's dad, and the minor deception or omission of information she and Cora presented. Ethan's mother had called not long after he arrived at her house the night before, and as Loretta spoke to her, reassuring her that Ethan was okay, she felt dishonest. Ethan was at her place all right, but he was definitely not okay.

+++

In the kitchen, Loretta and Cora ransacked the cabinets for something to eat, but they were depressingly empty. "Mother Hubbard's cupboard. This sucks," Cora said, her chin tucked into her shoulder, her hand propping open the refrigerator door.

"Let's hit the Penny Saver. I need sugar," Loretta said. "We'll pick up stuff for a picnic too, get enough for Granny and the others."

After the kitchen, Loretta and Cora wandered through the living room, the hall, and the downstairs bath, searching for clothes, shoes, a missing sock, hairbrushes, clips or hair ties. Toothpaste. Loretta could see Ethan still sitting on the couch, moving just enough to imply that he was more human than robot. She tried to forget about the bunker, concentrating instead on getting Toby fed, the wilted garden watered, a knocked-over gravestone righted, and Old Blue fired up and on the road.

They all three piled into the truck with their backpacks, one shoe in Ethan's hand, and Cora's hair still uncombed. Old Blue started up the first crank of the starter, much to Loretta's surprise. Cora sat next to the open passenger window putting on her socks, banging the dirt off her boots on the outside of the truck. She straightened her khaki shorts and tucked in her shirt, twisting on the bench seat as she finished dressing. "Stop bumping me," Ethan complained from his spot in the middle. "Please. Respect my private space."

"Are you kidding me? I can't believe this," Cora slammed back. "No sleep. No breakfast! Yesterday's socks and now you, Ethan, are Mr. Irritable. It's like the universe is trying to send me a message! Grumpy is as grumpy does. If my friends can't take it, neither can I. If something's going to go wrong, it will go wrong big. OK, Universe! I get it. What's next?"

Loretta turned on them both. "Damn! That's enough, just stop!" As soon as she said it, she wished she hadn't. Unable to retract her comment, she tightened her fingers around the steering wheel and drove.

Inside the Penny Saver Market, two young boys browsed the milk aisle; a man was pouring a coffee, a little girl pulling on his pant leg, and pointing her finger at the doughnuts. Loretta didn't bother with a basket; she, Cora, and Ethan made their selections and walked to the checkout counter, items in hand.

"Well, well, if it isn't the movie-trivia queen," Jemma

mocked, walking up behind them with a loaf of bread in her hand.

The checker ran their selections over the scanner: yogurt, pretzels, salami, cookies. And Ethan's peanut butter: Skippy's Natural, smooth, not chunky, and original Wheat Thins, regular size, not jumbo. An apple.

"Bug off, Jemma," Cora blasted. "I'm not in the mood…"

"Call off your dog, Loretta. Really." Jemma laughed, rolling her eyes.

"There's a name for you, Jemma," Ethan said, "but it's not appropriate to use in public."

Janice Blinn, the store manager, looked up from her task of stocking soup cans. "Is there a problem?" she asked, peering over her glasses.

"No ma'am, no problem," Jemma said. "Every customer's opinion is important here at the Penny Saver Market."

"Yeah, right," Cora added, with a barely concealed sneer.

"Oh, *yawn*," Jemma said, patting her mouth with her hand. "Take your Mutt-keteers back to the kennel, Loretta."

"OK, *Your Rudeness*. Really?" Cora fired back.

"Oh, really. You want to go there, *really*?" Jemma said, nodding her head toward Ethan.

"Just saying," Cora said. "If the *definition* fits."

The bag boy hurried through his packing job, his eyes darting from Jemma to Cora. In his rush to get out of the line of fire, he shoved the bag in Loretta's arms, knocking over the candy display at the end of the checkout counter. Ethan helped him pick it up, placing every bag of Jelly Bellies back in their rack.

"Nice to see ya, wouldn't want to be ya," Cora quipped, making sure she got the last word.

Loretta held the door open, and they marched outside and down the sidewalk toward the parking lot where they had left Old Blue. As they walked past the Eastside Deli, Ruby closed the shades. She didn't smile or wave as she usually did.

"What's up with that?" Cora asked Ethan.

"Two plus two," he mumbled.

As Ethan opened the door to the truck, Loretta translated, "He means it adds up. He means Ruby is one of them. He's saying Brock has gotten to her."

Back in the cab, no one spoke. Cora took the middle, scooting as close to Loretta as she could to give Ethan his space. Gray thunderheads capped Mt. Whitney. The air felt moist and thick and smelled caustic. Loretta flipped on the radio, and the news broadcaster mentioned a possible summer shower.

Boulders. Boulders. Acres of boulders. The lumpy Alabamas looked darker brown than usual, like shape-shifting granite transforming into an army of trolls.

"Your driving sucks," Cora teased. "Pedal to the metal, please, or we'll never get there."

A few droplets gathered on the windshield as the clouds

released some rain. It wasn't much, just enough to spatter the windows. Loretta turned on the wipers, and like a ticking metronome, they took up space where conversation lacked.

At the entrance to Willow Grove, the rain ceased, and a clap of thunder broke the sky revealing a rich patch of blue. There were two cars parked in the driveway: Clive's black Hummer and a tan Mercedes. Behind Loretta's truck, a cloud of dust announced another approaching car, this one moving at a fast clip.

"What the heck is going on?" Loretta asked, inching past the cars and into the yard in front of the house.

Ethan sat tall and stiff in his seat. As soon as the truck pulled to a stop, he opened the door and stepped out.

Two men stood near the vegetable garden, one dressed in a business suit, the other in a white, pearl-buttoned cowboy shirt, new Levis, and Tony Lama boots. The guy in the boots spun around and came at them in a hurry. Though he was dressed in western gear rather than a police uniform, Loretta recognized Clive immediately.

Clive approached her truck, looking smug. "Reinforcements?" he asked.

Sheriff Atkins pulled his police cruiser into the yard beside Old Blue, the cloud of dust made by his vehicle spiraling toward the creek. He didn't hesitate; he was out of the cruiser and walking toward Clive before Loretta could get out of the truck.

"What's this all about, Clive?" he asked.

"That's no longer your business, Neal. You saw to that when you fired me."

"This is not the time to go into that, Clive. What are you doing here?"

"I'm showing the property to Simon Brown. He's been here once but wanted another look around. The place is crap, as you can see, but Simon's ready to offer Noleen a good price if she's willing to take it."

"About the cease and desist order, Clive…"

"As real as the hand that signed it."

"I can argue with you about that until I'm blue in the face, man, but for now, Miss Noleen has issued a complaint of trespassing. And unless you can show just cause, I'm going to ask you to leave."

Clive rolled up the papers in his hand and slapped them against his thigh. He turned to Granny Noleen, who stood on her porch beside Earl. "This isn't over," he told her. "We *will* be back."

"Clive, that's enough. Pack yourself out of here. Now." Sheriff Atkins turned to the attorney. "I don't believe I've had the privilege," he said. "Simon? Is that correct?"

"Simon Brown," the attorney said, nodding.

"I'll be talking to you, Mr. Brown. Soon." Sheriff Atkins took a pad of paper from his back pants pocket and scribbled a note. "And Clive," he added. "Watch yourself, friend."

Clive chuckled and said, "Like that means a rat's ass."

He waved back-handed as he strutted down the driveway, followed closely by Simon. Sheriff Atkins trailed behind them, watching as they climbed into their cars and drove away. As if by magic, once the cars passed through the gate, the dust storm created by the Sheriff's police cruiser seemed to reenter from the creek, gyrating through the yard, whirring at the gate, and disbanding once Clive's Hummer was out of sight.

"Whoa," was all Loretta could say as she and Cora joined Ethan beside the porch.

Yoshi came out the front door with Pansy on his arm. He gently sat her in the rocking chair, and then leaned on the deck railing beside Noleen.

"Sorry about this, folks," Sheriff Atkins said as he approached them from the driveway. "I intend to speak with Clive and this…Mr. Brown. I will get to the bottom of things. But as I told you before, there are no legal grounds for the cease and desist that I can see. And as far as the vandalism that occurred here, I have no solid proof of who…"

"As a child, I was second-generation Japanese," Yoshi interjected. "When WWII started we had a home in Pasadena. My parents both worked. My father was a businessman. My mother was a seamstress. Our home got searched by military police one day. I never understood what they thought they would find. We were Americans. We had nothing to hide. A week later, we got a letter stating that we had six days to pack our belongings. We were told we could only take what we could carry. Seventy pounds. Our lives, our world, were limited to seventy pounds. We couldn't take our family dog. Or our furniture. Or my sister's piano. My mother cleaned every inch of our home; the kitchen, the bath, even the floorboards and baseboards were scrubbed." Yoshi paused. "She said our home reflected our pride. It spoke of who we were as a people, and whoever entered our door after we left would see that we were good and had no ill intent…that we were a proud *American* family." He paused.

"We were forced to board a train, hundreds of us. The blinds on the train were pulled so we could not see where we were going. When the train stopped, and as we piled out, we thought there had been a mistake. Military guards shuffled us into stables only recently vacated by horses. My mother took a deep breath, then began her work. She never complained or said a word, just cleaned as best she could and organized bedding for her family. I do not remember how long we were there, but it was long enough for me to realize it was a place we had been sent…that we did not *choose* to be there. From the stables, the guards brought us to the high desert by bus. To Manzanar, just miles from here. It was hot. And dry. And dusty. But again, my mother set her mind to creating a home out of nothing. We lined up for food, to use the bathroom, to take a shower. We slept in the dirt and breathed the dust and tasted it in everything we ate. The life we had known, the independence we were accustomed to, was gone. I remember the day my brother, my father, and mother were handed papers, requiring their signatures swearing their allegiance to the United States. My brother, then eighteen, enlisted in the Army. He fought the war against Japan. Against the Japanese. His people. Our people.

"Willow Grove is our home. We work hard to maintain it. It is clean and comfortable. I was too young during the war against Japan to stand up against prejudice and injustice, too young to understand what that meant. But today I am old enough to know that this is wrong. Today and tomorrow, I will fight with Noleen."

Sheriff Atkins stood quietly, head down, chewing his cheeks. "I was worried about how you folks might deal with Clive's threats," he said. "But I gotta say, I feel a little foolish. You're survivors. You'll do just fine."

"We can handle this little man's shit," Earl told him.

"All I got to say, is keep doing what you're doing, and I'll do my part to keep Clive at bay until I get this settled." Sheriff Atkins walked to his cruiser, opened the door, and then added: "Any of you. Call me anytime, day or night. Hear?"

Earl tipped his hat.

Sheriff Atkins pulled away slowly, checking his rear-view mirror as if he were expecting another dirt devil.

Loretta thought about the word "survivor," and how well it fit all those standing in front of her.

"Name them!" Cora said. "Underdog movies with a

happy ending. Go!"

"One. *The Goonies!*" Always Loretta's first choice when Cora suggested this category.

"Two. *Seabiscuit!*" No surprise: a horse movie title from Ethan.

"Three. *Shawshank Redemption!*" Loretta was on a roll. "Four. *Hunger Games!* Five. *Blindside! Holes!*" Her face reddened as she heard her own enthusiasm. *I'm turning into a nerd,* she thought. Then she thought: *Who cares?* "*Forrest Gump!*"

Cora gave her a standing ovation. "Better than a pity party, right?"

Ethan brushed his hands together. "Yes. And now we've got work to do." He trailed behind Earl to the ruined goat corral, picked up a broken timber and threw it to the side.

"Let's do this," Cora said. "Let's get 'er done."

+++

When they finished the goat pen, the remaining storm clouds were nestled in a gray halo around Whitney's peak. The air was humid, and even the chickens were searching for a respite from the heat, scratching holes in the dirt and settling in, taking dust baths. Yoshi nestled S'more on a bed of freshly seated straw, bringing her some grain, a pail of water, and an armload of alfalfa hay. Earl closed the gate and shook the fence line. "Yep. Well. It'll do just fine," he said. It felt good to see the little goat settled and nibbling on her hay, though the splint on her leg still caused her to look lopsided. Her body adjusted to the pain by tilting to the right with her weight balanced on her three good legs; the toes of the bad leg tested the ground tentatively, touching, jerking away, touching, jerking away.

Pansy sat rocking on the porch, staring at her flower-beds, the yard, the garden in the distance.

"Is she okay?" Loretta asked, brushing the hay off her arms.

"Everything that's happened, the cease and desist order, the vandalism...it's taken a toll on Pansy, brought on a bout of her Alzheimer's," said Earl. "The last few days, we've noticed changes. Yoshi drove her to the doctor, and yep, well... let's just say...Doc laid the cards on the table, and the hand she's been dealt ain't the greatest, I'm afraid."

There was no lipstick on Pansy's lips. Her cheeks were not the hot pink color Loretta had come to love. There was a hollow look in her eyes as if she were searching for some-thing—as if she were there but not there.

"Is she going to stay this way?" Cora asked.

"She'll come and go for a while," Earl explained. "The doctor said there will be good days and bad. It's a progressive disease, though, darlins', and I'm afraid we'll be seeing more of this side of it as time passes."

"Lunch!" Granny Noleen hollered from the doorway. Yoshi brought a large brass bowl from the barn and a fresh bar of soap. He filled the bowl with water and washed his hands, then dried them on one of several hand towels Noleen had strewn across the deck railing. When it was Loretta's turn, she washed her face and hands, reveling in the smell of lavender soap, the cool water in the bowl, the feel of an air-dried towel against her skin.

Pansy called out to her. "Girl? Help me up, will you please?" She was awkwardly polite; her childish manner of speech, bubbling smile, and joyful eyes were missing.

Loretta grasped Pansy's arms and lifted her to her feet. She took her hand then and led her to the house, in the door, and to the kitchen table. Yoshi pulled out Pansy's chair, helped her sit, and pushed her chair in closer to the table.

"Why all the fuss?" Pansy said, as if a breaker had flipped inside her head and the circuits had recharged. She lifted a jar of jam, smelled it, dipped a finger into it, and tasted. "Yum! Strawberry, my favorite!" She licked her lips and used a spoon to plop a huge dollop onto her plate. The jam sat on its own, shimmering on white porcelain. Pansy seemed intent on declaring it her main course.

Yoshi smiled and kissed her on the cheek, then sat beside her on the bench seat.

"Well, yep," Earl said, settling himself comfortably in his seat at the head of the table. "It's all good, then." He winked at Pansy. "Praise the grub and pass the bread."

Noleen bustled from counter to table, filling it with baskets of homemade sourdough bread. Bowls filled with peanut butter and jam. Trays of fruit: bananas, apples, and blackberries from the vines outside. A smorgasbord of chees-es: cheddar, jack, swiss, and muenster. Baby carrots from the garden. Last season's pickled beets.

Loretta remembered their groceries in the truck and thought of retrieving them, but decided against it. There was enough food at the table for everyone—no need adding more. She felt Ethan's foot touch hers as he stretched his long legs under the table. Earl and Yoshi talked, occasional laughter poking its way through their conversation. Noleen eventually sat down, but she seemed edgy. She filled her plate but only picked at her food, swallowing no more than a mouthful or two.

-CHAPTER 20-

When Ethan was a child, he called any flying insect a flutterbee. Once when he was little, a therapist asked him to describe the confusion in his brain, and he used that word to name it: Flutterbees. Years later, with another therapist, he gave the term a definition: a cacophony of voices in the midst of chaos. As he sat beside Cora in Loretta's old truck, those memories came back, and with them the flutterbees, stirring the airy breath inside him with their illogically patterned flight. The other definition that intruded on his thoughts attached to the word "brainwashing:" *to indoctrinate so intensively that one influences a radical transformation of beliefs and mental attitudes.* This issue of mind control popped up and disappeared, popped up and disappeared, until he could no longer dismiss it.

In spite of everything, it had been a good day. Ethan felt great about completing the repairs to the goat pen. And before that, in the pre-dawn hours, he and Loretta and

Cora had formulated a workable plan regarding the bunker. Loretta was right—she was usually right—though telling her so would be pointless. She was compassionate, loyal, and smart. Mindful. Character traits that should provide a degree of emotional stability, yet she never recognized these qualities in herself. Her points and Cora's as well had been spot-on. One. He had been going into the bunker with his father since construction first began. Two. His father had shown him the worksite and projects underway and completed. There were a couple of areas where he wasn't permitted—the munitions room and the garage—but he'd had access without question to the game room, the cafeteria, and the sleeping quarters. Three. Until the rules changed. Until Brock refused him entrance by way of the stairs. Which brought up point number four. What would happen if they chose not to use the stairs? What might the consequences be if they went into the bunker through the tunnel and steel door? Technically, he wouldn't be breaking any rule. Particularly one set by his father. And here lay the strongest convincer they had thrown at him. Five. Throughout his life, had not his parents told him that when a person was in danger, if there was a possibility of bodily harm, if someone was threatened, emotionally or physically, it was okay to break a rule? "It would be worse to stick your head in the sand and refuse to help the people you love," Loretta had said.

So the plan was set. He knew what he had to do. And

it wasn't dishonorable, since his father had given him the master access code, had him punch the numbers and open Brock's office after hours one day when he was busy and overtired. "I left my cell phone on Brock's desk," he had said while sweeping up a mess of sheetrock dust in the bunker's soon-to-be-completed infirmary. "In and out, okay? Be back here in five, no exploring, got it?"

Ethan flicked his fingers, knowing that his father had expected him to forget the code, but he hadn't, and could recite it as clearly now as he did that day in the bunker.

Ethan made a mental list of the rules he knew must be strictly adhered to: the speed limit, the number of fish you can catch per season, campfire regulations in the forest, the no-weapons policy at school. He also thought about other rules, like certain laws that should be indisputable, according to Loretta: relativity, cause and effect, the rhythm of life, and love. Fertility and gestation. Parental responsibility. Goodwill. Forgiveness. The right of all living things to be treated with dignity and respect.

He delved further, thinking about the gray rules—the ones that aren't as clearly understood. The ones that have nothing to do with safety or habitat or environmental concerns. These gray rules were the ones with which he had trouble. They existed outside the realm of rightness and wrongness and in his world, that was a point of confusion.

+++

Loretta pulled Old Blue onto a gravel turnoff near Ethan's house. "Remember," she said, squaring off to face him, "the only way to get close to the bunker is to use a vehicle that won't arouse suspicion. Under the circumstances, I feel better meeting you somewhere other than home. How about if we meet near Carmen's house? I'll leave my truck there."

The car thing had felt okay in the discussion phase of the plan, but now that they were near to implementing it, Ethan wasn't sure. As he walked up the path to the front door, he felt a chill, though the air was still warm. He had always thought this an odd time of day—when the sun and moon crossed paths, and the long evenings of summer kept the dark at bay. A gray squirrel chirped from a willow tree as Ethan walked beneath it. The neighbor's dog howled. "Shhh, Fritz, it's me," he said, peering over the fence, scratching the old German shepherd between the ears.

Ambient light filled the living room, which made the space feel homier and the house emptier. His mother's wind chimes tinkled a soft, soothing melody, and the large crystal prism she'd hung in the front window cast a rainbow of colors on the hearth. He walked into the kitchen and to the table, where his father's computer sat with the screen open. Ethan clicked on a folder named SECURITY. Inside was a calendar. Monday night: Bale – 7:00 pm to 7:00 am. Just as he thought.

The Subaru keys hung beside the kitchen door on a

dragonfly hook, its tail curved upward to hold keys. He had given this to his mother for her birthday one year, and he felt proud that he had purchased it with his own money, earned by mowing lawns around the neighborhood and doing chores around the house: chopping wood, raking the yard, cleaning the garage with his dad. With Sim. The name and the person rattled around in his brain. And the words "love" and "hypocrisy" floated to the top of everything else.

Ethan checked his wallet to make sure his license was there before he lifted the key off the hook. He crinkled his nose at his DMV picture, proof that he had refused to smile when the clerk asked him to, and that he had had a dime-sized zit on his chin that day. Still, the license was a reminder that he had passed both the written and behind-the-wheel tests in only one try—same with his motorcycle written and hands-on. "Easy-peasy for a vocabulary whiz," Loretta had told him when he picked her up for his first real on-his-own drive in the Subaru.

He had been driving for a year now, though admittedly he had cruised on his motorcycle more often than in the car. Feeling anxious, he fumbled with the keys, dropping them on the table. He found Raina's tablet and a pen near Sim's computer, and following the house rules, wrote a note: "Sim and Raina. I took the car. I'm with Loretta and Cora. Your son, Ethan."

The green Subaru Outback was in its stall. "An old-ie but goodie," his father always said. Ethan liked the trustworthiness of that statement. He fired up the car and drove to where Loretta said she'd meet him, near Miss Carmen's house. As he passed the house, he saluted, though there was no sign of Carmen. He had great respect for her—the woman was in her late seventies, but she never missed a weekday selling tamales at her stand. She was the sole support for her family: a disabled husband and several children, all the kids fruitful and thriving. One of them was in The Group, though he had never seen Lupita participate in bunker preparation activities. Come to think of it, he had noticed that Brock ignored her suggestions at meetings. Her hand often shot up, offering to volunteer for supply inventory or food management—but he couldn't remember a time when she'd been chosen.

Ethan parked less than twenty yards from the main intersection to Highway 395, and when Loretta opened the car door, he could smell the diesel fuel that powered the big trucks and the metallic stench of brakes. Loretta climbed into the front seat and Cora into the back. Both girls had secured their seatbelts before his foot hit the gas and the Subaru shot forward out into traffic, heading north.

Ethan's mind ticked thoughts like seconds on a stopwatch. Somewhere, in the midst of a chronological ordering of group picnics and meetings, bunker construction, and the presumptive insanity of Brock's mandatory declarations, lingered a question about Willow Grove and Clive and that too-smooth lawyer with the pencil-thin lips. Noleen's property was in decent shape but the house needed some repairs. The roof was missing shingles, the exterior paint was peeling, the windows needed re-caulking, and there was some earth-to-wood contact along the foundation—problems he learned to recognize working alongside his contractor father. But there was nothing major that would suggest the need for demolition. And the nuisance complaint, well, that was a matter to which he couldn't relate.

Cora leaned over the front seat and tapped Loretta's shoulder. "The thinking going on in this car is causing me brain strain. I need some tunes," she said. "Please."

Loretta turned the radio on and pushed the seek button to find the local station.

"...record heat continues," the DJ announced. "The Department of Water and Power is asking that you conserve water when irrigating your yards and gardens.

"At Friday's Board of Supervisor's meeting, an additional study was requested before supervisors would agree to take a final vote on the designation of wilderness areas.

"Sadly, a local resident was attacked and beaten last night in the alleyway behind the Eastside Deli. The man, identified as fifty-seven-year-old Lone Pine resident Shawn Bailey, was transported by ambulance to Southern Inyo Hospital for treatment."

Loretta flicked off the radio. "Enough bad news. Oh God, I sound like my mother."

"Shawn Bailey," Ethan blurted. "Shawn Bailey!"

"You know him?" Loretta asked.

"He was in The Group, a Committee member. He defected. He walked out in the middle of a meeting."

"Turn!" Cora shouted.

Words flew out of Ethan's mouth before he could stop them: "Clive replaced Shawn as Brock's bodyguard. Now Shawn's been hurt. Clive is threatening Noleen. Brock and the Committee have an agenda...the tunnels...the bunker...they're connected, we know that already, but they want Willow Grove. That's the missing piece! The house, the property...that's what's needed to complete the project!" He banged his palm on his temple.

"Turn, now!"

Loretta looked blank-eyed from Ethan to Cora. "What?"

"Act like you're going to my house, Ethan. Do it, now!" Cora demanded.

"Why? Your dad's not home." Ethan stared in the rear view mirror at Cora.

"He won't know that!"

"Who?"

"Clive! He's been following us for the last two blocks."

Ethan flipped the turn signal, braked, and turned right at the next corner.

"Your dad's car is in the driveway."

"Pull in behind it. The car's here but he isn't. The Cerro Coso College van picked him up this morning. He's leading a field trip at Manzanar today."

Ethan parked the Subaru behind Doc's Mini Cooper. "Get out," Cora said. "Follow me through the gate." Ethan did as he was asked, exiting the car and following Cora and Loretta to the fence and through the gate. They peered through the cracks between the cedar boards, watching as Clive's big black Hummer crept past Cora's house, turned near the end of the block and passed by once more, coming nearly to a stop behind the Subaru. Cora raced into the back door, flung it open, and flipped on the house lights. She ran inside, opened the front door, and grabbed the newspaper from the stoop.

"Dad, we're home!" she called out, louder than normal.

The Hummer sped up and drove away.

Cora fumbled in her father's desk, pulling out a pad of paper and a pen.

"What are you doing?" Loretta asked.

"I'm leaving a note for my father. Someone needs to know where we are."

Ethan couldn't argue with this logic.

They left the house the way they came in, through the back door. Cora double-checked the lock, circled around front, and checked the lock on the front door as well.

Ethan looked up and down the street for any sign of Clive. He glanced at Loretta to gauge her reaction, but all he saw was her watery eyes. He followed her to the car and opened the door for her, wondering if he had upset her somehow. Neither she nor Cora was talking, and the silence was *too* quiet. He bounced from foot to foot, flicking his fingers. Should he say something? Maybe, but he couldn't think what, so he bit his lip and climbed into the Subaru. As if on auto-drive, he continued their planned course of action down Highway 395, turning left on Whitney Portal Road.

"InYo Face, the Avenger!" Cora screamed abruptly.

Loretta jumped, then laughed, though she was still sniffling. "Great. You copped my line."

Ethan was glad to see Loretta smiling, and he knew what Cora was talking about: The aptly named InYo Face boulder, a large granite rock in the Alabama Hills of Inyo National Forest, had become a symbol over the years; of what, he couldn't say. Graffiti artists had painted eyes, lips, and a nose on the rock, and her expression and thus her mood changed yearly as people left their mark. Oddly enough, considering his dislike for defacement of natural resources, InYo Face seemed appropriate and excusable, for some reason. The three friends had spent many nights leaning against her smile or frown. Mean talkers and intentional rudeness had often been their topics of discussion, and *InYo Face* had become their war cry, a fist raised for change.

Yesterday in Lone Pine, bullies had beaten a man near the Eastside Deli. Today, he had mended a goat pen that had been maliciously destroyed, and now Clive was spying on him and his friends. At this very moment, his father was attending a meeting coordinated by an *evildoer* named Brock.

"Do you remember that rap we wrote together, the one with the line about haters, deflators, and label creators?" Loretta asked.

"Men who trap you, and zap you, who handicap and strap you," Ethan added.

"Yes, that's right. We talked about how it might feel to *be* someone like that; a person who *hurts* others, whose words "bite," as you might say." Loretta's voice sounded calm but serious, as if she wanted his full attention. "Ethan, I need you to think about something." She turned sideways in her seat, facing him now. "I know how important it is that you follow the rules your parents set for you. But we have a situation here where following those rules might put someone in danger. People you care about." She swiped at a strand of hair that had escaped her braid and stuck it behind her ear.

"Do you remember rapping this line? *"Bitter men bet on beastly experiments. Break your heart and your head until you bow to their regiments..."*

"Yes." And Ethan added: *"Men who drill you, mislead you, brow-beat, and force-feed you...sweet talking manipulators, assassinators, obliterators."* He scowled. "Brock got *so* mad at me when I rapped this at a Group picnic."

"Exactly."

"I won't chicken out."

"I know you won't."

The rap song he and Loretta wrote provided a useful comparison to his present situation. His thought fragments balled up into something more tangible and for this reason and others he did not fully grasp, he somehow knew the bunker break-in was appropriate. His finger flicking turned into a fist pump, and he yelled "InYo Face!" so loudly, his voice cracked.

"InYo Face! InYo Face!" Loretta and Cora echoed.

-CHAPTER 21-

"Best-case scenario, we go in, find the evidence to prove Brock's involvement in something illegal, get out, and then call the cops," Loretta said.

"Best-case scenario implies that there's a worst-case scenario." Ethan leaned over the steering wheel, focusing on the road ahead.

"As far as we know, Brock's done nothing illegal. The law can't go after someone just because they're creepy," Cora reminded Loretta.

"Of course not, silly," Loretta said. "We're chumming and will hopefully catch a big enough fish to pique the law's interest, that's all."

"You're such a dork."

"Dorkiness can be cool. So yeah, I'll own it."

"The definition of illegal can be vague," Ethan said.

"And..." said Cora, "What you mean by that *is?*"

Loretta shot her a look.

Ethan released the sardonic grin that had been frozen on his lips. "Illegal, according to Webster, is an action not authorized by law…not sanctioned by the rules of the game. But who sets the laws and who posts the rules? By what authority? Brock is the leader of The Group. The head of the Committee. His word is the ultimate truth, so accordingly, and not dismissing Webster, nothing he does is illegal."

The Subaru wheezed and sputtered and slowed to a roll. Ethan's white t-shirt draped his body in an uncharacteristic fashion; damp yellow circles stained his underarms, and perspiration glistened on his cheeks.

Loretta crossed her arms to conceal her own sweaty pits; she felt the moisture on her brow began to bead up and roll, etching trails through her mascara, bleeding salty liquid into her mouth. She turned up the air conditioner, but it only blasted warm air.

"Needs Freon," Ethan explained.

Loretta sighed and rolled down her window, sticking her head out to dry her face. The smells of creosote and high desert sage were oddly pleasant, but the road dust made her cough.

"Pick on, or off," Ethan said, with his hand on the air conditioner switch.

"On," Loretta said, as she rolled up her window. "It wasn't awful when it was set on low, but high is like a blast furnace."

"A little sweat is better than eating road dust," Cora added.

They were officially in the middle of nowhere, way past the entrance to Willow Grove, on a section of road Loretta had never traveled. Ethan braked and flipped his left-hand turn signal, though there were no other cars, and the main road had died out a good mile back.

An ancient bristlecone pine was an easy landmark for anyone who knew what they were looking for, but within a forest of native trees, it appeared nondescript until Loretta looked more closely. The tree displayed a myriad of scars, suggesting a history of wildfires and severe winter freezes; its twisted crown was indicative of heavy wind loads, and one lateral branch had suffered a lightning strike, yet the tree survived and held firm to the rocky ground. Loretta's mother had teasingly said to the *uncles* that her daughter's feet were tethered to the mountains like the roots of an old pine. Now, while admiring the tree, for the first time in her life she appreciated the analogy.

The dirt road dipped into a wide but low-flowing creek bed. Ethan drove against the gentle current, following the water's path up the hill and around to the right, where he pulled onto a large, flattened dirt pad. Here the road grew wider and was more clearly marked. A bulldozer was parked along the shoulder, also a dump truck, a Jeep with a large plow, and a brush chipper—all part of a staging area for some major construction site.

An electric swing gate with a keypad entry barred further progress up the road. Ethan keyed in his father's master passcode, the one shared with him that day in the bunker, and that he had watched his father punch in numerous times over the past year: "13-17-37-53-67," he recited. And then he explained: "Prime numbers equaling 187. The first three digits of my father's building contractor license number."

After a series of beeps, the steel doors swung open. Just inside, Ethan pointed out a large boulder marked by petroglyphs depicting deer, birds, and snakes, and one large disk that looked eerily like a flying saucer.

"Wow, look at that," said Cora. "These are better than the petroglyphs at Tuttle Creek."

A telescoping circle of light shone dimly over the top of a small hill.

"The bunker." Ethan's face was masked in shadow, but the disdain in his voice was apparent. He approached the area slowly, negotiating a turnout at the bottom of the rise, making a U-turn, and parking the car along the berm, facing downhill: a getaway maneuver Loretta was pleased to see. "The path to the tunnels is directly through these woods," Ethan said. "We need to hurry. The Group meeting will begin at 7 p.m. and run until 10. A projected three hours… but Brock can be very talkative, or not, so that timeframe might not be accurate."

When Ethan shut off the engine, the sudden quiet and anticipation of dusk were palpable. They closed the car doors as quietly as they could, but the clink of metal on metal was too loud, too conspicuous. Loretta scowled at the car door, wondering who else had heard and who might be coming to search them out.

+++

They stumbled through willow brush, following a deer path around the perimeter of the hill. Loretta scraped her leg on a sharp thorn and felt blood ooze from her shin down into her sock. "Ow," she whispered, rubbing the scratch without slowing her stride. At this point in the path, where the brush thickened, Ethan took a sharp left, dodging the worst of it with the skill of a tracker. Cora clumsily tried to mirror his steps, and Loretta flailed behind, wishing she'd worn her high-top hiking boots, as they had, rather than tennis shoes.

Loretta pulled her cell phone out of her pants pocket and clicked it on to check the time. 6:55 p.m. It seemed like they'd been walking for hours, but in truth, they had left the car no more than thirty minutes ago. She glanced at the phone icon, displaying a missed call notification. From her mother's cell. She hugged her phone to her chest before slipping it back into her pocket. Not listening to the voice mail was as difficult as resisting a call from Brady, but she couldn't—not now.

At the top of a small hill was the stone marker, the entrance to the cave that led to the tunnels. Cora and Ethan drank from their water bottles. Loretta's hands shook, and she felt sweaty, overheated. She fumbled in her pack for her water bottle as well, pulled it out, then struggled to open it.

Ethan reached for her bottle and unscrewed the cap. "Here," he said, "Drink. And eat this." He handed her and Cora a protein bar. "Carbohydrates," he added. "For energy."

Loretta gratefully accepted both, as Ethan checked and adjusted the other contents of his pack: flashlight, shorts, extra shirt, baseball cap, pocketknife, crackers with peanut butter, fruit-roll-ups, an apple.

As Loretta munched on her protein bar, she rummaged through her pack and found her flashlight, stuffed near the bottom under wadded-up socks and paper towels, pretzels (now smashed), yogurt (now liquid), warm salami. She rubbed her queasy stomach, wishing she had included Tums.

"Seven-ten," Ethan said, looking at his watch. "We've got to move."

Just as Loretta stood, a white flash popped through the brush, dotting the nearby trees. A second flash lit the rocks around the cave entrance, and Cora gasped, falling to her knees. Loretta pivoted and crouched, snapped her fingers to get Ethan's attention, and pointed in the direction of the flash. Familiar laughter lifted the thick air, and in an instant, they all three knew the source. Pansy. The flash must have come from the Nano-light she carried when berry picking – "So I can see what I'm putting my fingers into," she liked to say. It didn't matter the time of day; she used it religiously. The blackberry patch she frequented was a long, dense thicket that grew for miles along the creek bed, and

Pansy's presence reminded Loretta how close they were to Willow Grove's property line, half a mile, maybe a little more. Pansy loved picking berries this time of night: "The berries are ripest when the songbirds put their babies to sleep," she had said often enough. It made sense that she was scouring the thicket for the berries she used in pies, and cobblers, or sugared up, or eaten fresh, and it also made sense that someone else would be with her. Noleen had made it clear that she wouldn't allow Pansy to go out on her own, for a lot of reasons, but mostly because of her tendency to wander off with a pail in her hands—which meant that Earl or Yoshi, maybe even Bill, was nearby as well.

Cora laid a finger on her lips, then waved Loretta and Ethan forward and into the tunnel entrance. Cora went first this time, scooting on her bottom down the slope and into the hole. Ethan went in on hands and knees, disappearing in the dark before Loretta had time to protest. After one quick gulp of air, she followed. The rocky ground dug into her knees and the palms of her hands. Just as before, the lack of clean air left her feeling suffocated. She sucked a breath filled with tunnel dust and tried to stifle a cough, but couldn't. Ethan rounded to look at her, his eyes wide with concern. She signaled she was okay and tried to stand, but hit her head on the rock ceiling, fumbled for her flashlight and turned it on before crashing back to her knees.

Cora and Ethan sprinted ahead. Fighting the urge to groan a complaint, Loretta pushed forward, barely keeping up. The doorway to the bunker was as they left it, cold and menacing in its rocky tomb. Ethan punched his father's code into the keypad, and the red admission light blinked green. That quickly. That easily. He pushed the lever handle down and pulled the door open, exposing what appeared to be a detection center or control room.

"Brock's office," Ethan whispered, wide-eyed.

Loretta leaned over Cora's shoulder. "Breaking and entering. Not something I ever imagined myself doing."

At that, Ethan froze. Loretta admonished herself for saying it. She should have known it would give Ethan pause. Some long seconds later, she saw him lift his shoulders, flick his fingers once, and take a step.

Cora followed Ethan into the room. "We'll ask for adjoining cells," she squeaked. "Dad will bring us reading material. Your mom, chocolate."

Ethan propped the door open with a swivel chair and seemed to feel more comfortable once he'd established an escape route.

Loretta stood in the center of the room, arms at her sides, contemplating the unthinkable. Even though the break-in had been discussed at length and was planned preemptively, suddenly, and irrevocably, their mission was real. Now she was in the midst of it, in the office of someone she barely knew, and the reality of the offense hit her. She rebuked herself. Had she expected that the evidence they were seeking would stand up and shout: "Here I am!" No.

They needed to snoop, to spy—this was no movie scene.

Inside, near the back of the room, was a large mahogany desk. And a wall lined with computer monitors, each one featuring a still display of what appeared to be rooms within the bunker: kitchen, infirmary, library, conference room, munitions room, sleeping quarters, game room, supply rooms, garage. There also must have been cameras installed in the tunnels; a split screen on one computer showed the rocky walls, dimly lit, the area surrounding the cabinet where they found the ammunition—and also some junction within the tunnel, an intersect where it veered in two directions, perhaps nearer to Willow Grove.

Ethan stood in the middle of the room, arms at his sides, fingers flicking.

"Ethan," Loretta whispered, "Remember our deal. You're the guard. You know what to do, right?"

Ethan nodded, pointing toward a windowed door in the far right corner of the room.

Cora directed her flashlight beam at the wall of monitors, focusing on first one, and then the next. "Wait. Is this what I think it is?" she asked, waving Loretta over to get a closer look at the screen display—a wide-angle visual of Noleen's living room. Earl entered the room from the kitchen and sat in a recliner chair, picked up the paper, and shuffled through pages. Yoshi strode in, waving his arms, voicing what appeared to be some concern. Earl dropped the paper and trudged behind Yoshi out the front door. "My God, he's spying on them!" Cora whispered in an exhale. "This is so not cool. Hidden cameras? Are you serious?"

"Ethan was right," Loretta said. "The Committee, or Brock, wants Willow Grove, the property; its proximity to the bunker, the access through the tunnels is too valuable to overlook."

"Sneaky sons-of-bitches."

"Seriously."

A DVD player was attached to the central computer screen, and there was a camera set up to record. Dolphins leaped across the screensaver, but Cora bumped the mouse, chasing them away and displaying the desktop. An array of icons populated the screen, named and ordered by date. Cora took hold of the mouse and hovered the cursor over an icon nearest the taskbar. She hesitated. "I don't know…"

"Don't be afraid. Don't be that girl. Not now." Loretta cleared her throat, trying to rid herself of the nerve-ridden staccato in her voice.

"Is someone there?" A deep raspy shout came from inside the bunker proper—maybe in the hallway or in an adjoining room.

"Bale," Ethan mouthed. He pitched past Loretta, heading for the interior door. As he grabbed the handle, he turned back, and nodded a go-ahead. The door closed behind him with a snap of metal and puff of air.

"Bale! It's me. Ethan! I'm looking for my father," Ethan yelled.

The walls were a deterrent, but Loretta could still hear him. She could see his back, plastered against the small window glass in the door's top section. He was taking his job as their guard seriously.

"*Sim* is in town, Ethan, at the Committee meeting with Brock. Everyone's at the Grange Hall," the raspy voice replied.

"Mom won't be there. She's working. I doubt Ruby will be there. Unless she closes the diner. You won't be there because you're here. The term *everyone* is relative."

"*Sim* is at the meeting."

"Sim, *Sim*! The man you call Sim is my father. And according to the dictionary, a father is a man who has begotten a child. That child is me. Ethan is the name my father gave me. My father is Sim. The confusion comes by way of Brock's declaration stating that I can no longer call the man I have known all of my life as father, *Father*!"

"Stop blathering, boy. How'd you get in here anyway? I didn't hear…"

"According to the online dictionary, there are many definitions of the word *father*. One. A male parent. Two. The founder of a family. Three. The head of an organized crime family. Though, of course, in this instance that doesn't apply."

Loretta could no longer see Ethan's back, but she could hear his voice, farther away now, down the hallway, leading Bale away from Brock's office. "Four. The founder, or *father,* of a discipline or science. Now there is an interesting similitude. Stephen Hawking. According to Brock's terminology-based description of nondescript fatherhood, Stephen Hawking could be a person of relevant interest…"

"Oh, my God…" Bale said.

Though Loretta couldn't see Bale, she could hear his exasperation, and that made her smile.

Cora whistled softly and pointed at monitor A.

"How can we get man back to perfect?" Brock's image flashed on the monitor; the camera was focused on him, his pointer finger commanding attention. The room was filled with people faced away from the videographer. All but Brock—his curly hair neatly combed, parted to one side, his thick brows snaked across his forehead, and his eyes shining with an animal-like intensity. He wore a short-sleeved light blue shirt and a dark blue tie, loosened at the neck.

Brock was working the room, side to side, back and forth, dominating his audience with the intonation of his voice: "The only way we can do this is to defend ourselves from within. We must be ready. There's so much wrong with this world, friends. Think about it. We're being attacked from all directions, in the name of religion, democracy, political party affiliation, radicalism. Our kids are diagnosed at an alarming rate with autism, bipolar disorder, diseases of the blood and bone. We're being told to feed them medicines that are insanely addictive." At this point in the tape, Brock physically shrank. It was an incredible thing to watch, and

Loretta moved closer to the screen, unable to help herself. "And do you know what scares me the most? Jared, do you know? Mason, you?

"Let me tell you what, folks. I've discovered a little secret. The secret is purity. Family. But a new kind of family. And here's an example." The camera scanned the audience, and Frey stood up, walked toward the podium, to Brock. "My man Frey, here, is a Gulf War vet. You all know that, right?" Brock waited for the appropriate acknowledgments, the ooh's and aah's to die down. "When I found him, Frey was living at a VA Hospital. He has PTSD. Associated with his tour in the Middle East. Most of the time, Frey moves through life like the rest of you, doing daily tasks, working, relaxing. But there are moments, triggered by something he sees or hears, and he's drug backward into a storm that feels out of control. Windmills become helicopters. An acrid smell becomes gunpowder. The sound of gunfire...well...it takes Frey over the brink." Brock stopped talking, and put his arm around Frey's visibly shaking shoulders, pulled him tighter, then softened his tone. "It's okay, man, we're here. I'm here, remember?

"Our friend, Frey, has been attacked so many times in his mind, it's hard to distinguish sometimes whether he's here or in Iraq." Brock guided Frey to an empty chair in the front of the room.

"To be human is to be small, powerless, and subject to the forces of the world around you. Tomorrow it might

be your ass that gets blown up in the shitter, who knows?"
He paused again. "Wouldn't it be great to know that we're
safe? That these outside forces have no control over our lives?
That by our own devices we control our destiny? To have the
chance to test that theory…my God, my God, it's an answer
to our prayers. Control. Purity. Our choices, our decisions."

Someone in the audience returned a volley of questions:
"What do you mean? Purity by what means? Do you all not
see this is crazy?"

"Holy shit! You doubt my word, even now?"

"Brock, we *do not* doubt your word. We only want answers." This voice sounded like Sim's. "We've given ourselves,
our families, our time and our money to this project. We
want to be informed and included in the decisions, is all. A
lot of what you're saying is new information. And you have
to admit, it's a bit harsh."

In the video, Brock paced the floor. He closed his eyes.
"This spoken by a man on the Committee," he said, placing
his hands on his heart. "A man who helped write the bylaws of The Group. I ask you, friends, has this not been, a
democratic process? Have we not tried our best to address
all of your requests?"

"This can't be real," Loretta whispered.

"Carry on! We're with you!" came a cry from the middle
of the room.

"Thank you. Thank you. You people are…amazing.
"As I was about to explain," he continued, dusting off his

shirt sleeves as if wiping away the protests. "The bunker will become a depository of DNA and reproductive cells." He stopped and wiped his brow with a handkerchief he'd pulled from his pocket.

"With our cryogenics and nuclear transfer programs, we can help preserve the biodiversity of the planet from a possible life extinction event. This will assure the greatest chance of future restoration, regardless of the coming catastrophes. The bunker, and others like it, may be the next 'Genesis' for our Earth, providing a new beginning for life as we know it."

Cora clicked Pause, and the computer screen froze to a single image. "The guy's a wacko. I can't watch anymore."

"We have to keep going. Open another. The one titled 'Indoctrination Session.'"

Cora hesitated, then clicked open the second icon.

Brock sat in a chair this time, facing an individual seated directly across from him, no more than two feet away. The camera was set at an angle so only the back of the interviewee could be seen. Brock's face was again the focus of the video.

"What are you?" Brock asked.

"What do you mean?" the subject answered, a young boy, from the pitch of his voice.

"What are you?"

"A kid."

"What are you?"

"A trouble-making kid."

"Honesty. I like that. And you're right."

Brock sat quietly, his eyes ever focused on his subject.

"Who cares about you, boy?"

"You do, Brock."

"Who likes you, boy?"

"You do, Brock."

"Who takes care of you, boy?"

"You do, Brock."

"Yes, and I'm the only one. Not your drunk-ass parents. Me. I take care of you. I believe in you. Who believes in you, boy?"

"You do, Brock." The boy was tearful, his voice gurgling and strained.

"That's right, boy. Your parents, they don't give a shit about you. That's why they forget to pick you up from school some days, leave you there on the steps until dark. That's why they lock you outside in the cold while they party the night away, drinking and laughing and carrying on. Ever wonder about that, boy? Huh? Do you remember the night I found you wandering barefoot in the park, looking for an empty bench to sleep on?"

"Who *is* that?" Cora asked.

"I can't tell. He's crying too hard," Loretta said.

"Who believes in you, boy?"

"You do, Brock."

"Who believes in you, boy?"

"You do."

"This guy is nuts, just like Ethan said. He's got an agenda, and it's not global warming," said Cora.

"That's enough," said Loretta. "Let's get on with this and be done with it." She crossed the room to the mahogany desk. Her hands were careful but her heart betrayed her fear, beating so fast that she felt it in her ears. She rifled through papers in the top desk drawer, careful to replace what she had disturbed, reading file labels and picking through the contents of folders in the dim blue light. Suddenly, she grew afraid and wanted to give it up, get out, flee through the door and into the tunnel—to walk, run, crawl back to the safety of Willow Grove and into the arms of Granny Noleen. As if a bubble burst, an afterthought tickled her, and she realized how odd that sounded—fleeing to the safety of Willow Grove. A couple of months ago, she never would have considered this as any kind of option, let alone a viable one that made sense.

Turning back to the desk, she found a folder filled with receipts from the hardware store, and bar receipts from the Iron Gate. The Iron Gate? She snapped her fingers and held the receipts up for Cora to see, but Cora was facing away from her, digging in a file cabinet drawer.

"Bingo," Cora said, file in hand. "It's a duplicate of the cease and desist order presented to Granny Noleen...proof that this idiot is behind that too."

"The tunnels again...he needs them for an entrance or escape route, maybe both," Loretta said.

"And look at this," said Cora. She held up another file. "'Chemical Castration' is the heading on this one." She pulled an article out of the folder and skimmed the contents. "OMG. He's considering injecting someone…or someones…with Depo-Provera. It says here, an injection of this drug every three months will reduce a person's sexual desire. Chemical castration."

"And this, my God, he's got grenades, small bombs, enough ammunition to blow up…what is this guy planning?" Loretta held up sales receipts, an inventory list.

"Wait, there's more. Brock's excluding certain members of The Group. There's a list. When the time comes, he's going to refuse them access. Carmen's daughter is on this list. And the Bashara and Ameen families. Oh my God. So is Ethan, and F. MacNamara, whoever that is. This is master race-type stuff. Like Manzanar in reverse."

"Can you make copies?" Loretta asked.

Cora carried the files to a copy machine in the corner of the room, clicked the switch and waited for the machine to warm up. In the quiet, the Xerox's rollers thrummed and the paper feed shuffled, the light from the transparent screen casting shadows about the room.

Loretta bumped an ashtray on the desk, and the smell of tobacco found her nose, bringing on a stomachache and memories of other stomachaches caused by other men her mother had brought home. She coughed into her hand, and her foot kicked something beneath the desk. Bending down to look, she saw an old straw hat filled with money, lots of it.

There was a shuffling in the hall outside the door. Voices. Muffled, but close by. Cora put the files back in the cabinet drawer.

Suddenly, in the midst of a scuffle, Ethan yelled, "InYo Face! Run!"

Loretta ducked and ran, pushed past the swivel chair, the propped-open door through which they had entered, and plunged into the grotto—the tunnel.

Cora ran behind her, catching the heel of Loretta's shoe with the toe of her own. Loretta lurched forward, losing her balance, and Cora was on top of her, both of them landing in a heap on the rocky floor. Back in Brock's office, the interior door swung open, banging into the wall behind it, knocking a computer screen off its bracket and onto the tile floor. Boots crunched over the broken screen, stomping through the room.

The crack of a bullet stung Loretta's eardrums, though the shooter was a distance away. A bright orange flash held the caverned tunnel in a temporary freeze-frame. A bullet hit the rock above her head, ricocheted sideways.

Cora panted heavily. A second bullet whizzed past them and then a third. They were both on their feet now, running, running. The shooter was behind them but closing in rapidly.

Another gun fired, its bullet sounding like a hammer strike against the tunnel wall. Loretta fumbled in her backpack as she ran, grabbing her flashlight, flipping it on. The tunnel grew narrower, the passage leading up a slight incline toward the entrance they had used earlier that day. Someone was shouting: "Get her, stop her!"

"Help!" Cora screamed.

Loretta turned around, and Cora was on the ground, flailing beneath the body of a man.

One more bullet tore past, this one much closer, and as it hit the rock above her head, something cracked. It was a small noise at first, barely distinguishable. Loretta stopped, listening. Seconds passed, and then there was a rumble, and another crack, and another rumble in the distance, this one much louder, farther away. Rocks began to fall. Two, six. Many more. The air was thick with rock dust.

There were two men now, holding Cora down. Pulling her backward toward the bunker. Loretta flew at them, pounding one of them on the shoulder blades, screaming: "Let her go! Let her go!" From the direction of the bunker, a third man came. This one, though, joined Loretta, hitting, pounding the head and back of the first man who had tackled Cora. The smell of stale beer permeated his body, and then Loretta knew. Paiute Bill. It was Bill here now, and had been Bill watching them before, at her house, in the tunnels, ready to protect—to fight, if need be, Brock or whoever else might threaten to hurt them. Bill punched and kicked, bit and clawed, and threw his whole body into the attack, but then they had him, hit him from behind with a rock to the head. There was another shot fired. Bill collapsed in the dirt beside Cora, who was also not moving, and Loretta could see a puddle of blood beneath Bill's leg.

She shone her flashlight up and into the eyes of the man closest to her. Frey. Frey and…

The beam of light searched out the eyes of the second man, causing him to raise an elbow to shade them.

Pierce. He grabbed at the rock wall for support, scrambling toward her along its face. She expected something other than his hands as he reached out for her: snakes instead of fingers, fangs instead of teeth, a rusted heart, rocks for bones.

Loretta screamed and flew at Pierce, beating him with her arms, and scratching him with her fingernails. Her feet dug into dirt and rock as she scrambled to anchor them, and she stumbled over rubble, scarring the mealy earth as Pierce pulled her by the hair back into the blue light of the control room.

-CHAPTER 22-

*E*than had heard them before he saw them: Frey and Pierce thumping down the stairwell, blowing past him in the hallway. One of them punched him hard in the ear—then came a hollow rush of air, white light, and a whoosh of nausea as they knocked him to the ground. A moment later, he saw Paiute Bill plowing down the ladder, scuffling after the others toward the control room. Through the din came a voice he recognized. "Here you are, darling boy! We heard you from the thicket. What is this place? The stairs are so...ouch, oh. We were picking for a pie, don't you know."

Pansy.

Gunshots! From the control room. When Pierce ran past was he carrying his gun? Ethan thought so, though he couldn't be sure. The volley seemed too loud and too long, and afterward, there was rumbling and the sound of the rock falling, as on the side of the mountain when a boulder let loose and crashed to the ground. He pushed through the pain in his head. His legs moved of their own accord, projecting him forward and up the stairs; his only thought was to get Pansy out, away from the gunfire. He reached for her, shoving her back up the ladder, up to the rim of the bunker above ground. Bale was already there, pacing in the dirt, frantically pushing buttons on his cell phone. "Stop! Stay put!" he yelled, waving a Taser gun haphazardly at first, and then pointing it with intent at Ethan.

At the sight of the Taser, Pansy screeched. She covered her eyes and fell to the ground, a puddle of bright purple skirt. "What's happening? Somebody do something! Help!"

Ethan ran to and knelt beside her. He raised a hand to touch her shoulder, jerked it back, and flicked his fingers. "Pansy?" he said, softly. "Pansy!" Her skin looked soft and doughy, and she smelled of talcum powder. Pansy raised her berry-stained fingers and placed them over Ethan's hands, patting gently until he pulled away, stood up, and stormed toward Bale.

"Don't move!" Bale yelled.

Ethan stiffened, listening while Bale's call connected via cell. "They went nuts!" Bale said. "Shot rounds into your office, the tunnel!" Ethan could hear loud babble in response on the other end of the line. And Bale said: "I don't know who! I've got Ethan and the old lady from the house…No, not Noleen, the other one." Again the babble, so loud Bale moved the phone away from his ear. "I don't know how they got here! Damn, Brock! You better get down here! This is bad, really bad. I don't know where Frey is, or Pierce."

"Of course, you would report to Brock," Ethan said. "Underlings answer to their bosses."

"Shut up! I need to think!"

Ethan ignored the immediate threat and tried to create order out of chaos. He summarized his situation: He was held by force and Bale had a weapon, not technically a gun, but a Taser, which could still do damage, perhaps even prove lethal. He recalled a news story he had read a few years back. Granted, the article was old so he could assume the numbers had changed, but still, this article stated that the chances of dying from a Taser wound were one in eight hundred and seventy. Not an appealing statistic, but the odds were in his favor. Ethan flicked his fingers rapidly. Aside from Bale, Frey, and Clive, there was Pierce. His nemesis. He remembered Pierce, the yes-man, always in the background with his evil eyes and taunting smile. A working class soldier in Brock's army, executing Committee policies with an absolute lack of independent will.

Bale was shouting into the cell phone: "They went into the tunnels after the intruders...that's all I know, except there were multiple shots fired, and it sounded like a cave-in down there. Not a major rockslide, but enough to cause a pretty good jam-up.

"You want me to do what?" Bale finally said. "Is that necessary? Are you sure?"

Ethan could not make out Brock's exact words, but his garbled response was loud enough, angry enough, that even from a distance and through the crackling cell, he knew he was in trouble.

"Yes, sir. Yes, I…"

Bale turned the Taser gun at Ethan. His hand was shaking, but he fired.

The electricity ripped through Ethan's body. He fell to the ground, convulsing, unable to breath. The flutterbees swarmed and there was no room in his brain for anything else.

+++

According to Ethan's watch, an hour had passed since he had come out of the bunker with Pansy. He could remember the Taser gun and hitting his head on a rock. The rest was murky: tinted purple like the night sky, as blackened in places as the Hummer he now rode in. Dust raised by the truck's monster tires clogged Ethan's nose, and stung his eyes, his throat. He sat on the rear bench seat, bound with rope to Pansy in a knot of arms and legs, and tied not only to her but to the sidewall of the vehicle. He strained against the ropes but they held fast, and there was no wiggle room. He began to sweat and tried to free himself at least from Pansy's touch, but that was not an option either.

He blinked his eyes and tried to focus on the area around him. He turned his right foot sideways, noting that the floor space was ample; the mid-row bucket seats were missing. The power buttons for the windows were gone. Gun racks rode horizontally above the rear wheel wells, and the window glass was tinted dark gray, though one passenger window was open. This Hummer was top-of-the-line: an H3Alpha 300 horsepower with 320 pound-feet of torque. All the bells and whistles. In some other instance, he might have been impressed. He might even have obsessed over the qualities of the machine. Those darkened windows, the driver and passenger bucket seats, a full dashboard console with a compass and computer, and a high quality GPS system, its oversized screen lit up in bright blues and greens, displaying a map of unmarked roads that lead the driver to some plugged-in destination.

Ethan nudged Pansy's shoulder, and she moaned. "Pansy?" he whispered.

Pansy stirred a little but didn't respond. Ethan closed his eyes, flicked his fingers. His muscles twitched, and he ached deep in his bones. His mind was clear but his head pounded, each throb producing images of Loretta and Cora fleeing Brock's office, of Pierce and his rifle—not the .22 Ethan had seen him carry in the past, but an automatic that fired multiple times into the tunnels.

The gun and the gunfire made no sense to him. There had been no discussion; no one had interrogated him, or Loretta, or Cora. There was no time given for explanation, nor was any minor punishment dealt. Just the panic and the gunfire, and then, falling rock. Where was Loretta? Where was Cora? The law did not work this way, and every rule, as he knew them, had been broken. His own violation of Brock's commands seemed more justified than ever.

Ethan peered through the grayed window glass, trying to get his bearings. There were no homes nearby. He could see the tree-studded flanks of granite in the distance. Whitney: they were still close to home. The ground around them was flat, treeless, dotted with scrub, Manzanita, and pine. He imagined the cavalry on horseback coming to his rescue, bobbing and weaving between the rocks as they would have in old western movies.

A four-wheeler passed, headed in the opposite direction. Was that Brady? Yes, he was certain it was, and for the first time in his life, he wanted to call out to him and ask for his help. While watching the trail of dust the four-wheeler left behind, Ethan grew anxious. He counted to ten and took a deep breath to slow his heart rate. Stay, he told himself. Loretta needs you. Pansy, too. He wondered what his parents were doing and if they knew yet that he was in trouble. Surely they would be looking for him by now and might suspect something was wrong.

Brock was good, but he wasn't that good—what excuse could he possibly come up with for Ethan's absence? Not enough time had passed, but soon. Soon. He imagined Raina fixing dinner, enchiladas maybe or veggie lasagna or the cheesy eggplant parmesan he loved with homemade bread and butter and a green salad on the side. His mouth watered and his eyes fogged with tears. He blinked and blinked again. Flicked his fingers. By now, Raina would have noticed that the Subaru was gone; she would have found and read the note he left on the kitchen table and be anxiously waiting for him to return. It wouldn't be long then before she would call Sim or text him: HAVE YOU SEEN ETHAN?

The road had become more of a trail, and they began to climb. Ethan could hear voices now in the cab of the Hummer and static from the CB radio. "Destination shit-pile. Here we are. Ooh Rah," the driver announced, and the Hummer lurched to a stop. A distorted but recognizable voice responded after the customary "Break."

"Walk them up. No commotion. Just get them there without incident," Brock commanded.

"Roger," Clive replied, powering off the engine of the Hummer.

Through the windows, silhouetted by the night, Ethan could see cottonwood trees, clumps of brush, and low-lying rock, but couldn't tell exactly where they were. He knew these mountains, the Alabama Hills, as well as anyone, but there was something unfamiliar. The land appeared level, and rocks lay in piles along the perimeters. Rows of corn stood tall in a broad field, the leaves and tassels grayed in the blue-black night. What appeared to be a vegetable garden stretched into the distance, and behind it stood an orchard of young trees. Ethan squinted and tried to put a name to the expanse of space he saw: field, farm, *the* farm: The Group Farm.

Clive climbed out of the Hummer and disappeared into the night. "Pansy," Ethan said, trying to rouse her. "Pansy, wake up!"

Pansy groaned but didn't speak.

Ethan tried to remember what he had learned in first-aid class. Offered through the local YMCA, his mother made sure he attended. He watched Pansy's chest rise and fall, noting the speed of her breathing, which seemed a little rapid but steady. He touched her cheek with the back of his hand. Another good sign—it was cool, not hot or clammy. Her eyes were open, but her focus appeared cloudy, as if she were lost in the middle of a thought. It seemed plausible to Ethan that Alzheimer's was similar to Asperger's in this way; if Pansy had drifted into a corner of her brain where she felt safe, he would let her stay there for now.

Two beams of light from the headlights of an approaching vehicle appeared in the distance. Their glow was soft at first but quickly grew brighter. When it neared the Hummer, the truck spun a tight circle, brakes squealing, tires grabbing the dry ground. A cloud of dust twisted and swirled, entering the Hummer through the open window.

Pansy coughed and tried to sit up. Her voice was hoarse but discernable. "Where am I? I don't feel so good. Ethan, dear, is that you?" She pushed against the ropes binding her arms and legs. "What's going on? Billy? Earl! Where am I?"

The rear door to the Hummer opened, and Brock peered in. Ethan didn't want to look at him, but couldn't help it; from the corner of his eye he glanced at Brock's face, noting his tight-set jaw, dilated nostrils—enraged eyes.

Ethan tugged at the ropes, but they didn't budge.

"Damn, Clive! Shit!" Brock cursed. He pulled out a pocket knife and severed the rope around Ethan's wrists. He cut the rope binding Ethan to Pansy, but left the shackles around Ethan's ankles, dragging him from the Hummer and onto the ground. He then freed Pansy, pulling her, slumped but on her feet, nearer to Ethan.

Brock stood too close, the toes of his boots touching Ethan's leg. Ethan looked up and away. His breathing quickened, became shallow.

"Ethan," Brock said. "I tried." He pursed his lips and shook his head. "By God, I've given it my best. But you couldn't let it rest. You've pushed me, boy, and now, well. Here we are. In quite a mess." In the artificial light of the Hummer's headlight beams, he looked devilish. "Look at me when I speak to you, boy!" he screamed.

Clive grabbed Ethan from behind and pulled him to his feet. Brock glommed on to the collar of Ethan's shirt and drew him close, then pushed him away. Sweat ran down Brock's face. Even with Ethan's eyes averted, he knew what was coming.

Brock raised his hand and struck Ethan's jaw. Pansy screamed. Out of breath, Brock backed off, huffing out his anger, stomping enough dust in the air to cause Pansy to cough again. Clive cut the remaining ropes and freed Ethan's ankles as Brock walked to the Hummer, and foraged in the glove compartment, returning with a roll of duct tape. Clive pushed Ethan forward, forcing him to walk. Brock clutched Pansy's arm and she followed his lead, limping past the first rows of corn and a hydroponic nursery to the barn.

"Stop it! Let us go!" Ethan demanded, pulling his arm free of Clive's.

Brock turned on him again, grabbing at him, and Ethan backed away.

The rip of the duct tape was like fingernails on a chalkboard and the sound crippled Ethan's brain. Prior incidents flooded his thoughts: of his mother trying to administer first-aid by using Band-Aids; doctors and nurses and their attempts to apply surgical tape after stitching cuts or tending abrasions; Pierce chasing him through the playground at school with a roll of Scotch tape, sticking pieces to his skin. Clive held Ethan's head against his chest, and no amount of thrashing helped. Brock held up the strip of tape, and wagging it in front of his nose, said: "I've heard you love this stuff, boy."

Brock bound Ethan's arms to his body around his chest, each screeching pull off the tape roll reverberating in Ethan's ears. Brock jerked hard as he applied each strip, pressing more roughly and securing the adhesive ever more tightly. The tape burned and stung and stole Ethan's breath; it smelled red-hot. He flicked his fingers and bit his gums. Trying to resist, he fought to stay alert, but it was impossible. He felt himself slide deeper, deeper, until a quiet, black, circling space loomed perilously close.

Just then, words roared out of the gloom: "Don't you disappear on me! I need you to hear me and understand the trouble you've caused, you little shit."

Ethan opened his eyes. Brock's shadow loomed above him.

"I won't bind your mouth, because I *want* you to squeal," Brock taunted. He held the roll of tape under Ethan's nose, and Ethan could smell the chemical odor of adhesive.

Ethan squirmed and moaned.

"What, you can't handle this, boy? Too much for you?"

Brock slapped him on the ear, smacked the top of his head. "Tough," he said, as he walked away. "Deal with it."

Seconds or hours later—Ethan didn't know which—someone jerked him up by his belt and dragged him to his feet. Before he could react, the gate to a large chicken coop opened, and he was shoved inside. Several hens squawked and flapped their wings, running on their spindly little legs to get to the far side of the pen.

"You can thank your father for this one, kid. You might remind him to keep his mouth shut in Committee-counseling sessions. He loves to talk about you, you know. Blather on about your little idiosyncrasies, the things you fear, the things you loathe."

"Be quiet!" Pansy shrieked.

Clive ignored her. "Oh, yes, boy. Go ahead now. Let me see you disappear inside yourself, as your old man describes it. Let me see that *place* you go that gets even big bad Sim in a dither."

"You have no right!" Ethan yelled. "This is kidnapping! Two counts, one for me and one for Pansy! And where's Loretta? Cora?" He pulled from his mental dictionary: "Assault: an act carried out with the threat of bodily harm or, in this case, actual bodily harm. Kidnapping and assault are crimes, therefore, punishable by law!"

"Whoa. Wow. You've got me shaking in my boots." Clive laughed. "You're right, but sadly one has to be caught, victims need to be recovered, evidence needs to be collected before charges can be brought. I know this, you see, because I *was* a cop. Until your little escapades in town, the vandalism you and that alcoholic *loser* friend of yours perpetrated. Billy, Paiute Bill. Degenerate assholes, the two of you, nothing more." He walked closer, leaned down, then grabbed and shook Ethan's chin. "Did you know your parents issued a complaint against me, disputing my *treatment* of you during my investigation of your crime spree?" He hesitated, then hissed into Ethan's ear, "That's what got the ball rolling. Internal Affairs conducted an inquiry. Your friend, Sheriff Atkins, came up with some trumped-up crap, and bingo, bongo. No more uniform, no more cop.

"You. Your *father*. Well. Let's just say, I have a bone to pick."

The proximity of Clive's face to Ethan's, the chickens and their long spindly legs, the possibility of parasites and the probability of copious amounts of bird crap caused a frenzy of finger flicking. Ethan felt a familiar inward pull and searched his mind for a safe trigger, like the voice of his favorite rapper (Macklemore), or the vibration of his Enduro motorcycle beneath his body, but it was all too much, and he fell into the darkness.

+++

Ethan awoke to Pansy cooing in his ear. "There, there. It's okay." Slowly, gently, she unwrapped the duct tape from his chest and threw it across the chicken coop into a pile of old straw. She rocked and patted him on the arm, singing in a soft, nearly inaudible voice: "Hush, little baby, don't say a word. Pansy's gonna find you a dog named Rover." Ethan did not flinch. He did not move away. Pansy's touch felt good somehow. Safe. She appeared soft and fragile, like a puppy. And he noticed the hunched angle of her spine, the jugular vein pulsing in her neck. Waffled wrinkles trailed down her arms and to her hands, the aged skin resembling a topographical map.

"We're in a bit of high water," Pansy whispered, and Ethan nearly laughed.

"I believe the correct analogy is 'hot water'"

"High water, hot water. La de da."

Ethan lay there, unable to move. The sky was still a dark blue but brightening around the edges; it would be morning soon. As things cleared in his mind, he focused on Pansy. She was standing now, walking bowlegged, as if her hips had turned to stone. Her breathing was rapid, her skin pale and clammy, and it did not take a first-aid evaluation to understand that she needed medical care.

Ethan thought hard about it but was not sure what to say. All he could think of was, "We are getting out of here. Now."

Pansy stared into the distance. Ethan could see her mouth moving, but her eyes were shadowed. "Think of all the nights I've gone to sleep on a soft bed surrounded by people who love me, and the mornings I've risen healthy and spirited to the smell of blooming flowers and a sun-filled sky…

"I'm lucky, Ethan. I've had a good life."

"Quick. Untie me. We have to go."

"I was…indisposed…when they put us in here. I suppose that's why I'm not bound. I don't think they see me as much of a threat, don't you know." She worked the knots loose and freed his hands. "I hope it didn't hurt too much when I pulled the tape off your chest. Sorry about your hands. Guess I forgot…"

When Ethan stood, it felt as if a million tiny pins were poking his legs. As he took a deep breath, his ribs hurt.

The chickens huddled on the far side of the coop. He heard bleating goats, unnerved cries that seemed distressed. He checked the gate, padlocked from the outside.

"Stand back," he told Pansy. He picked up a grain bucket and pounded it against the chicken wire, again and again and again. In the spot where the wire buckled he kicked, rammed his body weight, and kicked again. The chickens screeched and he worked harder, forcing the wire, creating a hole just big enough for them to crawl through.

Once out, Ethan ran to a water spigot and drank directly from it, reminding himself to breathe. Then he filled his hands and took water to Pansy, over and over, until she refused any more.

"Can you walk?" he asked, flicking his fingers.

"Can you walk?" she repeated, looking through him, somewhere else.

He tried to help her stand, but she went limp in his arms. "Get up!" he said. "Pansy, get up!"

"I can't."

A mournful wail rose in his throat. All he could think to do was run, around the barn, the garden, and the cornfield to the goat pen, where he saw a wheelbarrow filled with hay.

One word came to mind, a single sequence: *escape, escape, escape.*

Ethan fluffed and straightened, fluffed and straightened the hay, then picked Pansy up and laid her on it.

"Let's go see S'more," he gently said, then grabbed the

handles and pushed, rolling forward and up a trail he knew would lead them away from the farm and the bunker, and toward Willow Grove. *Escape, escape, escape...*

-CHAPTER 23-

Pierce shoved Loretta onto the floor in Brock's office. Disoriented and dizzy, she struggled to sit up, spat a bit of blood, and licked her newly split lip. In front of her, the display on computer monitor T3 quivered and then settled on a blurry image of the bunker end of the tunnel, fallen rock and Bill lying motionless in the rubble.

There was a scream—loud and long and pain-filled—coming closer and closer still until Loretta could see Frey dragging Cora by the feet from the tunnel and into the center of the room. Cora moaned and fluttered her eyes, but otherwise was still.

"My God, what have you done!" Loretta cried, as she crawled to where he left her.

Frey growled something unintelligible, adjusted his belt, and gorilla-walked back into the tunnel. Loretta could hear him out there, cursing and ransacking the supply cabinet in the grotto.

Pierce stood hunched over with his finger in his mouth, staring blank-eyed at Cora.

"That's right, look at her, Pierce! You've hurt her, you emotionless dip-wad! What's the matter with you?" Loretta shouted, stumbling to her feet.

"Shut up," Pierce snapped.

"No!" Loretta said, "Let us go!"

"Words, words—now the dog speaks?" Pierce teased, blinking away the film in his eyes.

"You're crazy, you know that?"

"Not even, so shut up!" Pierce said, turning to walk away.

Loretta sprinted forward, caught him behind the knees, and knocked him to the ground. They rolled, and she kicked until someone yanked the back of her shirt. She felt Frey's fingers dig into her neck and heard him yell, "Stop! Now! Face to the floor!"

"No one touches me like that!" Pierce screamed, dusting off his jeans and then glaring at Loretta as she attempted to comply. "You screwed up! You shouldn't be here, and now you're dead…to me and everyone else! We busted your sorry little selves. It's Judgment Day!"

Loretta was still on hands and knees, and Pierce knocked her flat with a hard, swift boot to her back. "Ow!" she cried, barely raising her head. "What are you talking about? What Judgment Day? You have no right to hold us here!"

"Really? Breaking and entering are against the law, or

haven't you heard?" Pierce glowered at her and threatened to kick her again, but didn't.

"Both of you shut up! I need to think!" Frey paced and talked to himself, fumbling his sentences, rambling. "The boss isn't gonna like this. Shit!" He rubbed his face and ears. "Civil War, my ass! Freakin' tunnels! Granite caskets…that's all they are…and you, Pierce…you and your damn gun… the cops will come, and then what? It all falls apart! The Group. The bunker. The money. My…*job*. Brock's got rules, you know. Security concerns, special instructions. Give up nothing, leave nothing behind…"

"Brock won't be mad!" Pierce yelled. "The gun was his idea. He gave it to me. He told me to be a man, to take care of business when the time came, and I did."

"Shut up! You're no more than a pup…a pit bull pup, maybe…you got a good bite, but damn, boy. Learn some control." He rubbed his head again and stomped his foot. "Get 'em outta here. Take 'em up top."

As Pierce took hold of Loretta's arm, Frey turned, noticing the file cabinet with its middle drawer ajar. He walked to the far side of the desk and laid his hand on the warm copy machine, spotting one page of the document Cora had copied and dropped on the floor as she ran.

"What the hell," said Pierce, "is that."

Frey cocked his head and stared at Loretta. His eyes drilled into her, focusing on her mouth as if he were summoning her secrets and expecting her to spew them out.

Suddenly, as if she had ratted, as if he knew where to look, he lunged at Cora, flipped her over, and pulled the photocopies from under her shirt.

The large red letters on the top page were hard to miss: *EXCLUSIONS: HIGH-RISK GROUP MEMBERS.* Loretta remembered the first five names on the list as Cora had recited them: *Lupita Gonzales; Bashara family; Ameen family; Ethan Arnett; F. MacNamara.*

My God, she thought. *F. MacNamara—Frey MacNamara.*

Frey held the document close to his face, and read. As he spoke the words on the page, his hands shook and his jaw muscles contracted, his voice sounding brittle and detached. Minutes went by, and more, before he gripped the pages tighter, crushing and ripping the evidence while paper shrapnel wafted to the floor.

Pierce snickered. "You told *me* to learn some control? PTSD much, guy?"

Frey's face knotted and reddened. He turned and smacked Pierce in the ear. "Don't you ever," he screamed, "disrespect me like that!"

Pierce held his ear and whimpered.

"There's so much shit here, so much classified crap." Frey pivoted too effortlessly for someone wearing camo clothing and combat boots. He stared at the shredded paper on the floor, kicking a few pieces under the desk. "A commanding officer never turns on his men," he said to Brock's empty chair. "Errors in judgment regarding hostile acts can be critical to the success of a mission…the rules of engagement state…Murphy's Laws of Combat proves…I know this stuff, but I can't remember the details. What was it now? I can't recall!" He rubbed his temples, ran is fingers through his butch-cut hair. Outside, there was a loud bang. And another. And another. Someone screamed.

Frey's eyes glazed over. Standing stiff-kneed, he saluted. "Detention of civilians is authorized for security reasons, or in self-defense," he said, dropping his salute.

Loretta's eyes widened at she glanced at Pierce, who looked away, mumbling, *"Most of the time, Frey moves through life like the rest of you…but there are moments, triggered by something he sees or hears…"*

"What?" Loretta said.

"Nothing. Come on, move it now," said Pierce, shaking off his previous recitation. "You pick up one arm, I'll get the other," he added, reaching for Cora.

"Cora?" said Loretta. "We're going to lift you up. Do you think you can walk?"

Cora tried to stand but moaned when Pierce touched her left arm. "Let me do it!" Loretta fumed. "Back off!" She raised Cora slowly, guiding her to her feet.

"Faster," Pierce grumbled. He grabbed Cora around the waist, urging her and Loretta on.

In the doorway to the bunker proper they stopped and turned around, watching as Frey yanked computer screens off the walls, and carried towers and desktop computers, adding them to a pile on the floor. He crumpled paper, threw it into the heap, and, with his Bic lighter, lit it all on fire. "Get them out of here!" he yelled at Pierce. "Up the ladder! Pronto!" He then rambled and yelled, talking to his army of shadows: "Orders are, destroy the documents." He scratched his cheeks and pounded his temples. "Get out of my head! Turn down the noise!"

Cora screamed again when Pierce touched her arm. Her breathing seemed labored, and her head bobbed side to side.

"I said, let me do it!" Loretta yelled. "She'll walk if I ask her to walk! I'll get her out!"

Pierce threw up his hands and stepped back.

"Cora," Loretta said, shaking. The reality of where she was and what had happened bore down like her worst bout with claustrophobia. Suppressing her nausea was no longer an option, and she vomited on the floor. She gagged and wiped her mouth, then took hold of Cora's right arm. "Cora," she said, still feeling shaky, "I need you to walk now. We've got to get up the ladder and outside, do you understand? One step. That's it. Up we go."

+++

They stood in a grouping of trees with a view of the bunker. Pierce filled canteens from a nearby water spigot, throwing blankets, a hatchet, food and other provisions into a large backpack near the rear of his truck—*a truck with a shattered taillight cover.* Loretta gasped, remembering the horror at Granny Noleen's. *"Whoever it was had been headed toward Dakota, but Earl got to the horse first, with his shotgun. He fired three times, knocking out a taillight before the vehicle sped away,"* Yoshi had said that day.

The metallic clank of boots ascending metal stairs, the wheezing, wet cough of a long-time smoker, caused them all to look up.

Frey rose from the hatch, covered with soot, limping on his right side.

Loretta inched forward until she reached a stump, then helped Cora sit.

The roar of the fire intensified as live ammo exploded, and as flames leaped up from underground with a blast of hot air. At that moment, Loretta thought she might never see her mother again, or smell her hibiscus perfume, or watch her sashay across the room to the beat of a Willie Nelson song. She also knew that soon her mom would be looking for her, and in her own crazy way, would fight to the death to keep her, Cora, and Ethan alive.

"Breaker, breaker," Pierce called out, using the CB radio inside his truck. "Brock? You there? Somebody answer. Please, someone answer."

Frey grabbed the handset from Pierce's hand. "Frey here. It's done. We're nearly finished and heading out."

Pierce tied Loretta's wrists together and began to knot Cora's. "Let her be, Pierce, Loretta said. "She's not going anywhwere can't you see?"

Pierce dropped Cora's hands and walked back to the truck, sorted the items he'd pilfered from the bunker, stuffed waterproof vials of matches and candles into the pockets of his flak jacket, and verified that the CB was still on. "Breaker, breaker?"

Someone had taught him these things. Pierce was crafty but not survival-smart, and Loretta knew that someone had pulled him aside, trained and groomed him, and given him toys as encouragement.

The CB squawked and spit and then coughed up a response: "Pierce? Is that you?

Sounds like things are under control there, is that an affirmative?"

"Yes," Pierce said. "What about the others? What's happening with The Group?"

Static interrupted the silence that followed.

"The time is now. The end is near," Brock hissed.

"But the bunker. The fire…" said Pierce.

Frey grabbed the microphone again. "Shut up, you idiot!" he shouted. "I can't think when you're babbling like that!"

Radio silence. Crackle, crackle: "What fire?" Brock asked. "Frey? What fire? What did you do? Frey?"

Loretta remembered the interrogation video she and Cora watched in the bunker. "My God," she said to Pierce. "It was you. You were the kid in the video."

Pierce stared at her, oblivious to what she was saying. He had always been a jerk, but when he was younger, he'd been bullied. Even at his best, his clothes were thrift-store issue; in elementary school, when kids started out the school year with a new backpack and shoes, Pierce came with no backpack, wearing scuffed-up tennies with no laces. Things were different now, though, like his new Air Jordans, Gotcha t-shirts, and the big-ticket items on his truck such as new tires, a CB radio, and a stereo system that was the envy of the entire junior class. Today he had a new gun in his hand, far different from the .22 rifle he fired at the knoll weeks earlier and carried in his beater truck to knock squirrels from trees.

Regardless, no one deserved this. No one deserved to be demoralized and brainwashed. Loretta thought about the other people in The Group videos, their near-worship of Brock—this man who professed to be family and who called them "brother" and "sister" and "friend." They had all been duped. People that she knew and cared about had been lied to and tricked and cheated.

"I'm not here to pet your ego, Pierce. Let's move." Frey threw his backpack over the tailgate. "Hold still," he told Loretta, as he bound her eyes with a strip of cloth.

"Really?" Loretta said. "You have to do this?"

"Shut up!" Frey yelled, pulling the ties on the blindfold tighter.

+++

They drove in silence. It was not more than an hour, she thought, before the truck lunged to a stop—before she was dragged outside, her blindfold removed, and her hands untied.

"Hustle up," Frey said, pushing her from behind.

Though it was still dark, the landscape was vaguely familiar. "This is the trail to the Rock House," she said. "Is that where you're taking us?"

"Shut up and move. Get your friend here off her ass and let's go," Frey said.

It was hard to know how best to help her, but somehow, Cora managed to stand. "You okay?" Loretta asked.

Cora struggled to breathe, as her answer came in crisp, short bursts. "Yes. No. Not…really…"

"Sling Cora's arm, at least," Loretta said. "And give her some water. *Then* we'll walk."

"You're in no position to make demands," Frey growled, but he scrounged a stick from under some scrub brush, pulled a bandana from his pocket, and fashioned a crude sling. "Hold your arm bent at the elbow and against your belly," he grumbled. Cora followed Frey's instruction, and he tied the sling under her arm and over her shoulder. "Ow! Take it easy," she told him, "Please!"

"Stop whining. I'd just as soon leave you behind, tied to a tree somewhere where no one will ever find your sniveling ass." Frey laughed. "Imagine how that might look, a tree hugger hugging a tree. Score one for me."

Pierce thrust a canteen into Loretta's hands. It was an old military issue, with a chain that held the cap to the canteen. She unscrewed the cap and helped Cora drink, then took a turn herself. The water slid down her throat, soothing her parched and irritated lips. She pressed the cool canvas cover against her cheek, luxuriating in its brief relief.

"Let's go!" Frey yelled again, gruffly.

Loretta followed Frey up the trail. Behind her Pierce stumbled, tumbling sideways. Choke on your own dust, she wanted to say. Instead, her grip tightened on Cora's arm, and she kept her eyes on the moonlit ground, knowing that the trail would narrow soon and Cora would have to manage on her own. She let go of Cora's arm and urged her to walk ahead. "I'm right behind you," she told Cora. "Call out if you need me. If you feel like you can't make it, anything at all, just signal."

Cora flipped her the bird.

"Alrighty then. At least I know your sense of humor is intact."

As they climbed, the sky began to lighten; only a sliver of moonlight remained. Though Loretta was fatigued, the promise of a sunrise felt hopeful. She recalled stories Doc had shared with her and Cora about the old Stone House. The original tale was romantic and inspiring, and she had paid close attention to its retelling. The first recollection that came to her now was the phrase *"seclusion and defendable space, a bird's-eye view of anyone approaching the area."* How perfect, she thought, that this was the spot Frey chose to bring them. No one would think to look for them here, and the chance of a random encounter with hikers or climbers was slim to none.

According to Doc, Franklin and Sherifa Wolff built the Stone House in the 1920s. They believed that the most spiritual place is the highest place, and thus leased a parcel of land from the federal government and began work on a sanctuary where they and their friends could come and meditate while enjoying the solitude of the mountainous environment. They used burros to carry cement and the supplies they needed for building and their own backs to do the labor.

Loretta examined the brush-burdened foot trail she followed, amazed that the forest had so thoroughly reclaimed it. Frey's decision to take them captive and lead them to the Stone House was fouling both the path that took so much effort to create and the Wolffs' legacy—the spirituality and peace they had felt while living here. Thinking of that, her heart pounded faster and her legs pumped harder, and she felt fiercely proud that Cora was persisting, let alone keeping up with Frey's hard-driving pace.

"Seventy-six...hundred...feet. Is that what my dad said?" Cora asked, her voice sounding as strained as her breathing.

"Yeah," Loretta told her, not surprised that even in

this circumstance their brains were connecting with such synchronicity.

Sweat ran down Loretta's forehead and into her eyes. She slowed her pace and swiped at them with the sleeve of her t-shirt.

"Move!" Frey's gravelly voice was an assault, rough and crude, and she wanted to cover her ears to it and say "la, la, la, la," to block it out as she had done as a child and as her mother still did while pretending not to listen to Loretta's favorite songs. Where were Ethan and Pansy and Bill? Cora was now six paces in front of her. She could hear her ragged breath but Cora never stopped trucking. Loretta understood what she was trying to pull off, and wanted to give her a high-five, to tell Frey and Pierce that Cora was one-upping them because she was tough and stubborn, and she would never, ever let them feel like they had the upper hand. That's who she was. Who she had always been.

And there was nothing Loretta could do for Cora. Except maybe...play the game.

"Movie trivia," Loretta said. "Best guess.

"NASA suddenly becomes aware that an asteroid is on a collision course with Earth. The only way to knock it off course is to land a spaceship on the asteroid, have some astronauts drill a hole, plant a bomb, and kaboom!"

"Oh, *Armageddon*. More," Cora said hoarsely.

"Another one? Okay, how about this. There's an alien invasion..."

"Shut the hell up!" Frey said, shoving Loretta from behind.

Loretta twisted around, rubbed the spot on her back that Frey had jabbed. "Why? What's it going to hurt?" she asked. "What have you got to gain here, anyway? This is nuts. When my mom catches you, and she will, she'll hang you by the balls to the nearest tree and rub with you honey and let the bears have their way with you."

"Shut up."

"You. Are. Toast."

"Pathetic losers. Your mom...you and your friends...are a big-ass joke." Frey kicked Loretta on the heel of her shoe.

She wished that she had kept her mouth shut, that she could find some peace and time to think, or cover her head with a blanket and disappear for a while—anything to keep Frey's eyes off of her and his ugly insinuations from invading her space.

The trail grew steeper, and her breath came harder. She could see the sun now, perched low in the sky, a pinkish-red glow crowning the top of the mountain. She scanned the forest in front of her, trying to catch a glimpse of the Stone House.

"The creek is up ahead!" Pierce yelled over his shoulder. "Let's break."

Frey pushed past Loretta, knocking her to the side of the trail. Cora dodged his weight as he threw it at her, flinching, protecting her left arm with the right. "Hold off," he hollered. "Let me check it out first. Keep your eye on them. No funny business, kid."

Pierce fumbled back down the trail carrying his gun and a large pack filled with the supplies. This is it, Loretta realized, the disaster Brock had prepared them for, and they were ready to dig in for the duration. She felt nauseous again, and her heartburn kicked in. Where were her Tums? Where was her mother?

"Bring 'em in," Frey called out. "Five minutes. That's it."

Loretta's leg muscles quivered and strained against her effort to kneel, and the creek water was snow-cold, but she didn't care. She cupped her hands and drew the water to her face, feeding her dry, parched skin. If help arrived at that moment, she thought, it would be hard to scream, to run, to work out the stiffness that had settled in her body. She rotated her ankles in a circular motion, flexed her calves, clenched and unclenched her fists.

"I can't," Cora whispered, "get down."

Loretta opened the canteen and tipped it to Cora's lips. Then she drank as well, and poured the last bit of fresh water into her hand and washed the dirt from Cora's face. She helped Cora sit, and she sat down too, grimacing when she felt a stab of pain, the hard lump in her front pocket pressing into her groin.

Cell phone, Loretta remembered with a hiss. She snuck a peek at Cora, and at Pierce and Frey, who were standing just out of sight, squabbling and attempting to speak in private. She coaxed the phone from her pocket, and, using one finger, pushed the Home button, and the Contacts icon, scrolled to Ethan's name, and pecked out a two-word text: STONE HOUSE.

Then she checked the battery: LOW.

And the signal level: one bar—little or none.

It would take a miracle, she realized, to get her message out, but still she held her breath and prayed. She dropped her phone between her knees and buried it in the dirt.

In the next instant, Frey was on her, pulling her to her feet. She didn't dare look back as he urged her on. But she could wonder. She could hope. She could dream that Ethan's typically simple text response had popped up on the screen by now. I'M COMING, he might say. And that's all she would need to know.

+++

A few more switchbacks and she saw it. It was not there, and then it was, as if created by elves and with its own bit of magic, and rising from the base of the cliff—the great Stone House. Made of the same granite that comprised its foundation, the building appeared as if it were nature-made; there were window casings but no glass, a portal, but no door to bar entry. Loretta forgot the reason she was there for a moment and marveled at the beauty of the place.

Cora stumbled through the doorframe and lost her balance, landing on the cement floor face down. Loretta raced inside to grab her and help her to a sitting position against the back wall. She settled Cora, then sat beside her, breathing hard, her mouth dry, her eyes so irritated from stress and dust, it felt as if they would burst from her head.

Cora's lips bent in an uncomfortable scowl; she quivered. Tears slipped out of the corners of her eyes. "So tired," she mumbled. "Have to sleep."

"No, Cora, please. You hit your head hard in the tunnel. You may have a concussion. You've gotta stay awake."

Cora moaned but nodded.

In the center stood an altar, rugged yet graceful: a heart-rock, she thought, as pure as the hearts of the people who built it. Yet on it now sat Frey, and he struck a match across its face and lit his cigarette. There were candle-sized recesses along the walls and a stone cistern, and she thirsted for the water that might have filled it at one time, wishing she had not finished the last of the water in her canteen. She wondered where her backpack was, filled with all the goodies she'd purchased at the store, and her water bottle. Oh, her water bottle.

She wondered how many miles they were from the Penny Saver, from home. She didn't know how long it had taken them to climb the trail, or what time it was; she only knew that her tongue was stuck to the roof of her mouth, and her lips felt swollen, and the sun was rising in the sky. "Fritos and Pepsi. Fritos and Pepsi," she repeated, for no reason other than to keep herself sane. "We need water," she finally told Frey. "Cora first, please, we need water. And food."

"Snivel, snivel." Frey snuffed his cigarette out on the heel of his boot. "Pierce," he commanded, "Do something useful. Get these whiners some water, something to eat."

Pierce pivoted away from the corner where he had dropped his pack. "You're not the boss of me, Frey. Quit telling me what to do!"

Frey rushed Pierce and knocked him to the ground, then brushed off his hands and stood back, watching as Pierce scrambled to his feet. "I'm going to say this once, so listen up," he warned. "I *am* your boss unless your wanna-be-daddy shows up, so get your ass moving and do as I say!"

Pierce rummaged in his backpack, grabbed a thermos, and tossed it in Loretta's lap. "Brock's gonna be so pissed at you," he said to Frey.

Frey threw his head back and laughed. "At me? Really? I'm not the one who fired live rounds into the tunnel. It's your ass on the stick, not mine."

"But you *did* start the fire," Pierce mumbled, with his hand sweeping his lips.

Frey balled his fist and drew back his arm as if daring Pierce to say another word.

Loretta unscrewed the cap off the thermos and took a long drink. When she held the canteen to Cora's lips, she gulped the water too quickly, coughing it up as soon as it went down.

Cora fell onto her back, moaned, and clutched her side, trying to right herself.

Pierce stood watching now, nearly on his tiptoes, swaying back and forth as if he wasn't sure whether to stay or run. He bounced over to his backpack, pulled out a sweatshirt and threw it to Loretta. "Pillow," he said, lifting his chin at Cora.

Loretta rolled the sweatshirt into an oblong ball and placed it beneath Cora's head. She caught the strip of beef jerky Pierce tossed, broke it in half, and handed Cora her share. Cora held it but didn't take a bite, staring blank-eyed at the doorway. Loretta ripped a chunk off the jerky, but it was hard to swallow, knowing Cora couldn't eat.

+++

Hours passed, and Loretta watched Cora doze, waking her often to check the dilation of her pupils, to ask her simple questions: Where were you born; what's your dad's name; what street do you live on? Day had turned to night, but the hours were smeared together, plummeting rapidly, passing so slowly sometimes, she wasn't sure she herself knew what time it was. The only clue she had right now shone through the glassless windows. The sun clutched the side of the mountain like a two-year-old throwing a tantrum, screaming fits of color, reds, and oranges, pinks and yellows, flung along the horizon as far as she could see.

Pierce was the only one who had passed the day sleeping.

Curled up in the corner, he cradled his rifle, his fingers flexing on the barrel as if he dreamed of shooting rounds. Outside the Stone House, Frey paced. Like an apparition, he appeared in front of the doorway and then disappeared, building a tent of twigs in the campfire ring, adding tinder, and lighting it. Loretta watched him add each stick, fueling the blaze to a sizable burn.

The wood popped and spit, and Frey rocked on his haunches, pulling at his hair, talking to himself in a babble of words that sounded sharp and angular.

As the light slipped away, Loretta thought of one *teachable moment*, as her mom called them, when she had preached this advice: *"Pay attention, Loretta. A man treats you rough, nail him where it hurts. He's out. No excuses. Period."*

She thought about the ramshackle graves in her front yard, one for each bad relationship her mother had endured—*and* the secret marker she had erected herself, for her father, for the *whole complete family* she dreamed of having one day. How many times had she grilled her mother about popping out a kid—a brother or sister to keep her company when things got wild, or when she felt lonely? Every time she asked, and each time he mother said "NO," Loretta added a pebble to the pile. Recalling this now in the craziness of her present situation felt so comical, so absurd, that she couldn't help but laugh.

Suddenly, Frey was on her, shaking her by the shoulders, pulling her hair into a tight ball with his fist and jerking her backward. His stale breath poured into her nose and bursts of spittle hit her in the eye. "You think this is *funny*? I'll show you funny," he said, and he kicked Cora in the ribs.

Cora screamed.

"Things were moving along…everyone was buying into Brock's crap…I would have been second in command. A soldier in the army…only, this time, I wouldn't have been fighting in Iraq. Difference is…these terrorists are radical homeboys, politicians, crap-ass environmentalists who think they know what's best for this country…"

"Frey, pull it together," said Pierce. "This is not Iraq, man." He stood up, still holding his gun.

Frey dropped Loretta and rubbed his ears, then stomped away; still mumbling to himself, he squatted heavily beside his fire.

Everything hurt: her head, her neck, her shoulders and arms. For some odd reason, Loretta pictured Ethan with his dictionary, flipping pages, calling up the definition of a term she'd often questioned: Laws of nature: regularly occurring or apparently inevitable phenomenon observable in human society. Everything in her life was catawampus. Everything she knew, or thought she knew about how her universe worked, had tumbled upside-down.

A pair of golden eyes peered at her from the brush just outside. In the distance, a coyote howled. Here lived mountain lions, bears, bobcats, coyotes, and other predators that usually felt threatening, but somehow, this night, their presence was reassuring.

Loretta stroked Cora's hair and sang softly: *"I'm your friend, you're my friend, we'll stick together until the end…we share a history, nothing's a mystery…"*

There was more to this song that they had learned in kindergarten, but Loretta's mouth and jaw hurt too badly to continue; she was too tired and frazzled to keep her eyes open or to help Cora stay awake. Leaning against a wall of granite, within the sanctuary of stone, she closed them, allowed her breathing to slow, and fell into a deep but restless sleep.

-CHAPTER 24-

*E*than watched Dakota, his eyes focused on the bend of the horse's neck, the way his ears lay back, his flared nostrils. Dakota stomped his right front hoof, prancing on his back feet, eager and ready to run. Ethan knew the stance and felt the same urge—standing still, minding his composure was almost more than he could bear.

Burned, battered, and bruised, Bill teetered on the top step of the porch. His fingers flew as he described the attack in the bunker, the fire, the cave-in, and his escape—fleeing the flames, climbing over piles of rock and debris, struggling in the dark through the passageways of the tunnel until he finally found the familiar chambers, the sleeping quarters, the stairs.

It was his third time telling the story—the first for Sheriff Atkins, the second for Ethan's parents, and now again, for Greer. As Greer listened, every so often, she would turn and look at Ethan as if verifying Bill's version of events, and assuming that Ethan would interrupt, and interject facts if needed.

But Ethan was done talking. He had already told the Sheriff everything—about the break-in and the bunker, his abduction—his and Pansy's—about Brock and Clive and what happened at The Group farm. The only bits he left out were The Group's Doomsday activities, and those parts were not his responsibility to confess. Ownership of that burden belonged to Sim. And Brock. And Clive. *Burden of proof: the obligation to offer evidence that a court or jury could reasonably believe.* Would it come to that, he wondered? Yes, he thought. At this point, yes.

By the time Sim and Raina arrived at Willow Grove, the billowing smoke around the bunker had thinned to a gray tail, spiraling upward. Ethan didn't know whether it was Committee members who put the fire out or the Lone Pine Fire Department. It didn't matter much either way. What had happened had happened, and his head hurt to think about it.

It was twenty-two hours since they first entered the cave. From what Ethan could tell, Sheriff Atkins had received a barrage of missing persons reports early in the morning: one for him, another for Pansy and Bill—and when Doc discovered that Loretta and Cora were nowhere to be found, his was the third call, the most distressing of all because he had found Cora's note—a cryptic message, and a crudely drawn map showing where they planned to enter the tunnels.

The message read: "In case we're not back by dawn. Love you, Pops."

At this hour, all of Lone Pine's on-duty officers, fire personnel, and first responders were either with the Sheriff and Sim at the bunker or part of a search party scouring the local area on foot and in four-wheel-drive vehicles. A single officer stationed inside the house at Willow Grove manned the phone, the Internet, and a CB radio unit set up on the kitchen table, and was in contact with a local back-country horseman's group, whom he had put on standby in case they were needed. Ethan listened to all of this, the plans, the shifting scenarios—from horses to SWAT teams—and he wanted to scream. There were too many people involved, too much hustle and bustle since he first arrived with Pansy in the wheelbarrow. Police and paramedics had crowded him, asking questions, checking his vital signs, applying peroxide and antibiotics to his cuts, and stitching one deep wound on his left forearm. Expecting him to talk and talk and talk some more.

"Tell me again, please. About the girls," Greer said, speaking to Bill.

Yoshi translated: "Cora is hurt. Bill thinks she may have broken ribs, and possibly a broken arm. Loretta is all right, or at least she was the last time Bill saw her." Bill wiggled his fingers in an upward spiral, a signal that he had more to say. Yoshi translated once again: "Loretta fought the men who attacked them, and Bill was fighting too. Then someone hit him from behind and knocked him unconscious. He doesn't know how long he was out, but after he had come to, the girls were gone."

Yoshi watched as Bill's fingers worked out his next sentence. He lowered his eyes as if waiting for Bill to change his mind, to reconsider what he was about to share. Finally, he finished translating: "I am sorry to say this, but Bill has no doubt that Frey, or even Pierce, could hurt Loretta. They are armed, and undoubtedly feeling desperate." Yoshi flexed his upper torso to reposition his white button-down shirt, his eyebrows sewn together in an expression of concern.

Dried blood still colored Bill's dirt-caked t-shirt; his head and leg wounds were bandaged, but reddened welts and bruises ran up and down his arms, and on his face and neck. His skin was pale, his cheeks heavily whiskered, and his eyes begged for respite. He cupped one hand and raised it to his mouth, tipping as if he held a glass. On the porch beside him, Pansy rocked a hard and steady rhythm, thumping her feet with each back swing of the old chair. *"It's a grand old flag, it's a high flying flag,"* she sang. Noleen dropped the cloth she'd been using to wash Pansy's hands into a bowl of water, poured two glasses of lemonade from a pitcher and handed one to Bill and one to Pansy. Bill frowned but drank anyway.

Ethan watched Bill's Adam's apple slide up and down, saw his hand shake so badly he could barely hold the glass. He remembered that day at the Penny Saver when he threw

Bill's bottle of gin into the dumpster, his pleading eyes and that helpless longing. Oddly, at this moment, the same sense of uselessness—yearning—poured through Greer's eyes, and though her hands didn't shake, and she appeared to be in control, Ethan knew otherwise.

Greer rubbed her cheeks with both hands, and then wiped her eyes, smearing a bit of mascara. "I can't just stand here doing nothing," she said. "I'm tired, and I'm dirty, and my daughter is missing. I can't stand here and do nothing." Ethan pictured Greer's four-hour bus ride from Las Vegas to Lone Pine—what it must have felt like to get home and discover a phone recorder filled with messages from Granny Noleen, Sheriff Atkins, Doc, Raina—and who knows how many others regarding the whereabouts of her daughter. According to Greer, she'd raced out of the house in the same clothes she'd traveled in—a rumpled pair of pink culottes and matching peasant blouse and a pair of toe-pinching white clogs. She'd first had to locate her truck, then battled backed-up traffic at the gas pumps (this piece of the story included a rant aimed at Loretta for leaving the truck's tank on empty), tourist-filled crosswalks in downtown Lone Pine, a gang of wanna-be bikers en route to the Alabama Hills, a wayward mallard duck that nearly collided with her windshield on Horseshoe Bend Road. As she talked, Ethan watched her pace back and forth in the driveway, her usually well-coiffed hair falling askew, the curly red tendrils clinging to her face and neck. He noticed her sullied eye makeup and au naturel brows, appearing blonde rather than penciled-on auburn—a no-no for Greer, under any circumstances. She had lost a fake fingernail and was picking at it incessantly, swearing when she tore it too close to her nailbed and made it bleed. She leaned inside Old Blue's open passenger window and pulled a tissue from her stash inside the door panel. The truck was parked at a peculiar angle, followed by its own frenzied tire tracks, the result of Greer fishtailing down the drive and into the yard when she'd first arrived.

"Sheriff Atkins has been out for hours, searching the bunker, the Farm. He's got folks in the hills, looking near the river and creeks," Noleen said. "They're doing everything they can."

"How did these crazy-ass people end up with the kids anyway?" Greer brushed the hair out of her face, wiping the sweat from her brow. "What's been going on around here, Noleen? I leave for a few weeks and all hell breaks loose."

"I'll let that one go. But the next one'll get zinged back at ya, Greer, and I don't believe you want that right now." Noleen's tired eyes held the fire locals feared, that temper-smacked indicator people tried to avoid.

The old blonde horse shook his head and stomped his right front hoof.

"He's like me," Ethan said. "When he's anxious he stims…you know…like my finger flicking. Like me." Ethan ran his hand over Dakota's muzzle and grabbed a handful of mane.

Earl dropped the flake of hay he carried and dou-ble-checked Dakota's water bucket, then nodded. "Yep. Well. This 'ol guy, he's been around long enough to recognize a thing or two. He knows a fella's heart. Feels it to his bones," he said.

"Bones, bones, he feels it to his bones," Pansy said, rubbing her arms.

Greer held her finger up as if she were listening to the wind, as if somewhere within it, she might hear Loretta's cry. "Dammit. I've got to do something," she said again. "I'll go nuts just standing here. I need to find my daughter."

Ethan listened, and his mind raced. His fingers flicked more often than usual, and he traced circles in the dirt with his boots.

Raina stood to the side of the porch and rubbed her swollen eyes. "I'm so sorry," she said. "I can't believe it's come to this, I mean, I knew things were bad, but…"

"It's not your fault, darlin'," Earl told her. "You got duped, same as the lot of 'em."

"I've gotta go," Greer said, still pacing. "The rest of you can come or stay."

"Deputy Scoggins," Noleen called out to the officer staff-ing the phones. "Where is the search party at this particular moment?"

"Out near Movie Flats, down near the canyon."

"Stunt Man Canyon," Earl advised.

"And an ambulance is on its way out to pick up Bill,"

said Deputy Scoggins.

Bill tapped his middle and index fingers against his thumb, repeatedly. No, *no, no.* But Noleen shook her head. "You're going, Billy. I'm not arguing anymore about this."

Greer pulled her cell phone from the pocket of her oversized silver purse. "Just one minute. Just…" she said, scrolling through her list of contacts.

"She's making a phone call?" Raina's eyes bulged, and she squeaked a single word, "Now?"

"Trust her," Doc said. "I know that look. There may not be a method to Greer's madness, but there's usually a reason behind it."

Greer ran her fingers through her disheveled hair, and curled the index finger of her free hand through the belt loop on her culottes. She inhaled sharply and screamed into the cell phone: "Let my daughter and Cora go, you scumbag! I'll say this once, and you better listen. You talk a lot when you're drunk, *Brock.* You say things. I *know* things. Like about misappropriated money. Bullying Mo out of business, blackmailing him, forgiving his gambling debt after he signed over the Iron Gate. Let the girls go, or I'll go straight to the cops!" In one quick motion, she twirled around and pocketed her phone. "Sorry," she told the others. "I tend to rant."

"Rant," Ethan said, "means to speak or shout in an impassioned way." He flicked his fingers, gave her a thumbs-up.

Doc exchanged looks with Greer, his eyebrows tilted

in a way that suggested he had questions to ask her later.

Ethan glanced from one to the other. "Beloved." He slowed down and said it again: "Be-loved."

"What?" Greer looked fish-eyed, as if the relevance of the word were as complicated as her scrabbling for its definition.

Doc smiled, frowned. Blushed.

"It's nearly five o'clock," Earl said. "We best get movin'."

"I'll stay here," Yoshi said, his eyes following his words to Bill, to Pansy.

"I'll stay as well," Raina said. "With Ethan, in case he needs me."

"I won't. Need you. Because I'm going with them," Ethan said.

"No!" Raina spun around, projecting her fear with her finger.

"I'm going. You can't stop me. No one can."

"Ethan, listen to me. Sim, your father, will be back soon…"

"I'm going!"

"Sorry, but no can do." Greer steadied herself beside Raina. "It's not having you go with us that we're worried about, Ethan. It's what happens after."

"I'm capable. I'm strong. Don't tell me I can't help."

"Wait. Stop," Doc said calmly. "Ethan, it's obvious that you're capable. Good heavens. Look what you did to save yourself and Pansy.

"But as much as I appreciate your willingness to help, I agree with your mother. Our efforts need to be focused on the girls right now, and if you were with us, we'd be worried about you as well."

Earl strolled over, pulled a sugar cube from his pocket and slipped it to Dakota. He scratched the horse's forehead and rubbed his muzzle. "Ethan, buddy, you could do me a big favor," he said. "Take care of Dakota while we're gone. Can you do that, son?"

Ethan flicked his fingers, looked up and away. "Okay," he said. "I'll stay. For the moment, I'll stay. But I don't like this plan. I don't like it at all."

Granny Noleen stepped off the porch and walked toward her Buick. "Let's be off then," she said. "Doc. Earl. You ready?"

Noleen shadowed Greer's footsteps, instructing as she walked, "Those of you staying here, be safe. If Brock shows up, if anything happens, don't try to be a hero. Call for help. Billy…get in the damn ambulance when it comes, hear? I'll get to the hospital as soon as I can."

+++

Ethan watched the Buick pull out of the yard. It was hard to stand still, to see Greer and the others leave. He shouted after the car: "Check the berry bushes near the creek! Check above the campgrounds in the boulders there."

"Come, Ethan. Let's go and get something to eat,"

Yoshi said. He helped Pansy stand. Raina helped Bill, and they walked into the house, the screen door slapping shut behind them.

From inside, Raina called again: "Ethan. Come put something in your stomach. It will settle your nerves, son. Please."

Ethan stared at the house, the door, but didn't move. A ping on his cell phone startled him, and he flinched; he pulled the phone from his pocket and saw the text: STONE HOUSE.

Loretta.

No doubt the message was late in coming. No doubt he was lucky to have received it at all. He ran to the end of the driveway, but the car was gone. He started toward the house, but thought of Pansy eating cookies, thought of Raina and Yoshi tending the bandages on Bill's forehead and arms and leg. He strode in circles, kicking up dirt as he walked.

Dakota whinnied and stomped his foot. Swished his tail.

Ethan made a mental list of all the rules he had broken in the last twenty-four hours and wondered if there was a specific number regarding allowable mistakes—another rule about breaking the rules that might allow for one more. And then he thought of Loretta. And what she had said to him before they went into the bunker: "I know how important it is that you follow the rules your parents set for you. But we have a situation here where following those rules might put someone in danger. People you care about."

He didn't want to think about it anymore, or wait around to appease his mother and Greer. His feet crossed the yard before his mind could count his paces. He rested his phone face-up on Noleen's rocking chair and didn't look back as he sprinted to Dakota. Didn't check his watch when he saddled and reined him.

The muscles in Dakota's neck stiffened and popped; his tail spun like a propeller. Ethan slipped his foot in the stirrup and swung himself up, using his seat and his inside leg to turn the horse toward the creek and set him to a gallop.

+++

Dust pattered Ethan's clothes with a gritty waterless rain. The clack of Dakota's hoofs over rocks and through crusty washes was the only discernable sound: monotonous yet intentional. The horse had a steady gait and did what Ethan asked of him, responding to his subtle shifts in weight, a slight rotation of his pelvis, minimal pressure with his calves and knees. Other horses Ethan had ridden in his life streamed through his mind: Blossom, a Shetland Pony; Buckwheat, a buckskin mare—his first serious horse-crush; and Beau, the beautiful black quarter horse that was his last ride at Shady Lawn Farm Horsemanship Camp. Ethan kept off the main roads, riding through hills he knew well and could navigate with ease. He felt the horse's body beneath him, every muscle in his shoulders, barrel, and legs, moving in a coordinated effort with his own, his chest heaving as Ethan's did. He loped over the uneven ground, as anxious, it seemed, as Ethan was, to get to the trailhead that would lead them to Loretta and Cora. To keep his mind off the girls, Ethan challenged himself with Loretta's game, scrolling through movie titles and plotlines in much the same way she memorized trivia. His favorites first. Second: plot-driven and meaningful films. Third: his least favorites, but those he had watched to the end. When that challenge tired him, he thought of the Stone House. He'd been there twice with his parents—on a day hike once, and an overnight campout the second time. He had scouted, and surveyed the ground and discovered most of the rocky treasures nearest the building. He had ideas now of where to position himself once he got there, places he wouldn't be seen but where he would have a good view of everything, inside and outside the old Stone House. Ethan shaded his eyes with his hands, straining to see Whitney Portal—the old Hunter's Camp where Franklin and Sherifa Wolff first pitched their tent when visiting Mt. Whitney. The Wolffs' story fascinated him. According to his mother, they were "freethinkers" and loved to write in their journals. They studied philosophy, mysticism, and religion. And most importantly, they fell in love with the mountain, just as Ethan loved it—and they built the Stone House. Ethan shivered, thinking of Loretta and Cora being held there against their wills. Of the gentle way his mother described the Wolffs' intentions for the place and the words they had inscribed on the stone altar inside: *Father, Into Thy eternal wisdom, all creative love, and infinite power I direct my thoughts, give my devotion and manifest my energy, that I may know, love, and serve Thee.* Even now, Ethan pondered the meaning of this phrase, marveling at what Raina called its strength and beauty. He remembered sitting beside her, examining the fine cut of the scroll with his fingers, reading, scrutinizing the phrase *Father, Into Thy eternal wisdom.* Father as in a *male parent,* or father as in *an old man,* or father as in *Our Father in Heaven*; and into the eternal wisdom, eternal as in *endless*—really? How could that be? Could time really be endless? To visualize a concept that meant *forever, for all time,* was complicated and did not fit into a category that he understood.

One minute became two became thirty and more, but finally, near the edge of a briny lake bed Ethan relaxed. The trailhead to the Stone House was poorly marked, but he drove Dakota to it, and the horse changed his gait to a slow trot, sidestepping desert scrub brush and low-growth manzanita until he reached a narrow footpath heading up-mountain. At the base of the path, Ethan slowed the horse to a walk, pulling gently on the reins. "Whoa, boy. Shhh…" He leaned forward in the saddle, listening, though he wasn't sure what he expected to hear. Birds were chirping. Leaves were rustling. Other than that, there was nothing. He clicked Dakota forward again, moving cautiously, wondering whether he should stay on the main path or detour through the brush. He argued with himself regarding the wisest choice, how the *wisest choice* could be the wrong choice and prove disastrous.

Dakota snorted as if frustrated with Ethan's indecision. Then he took the lead, heading off the path, his legs hammering up the mountain. Maybe in a direction Earl had taken him before, Ethan thought—maybe not—but the horse was determined, chugging through brush, weaving around trees, stumbling once on a root and nearly going down. Before long Ethan heard the rush of water, and his dry mouth felt drier still until suddenly Dakota was ankle-deep in the creek and he didn't wait for Ethan's cue, but drank, and drank, and drank. Ethan slid off the saddle, pulled his pack off his shoulders, found his canteen, and did the same.

Once done, Ethan took the reins and led Dakota through the creek, up the far bank and into a stand of trees. He eyed the surrounding forest, found a slim but sturdy cedar, and tied Dakota to it, wishing he had thought to grab an armful of hay and stow it in a saddlebag—something to keep the horse satisfied and busy. What he did have, he realized, was an apple. He pulled it from his pack, bit it into pieces and fed it to Dakota.

"I'll be back," he whispered, and Dakota flicked his tail and dropped his muzzle into Ethan's hand. Ethan leaned into him. "Stay here," he said. "Good boy." He let go of Dakota's mane and darted up the hill. He tried to still his breathing, but every inhale and exhale seemed wired for amplification, as he imagined what, or who, might be listening. He tried to quantify the one-eighth measure of Native American blood that ran through his veins and told himself that he could creep more quietly, hunch lower. In his mind, the crunch of every twig, each stumble and kicked rock intensified times two. Up the next ridge and around a bend was the house made of stone, and as it came into view, perched like a wonder on the side of the mountain, his heart raced and his palms grew sweaty, and he marveled again that it stood there at all. When he reached a large granite boulder, he scoured it, found its cracks and ridges, and climbed to the top, a vantage point as good as he had hoped it would be.

On the other side, stood Frey. Ethan's skin prickled; he instinctively withdrew like a turtle into his shell, though he kept his eyes locked on the man, this person who, even now, from this distance appeared anxious and ready to fight. When Ethan dared to look away, it was only for a moment to assess what he saw on the ground: random supplies, a pack, a bear-proof food canister, a thermos, a pile of kindling. A large hunting knife jabbed into a stump beside the fire pit where Frey was now piling tinder, and lighting it with a match. Time passed slowly and the daylight held; Ethan questioned his own judgment, coming here without a plan, and he ached for his journal and his pen, wanting to write and make lists and diagram an escape route. His eyes began to burn and his fingers let loose their grip on the rock. He wondered where his father and Sheriff Atkins might be. Did his mother or Yoshi suspect yet that he had taken the horse and left? Maybe. But maybe not. Raina would expect him to keep his distance from her and the others, to wander off and write in his journal. She would respectfully give him space until someone found the phone and Loretta's text, or until it got dark outside, or until Earl got home and discovered Dakota missing.

Night came then, the first stars reluctantly surrendering their position. Ethan reached for his flashlight, still snug in the waistband of his pants. He pulled it out and laid it beside him on the rock. He reached for it again, and again, securing its position in his mind. There had been no movement within the house, but he kept his eyes trained there, even as a mosquito buzzed his ear and his nose, and a big brown bat scooped away the air in front of him, causing him to flick and blink and hold his breath.

He had no more than settled when a shrill cry stilled the night sky. Then a voice blasted through the doorway of the Stone House, gritty, and agitated. "If Brock hadn't insisted you come, I'd a dumped your ass on the road somewhere!"

Then came another voice, this one breaking pitch from high to low: "Don't push me! Get your hands off me, you asshole!"

And another: "Both of you stop it! Stay away from Cora!"

"Loretta!" Then Ethan couldn't help himself, and from his perch on the rock, he yelled, "InYo Face!"

There was a scrambling within the house, a string of

mumbled curse words. A flashlight beam cut a hole in the dark, a bouncing tube of light graying the brush, the trees, the ground around the fire pit. "Who's there?" Frey hollered.

"If you can hear me, listen, don't give yourself to haters, deflators, label creators. Men who trap you, and zap you, who handicap and strap you..." Ethan knew that Loretta would recognize this snippet of the rap song they had written together. He felt invigorated.

"Shut up! Show yourself!" Frey screamed.

"No."

"This is not a request, it's an order. Show yourself!"

"Men who enslave you, berate you...who drill you, mislead you, brow-beat, and force-feed you...Do not despair!"

Loretta heard him and answered. *"Bitter men bet on beastly experiments. Break your heart and your head until you bow to their regiments..."*

"Shut up! You little bitch. You know who's out there, don't you..."

Ethan could see Frey through the window, scudding forward, bending down and out of sight. He knew that it was Loretta, Frey was after, and he screamed, continuing his bit of dialogue where Loretta left off: *"...Men who drill you, mislead you, brow-beat, and force-feed you...sweet talking manipulators, assassinators, obliterators. Indoctrinators: critical, literal, insanely political..."*

Throughout his oration, the beam of light probed the brush surrounding the rock, and Frey was yelling, "Quiet!

Shut up! Quiet!"

The ground blackened then as if the moon had deserted the sky, but inside the Stone House, Frey's flashlight beam whipped the rock walls and rode on faces, exaggerating every bit of puckered skin, stretched lips, rounded eyes. Ethan watched through the side window as Frey pulled Loretta up and shoved her into the wall. As he backhanded her across the face.

"Stop!" Ethan yelled, standing tall on his rock. "You are breaking the law! Arson! Kidnapping! Inflicting bodily harm!"

"Ethan. I should have known." Frey laughed, and his tone was wicked.

"Citizen's arrest!" Ethan yelled.

"Come get me, I dare you."

"Greed breeds tyranny and hate. Haters think too much and feel too little. There is no middle…" Ethan recited.

Once again, Loretta answered: *"Reject their faction, find your own passion, be ready to dash-in, and lead with compassion…"*

"Shut up, I told you to shut up!" Frey grabbed Cora this time, and her scream was shrill, painful to hear. "You idiots! Shut the hell up!" he screamed.

"Enough!" Pierce stammered. Ethan saw him leap at Frey, sucker-punch him once, twice, in the ribs. Frey flew at him, punching him in the jaw and solar plexus, knocking him to the ground. Pierce gasped for breath and struggled to his feet, lurching sideways, toward the wall of the Stone House. He reached for his gun, grabbed it, turned and leveled it at Frey.

Frey wiped his bloody mouth with the back of his hand and stumbled out of the building, hands clasped behind his neck in surrender. He opened his mouth to speak, but Pierce yelled, "Stop. Don't say a word."

"All that crap," said Frey. "That shit Brock told you about you being like a son to him. It's all bullshit, Pierce. And you're too stupid to see it." Frey turned and stumbled, fell on his knees, crawled to the stump beside the fire pit. He gripped his knife, fingering it, waving it tauntingly, jabbing at nothing, as if he were sticking invisible people. "Flank left, move fast and clear those murder holes!" He crouched beside the fire pit now, screaming, flailing his arms. He kissed the dog-tags around his neck. "Cover fast! To your left, your left!" He rolled on the ground, too close to the fire and the sleeve of his shirt sparked and began to burn. He screamed and rolled, batting at his arm, beating the flame to black embers.

In the harshness of the moment, Ethan saw Frey's torment—the anguish in his eyes, the battleground in his mind. He understood what it felt like to be labeled with an acronym. For Frey it was PTSD. Post-Traumatic Stress Disorder: a mental health condition triggered by seeing or experiencing a traumatic event.

"Frey. This is Sheriff Atkins." The voice came out of

nowhere, amplified, a whooshing of words through a mega-phone and directional loudspeakers. "I understand you must be frightened and confused. Let's talk. What do you need tonight, Frey? What do you need?"

The microphone squealed, and there was a rustling sound. A woman yelled, "Gimme that micro-thingy! Lo-retta!"

Loretta shrieked, and screamed, "Mom!"

"If you hurt any of those kids, I'll hang you by your twisted little dick, hear me?"

After a minute, Sheriff Atkins spoke again. "I don't believe you intend to harm anyone, Frey. If you can hear me, give me a sign. If the kids are okay, please, give me a sign."

A rifle shot echoed over the lakebed.

Ethan jumped from the rock and ran into the Stone House, just as Frey ran in and knocked Pierce to the ground. They rolled and punched, a jumble of arms and legs, until Frey scissor-locked Pierce, pinning his arm with a bone-wrenching tug. Pierce's gun lay a few feet away, and Loretta was on her stomach, crawling toward it. Ethan's body was in motion, but his mind was stuck on one cru-cial detail: he had never been in a physical fight before. He wasn't sure what to do. Thinking of pictures he had seen, movies he had watched, he forged ahead, arms flailing, fists pounding the air. He jumped on Frey's back and his fists kept up the assault. Frey was on him now and Pierce was rolling free. Then Ethan was on his back, and dirt was in his hair, and Frey's arms, his face, the morbidity of his breath became an assault on their own, stinging with their proximity. Ethan felt the arrival of his flutterbees, thousands of them, and they swarmed, and he screamed, then chanted, "You're in my space! My space! My space!" He grabbed a handful of dirt and threw it in Frey's face, and in the second that Frey rubbed his eyes, Ethan freed his leg and kicked Frey in the side. He scrambled from beneath him and stood jumping up and down. "Assault with a deadly weapon! Kidnapping! Child abuse! Arson! Abuse of power! Harassment! Intimidation!"

An ear-splitting explosion at close range shook him to his knees. He turned and saw Loretta with Pierce's rifle, pointed up and out the window. Her hands were trembling. Her eyes looked manic and were tear-filled. She wiped at them with the sleeve of her t-shirt, stained with blood and dirt and sweat.

A cacophony of screams rose up the granite walls, a scramble of words, a raucous mix of voices carrying panic. "Lo-retta!" Greer wailed from afar.

"InYo face," coughed Cora. "You messed with the wrong *idiots*, assholes."

"Over there, both of you," Loretta said, pointing the gun to the wall closest to the door. "There is no reason for any of this. Your boss screwed up. You don't have to go along with his craziness..."

"You have no idea what you're talking about!" Pierce

said.

"Oh, yes, Pierce, we do. We saw tapes. We've copied records. What I don't know is how deep you are into all of this, if you know about money laundering and plans to seize property. Genetic crap, like serious messing with families and, my God..."

"Shut up!"

"Best thing you can do is give 'em the dirt. Rat out your leader," Cora said, smiling despite her pain.

"Frey!" Sheriff Atkin's voice thundered from below. "You are surrounded. My deputies are armed and ready to fire. You have nowhere to go. Free the hostages. Now."

Frey crouched down and his eyes darted from one rocky outcrop to the next, as if he were waiting for an inevitable ambush.

Ethan dusted himself off. He flicked his fingers. He stared at Loretta, seeing some new thing in her, something unfamiliar but awesome.

Armed men in flak jackets stormed the Stone House. Ethan dashed to the altar in the center of the room, covering it and part of Cora with his body. "Watch out!" he yelled. "Be careful here!"

Pierce slumped to the ground, chewing on his fingers. "Go fart peas on the moon!" he yelled at Ethan.

"You look like you don't know whether to save yourself or swallow your pretzels," Loretta told Pierce, repeating what he had said at Jemma's party. "Sound familiar? Score one for our side. You're swinging for the wrong team." She handed the rifle to the officer closest to her and then returned to Cora and the medic now treating her.

The small sanctuary filled with people. One deputy held Frey facedown on the ground; another had backed Pierce against a wall, handcuffing him and reading him his rights. The medic took Cora's vitals, cleaned and rebound her arm, and checked her ribs and legs. He then cleaned and bandaged the gash on Loretta's forehead and various smaller lacerations on her arms and legs.

"No," Ethan said, as the medic approached him. "Don't."

"Stay put," Loretta said. "Ethan chooses who and when to allow someone into his space, and I think he's had enough people messing with him for now. We'll manage from here, truly."

"Better do as she says," Cora told the medic. "She's badass."

Loretta stood and walked to the altar and to Ethan. He inched toward her then, arms at his sides, until his joy brought him to her with no holding back. The hug felt good, safe, and Loretta held him close.

"Sheriff says the helicopter is busy on another rescue near Mammoth. Do you need the Stokes?" asked a flak-jacketed deputy just entering the Stone House.

"Stokes?" Cora asked, frowning.

"Stokes basket," the medic said.

"I'm not getting in a basket," Cora told him. "No way."

"I've got a horse," Ethan said. "She can ride him. He's gentle."

"We know about the horse," the deputy said. "Your opinion?" he asked the medic.

"She's ambulatory. And stable. It's doable."

"Can you walk to where the horse is tethered?" the deputy asked Cora.

"We'll help Cora," Loretta said. "Me and Ethan. That's how this started, and the way it should end. Just the three of us. Together."

-CHAPTER 25-

*B*y the time they left the Stone House, a pale yellow light had outlined the granite cliffs, the sun's round eye rising behind the mountain and scattering colors amongst the clouds. The oranges, grays, and blues were more vivid than Loretta remembered seeing, a reminder that they had made it through the night.

The walk from the house to where Ethan had tethered Dakota was long and tedious. She and Ethan shouldered Cora's weight, positioning their arms just so around her waist, but her legs often faltered, her knees buckled more than once, and she groaned, drawing a series of short breaths as if to keep the pain from spreading.

Ethan did not hesitate when he lifted Cora onto Dakota's back, or when he entwined his hands under Loretta's feet to give her a boost and help her seat herself behind Cora on the saddle. He did not blink, or flick, or falter in any way as he led the surefooted horse, stepping carefully over rocks and tree roots and covering ground much more quickly than she and Cora had walked it the day before.

Dakota swished flies with his tail. His head was down, and his gait was as relaxed as if he were on a trail ride on any random day. Loretta thought of the few times she'd ridden a horse—at a summer carnival when she was five or six, and with Ethan at his riding lessons on occasion. More often, she had leaned on the round corral at Shady Lawn Farm, just watching Ethan ride, always impressed by his connection with the animal and his focus on the training. His instructor would speak a single-word command, and Ethan responded; his horse responded. It was a beautiful thing to see and had always left Loretta in awe, of both Ethan and the horses. The one-word thing, the simplicity of it, had always left her wishing it was the same for her, that all she had to do was speak, and others would listen—that communicating was as easy as that, as simple as having someone care enough to hear your one word.

In front of her on the saddle, Cora moaned. Loretta scooched a little closer, readjusting her position to accept more of Cora's body weight and to ease the pressure on her ribs.

"You're alive," Cora said, patting Loretta's knee.

"Yeah, I'm alive. You?"

"I'm too stubborn to die."

"Well, yeah…you're just figuring that out?" Loretta said, holding her tighter.

"Takes me awhile sometimes. I, ow, easy on the ribs, Batgirl."

"Stop whining.

"Just watch the trail, will you? Make sure this horse is taking us home."

Frey and Pierce walked behind them, in and out of step with Dakota's gait: too close, too far, pushing them faster, slowing them down. Even handcuffed and flanked by officers, Frey's eyes on the back of Loretta's head intimidated her. All along the trail, he carried on his ghostly conversation, mumbling like a wild child, screeching like a madman. Pierce's sobs were background noise and she tried to ignore them, but it was difficult. "Someday I might feel sorry for you," she told him, "but right now…" She glanced at Cora's wobbling head. "Not so much."

Dakota eased around a section of trail that had eroded—loose dirt, a slide of fractured pebbles. Ethan locked his fingers around her ankle, and Cora's shoulders rocked against her chest. For the first time since the rescue, Loretta began to cry.

+++

At the trailhead stood a throng of people: Sheriff Atkins, deputies, and many volunteers—Granny Noleen and Earl, Doc. Sim. The police had stationed their patrol cars in a broad semicircle. There was an off-road police vehicle, manned with loud speakers. An ambulance. A fire engine.

Granny's Buick and Sim's Jeep Cherokee. Where was Old Blue, Loretta wondered? Where was her mother?

Sim's voice carried over the huddled talkers, the static on the police radio, and Noleen's raspy-throated wail. "Yeah, this is Sim, leaving my message after the beep. We trusted you, Brock," he screamed into his cell phone. "And look what you've done. If my son is harmed, if those girls are hurt, you *will* pay. Understand me, *brother?*"

Loretta watched Ethan carefully, concerned that he might have a T-Rex-sized meltdown after hearing his father's voice—bolting with or without Dakota's reins in his hands. But he didn't. Instead, he completed his task and walked Dakota into the middle of the crowd.

Earl hobbled more than ran, shoving past the officer and to Dakota. His eyes pored over each of them, settling on Cora. "You kids all right?" he asked. Doc was beside him now, and together they lifted Cora down. Earl helped Loretta drop from the saddle as well, and like a newborn calf, her legs wobbled and her hips resisted as she tried to stand. Earl offered his arm for support while she steadied herself, running his free hand over Dakota's flank, his neck and ears. "Good boy," he told the horse. "You're a good ol' fella."

When Loretta let go of Earl, he turned to Ethan. "I'd be pissed if I wasn't so happy," he said, wiping away tears with his shirt sleeve.

Ethan nodded. Looked up and away.

"Truth is, you got some balls, kid."

"Of course I do," Ethan said.

Earl chuckled. "I'd be proud to have you ride beside me any day. Anytime," he said.

"Okay, but for safety's sake, it's best to ride in pairs, with a friend or an associate. That means we'd need two horses, so I'd have to buy one of my own. Preferably, I'd board him at Willow Grove. Near Dakota. Of course, I'd pay for room and board. But I can speak with Granny about that later. Maybe tomorrow. How about tomorrow?"

Earl shook his head and tipped his hat. "Yep. Well. I figure we can work that out," he said. "You're somethin', Buckaroo, somethin' real special."

The paramedics settled Cora on a gurney, and Loretta watched as they navigated the rough ground toward the ambulance. Satisfied that Cora was safe, she searched the crowd again for her mother.

Greer stood apart from the rest, chewing her finger-nails and glaring at the deputy who restrained her. Loretta could only imagine why her mother was being held: too mouthy, too accusatory, too cynical, too brash, too jittery, too pushy—the list went on and on.

Loretta rushed toward her as Greer shoved the deputy aside. "Let me go!" she bellowed. "That's my daughter!"

Loretta threw her arms around her mother's neck and sobbed.

"What were you thinking?" Greer asked, hugging her back. "You could have been killed!"

"Yeah," Loretta said, "But I wasn't. So." She dropped her arms and backed away.

"I told you to stay clear of Brock," Greer continued, "I can't believe you put yourself in this position…"

"Greer," Loretta said, squaring up. "I'm not going to argue about this. Ethan, Cora, and I…we made a decision. And based on the stuff we found in the bunker, I'd do it all again. It was only a matter of time, Mom. The guy had plans. People would have been hurt. Lots of people. You should be saying thank you. I mean, really." The sharpness in her voice surprised even her.

Earl laid his hand on Greer's shoulder and nodded at Loretta. "This girl of yours is bright, Greer. She's got a lot to say and more spunk than a blue-tick puppy."

Greer stared at Loretta as if she didn't recognize her. She paused, then shrugged her shoulders and relaxed. "Who are you and what have you done with my daughter?" she teased.

Loretta kicked at the dirt with her tennis shoe. "Is that an apology?"

"Quite possibly."

"It would be a first."

"Now, wait a minute. I apologize all the time. When I'm wrong…which isn't often, like, almost never," Greer said, grinning.

"I heard you yelling at Frey on the bullhorn," Loretta said.

"Yeah, well…he'll be lucky if I don't hang him to a tree and…"

"That's what *I* told him." They both laughed and hugged again.

Greer held Loretta at arm's length. "Now let me look at you," she said, wiping the dirt from Loretta's cheeks. "You're a little worse for wear, but you'll do," she said, her lips quivering, her eyes filling with tears.

Loretta nodded, smiled. "Hey…how's Mr. Fancy Boots?"

"The guy in Vegas? Didn't work out."

"Was he worth a gravestone, at least?" Loretta asked.

"A groovy one," Greer said. "Maybe soon we'll do that together."

"Cool. Yeah, together."

Loretta's hair blew over her eyes and about her shoulders, tangled, blood-smeared, and sticky with sweat. Her arm and leg muscles ached, and her forehead throbbed behind the gash in her head, but she felt happy. She hugged her mother once more, then marched toward the ambulance and stepped inside. "Only one can ride along," the paramedic said. "Sorry."

"You stay," Doc told her. "I've had my visit. It should be the two of you on this ride anyway, am I right?"

"Do you mind?" Cora asked.

Doc backed out of the ambulance. "I'll follow just behind, my darlings," he said, as he stepped out of the vehicle. He stopped and gazed back at them, his eyes damp and reflective; he cleared his throat and swallowed. "I'm so thankful," he said, "that you both are safe." He turned to the driver. "Take care of my girls." Then he blew them a kiss. "Mi corazón, mi alegría," he said, before walking away.

"Wait! Loretta shouted. She slid past the gurney, jumped out of the ambulance and ran to Ethan. Dakota sidestepped as she approached, flicked his tail and went back to chewing a mouthful of hay. Sim looked like a bookend, standing stiff and somber at Ethan's side.

Earl took the reins from Ethan and Sim took a step back. Ethan blinked his black-button eyes. His arms hung at his sides, and he flicked his fingers and smiled. Loretta reached out, but held off, waiting for him to give her permission. He hung his head, stepped toward her, and accepted her hug, hugging back.

+++

At the hospital, Loretta told her story so many times that her voice grew hoarse. There was a steady parade of police detectives through her patient room in the ER. Cora's room was just across the hall, and she could see the same scenario playing out over there. She knew Ethan was nearby, assumed he was being cross-examined even more closely, and could only imagine the room-pacing, finger-flicking, dictionary-quoting energy he must be displaying. She wanted desperately to drag her hospital-gowned butt off the table and tiptoe barefoot down the corridor until she found him.

She imagined it wouldn't take long; she would most likely hear him doors away.

Nearly eight hours later, they sat side-by-side in the waiting room. Ethan stared at the ceiling. Loretta answered a volley of Greer's questions.

"Are you okay?"

"Yes."

"Do you hurt?"

"No." This was a lie. A nurse had cleaned and dressed her lacerations, but their synchronized throbbing was driving her nuts.

"Do you need anything? An aspirin? A snack? Something to drink? Either of you?"

"No thanks. Ethan?"

Ethan flicked his fingers, looked up and away.

"What? I know I'm obnoxious, but I'm still loveable, right?" said Greer, fluttering her eyelashes. Watching her now, Loretta wondered how her mother had managed to make it through the day without flirting with the doctor—sticking a daisy in his stethoscope.

Ethan crossed the room to the vending machine. "The healing power of chocolate should never be underestimated," he said, staring at the selections.

Everyone laughed.

Sim offered Raina his hand and helped her up. They had been sitting by themselves across the room, touching but not cuddling and occasionally sobbing. "I don't know what to say, except, 'I'm sorry,'" he said. Dark circles framed Raina's eyes; she tried to speak but couldn't.

"This isn't your fault," Doc said. "The kids are okay, and that's all that matters."

"Brock *will* be caught," said Greer. "In the meantime, can you get your hands on the pink slip for that Hummer?"

Sim snickered and nodded. His Adam's apple bobbed up and down in his throat as if he needed to choke out another apology. "We're tired. Let's go home," he said to Ethan and Raina, extending his hands to them both.

"No, I'm going to stay here," Ethan said.

"Ethan, please." Sim sighed, his eyes drooping as much as his mouth. "Your mother and I need you with us. We want to go home."

"*Need* is an interesting word," said Ethan. He flicked his fingers, turned to Loretta, and with his eyes focused elsewhere, said, "They need me. See you tomorrow."

"Tomorrow," Loretta said. Suddenly, all she wanted was to be in her own bed, in her own room, with her mother in *her* own room, in *her* own bed, just feet away.

"You know, once I get you home, I'll lock you in," Greer said. "No sleepovers, no four-wheeling, or cruising the main drag in Old Blue."

"Don't mess with me, Mom. Besides, there isn't a *main* drag in Lone Pine, Main Street is the *only* drag there is."

Greer chuckled, then leaned down and kissed Loretta's cheek. "I love you, baby," she said, wetting her fingers with her tongue and slicking Loretta's hair behind her ears.

"Aww, don't!" Loretta frowned and walked away, following Doc down the hall and to Cora's room. "I'll be back," she called out to her mother. "Behave yourself," she said.

Doc placed his index finger on his lips. He opened the door quietly. Inside, Cora was asleep in her hospital bed; her breathing was still ragged, and a sling and swathe held her broken shoulder in place.

"Her shoulder should heal just fine," Doc said. "Please try not to worry."

"What about her ribs?"

"Six weeks and she'll be back to normal." He hesitated a moment, then continued. "I spoke with Noleen. As you know, Bill didn't fare so well. It took the paramedics a while to convince him that cleaning and dressing the gunshot wound was not enough and that he should go to the hospital. The wound is infected, and his long-term prognosis is complicated by his liver disease—cirrhosis—the result of his alcohol addiction."

"Is he going to be okay?"

I think so, but he may lose his leg."

Loretta sighed. Her eyes spilled over with tears. "And Pansy?" she asked.

"Pansy is okay, though she's badly bruised. She has some major lacerations on her arms and one on her head. She's pretty disoriented, but she's home with Earl and Yoshi. Noleen's here with Bill, of course."

Doc handed Loretta a box of Kleenex. "You were all very lucky. This could have been much worse."

"Bill saved us, you know. If it hadn't been for him... him and Ethan..."

"I know. We all do." Doc sighed. "Bill told us what happened, part of it anyway."

Loretta's chest constricted and she felt nauseous. She glanced at Doc and then at Cora. "I'm sorry," she said. "I told my mother otherwise, but we shouldn't have gone to the bunker. We shouldn't have made plans without talking to you first."

"Yes, darling girl, that would have been best." He placed his hand over Loretta's as she sobbed. After a minute, when he had control of his own tears, he said, "I'm not saying what you did was right, but truth be told, your actions were honorable and brave. You were concerned about your friends. People you've grown to love, just as I love you and my precious Cora."

Loretta leaned into Doc's chest and closed her eyes.

+++

Granny decided a get-together was in order. Simple, but celebratory. "A Thanksgiving minus the capital T," she said. To be followed by work days, many work days, but those would commence tomorrow. It had been three weeks since the bunker incident. The dust had settled. Sim's construction crew had shored up the tunnels, but repairs to the house were still to come: extra support for the substructure, new posts, and beams to replace the old. A new staircase—not because the original was damaged but to create safer access for the anthropologists, news reporters, and the occasional lookie-loo Noleen was reluctantly allowing inside.

Sim and Raina sat side by side in chairs under a cottonwood near the porch, holding hands. Loretta glanced at Sim, thankful for his help, knowing that he had offered Noleen more than just fixing the beams and supports. He was giving Willow Grove a new roof, fresh paint, and a sturdier porch. "Please," he had said. "I want to help, and who knows, what with the history here, the tunnels, Underground Railroad and Japanese, this house could someday end up storied in a textbook or even a novel."

Ice tinkled in glasses of lemonade. Shade filtered through tree branches and mirrored the sides of the house and sheds. Bill sat, bandaged and bruised and minus his left leg, on a wheelchair just off the porch, head tilted upward, eyes closed.

Cora crinkled her nose, not happy that she had to rest while Loretta readied the picnic table: covering it with a tablecloth, setting it with tableware, hauling folding camp chairs from the barn. "Ah hum," she complained, noting Loretta's improper placement of forks to the right instead of to the left of the plates.

Yoshi translated as Bill signed. "Cora's doing that thing with her jaw again." Bill opened and closed his fingers. *"Blah, blah, blah."*

"Really? Such a comedian," Cora teased back. "What a comedian."

Granny Noleen and Greer walked out of the house carrying platters of bread, and cheese, and bowls of fresh honey and blackberry jam. "Earl, how's the barbecue?" Noleen asked.

"Give 'er five. Maybe ten," Earl said, as he closed the lid on the grill.

Sim stood up, rubbing his hands on his pants. "I've got some news about Brock. But if you'd rather, I'll wait..."

Ethan dropped the currycomb, patted Dakota, and let the horse have his lead, free-feeding on the sun-parched Bermuda grass. He jumped the stairs two at a time, landing on the bench near Loretta.

"No time's a good time when you're dealing with Brock," Greer said. "Let's get it over with. Details, please."

Sim nodded. "We spent the morning with Sheriff Atkins," he said. "Group bank accounts have been emptied. Supplies were taken from both the Iron Gate and the bunker the night of the assault. Food. Liquor. Guns. Not heavyweight stuff, but pistols and ammo. Unfortunately, there have been no sightings of Brock or Clive. Atkins ran background checks on both of them. Clive's was clean. Until recently. But Brock has been a busy boy. What was it, Raina?"

Raina fidgeted in her chair, ran her hand over her cheek, and cleared her throat. "Alias one: Frank Quader, accountant. Alias two: Jimmy Schook, minister. Alias three:

Matt Capwell, motivational speaker. This wasn't Brock's first go-round with mind control and end-of-times prophecy according to APB responses from out of state. Many people claim to have been duped, coerced out of money and property. Sheriff Atkins does believe, however, that the bunker is the most sophisticated plan Brock's implemented thus far."

The afternoon sun hit Sim just right, exposing the pallor of his skin. "I can recoup some money by selling furniture, medical supplies, some other items that didn't get destroyed in the fire. At least get something back to the folks who invested in Brock's lies." He sat down and cradled his head in his hands. Raina rubbed his shoulders.

"We're smart people. All of us. How did this happen? How were we so gullible?" she asked.

"Brock's greatest asset was his ability to determine what his listeners wanted to hear and give it to them in simple language that appealed to them," Doc said. "He was good at it, and apparently perfected his technique on others beforehand."

"Fertile minds are productive for farming," Yoshi said.

Granny swished flies away from the food table. "Let's eat," she said. "Earl, we 'bout ready? Greer, get the condiments, lettuce, tomatoes and such."

Toby ran out from under the porch, barking. A horn honked in the distance; a vehicle moving at a fast clip drove up the road and into the driveway.

Brady's four-wheeler came to an abrupt stop, sending a

cloud of dust toward the barbecue. "Hey," he said, jumping out of the Jeep. "We thought you might be here, Loretta. Hope you don't mind that we stopped by."

The passenger door opened, and Jemma stepped down. "My parents are just sick about the whole Group thing," she said. "Luckily, they were smart enough to walk away before the worst of it happened." She flipped her hair back off her face. "Scary as hell, though, right? I mean, I was petrified through this whole ordeal."

Sim cleared his throat. Earl slammed the lid of the barbecue grill down a little too hard.

"It was thoughtful of you to come by," Loretta said. "But we were just about to…"

"I can't believe Pierce was involved in this stuff. I mean, the dude royally flipped out," said Brady, walking toward her. "So, yeah. Are you okay? Is everybody okay?"

"It's been three weeks. But thanks. Yeah. We're all right."

"He's still at the Juvenile Detention Center. My parents said I should try to go see him, but I don't know…"

"You should," Loretta said. "I'm sure he could use a friend."

"I heard you were amazing. Balls-ass tough." Brady strolled along the porch, hung his arm over the railing. "Can I talk to you a minute?" he said in a low voice.

"You can say what you need to say right there," Loretta said.

Brady's jaw hung a little. "Well, okay. I guess. Really?"

Loretta nodded.

Brady squared his shoulders. "I'd like to hang out," he said. "I mean, like, do something. For real. You know, when you're better."

"Humph," Jemma snorted, red-faced, arms crossed, thrumming her fingers.

Loretta straightened the legs of her jeans, and stepped off the porch. "Seriously?" she said, sidling up to him. "You're asking me this *now?*"

Brady shrugged his shoulders.

"A month ago, this would have meant everything," Loretta said. "But, now…Sorry. No. My answer is no." She pivoted and walked back up the stairs and sat next to Ethan.

"*What?*" Jemma sneered. "Are you kidding me?"

"Dinner?" asked Greer. "You're welcome to stay."

Jemma waved Greer off and rolled her eyes. "We drive all the way out, this, this, bramble-rut road…" she said, "…to, to Willow…Willow…whatever it's called. Brady asks you out, Loretta, and *you* say no? How funny is that?"

"Not very," said Loretta. "I'm sorry."

"You're sorry. Well, so am I. You know, this day sucks. First, Brady, you ask me to drive all the way out here with you…so you can see *her*…so you can ask *her* out? Jemma said, pointing to Loretta.

"Jemma, stop," said Brady.

"No, I don't want to stop. I'm tired. And I'm dirty. And I want to go home. You *asked* me to come out here with you,

Brady. I thought, maybe…"

"You *begged* me to bring you…" said Brady, his face flushed, his voice barely a whisper. "Stop, seriously," he added, louder now. "This is *so* not cool."

"What? Do you blame me for being upset? Jemma said, facing him.

"We were never a *thing*, Jemma," Brady told her flatly. "You know that. Everyone knows that. We've *hung* out, we're friends, but we've never officially *gone* out."

"Never a thing? Really? *Hung* out, but never *gone* out? What does that even mean?"

"We've never *dated*, Jemma. Do I need to spell it out?" Brady shook his head and turned away. "This is embarrassing, man. Stop. It's not the time or place…"

"You best listen, little missy," Noleen said, tapping a wooden spoon against her wrist.

"Little missy? Really? Are you *advising* me, Noleen?"

"No ma'am, just making sure you understand…"

"Loretta, seriously. You'd rather hang with this *witch*, and her family of goony birds…that, that autistic kid," Jemma said, pointing at Ethan, "than with me?"

"Goony birds," Ethan said, "are egg-laying feathered vertebrates with wings."

"Jemma, I understand that you're upset, but…" said Greer.

"You *understand*? Really? *Dang*," she sneered. "Like I said, I drove all the way out here…and you people, all of you, including you, Greer Duvall…stand there like you're *all that*," Jemma said, her face screwing up, her voice whiny and high-pitched.

"Now, wait just a minute," said Greer.

Loretta stood up and stepped off the porch. "Whoa, Jemma. Stop. These *people* are my family. Ethan, he's a guy, a really cool guy. Don't put a label on him. Period. And as far as the *witch* goes, if you were referring to Granny Noleen, she deserves so much better than to be insulted by you. Honest to God. Both you and Brady have humiliated Cora and Ethan and me and made us feel like we were crap from the time we were little. Enough. That's over now. Get it? You may have the looks. You may be popular. But you've got no manners. And none of us should have to put up with your crap."

"You go, girl," Greer shouted.

"Oh, and Jemma, my mom may not be traditional, but she loves me. And she's taught me that every person deserves respect…even if that person is a royal *bitch*. So I respect you, Jemma. If you wanna play nice, pick up a hammer and stick around. Otherwise, have a nice day, and don't let Brady's Jeep door hit you in the ass on your way out of here."

Brady picked up a shovel. Grinned.

Jemma sideswiped him, knocking the shovel out of his hands. "Take me home. Now!" she screamed, storming to the Jeep and crawling inside.

"Come back when you're ready to work with us, Jemma,"

Loretta said. "I'll keep that hammer handy for you. You're welcome anytime."

Jemma cleared her throat, opened her mouth to speak, but said nothing, wiggling into her seat instead, fastening her seatbelt and signaling Brady to come.

Brady shrugged his shoulders, still grinning. He hopped into the driver's seat, clucking his tongue. *"Balls-ass tough,"* he said to Loretta, as he turned the key and drove away.

"Life's full of boulders," Loretta said. "We climb and then we move on." She turned around and stared at the others, as they stared at her. "What's the matter?" she said. "You all have a hitch in your gitty-up? Come on now, day's-a-wastin'!"

Greer smiled. "Movie trivia game, Loretta. Here we go. *Wizard of Oz*. Glinda, the Good Witch of the North. Famous quote."

Loretta blushed.

Granny Noleen answered this time. "You've always had the power, my dear. You just had to learn it for yourself."

+++

That evening, the bunker and the Stone House seemed a lifetime ago. On Granny's porch, Loretta and Cora watched the sun cuddle with the mountain while Ethan read from his dictionary: condiments, he said, were something (such as salt, mustard, or ketchup) that is added to food to give it more flavor, not foods like pickles and tomatoes, etc. Sim and Raina brushed Dakota as he munched his hay; Raina giggled at some joke Sim told, something private between them. Pansy, Yoshi, and Bill played with S'more in her pen while Granny Noleen replenished their glasses of lemonade. Greer and Doc smiled so hard it seemed as if their mouths might freeze, and they laughed and talked and told stories about when Loretta and Cora were kids.

Loretta's *job* had ended long ago, yet every day, every single day since the bunker incident she had returned to Willow Grove. From her viewpoint on the deck, she noticed all these things, and several more, wondering how she had missed them before: the sound of the creek mingling with the rustle of leaves; how the gentle swish of the old wooden chair matched the rustle of Pansy's slip beneath her square-dancing skirt. The grace of Yoshi's hands as he *talked* for Bill, wiped Pansy's chin with his napkin and changed the dressing on Bill's stump of a leg; the deep-throated joy of Granny's laugh, and the sparkle in Earl's eyes as he told his stories. The smells of horse and goat and chickens and hay, combined with lavender and sage, the scent of cedar blowing off the mountain, blackberry jam, homemade biscuits, and barbecue. Sweet and savory, just like the house. Just like the people who lived there. Just like the mothers and fathers and friends who surrounded her now.

The sky was empty but for a single cloud hovering in a windless sky. The cloud puffed up and contracted, puffed up and contracted, forming one thing and then another:

an eagle, a bear, a butterfly. A heart. Each incarnation was surprising yet wondrous—a birthing, in a way, of a brand-new life. Loretta smiled, content with the moment.

ACKNOWLEDGMENTS

My sincere thanks to the editors, family, and friends who contributed to this book: Dr. Kate Evans, Joan Canty, M.A., Nick Chase, Carol Dali, Jan Zukal, Jan Lekas, Sharon Marshall, Patricia Kinley, Kris Osward, Debra Kushnir, Melissa Colon, and Jonathon Andrews.

Special thanks to my writer's group, WOW: Ellen Stewart, Ann St. James, Patricia Harrelson, Suzan Still, Blanche Abrams, Carol Biederman, Sally McClellan, Kristin Miller, and Cynthia Restivo. Much appreciation to Columbia College Fire Instructor, Shane Warner, for advising me regarding high country search and rescue techniques.

And to Word Project Press, my gratitude, as always: Melody Baker, Sy Baldwin, Gillian Herbert, Patricia Harrelson, and Sally McClellan.

ABOUT THE AUTHOR

Shelley Muniz has short stories in these journals: Wild Edges by Manzanita Press; Wisdom Has a Voice: Every daughter's memories of mother by First Edition Paperback. Her narrative non-fiction book, *Eagle Feathers and Angel Wings: Micah's Story* was published by Word Project Press in 2013; her children's picture book, *One Great Tribe*, illustrated by Bear Dyken, in 2017. Shelley has been a teacher's aide, elementary school librarian, and a library specialist for thirty years. She lives in Sonora, CA.